MW00718438

ENEMY WAY

A JESSIE RICHTER NOVEL

STEPHEN EAGLES

Enemy Way

Copyright © 2020 by Stephen Eagles

All rights reserved.

No part of this book may be reproduced in any form or by any electronic or mechanical means, including information storage and retrieval systems, without written permission from the author, except for the use of brief quotations in a book review.

CONTENTS

PROLOGUE

J essie Richter sat in the comfortable oversized chair bolted into the floor of the company's Lockheed AC-130 gunship communications pod and glared at the blue folder her co-worker, Juanita Johnson had handed to her almost an hour ago. She had read the cover pages, containing cursory information of a brutal homicide in San Antonio, Texas, while quite literally standing in the middle of a wreckage from her somewhat successful mission. She had that glass-half-empty feeling sitting in the pit of her stomach like a brick. It was the kind of feeling one might get when innocent people died.

Her eyes went out of focus as she thought about those souls who were killed a few hours ago, the victims of a greedy scientist who had even sacrificed some of his own employees to affect his escape. Ultimately, that traitor had also paid The Ferryman full price for his treachery. Jessie felt no guilt for at least some of the dead, but for the unfortunate innocents who were just in the wrong place at the wrong time, she felt the heaviness of their lost lives on her shoulders. Mistakes were made. Some of which might have been prevented. What's more, she could have been among them, torn apart by the concussion of the blast or a piece of shrapnel.

It is what it is, she thought, and then a shiver shot through her, surprised at her feigned attempt at a cold dismissal of it all.

1

She hadn't been trained as an assassin, and although she had killed, it had been in the defense of others.

Well, for the most part.

She wondered if making mistakes that led to the deaths of others might be no different than pulling the trigger. She rubbed at her temple, exhausted by the weight of running scenario's through her mind about what she *shoulda, coulda, woulda* done if she could do it all over again.

Too late. It is what it is. Lessons learned.

She fingered the folder once again and then latched on to the catalyst for her reluctance to delve deeper into the file. It had nothing to do with her next mission. It had everything to do with fear.

Fear.

For years, Jessie and her co-workers at Crue Intellis, a Private Military Company, or PMC, specializing in the collection of intelligence, both domestic and abroad, had searched far and wide for the information contained within the folder she now possessed. After almost ten years, they had found it — proof of the existence of another Walker like her. She ran her finger along the edge of the thick paper cover and hefted the weight. A lot of information compiled in a very short time.

"I sure as hell hope you're going to crack it open and read." Jessie looked up to see Juanita, a former, and now the Crue's in-house CIA analyst, staring at her as she leaned against the comm-pod's doorframe. "I mean, we're on our way. You got about three more hours before we land."

"Yeah, I know," Jessie said, looking again at the folder.

"Still thinking about Kore and the attack? Do we need to talk about this again?"

Jessie shook her head and wrinkled her nose. "Other than smelling too ripe and needing a shower, no," she said. *No,* she thought, *that fucking traitor got his comeuppance.* "I'm just . . ." she tapered off, not willing to speak her mind.

"Concerned as to what you might find?" Juanita asked, coming around and sitting in the chair next to hers.

"A little. But in reality? I'm feeling a little deflated."

"What do you mean?"

"Well, for years, I've been running around doing all this crazy stuff, thinking that I am the only one of my kind on the entire planet. Unique. Special. I know it sounds selfish, but now . . ."

"There's another," Juanita finished.

"Yes. Exactly. And to be honest . . ."

"Honey, you can't be honest about anything pinging around inside your head until you read the whole file. This is bigger than you, and what's in that envelope is too close to home to be coincidence. Another thing you need to accept is that you're the one who needs to come up with a plan." Juanita reached over and pinched Jessie's arm until she made eye contact. "Because no one else can." Juanita got up, walked across the comm-pod to the data console, and sat down.

Jessie nodded, curled up in the chair, and opened the file. Within minutes, she found herself sucked into the detailed police reports and the story of her new target.

The date of the incident grabbed her attention. September 21st. Almost two weeks ago. The exact day she slip-streamed into Kore. She wondered if this might be yet another coincidence and rubbed the goosebumps from the skin of her forearms.

"Time to get to business," she whispered to no one.

Besides, she thought. *What's there to be afraid of?*

THE OTHER

Monday, September 21, 2020
The Miller Residence
San Antonio, Texas: South Side

Matthew Miller positioned his motorized wheelchair in the shadow of the front bay window, and then double-checked the video monitor attached to the arm rest. He flicked the controller with his right hand, his good hand, until his knees were no longer visible from the street. He glanced at the time: 3:15 p.m. He smiled knowing Kristi Sellers, the most beautiful girl in the world and the love of his life, would be arriving for Calculus tutoring in about ten minutes. He let out a breath of despair. If she only knew.

A week earlier, his mother had successfully shamed Kristi into asking Matthew to the prom. Matthew couldn't hear the details of the conversation, but he had caught bits and pieces about how Matthew had crushed on her since they were children, how close they were, how he intended not to go to prom if he couldn't come up with a date . . . *yada, yada, yada.* All the proper seeds of guilt his mother had expertly sowed. When

Kristi approached him last week, he saw it in her ashen face. She had taken a beating. Although she had said she'd be honored to escort him to graduation, he saw it as pity and guilt. He came close, so close to calling her out on it, but it had been Kristi. So, he had said yes.

"I won't embarrass you, Kristi, I promise," he'd said, and then he had added, "If you'll honor me with just one dance, I'll release you from your bond so you can have fun for the rest of the night."

The memory of her hesitant, teary-eyed agreement resonated with him even now. *I'm such a punk.*

He'd also fought with his mother again about the whole matter the previous night. She had tried to convince him to tell Kristi how he felt before time ran out.

"You have nothing to lose," his mother said.

Of course, she had always looked out for his heart, but Matthew couldn't bring himself to do it. Instead, he lurked in the shadow of his bay window spying on her approach, hoping that Kristi would one day look past his imminent demise and perhaps love him the way he loved her. As his mother put it, before time ran out.

Matthew blushed at his selfishness. A tiny pang of guilt rose in his chest because he spent way too much private time fantasizing about Kristi.

3:23 p.m.

She would be turning the corner any second. Matthew tinkered with the video monitors on his chair and thought about the early days when he and Kristi used to hang out together. They had almost been inseparable as children before the Motor Neuron Disease had taken over. Before he had lost control of his left hand. Before he had lost the ability to walk, lost control of his bowels, kept the drool in his mouth, and everything that used to be *him* fell apart. The inevitability of death registered with Kristy as soon as she researched and understood the disease. Why would anyone want any kind of relationship with someone who would be gone in a couple of years?

Or less?

These days, Kristi only came over for one reason: to get tutored in Calculus. But back then, before he became disgusting even to himself, she had kissed him.

He wondered if she remembered the breathtaking moment that had occurred over a year ago. Probably not. He closed his eyes and slipped into the memory of the day that had changed his life, and then, with a gasp, began to relive it.

Her azure eyes opened and fix him with their gaze. The smell of her perfume covered him like a warm blanket. She pulled a tissue from a box, leaned toward him to wipe the drool off his chin, and caught him staring, wide-eyed, down her shirt.

"Matthew Miller!" she scolded.

"Oh, I'm sorry. I just . . . uh, I'm sorry . . ." He felt the heat rise to his face and tried to look anywhere but at her.

She giggled, pulled up a chair, and planted herself in front of him. "Well, I guess it's only natural," she said, her angelic voice causing a stir in his underwear. "Look at me, Matthew," she said. Slowly, he turned to look at her. "Have you ever been kissed?" Matthew nodded, sighed, and then shook his head. Gazing so deeply into his eyes, she asked, "Can I kiss you?" He about passed out.

In a flash of excitement, he felt like Rhett Butler in Gone with the Wind—ready to launch from his chair, grasp Kristi by the shoulders and say, "No more of that talk," before planting a kiss on her that would leave her breathless. Instead, he managed a weak nod.

With her index finger, Kristi lifted Matthew's chin, forcing his line of sight from her cleavage. "Tilt your head," she whispered, "and open your mouth a little bit. There," she said, then pressed her lips to his lips. After much too short a moment, she pulled back and asked, "Did you like that?"

Terrified of saying or doing anything that might screw it up, all he could do was smile. Maybe, just maybe, if she didn't notice his full-on boner, she might kiss him again. And she did, harder this time, tickling his lips with her tongue. She somehow had his hand, and she pressed it against her . . .

The doorbell rang, startling him out of his daydream.

Matthew's body jerked up straight. He pulled his drool towel into his lap and cycled through the video channels on his chair's monitor. He saw nothing but black screens where there should have been an image. He rolled forward to glance out the front window.

Hmmm, no one there.

He checked the time — still too early. He leaned in closer to the video screen, flicked at it with his good hand, and checked the connection. He took a deep breath, rolled his chair right up to the windowsill and leaned as far forward into the bay window as his chair restraints would allow. The sun came in strong from that angle, forcing him to squint, but he could see clear enough to register a presence in the vestibule — someone wearing blue jeans. His heart skipped a beat. Matthew grinned and maneuvered his chair toward the front door.

"Wow, Kristi," he called out, "you're early for a change." No reply. Worried that his joke had offended her. He reached for the deadbolt and twisted the lock open. "Kristi, I'm just kidding, I —"

The door exploded inward.

Three young males poured into the room, gliding past Matthew as if he did not exist. Instinctively, he pressed the red med-alert button on his chair, then slammed the toggle hard to the right. His chair spun around to face the invaders. One looked Hispanic or black, *or a mix of both.* One white. The third one was also Hispanic but much taller, broader, and older than the other two. He grinned at Matthew with brilliant white teeth that made the guy look like a wild animal. He had no doubt this last one was the Boss.

"What do you want?" Matthew asked, putting on his toughest face to hide the fear flooding through him. But he felt something else, too. A faint tickle, like static electricity, igniting deep inside his head. The energy crackled in his ears, yet it also sounded distant. The power almost distracted him from the event unfolding before his eyes.

The Boss tousled Matthew's hair. Then without a word, but with practiced efficiency, the three young men disappeared into different parts of the house and began to ransack the rooms, starting with his.

"Hey, get out of here or I'm calling the police!" Matthew shouted over the bang and crash of worthless items being smashed and tossed aside.

"Let's hurry it up!" a voice called out. From his bedroom maybe? "We got about ten more minutes before his girlfriend shows up."

The comment struck Matthew like an invisible slap. Terrible thoughts flashed through his mind.

Kristi set me up? No, she didn't. She wouldn't. They cased my house, that's all.

He resisted the urge to press the red button again. He knew that wouldn't speed anyone up, least of all him. Instead, he focused on the struggle to keep his fear in check by adding to his mental notes. Asshole number one: Dark. Skinny as a zipper. Head too big for his body. He smiled at the nicknames as they came to him. This one he would call Skinny-Fathead. He looked closer at the white kid. His skin looked Pasty. White. With brown freckles.

Oh! Oh! Oh! I know you. I know you.

Matthew pressed his eyes closed in recollection — and to shut out the sounds of items breaking throughout the house — as that tickle of power grew louder in his head. Matthew paused a moment to be sure. Yes. He had never met him in person, but he convinced himself that he recognized Pasty-

White's freckled face from the science class he attended remotely.

His heart sank: Kristi attended that class, too.

Skinny whistled and tossed a pillowcase past Matthew's head. Pasty snatched it out of the air. He then turned to face the wall full of electronics equipment, given to Matthew by the University of Texas, and started unplugging the gear.

"You were right," Pasty said as asshole three, the Boss, reentered the room. "This place is a jackpot, J —"

Boss glared, cutting Pasty off before he said his name. Then Boss bounded across the room and shoved Pasty aside.

"Too slow, white boy," Boss barked, as he ripped the pillowcase from Pasty's hands and began shoving electronics into it. Skinny snickered as he headed for the kitchen.

"That's my stuff. I need that!" Matthew screamed at Boss, swiveling his chair in a wild attempt to guard the electronics that remained on the shelf. Boss reached around him effortlessly and flashed another brilliant smile that drove Matthew to despair. "My mom's got jewelry in her bedroom," he pleaded. "On the top shelf of her closet. Take all you want, but not my school stuff, please."

Boss took hold of Matthew's chair and looked him dead in the eyes. When Matthew least expected it, Boss jerked the chair — hard. Matthew spluttered in surprise. Boss threw his head back, laughing maniacally. After catching his breath, Boss reached out and patted Matthew on the head.

"Just stay out of the way, and we'll be out of here in no time flat," Boss said, and then he got back to work. When Skinny reentered from the kitchen, Boss told him, "Go check the back-bedroom closet, top shelf, for jewelry."

Matthew frowned. "I said get out of my fucking house." The intense fear he felt blended with a growing fury. He grew light-headed as the power thing swelled up within and swept through him.

The thieves stopped for a moment to look at him and then at each other before they burst into laughter.

"What are you assholes laughin' at?" Matthew said defiantly. "Get the hell out!"

"Shut him up," Boss said to Pasty. He went back to clearing the wall in front of him.

In a flash of revelation, Pasty's name came to Matthew from the science class. *Christopher. Chris Storey.* Matthew had watched enough CSI on television to know not to tip his hand to the thieves.

I know who you are, white boy.

Chris pulled a piece of duct tape off a roll and slapped it hard across Matthew's mouth. Boss pointed toward the kitchen. Chris tilted the chair and started dragging it in that direction.

"Fuck, this thing is heavy," he said.

Matthew saw his chance and pressed the toggle forward, sending Chris flying backwards where he tripped over the half-filled pillowcase. Chris got up, punched Matthew in the side of the face, then pulled Matthew's useless arm across his own throat.

"Do that again, fuck-head, and see if I don't break your arm." Maintaining the choke hold, Chris used the toggle to guide the chair back into the kitchen. "Stay the fuck out of our way, and nothing bad will happen." He released Matthew's arm and leaned in, whispering in Matthew's ear. "It's just stuff, right?" Chris stood up straight, his voice louder now. "You just sit here like a good little Timmy." Matthew nodded and Chris patted him on the head like some kind of pet, cheering, "Timmy!"

From the living room, Skinny and Boss echoed him. "Timmy!"

It finally clicked. Oh! That Timmy. South Park's cartoon Timmy. Matthew fumed. He had to do something, anything. Scanning his chair, his eyes fell on the huge battery that made it heavy and fast. His line of sight rose to the back of Boss, who was crouched low, ripping electronics off the shelf.

He gritted his teeth and threw the toggle forward. Rubber tires squeaked across the kitchen's linoleum floor then bit into the living room carpet. The chair lurched toward Boss who moved just a little too late.

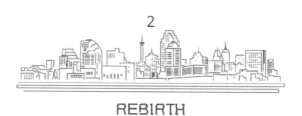

2

REBIRTH

3:30 P.M.
MATTHEW MILLER HOME
SAN ANTONIO, TEXAS

The steel chassis slammed into the back of Boss's legs, forcing him into the shelving face-first. The edge of the wood cut a deep gash across his forehead. Blood poured from the wound and down his face. Jamming the toggle forward once more, Matthew's chair pinned Boss, his face smearing blood against the wall like a foot-wide paint brush. When Boss tried to kick the chair away. Matthew held the toggle forward for dear life as the chair lurched forward again and again, forcing Boss's head through a growing hole in the sheetrock.

Boss looked like some kind of voodoo demon: white plaster mixed with blood smeared from head to chest. As he pulled himself from the wall and tried to stand up, the bottom of the chair caught his ankle and sent him crashing back to the floor, howling in pain. Matthew laughed through the tape, thinking he had the upper hand. But his ears were pulsing from that weird energy surging through his veins, feeding his confidence like never before.

As they watched the deformed-boy-in-wheelchair kick their leader's ass, Skinny and Chris couldn't restrain their own laughter. Matthew laughed with them through the tape, his head bobbing up and down in joy, sure he had won, certain they were all about to run. Then Boss let out a roar, planted both feet on the side of the chair and shoved. Matthew's wheelchair tilted over on two wheels as he leaned his body toward Boss, trying to provide a counterweight, but it wasn't enough. In slow motion, the chair passed the point of balance and toppled over sideways. Matthew's head struck the floor with a loud smack where the linoleum met the carpet. Stars shot into his vision as dizziness overwhelmed him and rendered him helpless.

"You're dead, you crippled bitch," Boss said, scrambling on his knees to the wheelchair. Matthew's eyes went wide as Boss's hands wrapped around his throat. Panic seized him. The sucking sound he heard as he tried to draw breath meant death, and Matthew knew it. He bucked as hard as his body would allow, but the chair wouldn't budge. He could not escape Boss's grip.

"Get off him!"

All eyes turned to the front door where Kristi stood behind freckle-faced Chris and Skinny with her fists clenched and her expression fiery with anger.

She's not part of this, Matthew realized, elated to discover that she had not betrayed him. Then he looked up into the face of Boss and saw that the maniac's focus had shifted to Kristi. *Oh no.* His heart stopped.

Boss loosened his grip enough for Matthew to suck in air through his nose. Spots swirled before his eyes while he frantically tried to signal Kristi with his good hand, but the words "Run, Kristi, run" were muffled behind the duct tape.

Kristi made eye contact with Matthew, and her brow rose in understanding. She nodded once and turned to flee, but before she reached the door, Boss sprang to his feet and launched himself at her. He grabbed a handful of hair with one hand and wrapped the other around her face then jerked her off her feet, tossing her like a rag doll into the wall of electronics. When her head connected to the remaining shelves, Matthew heard a sickening crack. She landed on her back and laid still for a moment, her face less than a foot from Matthew's. He watched her eyes roll back in her head, but then she managed to come around and focus on Matthew's face. She frowned; brows furrowed in anger. Helpless to do anything, Matthew could only cry. He looked up at Boss just as the demon bent over Kristi, eyeing her body as his own dripped with sweat, blood, and plaster. His stench reached Matthew's nose just as Kristi kicked Boss square in the face.

The loud crunch of Boss's nose breaking sent a shiver through Matthew. Watching fresh blood stream down his face, Matthew dared to hope.

Go, Kristi! Kick his ass!

Then Boss roared like some kind of beast. Kristi's blow to his nose had just pressed the berserker button.

Matthew looked up and over to Skinny and Christopher, but they were frozen in horror, transfixed as Boss snatched Kristi by the neck with both hands, lifted her completely from the floor, and flung her into the far wall. Before she could recover, Boss leapt onto her back. With one hand, he picked her up by the throat and with a savage grunt, chucked her back into the bottom shelf of electronics. For a second time, she landed in a heap beside Matthew.

Stay down, Kristi, Matthew begged through the duct tape. *Play dead. They only want the stuff. Play dead.*

"Help me," she said.

And then came the stomping.

To Matthew, her head seemed to bounce in slow motion before her eyes rolled back in her head, as Boss stomped again, and again, and again.

"You like to kick? Here's some kicks, bitch," Boss yelled, his eyes wide and wild.

Matthew shook his head in protest. He begged as best he could through the tape for Boss to stop. He did not. Matthew twisted his neck around and shot another pleading look at Chris and Skinny. But they were just as useless, and like him, paralyzed.

Do something you fucking cowards.

The Boss's eyes bulged. He had lost control. He stomped and stomped until Kristi's skull gave way to the pressure. Matthew froze in surprise as her blood and brains dripped down his face. He had been forced to watch every moment in torturous, slow motion because his sideways chair refused to let him turn his head. He rolled his eyes up to look at Boss, who looked crazed with horror, mixed with fascination, at what he had just done. Boss's transformation from thief to murderer, from street thug to maniac, was now complete.

Kristi's caved in skull sent a painful surge of power cascading through Matthew's body, the electricity on his skin sizzled in his ears. He saw the high-voltage charge dance in the air around him. At first, Matthew thought his body had gone into shock and he was about to lose consciousness.

No! Stay with it.

Little sparks of light lifted from his skin, then blinked out after rising a couple of inches into the air. Calm enveloped him but sounds were muffled due to the surge of power rushing in his ears.

Matthew's eyes flicked to Chris and Skinny, not surprised when the cowards backed up and skittered through the kitchen before hurtling out the back door. When his eyes flicked back, he saw that Boss had now turned his attention from Kristi to him. The pulsing veins in his face and neck made him look like some crazed monster.

"See what you made me do, motherfucker?" Boss said

through clenched teeth as he yanked Matthew by the neck and dragged him from his chair. For a second time, Boss's hands wrapped themselves around Matthew's throat and squeezed.

Whatever, Matthew thought. Without Kristi, he had lost all hope. He felt numb. Nothing to live for. *Just do it. I don't want to live.*

Something popped in Matthew's neck, and his body convulsed as if he had jammed a metal fork into a power outlet. His vision shrank into a dark tunnel. *I am going to die. Finally, I am going to die.* But as his vision faded to black, a burst of power emerged from a deep, dark place within.

Fight, dammit! the power said.

Or is that me?

Matthew now understood. The calm he felt had tried to wash away the last remnant of his will to survive. He concentrated, calling upon whatever power coursed through him to provide the strength to fight. Without thinking about it, he thrust his good right hand into the unprepared Boss's face, catching his broken nose. Then, mustering every ounce of strength left in him, he dug his fingernails in the soft cheek tissue. Boss unleashed a scream of agony that encouraged Matthew to bear down harder.

Scream, punk. Scream. You will never smile again.

Another pop and stars shot through Matthew's vision, making it almost impossible to focus, but his fingernails refused to release.

Matthew willed the power to flow through his useless left arm until it floated away from the armrest and began to shake. Energy filled the long-atrophied muscles. The sparkles of light continued floating away from his skin as the crooked, disfigured hand slowly opened.

It's working.

He breathed deep, visualized the twisted fingers turning into a raptor's talons, and looked Boss straight in the eyes. Before

Boss could react, the talons struck, rooting themselves into the other side of Boss's face. The instant his hands made contact, Matthew felt a distinct connection, like flipping the switch on a lamp. He set the power free and the world, all motion and time, stopped. Matthew heard nothing but two thunderous beats of his heart.

Thu-thump. Thu-thump.

Then the room erupted into movement. Matthew felt as if he were spinning, caught up in some tornado of motion and pain. His stomach lurched as dark shadows reached inside his chest, tore out his backbone from the inside, ripped him apart limb from limb, and slammed him back together again in one, swift movement. In an instant, pain overwhelmed him. The roar of power filled his ears. He tried to scream, but his voice sounded muted inside and out. Some part of him disconnected from the power and shifted outside of his body as, just for an instant, the image of his attacker crying out in pain flashed in his mind's eye.

Then it ended.

The colors and light dissipated as the world slowly came back into focus, and time seemed to have resumed its normal pace.

"Let go!" Matthew yelled, then froze. "What the . . ." Shocked to find himself standing, he gasped, stunned by the sight of his hands wrapped around — his own neck? And the voice — not his voice. "What the hell is this?" he said, feeling unsteady on feet that were not his. He opened his hands, stumbled back a couple of steps, and watched in shock as his own ravaged body collapsed, totally lifeless, to the floor.

Out of nowhere, something slammed into the side of his head, and his vision faded to black.

3

INVESTIGATION

H<small>ALF AN HOUR LATER</small>
M<small>ATTHEW</small> M<small>ILLER</small> H<small>OME</small>
S<small>AN</small> A<small>NTONIO</small>, T<small>EXAS</small>

J olted into consciousness by the sting of ammonia in his
nostrils, Matthew woke up to find a medic leaning over
him. He tried to get up but a hand on his chest prevented
it.

"Whoa now, you just lie still," the medic said.

Dizzy and out of sorts, Matthew licked his dry lips and
tasted blood. When his eyes came into focus, he realized that he
knew the medic from many a ride to the emergency room.

"Hey, Richard," he said in an uncharacteristically deep voice.
Richard shot him a perplexed look. "It took you guys long
enough —" Matthew couldn't finish what he wanted to say. He
couldn't breathe. His head turned to the side, and he did a
double-take at the gurney to his right. A different medic
working on . . . *him*. A wave of electricity blasted through his
body, producing an eerie scream from his throat.

"No! No! No! This is not possible!"

He squeezed his eyes shut, willing the vision away. He

opened them slowly, then gasped at the sight of a medic working on *him*. A realization slammed into him: he saw his own ALS ridden body from . . .

"Oh my God, NO! This can't be real. Richard!?"

Panic flooded into his veins and that same energy from before surged through him. He tried to sit up again, but the medic roughly pressed him back down into the cot.

"Just relax, young man," Richard said, cinching the restraints around Matthew's chest one notch tighter.

Matthew writhed, then feeling exhausted, he collapsed. His eyes drifted down to the arms by his side: they were dark and tattooed. He squealed at the sight and started bucking wildly. "What's happening to me?" he demanded.

"Just relax," Richard said. "We're going to take care of you."

"No! You don't understand," Matthew said, bending his hand as best he could in the metal handcuffs and pointing at the body to his right. "That's me! That's *me*, Richard," he pleaded, looking deep into the medic's eyes. "I'm Matthew. You've got to believe me. I'm Matthew Miller!"

In an instant, a man appeared to Matthew's left. Matthew's head turned toward the movement. His eyes leveled on a gold detective's badge clipped to the man's waist belt. Matthew sighed. Help at last. "Detective, listen to me, I . . ."

The man, now standing closer to him, seized Matthew by the hair and jerked his head up to examine his face. He looked into Matthew's eyes, pulled back, then looked out the front door and around the room at the red-flashing emergency lights reflecting off the white walls of the living room. The detective moved in even closer. Matthew recognized the violence in the detective's eyes.

"Shut . . . your . . . mouth," the detective said, then leaned in closer, looking into Matthew's face. The detective glanced up at the medic. "What's wrong with his eyes? They're . . . glowing, or something."

"I don't know, Detective. I noticed it, too. Freaked me out. Maybe it's drugs or something?"

Without warning, the detective yanked Matthew's head to the right toward his own lifeless body on the other gurney. "That's Matthew Miller, motherfucker." Then he whipped Matthew's head back toward a different bloody gurney on his left. "And that's what you did to his girlfriend, you filthy, fucking piece of shit."

The sight of Kristi's crushed face, only partially covered by the blood-soaked yellow sheet, sent tears flowing down Matthew's face again.

"No, no, no, this can't be. This just can't be happening," Matthew said, sobbing.

"Don't you dare cry, asshole," the detective said, rage flooding his features.

"No! This isn't real!" Matthew screamed and started to turn away.

"Oh, yes it is," the detective said, locking Matthew's head in place. "It's real all right. It's all too fucking real."

Unable to endure one moment more, Matthew threw up and fainted dead away.

INSIDE THE LIVING ROOM OF THE MILLER HOUSE, DETECTIVE Randy D'Agostino stepped away from the front door, allowing the crime scene crew to exit and the cleaning crew to enter. The bio-suit-clad cleaning team carried in specialized equipment to tackle the gruesome task of removing blood spatter and brain matter.

They have their work cut out for them tonight, he thought.

"Randy, I'm ready." The detective glanced back over his shoulder to see one of the critical crime scene techs, a young computer nerd everybody called Will, seated at the dining room table at the back of the room. Randy walked across the living room, his eyes glued to the floor, taking care to show reverence for what remained of Kristi Sellers by not traipsing through it.

Lowering himself into the seat next to tech, he asked, "What ya got?"

"Making final adjustments," Will replied, not bothering to look up. "Reconnecting the DVR . . . now." He hit the play button and video started to roll. As the attack unfolded on the screen, Will remarked, "This is some kind of fucked up, Randy."

Randy's brow furrowed at the recording of the attack on Kristi.

Will gasped and whispered, "Holy shit."

Another minute went by and Randy's eyes went wide as he sat up straight in his chair. "What the . . . Will, did you see that?" He pulled his chair in a little closer. "Play it again from the start of the attack on Miller." Will didn't answer but reversed the video. The attack on Miller unfolded again until Randy pointed at the screen and said, "Whoa! What is that? Rewind a few seconds. See? There it is again. What is that flicker? A glitch?"

"This is a pretty good video system, all high definition stuff," Will said. "So, let's find out." Will twisted the scrubber knob, running the image forward and back a few times. "Might be static electricity. It's definitely not a glitch."

"How do you know?"

"Watch," Will said, inching the video forward a few frames at a time. "The effect is isolated to his hands. It's not a ghost image created by the system. It's really there. It's on the recording."

"Can you zoom in? On his hands?"

"Not here, but we can do it at the lab."

Randy's phone rang and he answered. "Hey Mel, what you got?"

Mel, aka Detective Melissa Santos, had been Randy's partner for the past seven years. Their working relationship had a solid foundation built upon Randy's hatred for crime-related family interactions and Mel's weak stomach for crime-related gore.

"At the hospital," Santos replied. "Handling a bunch of parents."

"How's the Miller boy?" Randy asked.

"He's in bad shape."

"Is he going to make it?"

"How the hell should I know?" Mel said softly. "Only time will tell. The docs say his throat is crushed, and considering his already fragile medical condition, it's not looking good. It's really sad. I feel bad for the kid."

Randy shook his head and thought about how much sorrow came with his line of work. Too much.

"What about the asshole?"

"Well, Asshole has been identified as Mr. Jeffrey Cruz," Mel said.

"Is Asshole Mr. Jeffrey Cruz awake yet?"

"You could say that," Mel said. "He woke up screaming bloody hell about how he's Matthew Miller."

"Give it up, Cruz," Randy said, not meaning to vocalize his thoughts.

"What?" Mel asked.

"Cruz tried that crazy shit here at the scene."

"Really?" Mel asked, surprised. "Well, now he's added some other crazy shit about the girl."

"It doesn't matter," Randy replied. "I just watched him murder the Sellers girl in full HD. When the court sees what I saw, there is no way he's going to be able to plead insanity."

"Isn't going to stop him from trying," Mel said.

"What are you talking about?" Randy asked.

"Two minutes ago, he went wild," she explained. "Tried to tear his wrists out of the handcuffs. They had to sedate him. It took four of them to hold him down and a few shots before he stopped bucking. I guess Cruz has developed a tolerance."

"Imagine that," Randy said. "What's his background? No, wait, let me guess: Drug dealing, theft, burglary."

"Very good. The only one you forgot was aggravated assault. His rap sheet is as long as your arm."

"And yet our beloved system still let him out to walk our streets, murdering people," Randy said, disgusted.

"Probably because he committed most of his offenses as a minor," Mel said. "He just turned eighteen yesterday."

"Shit," Randy said. "Celebrates his manhood by adding murder to his file. His parents must be so proud." No reply. "Mel?" Nothing. Randy pressed the phone into his ear: in the background, he heard something that sounded like a scuffle.

"Sorry, Randy," Mel said, coming back on the line, breathing heavy. "I had to stop Miller's father from killing Cruz. Hold on."

Randy heard the unmistakable screech of a Hispanic mother verbally defending her son in the background.

"What?" he asked. "Mel? Mel?"

A moment later, she answered, this time completely breathless. "Sorry, Randy. What a shit-hot-mess. Miller's Dad landed a couple good punches. I finally had to restrain him."

"Who gives a crap?" Randy exploded.

"Cruz' mother!" Mel shouted back. "She's insisting her son be moved to a different room."

"We ought to move his ass to the morgue," Randy hissed.

"Randy," Mel said, pushing back.

Randy reached up and pressed three fingers into his left pectoral muscle, massaging with pressure. Despite the training he had received, teaching cops how to disconnect and not take these crimes personally, this one made his chest hurt. One beautiful young girl brutally murdered and one wheelchair bound, innocent boy sent to his deathbed by the hands of a thug-punk-kid.

"Yeah," he said. "I know, I know. It just sucks. It always sucks."

4

INCARCERATION

9:00 A.M.
Two Days Later
Bexar County Jail
San Antonio, Texas

From his position on the floor, Matthew stared at the stark ceiling above his bunk. He had spent most of his time staring at it since he'd arrived at the Bexar County Jail three days earlier. A sudden *bang, bang, bang* against his cell door startled him. He jumped up and rubbed at his temples, the sound resonated painfully behind his eyes. He pushed himself to his feet with a groan.

His body felt sore from head to toe thanks to the thrashing he'd received three nights earlier. Ironically, he was at the hospital at the time; even more ironically, his father had been the one who had pummeled him.

Stupidly, Matthew had tried to forestall the beating by saying, "Dad, it's me! Matthew!" Of course, claiming to be the man's dead son had only infuriated him.

He squinted across the cell with his one good eye before starting toward the door. He reached up, touched the swollen eye, and smiled, knowing his father had tried to punish Cruz. Until that beating, Matthew had questioned his father's love for him. As the Motor Neuron Disease took hold and Matthew's condition deteriorated, his dad's role had turned more clinical, less fatherly.

At the door, he peered through the tiny window at a jailer who stared back at him with a blank face.

"Assume the position, Cruz," the jailer said in a voice just as blank.

Unlike the police detective, Matthew felt the jailers bore him no malice. They were simply doing their jobs. *Or were they?* It struck Matthew that he had been through this routine every few hours over the past couple of days. He would just fall asleep and then be moved. No doubt the detention staff knew Jeffery Cruz had been incarcerated for the murder of an invalid kid.

So maybe this is their way of delivering justice, he thought.

A new expression painted the jailer's face. Impatience. And something else.

Is that fear?

"What the fuck is wrong with your eyes. Hey, John, come look at this." The other jailer's equally placid face pushed into view, and he gasped. "What the . . ." Then they moved back. The men left for a couple of minutes, and just as Matthew moved to sit back on the bunk, they returned.

"Assume the position."

Matthew glanced at the door. The first, blank-faced guard had returned, but this time, a stern expression painted his face.

Matthew knew what they expected of him. He walked back up to the window and looked the man in the eyes. This time, the man did not flinch. Matthew thought it might not be a good idea to push this new revelation about his eyes, whatever it meant, so he turned his back to the door and slid his hands behind him through the chow hole. He felt strong fingers lock down his thumbs, and the soft, sheepskin wraps fastened around his wrists. Together, they created an excruciating lock-hold he would be a fool to resist, so he did not.

He winced as the lined, leather cuffs were tightened over his bandaged wrists. The bandages covered bruises and lacerations he'd inflicted on himself, ironically, also while at the hospital. He got the bruises on the first night while attempting to squeeze out of the detective's steel handcuffs. Then he received lacerations on the second night while trying to slash his wrists with a bedspring from the infirmary's cot mattress. The bunk in this cell had a one hundred percent cotton mat about three inches thick.

"Move to the spot," the voice said in the same colorless tone he'd started getting used to. "Step to, boy, hurry up."

Matthew shuffled his feet forward until they filled a pair of black footprints painted on the floor. Then he leaned toward the wall in front of him where a simple black circle had been painted just above eye level. The footprints and head target were designed to keep dangerous criminals off balance. He tried to resist gravity, but he inexorably tipped forward, and his forehead struck the circle with a dull thud. Too short a distance to be physically painful, Matthew immediately understood the passively demeaning form of control to be another variation of punishment.

To punish dangerous criminals like me! Matthew thought. *No! Not like me. Like Cruz. I'm not like him.*

The two Jailers entered the cell.

"Stay still, boy," the blank one said while the other one pressed Matthew's head into the wall unnecessarily hard. Without another word, they wrapped a leather belt around Matthew's waist, then locked the cuffs to a ring on the belt near the center of his back. After they completed the ensemble with ankle cuffs, the jailer with the dead voice said, "Go."

As the trio shuffled down the hall, Matthew decided Cruz's

subconscious had caused the suicide attempt, probably as a side effect of whatever drugs he'd been given.

Maybe, he thought, but he couldn't quite get himself to believe it.

"Where are you taking me?" Matthew asked.

"Shut up and keep walking."

The clanging from his leg irons, which seemed to get louder with each step, made it hard for Matthew to shake the idea that they were leading him directly to the electric chair.

That ain't going to happen, he thought, trying to calm himself, *because in Texas these days, we convicted murderers get to choose our form of execution: lethal injection or firing squad.*

Before he could laugh at his maudlin joke, the guards jerked him to a stop in front of an unmarked door.

When his guards forced him inside, Matthew realized that he had seen rooms like this on television a hundred times before. Bulletproof glass: check. Chair facing glass: check. Two-way phone connecting prisoner to person on other side of glass: check.

"You have a visitor," the blank guard said.

A powerful hope rose in Matthew's chest that his father had somehow understood the truth and came to visit.

The bigger guard uncuffed his right hand. His left hand remained secured to the steel ring affixed to the leather belt around his waist. When they jostled him to sit, a sudden, over-whelming need to apologize to his parents for failing them brought tears to his eyes. That feeling died instantly when a puffy-eyed, round-faced Latina woman appeared on the other side of the glass. Her heavy red lipstick and gaudy makeup nauseated him. Nonetheless, when she picked up the handset and motioned for him to do the same, he grabbed the old-fashioned phone and brought it slowly to his ear.

"Hijo querido, querido. Te amo, te amo," she blubbered.

Oh, Jesus. Don't waste your time, he thought. *I don't speak*

Spanish. "Que quieres?" he asked, stalling for time and pretty much exhausting his Spanish skills. "Se hablas Inglés?"

But the woman seemed too upset to listen or to hear. Instead, she erupted into a flood of Spanish that Matthew sensed to be a mix of pity, rage, confusion, grief, and shock. Shock that finally shut her down. Shock that made her stare into his eyes. Shock because whatever she saw there sent huge tears rolling down her face.

"My sweet baby's eyes."

Matthew let out a sigh of relief hearing the woman speak broken English and had a sense that Cruz's Spanish might be as bad as Matthew's.

"Oh, Dios Mio, mi hijo, mi hijo. What did they do to you?" she asked, weeping.

Weeping? Really? Over your lowlife, murdering son?

Matthew gasped. The woman wasn't speaking English. Something inside Matthew had switched. He understood her. He wondered how but pushed the question aside.

"What?" he asked, speaking Spanish easily now. "What's wrong with my eyes?"

"One is swollen, and the other looks kinda red or something. You never had no red eyes. They are . . ." she leaned forward and squinted, ". . . kinda glowing. Oh mijo, estas poseido?"

Matthew sat back in the chair, his brow furrowing in thought. The guards had also said something about his eyes.

But possessed?

He thought that made some sense. Cruz was most certainly possessed. By him. Matthew focused from Cruz's mother to his ghostly reflection in the bulletproof glass, trying to inspect his eyes, but the reflection appeared too fuzzy to see details. He leaned back. Dozens of questions flooded him. He thought about the attack. Wondered if the reason . . .

"Son, are you listening to me?" Jeffrey's mother asked. "Has the doctor seen you yet? They said they were going to send you to a doctor."

Really? They hadn't told him that. Maybe Cruz is dying. *Good.* He deserved to, but then . . . *Dammit, where does that leave me?*

Finally, he asked, "Why do they want me to see a doctor?"

"Because you say you are not mi hijo. You say tu nombre es Matthew Miller. Crazy things como eso."

"Is Matthew Miller still alive?" So weird to be asking about himself in the third person.

"No sé, mi hijo. I know you didn't mean to hurt him," she said, mistakenly believing her son to be concerned about Matthew's life. "Cariño," she added, rapping on the glass with heavily ringed fingers. "Tu no diga nada a estes cabrones. You wait for your lawyer."

Good idea.

Here he thought nothing good would come of this conversation, but her words rang true: the police were only interested in a confession.

Good thinking, lady. He smiled at her.

"I know you, cariño," she said, weeping again. "You're a good boy."

Matthew's smile disappeared. A wave of uncontrollable anger surged through him because he knew damn well what Jeffery had done, and also knew, somehow, that Cruz's mother had to be well aware of her son's criminal nature. "What are you talking about, lady?"

The woman across the glass stared back at him blankly and blinked. "Que? What?"

"If you think he's a good boy, then you have never known your son. Because he's a murdering street thug who stomped on the head of the woman I loved until her brains splattered all over the walls." He spit onto the thick glass.

Alarmed, the woman raised her hands and glanced around at

other visitors in embarrassment. "Ssh, ssh," she whispered. "You don't know what you're saying, mijo."

"I'm not your son," he growled, "I *am* Matthew Miller." Her brow furrowed in disbelief. He rubbed his free forearm against his thigh to chase away the electricity crawling beneath his skin. Then another realization struck him. He enjoyed the fear reflected in the woman's eyes.

"Your son is not a good boy," he continued in Spanish. "He murdered an innocent girl and then attacked a helpless cripple. Me. That pissed me off. So, I stole his body from him. You're not looking at him. You're looking at me. Me llamo es Matthew Miller. Comprendes, puta?"

"I believe you," she said, her voice quivering. "You are not my son because my son would never tell such ugly lies or speak to his mother that way." She dropped the phone and almost fell as she stumbled toward the exit.

"He's a fucking murderer! You hear me, puta?" His screams echoed off the walls as she fled the room. "You raised a monster, and now look what he's done! He's a fucking maniac, lady. He's a fucking murderer, do you hear me? Tu hijo es a cold-blooded killer!"

Guards rushed in and slammed Matthew's face into the glass. He felt the energy flow down his arms and into his fingertips, but before he could explore it, the guards cuffed his right hand again. "I don't want to see that bitch ever again!" he screamed, as they dragged him back into the bowels of the jail. Strangely, when they hurled him back into his cell, his mind suddenly quieted, and Matthew found himself able to use his Calculus brain to calmly analyze what had just happened.

Why did feelings of rage flood me with power? And if my hands had been free, what would I have been capable of?

5

ES-CA-PE'

9:30 A.M.
BEXAR COUNTY JAIL
SAN ANTONIO, TEXAS

"Stand up."

The command came to Matthew as an echo, as part of a dream. In the dream, he laid on the floor of a jail cell as power and anger racked his body and mind. He screamed again and again, desperate to release the pain and the power, but the screaming did not help. Some entity approached from the shadow and worked against him. The shapeless form worked to wrap Matthew in a blanket of nothingness. Matthew tried to hang on, working against the force as it defeated him, slowly creeping up to cover every inch of his body. The blanket was death, the entity wanted Matthew to pass on. At the last moment, as if holding on to the hand of a savior as he hung from the edge of a cliff, Matthew let go. Free of his body, he cried as the last bit of light from his eyes — wide and filled with terror — disappeared into the depths of darkness.

"Cruz," the voice intruded again. "I said stand up!"

The dream ended abruptly, and Matthew's eyes flew open.

He tried to lift his head, but his face stuck firm to the concrete from dry saliva that had drooled from his lips hours earlier. When he attempted to push away from the floor, he found his hands were cuffed. Instead, he struggled through rolling over and sitting up. A million needles pricked his arms and legs as the blood flow returned to his muscles. Matthew discovered his eyes were also glued shut. Flexible enough to reach around, he bent his head down to his side and pawed at his face. A crusty substance crumbled under his fingertips.

Great, he thought. *Cruz is sick. Perfect.*

"Your lawyer is here," said a different guard. His voice, and Matthew imagined his facial features, were just as flat as the other guy's. "Time to get pretty."

Thirty minutes later, Matthew, as dry as time would allow, worked his sore body into a clean orange jumpsuit. Once he zipped up the front, he slipped his feet into the jail-issued shower shoes and stood there, looking at the guards. "How do I look?" Matthew said, as there were no mirrors in the jail wash facilities.

"Like a fucking murderer," the second guard said. Although Matthew had scrubbed the sick-crust from his eyes, some kind of goo had already started forming up at the corners. It blurred his vision, like looking at the guards through a thin smear of Vaseline. The guy who had just spoken shoved Matthew hard in the shoulder, enticing him to either move forward or strike back. This new guard appeared to be a whole lot meaner than the others.

Matthew felt the blood rush to his face. "I am not a murderer."

"Who cares?" the first guard replied.

"What's your name?" Matthew asked. "There are no names on your uniforms."

"None-ya," the mean guard growled. Matthew knew the rest of the joke. *Business is my last name.*

They took hold of Matthew's arms and, once again, began the long walk of shame past the other prisoners. Matthew's mind became muddled with terrifying thoughts. He had no clue what to expect from the lawyer and no clue what to say to him. He wondered if the lawyer had already struck a plea deal, like on television? While his mind raced with possibilities, the guards stopped and unceremoniously deposited him into another cell that had a steel table bolted to the wall and two chairs, one on each side of the table. A dark haired, slick-looking man wearing a tan sport coat, holding what appeared to be a case file, stood up and smiled. The guards both turned to leave.

"Hold on," the lawyer said. "Take his handcuffs off, please."

The two guards looked at each other, then back at the lawyer.

"No can do, sir," one said. "This man is a violent criminal, and he's on suicide watch. Our orders are to leave him cuffed."

"You can stand outside the door, but you will un-cuff my client."

After a brief stare-down, the mean guard huffed, rolled his eyes, and removed the restraints. After Matthew spent a moment rubbing his not-entirely-healed wrists, he glanced at the lawyer's face. Even though he couldn't quite make out what the man's face looked like through the sheen of goo coating his eyes, Matthew gave him a small nod.

The lawyer studied him with what he guessed to be either genuine concern or disgust.

"How old is this body?" Matthew asked.

"Excuse me?"

Matthew leaned in and glared at the lawyer, "I said, how old is this body?"

The lawyer seemed mesmerized for a moment, then unlocked his gaze from Matthew's, and flipped through the file. "Looks like you're . . . eighteen."

Matthew leaned back and nodded. *Officially an adult,* he thought. *This won't be good.*

"Have they hurt or mistreated you in any way? What's wrong with your eyes?"

Matthew shook his head. "My dad did the face," he said, pointing to his still partially swollen cheek, not sure how to explain that *he* had delivered the cuts and bruises. "But I did this." He held his wrists higher and rubbed them again. "My eyes are crusty . . ." he paused, understanding the lawyer wasn't talking about the crust, "and bloodshot because this body is going through some kind of withdrawal, I think. Drugs."

The lawyer handed Matthew a white handkerchief from his leather briefcase. "For your eyes," he said. "Keep it."

Matthew took the kerchief, wiped away the fresh batch of yellow goo, and nodded. "Thanks." His vision cleared up just enough to make out the man's features. The lawyer wrote something on a pad and then settled down to business. "My name is Ruben White. I'm the attorney who has been assigned to represent your case to the court, Mr. Cruz."

"My name's not Cruz," Matthew said, gritting his teeth. Since he awoke in Cruz's body, now eight days ago, he found that something about Cruz's biology made him quick to anger. There hadn't been a day since he'd arrived at the Bexar County lockup where he hadn't gotten into a fight of some kind. "It's Miller. Matthew Mill —"

"I've read the brief on your claim. That's not my main concern right now because no matter who you are on the inside," he said, pointing at Matthew, "Jeffrey Cruz is sitting in front of me."

Matthew thought about his comment. "I can't argue with that," he said.

"I've scheduled an appointment for you to visit with a court appointed psychologist later today." The lawyer slid an appointment confirmation card across the desk for Matthew to read.

"You think I'm crazy?"

"What I think doesn't matter. Only what I can prove." Matthew snorted. "Do not scoff," White advised him. "You need to understand that your beliefs do not refute the fact that Mr. Cruz, whom you appear to be, is going to be put on trial for two counts of murder."

A bolt of fear forced Matthew to sit up straight. "Two counts? No. Only one. Kristi —"

"Two," White interrupted. "Yes, the Sellers girl, but Miller's dead, also."

"No, he's not. I saw the EMT's working on him at my . . . at the house."

"He died last night," White said and paused. "I can see by the look on your face they didn't tell you. I'm not surprised."

Matthew froze, and the energy within him kicked to life.

Last night's dream wasn't a dream. Matthew felt the skin of his face begin to tingle. Things had become far, far worse than he'd imagined. His plans, however vague and half-formed, of escaping Cruz's body had just turned to ash. "I'm dead?"

"No, Mr. Cruz, you're fine. You're talking to me."

"No, you don't understand. This is just a body, a jail I'm stuck in. Much like the one around me," Matthew said, pulling on the front of his jumpsuit and beginning to hyperventilate. "I'm. Not. Jeffrey Cruz." Matthew just barely resisted a powerful urge to prove his point by ripping Cruz's heart from his chest. "So, what you're saying is that my . . . my physical body has died?"

Matthew saw the attorney trying his best to figure out how to phrase his next words. When he opened his mouth, he spoke with deliberate kindness and caution. "If by 'my body' you mean the body of Matthew Miller, then —"

"Yes! Yes! Of course, that's what I mean! I'm Matthew Miller! Didn't you hear me?" Matthew's eyes rolled back in his head as the lack of oxygen caught up with him. When he suddenly slumped forward, the attorney jumped from his chair and caught Matthew's head in his hands just before it collided with the tabletop. Then Matthew heard the echo of keys jangle in the lock. "No. Please. Tell them not to come in. I'm okay."

"You are not okay."

"Give me a minute, and I will be."

White signaled the guards to stand down. "Do you need medical?"

"No. I'm okay now. Just tell me what the paper says." Since his situation seemed hopeless, Matthew questioned if he even cared anymore.

"I'm sorry. What paper do you mean . . . son?" White wisely avoided referring to Matthew as Cruz.

"The one that says how . . . how Miller died," Matthew replied, practicing some wise avoidance of his own.

A wave of calm enveloped Matthew, surprising him by how quickly the panic faded. At the same time, he noticed the return of the strange tickle of energy that had accompanied Cruz's attack, not to mention the incident with Cruz's mother during her visit a few days ago. Something ignited deep in his mind, and he knew that something to be his inner voice, telling him it was time to go.

If you stay here, you die. You have to get out.

As if encouraged by the words, the something deep inside flooded into him like water busting out of a broken dam, the power so pervasive that his hands began to twitch. A small smile lifted at the edge of Matthew's lips. He nodded at the lawyer. "Go on. Tell me."

The lawyer hesitated a moment before scanning to the bottom of the medical report. "According to the autopsy, the cause of death is listed as asphyxiation."

Matthew's face went numb, just like it had on the gurney back at his house. He thought it very likely that a moment from now, he would be throwing up on the lawyer, just like he had thrown up on the detective.

"Can you, please, tell me everything it says?" Matthew asked, stalling for time. The river roared in his ears, and the power swelled. He sensed the power rising to an almost maximum level. In a matter of seconds, it would be ready for release.

The lawyer's eyes returned to the top of the form, and he began to read. The drone of medical jargon soothed Matthew. Much of it written in words he understood, having been the subject of hundreds of medical tests over the past ten or so years. He closed his eyes, spread his arms, turned up his palms, and listened until he heard "the cause of death determined to be asphyxiation" for the second time. "Thank you. Now read me the charges," he said.

"Look," White replied, "before we get to the legal end, we really need a psychologist to examine you."

Matthew heard the anxiety in the lawyer's voice, but he remained calm.

Is that because of the power working its way through my body? he wondered again.

"Can you, please, read the report to me?" he asked. While White read the charges, Matthew allowed his eyes to close and let the thrum of energy pulse through him like some Native American drum. The rhythmic pulse felt so complete and synchronous, it made him sleepy.

"Charge one is first degree, premeditated murder of . . ."

The unspoken name "Matthew Miller" hung in the air causing Matthew to open his eyes only to see tiny dots of light lifting from his skin. The feeling of power coursed through him like a locomotive.

This energy is malleable and tractable. He chuckled. *Jeffrey wouldn't have a clue what in the hell those words meant.* He felt a swell of malevolence rise in his throat and embraced it.

"Can you see the lights?" he asked White.

"Lights?" The lawyer looked around the room, confused.

Matthew enjoyed the puzzled look on the lawyer's face. "Never mind. What about the other guys?"

"What other guys?" White asked.

"The guys who just stood there and watched while Jeffrey killed Kristi. The guys that did nothing to help us."

"What about them?"

"Have they been caught?"

"I don't know," White replied, quickly flipping through pages in Matthew's files. The tremble in the lawyer's voice told Matthew that the man struggled to maintain control. A moment later, the lawyer tried to signal the guards at the door. Matthew slowly followed the lawyer's gaze and turned to look back over his shoulder. The window appeared to be empty of blank faces.

Too bad.

Matthew's head snapped around to face White, and he shot the lawyer one of Jeffrey's unnerving smiles.

"I know one of them," Matthew said. "He takes class with me."

White made a note, keeping his eyes down, but he failed to keep his voice or hand steady. "Can you describe him?"

"Yeah, he's a pasty white boy. His name is Christopher Storey. He doesn't live in my, er, Matthew's neighborhood. But you know what? You don't have to worry about him."

"Why not?" The look of curiosity on the lawyer's face made Matthew want to laugh.

"Because when I find out where he lives, he's going to pay for what he didn't do."

"Let's stay away from those kinds of comments," White said. "Tell me more about Storey. That will show the police that you're cooperating."

"Cooperating?" Matthew asked.

"Yes, Jeffrey. By giving them information . . ." White hesitated. Matthew sniffed the air. His senses were now hypersensitive. He smiled at the smell of fear oozing from the lawyer. "About . . . your accomplices."

"My accomplices?" Matthew shouted, violence undulating through his body. "I'm not fucking Jeffrey Cruz, you goddamned jackass!"

He lunged over the steel table, grabbed White by the collar, and drove the squealing man to the concrete floor. He heard the guards rush in. He felt their batons strike his, *Jeffery's*, legs and back. A moment later their blows didn't matter because Matthew had already reached up and touched the sides of Ruben White's face.

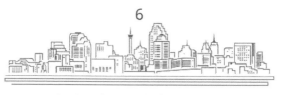

6

WINDOWS TO THE SOUL

12:30 P.M.
BEXAR COUNTY JAIL
SAN ANTONIO, TEXAS

R andy and Melissa entered the jail infirmary to find White sitting slouched on a bed. Randy's gaze followed his partner's eyes to the lawyer. White briskly rubbed his hands together, his right foot bouncing rapidly up and down. When White finally glanced up at the detectives, they exchanged a look of surprise. White's irises seemed to undulate with a reddish glow. Randy gently elbowed Mel. Randy saw her jolt a little when she caught on. She tried to move closer, but the lawyer got up and slowly moved around the bed, putting a barrier between him and the detectives.

Randy said, "We just wanted to get a closer look at your eyes. Are you okay?"

"You don't need to stand closer to me. Please keep your distance. I'm fine," White said, a tinge of anger in his voice. Then he added, "Thank you for asking." Both detectives noticed White's eyes were working double time in their sockets, darting around the room, as if looking for an escape route.

43

"Are you sure?" Mel asked.

"Well, I've never been attacked by a client before, so I guess maybe I'm not okay," he snapped. "My head hurts, and I'm seriously creeped out. I just want to go home."

"No problem, Mr. White," Randy replied with practiced calm, even though, for the first time in a dozen years on the force, he felt a little creeped out, too. Randy had seen those eyes before. "We can get a detailed statement from you later." Randy sneaked a peek at Melissa. She simply raised an eyebrow. "What we need right now will only take a minute." Randy couldn't shake the feeling that White looked ready to break and run. "Before you talk to us, maybe you want to see a doctor?"

"I don't need a doctor," White flared, then collected himself, "but again, thank you for your concern." His eyes flicked everywhere except at Randy. "There's not much to tell. I was trying to explain to —" He interrupted himself with a manufactured cough that Randy took note of. "— my client, Mr. Cruz, that we schedule a psychologist to see him when he snapped."

"Did he say anything before the attack?" Melissa asked.

"No. I was just getting ready to call for the guard when he attacked me." White did everything possible not to look the detectives in the eye.

"You sure he didn't say anything?" Randy asked. White's behavior had him on high alert.

"No. Before I knew it, he'd jumped me and beat my head into the concrete," White said. He folded his arms defensively across his chest and started tapping his foot again. The detectives turned away to have counsel.

"What do you think? Concussion?" Randy whispered to Melissa.

"Yeah, could be. If the beating was that severe, short-term memory loss fits too," she said quietly.

"I'm standing right here, you know," White interrupted. The

detectives turned to face him. White looked guiltier than ever. "I do remember one thing Cruz said."

"What's that?" Mel asked.

"He kept saying, 'My name is Matthew Miller' over and over."

"Why would he say that?" Randy asked.

"How should I know?"

Randy narrowed his gaze at the lawyer but said nothing.

"I don't feel well," White continued. "I think you're right. I will see my doctor. Can I go now?"

"Sure," Randy said and signaled the guard outside. White collected his leather satchel and moved from around the bed, careful to keep more than an arm's distance from the detectives. Randy and Melissa's eyes were glued to the man. White went to the door as the guard on the other side unlocked it. White fidgeted, tapped his leg, and repeatedly glanced backward.

When the door finally opened, Melissa stepped in front of White and said, "Just leave us your card."

"My . . . what?" White stammered. His leg tensed, ready to bolt. His strange eyes pleaded to be released.

The detectives said nothing for a long moment, until Melissa said, "Your business card, Mr. White. We need a way to contact you."

"Oh, yeah," White said. He looked around him, opened the flap to his messenger bag, and nervously rifled through it. "Ah, here we go." He smiled and handed a card to Melissa, his hand trembling.

"Seriously, Mr. White, maybe we should call the doc," Mel said.

"No, no. I'll go in myself. It's just nerves. Fucking disrespectful kids." Mel nodded and let White pass.

"Sorry about Kristi," Randy said unexpectedly.

White froze, his head snapping up, but he didn't look at the detective. "Yes, detective, those victims did not deserve what

Cruz did to them." Without another word, Lawyer Ruben White charged through the door.

Melissa turned to Randy. "What was all that about?"

Randy shrugged. "Just a hunch. He didn't even ask about the condition of his client, who is in a coma. And what lawyer doesn't say 'what my client is alleged to have done'? If that guy isn't hiding something serious, then my name is Mudd."

"The guards say they never touched him," Melissa reminded him. "And the video feed to the room for those few moments has just oh-so-conveniently disappeared. Why would they do that?" she asked. Randy folded his arms, deep in thought, as his partner continued. "They couldn't know any of this was going to happen. And as far as I'm concerned, they didn't do anything wrong. As far as I'm concerned, it's White's fault for insisting they un-cuff his client." Randy still didn't respond. "Uh oh, Detective D'Agostino," Mel said, poking him in the chest. "You're thinking again."

"How do you know?" Randy laughed.

"I can smell the wood burning," she said.

"Something isn't right," Randy replied.

"How do you know?"

"I don't," Randy said, "but did you see his eyes?"

HAVING SUCCESSFULLY COMMANDEERED THE BODY OF RUBEN White, Matthew wandered through the visitor's parking lot of the County Jail. Although elated by his freedom, the lawyer's heart pounded in his chest because Matthew felt equally terrified of getting caught again. He'd come too close to blowing it with the detectives, especially the one called D'Agostino. This thing he did, he hadn't even thought about what to call it, *shifting maybe,* felt too surreal, too unbelievable. He felt certain he walked a tightrope of insanity that he would lose himself in if he made one more mistake. But now, just like in the jail, a voice — maybe it was God after all — echoed in his mind, repeating over and over that he had been given a path of opportunity.

Keep it together, dumb ass.

He calmed himself with a few deep breaths, and then he committed to behaving as normally as possible.

Now what? He looked around the parking lot, fighting off the panic that threatened to overwhelm him. *Find the car, dumbass.*

He patted the outside of the pants he wore and felt the form of keys. He pulled them out, held the remote high in the air, and pressed the button. *Beep, beep.* He made his way toward the sound but had to hit the button a second time to locate the car. He got in, put the key in the ignition, and started the engine.

"Now what, dumb ass?" he said. "I don't know how to drive." And yet, his right hand automatically draped over the gear shift, and his right foot rested comfortably on the gas pedal. It felt familiar. Matthew thought driving might be part of White's ingrained abilities.

I can do this.

He turned to look behind him, pulled the shift lever down, and eased off the brake. Matthew allowed Ruben's subconscious mechanics to take over. As the car took him down the road, just below the speed limit, he laughed.

"I'm . . . fucking . . . driving," he said under his breath, almost as if he were doing something wrong. Then the realization filled him with joy as he roared with laughter. "I'm driving!"

He had read about muscle memory, mostly because his own muscles were forgetting everything. He had read just about every book on everything you could imagine while stuck in the chair. But that chair would never be part of his life again.

Holy shit, he thought. *I'm not about to die anymore. My old body is dead, and I've escaped.*

Matthew drove. He had no idea where he might go or end up. No idea what to do next. Then thoughts of Kristi erupted in his head and, just like that, he had a plan. He pulled to the curb, reached into White's briefcase, and pulled out the case file. When he flipped it open, a flash drive and small adapter fell into his lap. He retrieved White's tablet and powered it up, then he located the mini port and shoved the flash-drive into it. It contained exactly one file: Case number 18-018619, Miller Crime scene video. He double tapped the MPEG icon to open the video file and his heart began to pound.

After a moment, his living room appeared on the screen. And watched himself, chair-bound. Helpless. Worthless. And then came Cruz. Attacking Kristi. Matthew turned away. He couldn't stand to watch it again. But suddenly, he felt like a coward and forced himself to watch. There they were on camera. All of them. Even Jeffery's crew sporting the same stupid look on their faces. He remembered them watching, doing nothing — nothing — while their buddy killed Kristi and then killed him.

"I swear, as God is my witness, if I ever find you two . . ." and the answer came to him. He knew where to start. "Christopher Storey," he said. A concoction of anger, fear, and excitement pulsed through him. Matthew picked up a pair of sunglasses from the passenger seat, put them on, and looked in the rearview mirror. "Better," he said. His lips tightened with deter-mination as he put the car in gear and peeled away from the curb.

IN THE JAIL'S CENTRAL CONTROL CENTER, RANDY AND MELISSA leaned in over the backs of the shift lieutenant and the Central Control video operator to review the "lost" footage from the interview between Cruz and White. The segment just so happened to magically reappear once Randy started making threats.

"So glad you found it," Randy quipped to the video op. Wisely, the operator refused to take the bait.

"Our guys didn't do anything wrong," the lieutenant replied, bristling.

"Except maybe allowing the cuffs to come off," Melissa observed. The operator covered a grimace with his hand.

They watched the video in silence until Cruz grabbed the lawyer. "Freeze it," Randy said. "Then back it up a little."

The operator scrubbed back the video.

"Stop! There," Randy said. "Move it forward frame by frame."

The images clicked forward. Cruz's hands rose and reached for White. Cruz's hands touched the sides of White's face.

"Stop!" Randy said, studying the still frame. "What is that?"

"What?" the lieutenant asked.

"Can't you see it? There's like a spark of light, or something, jumping from Cruz's hands to White's face. Right there." He jabbed the screen again for emphasis.

Shit. Just like the Miller kid's home video. Shit. Shit. Shit. Fool me twice, shame on me!

"It's a glitch," the lieutenant said.

"I smell the wood burning, partner," Melissa said.

The lieutenant snorted. "Can we move on to the part that clears my guys?"

"Your guys?" Randy barked. "I don't give a shit about your guys. Make me a copy of the video to the point just before your guys pummel Cruz. I trust you'll handle their excessive use of force appropriately." The video op looked to the lieutenant. "Don't look at him. Do it now or I call County Internal Affairs." As an afterthought, Randy slid his hand into his pants pocket and pulled out a small USB thumb drive. "Copy that video onto this, maximum resolution. There's plenty of space."

The op reached for the USB but didn't actually take it until the lieutenant nodded. Then he quickly swiveled back to his console and plugged it in. "OK, copying now."

"How long?" Randy hissed.

"Seven minutes. And no, I can't make it copy any faster. The file is non-compressed MPEG format so you can view it on any platform and enlarge it without losing resolution. That's what you want, right?"

Randy nodded but glared at the progress bar on the console. "Mel, you got your radio?"

"No, it's in the car. What's going on? Talk to me."

"Can you run outside and see if White is still in the parking lot? We need to get White, now."

"Why?"

"I can't explain it. It's just a feeling I have . . . a bad, bad feeling. Please. If he's not out there, see if you can get a call in for his car registration and put out a BOLO."

The second Melissa buzzed out, she made for the exit at a dead sprint.

Randy rested a hand on the op's shoulder and squeezed. "Come on, man. You're killing me."

"Another five minutes, detective. I . . ."

"Yeah, yeah, I know, you can't make it go any faster. I get it." Randy paced the room like a rabid dog, not saying a word until the op said, "And, done!" He ejected the thumb drive and handed it to the detective. Randy bolted out the door.

"You're welcome, Detective!"

7

ONE DOWN

SAN ANTONIO, TEXAS: SOUTH SIDE

At 4:30 p.m., Melissa pulled the car up to a house with four police vehicles and a crime scene van parked in front. She turned toward Randy in the passenger seat and waited. He looked first to the house, then turned back to her.

"I'm guessing you're going to tell me why we're here?" he asked.

"Sure. We're doing our job," Melissa said flatly. "You know, we get a call, we answer it."

"When did we get the call?"

"While walking the jail parking lot, looking for that weirdo attorney."

"We should be on our way to weirdo White's residence," Randy said.

"Why? You've got Cruz on video. Case closed."

"That's right. Twice now. Are you going to tell me that White's behaving normally?" Randy looked at his partner with unwarranted expectation. Melissa didn't take the bait.

"Are you going to tell me that you are?" she asked. Randy rolled his eyes. "You watched Cruz stomp that girl's head until it

51

exploded. He's in jail. We got him. And that's exactly what the captain's going to say: 'You got your guy, so what the fuck?' We skip out on this fresh meat, and the captain will have both our asses."

"I told you," Randy pleaded, "I have a hunch we need to follow up on White."

Melissa turned to her partner with a raised eyebrow. "A hunch? Look, I know your gut feelings are pretty good, but . . ." Randy started to open his mouth, but Melissa held up a finger. "Yes, I know, damn good. So, let's just get a quick look at this, and we can hand it off *after* we cover our asses. Cool?"

"Fine. Let's just get this over with. What was it called in as?"

"Probable gang-related homicide."

"The second we determine this is gang-related," Randy said, as he slid out of the car, "we hand it off to the gang unit and head straight to White's residence. Fair?"

Melissa shook her head. "Not fair, but whatever."

After he closed the door, Randy's attention focused on a uniformed officer trying his best to console a distraught woman.

"Awesome," Randy said. "I'll take the house. You take the screaming relative."

"I wouldn't have it any other way," Melissa said.

On his way to the house, Randy turned and said, "Oh, and switch your radio over to Tac-2."

"Nobody's listening," Melissa said.

"Bullshit. Those stalkers who call themselves the news media are always listening."

"Asshole," she called after him, but still switched her radio to channel two. She glanced toward the wailing woman, turned the air conditioner on high, and rolled up the passenger window Randy had left down. Leaving the car running, she got out, straightened her blouse, and headed for the woman. The uniformed officer turned to Melissa.

"This is the victim's adopted mother," the officer said, turning back to the woman. "Mrs. Storey, this Detective would like to talk to you, okay?" The woman blew her nose in a dishrag and nodded.

"Good afternoon, ma'am, I'm Detective Santos. I'd like to talk to you."

The woman nodded. "Yes. Si. I don speak good Ingles," she said.

Melissa switched to Spanish, "Tu prefieres hablar en español?"

"Si. Gracias."

"How about we talk in my car where it's quiet and cool?" Melissa's calm demeanor won the woman over. Moments later, Melissa gently ushered her into the backseat, and once she settled in, she pushed the door closed with a quiet click. She turned and spotted another uniformed officer coming out of the front door. She whistled and waved him over. "Are you the reporting officer?"

"Yes ma'am," replied the young man.

Cute, but not my type, she thought and bent toward his name tag.

"De La Rosa?"

"Yes, ma'am."

"Call me ma'am again, and we'll have a problem. You can call me Mel or Detective."

"Fair enough, Detective," he said, giving her his best poker face.

"Who called this in as a gang-related homicide?"

"That would be me ma . . . uh, Detective."

"And how did you determine this is gang-related?"

"Age and neighborhood."

"Shit," Santos said, raising an eyebrow. "So, every teenager is a gang-banger in your book?"

"I . . ."

"Have you even talked to this woman?"

"No, ma'am, I mean detective. I don't speak Spanish well enough for an interview. We were waiting for you." He handed the detective the woman's driver license. Melissa nodded, then went around to the driver's side and got into the back seat with the woman. "You are Mrs. Storey, yes? I take it your husband is not Latino?"

"Si. My husband was Ronald Storey. He died last year of a heart attack. He was white, well, Irish. We were only married a few years. Christopher's real mother died in a car accident several years ago." The older woman crossed herself and tears flowed again. "Poor Christopher," she said just as her face morphed into a mask of desperation and pain amid a relentless flow of tears.

"How old is your son?" Melissa asked.

"He was seventeen, poor boy. He was my adopted son. I tried to be a good mother, but once his papa died, he started to hang out with the wrong people. I did everything I could to help him. But he . . . he . . ." She couldn't continue. Melissa held her and let her cry.

Real father and mother dead? This could be gang related after all, Melissa thought.

After a few minutes, she gently pulled away and looked into the woman's face. "I'm so sorry for your loss. Both of them, Ms. Storey, and I'm sorry to be so abrupt, but we need information, and we need it quickly."

"It's okay. I know you're here to help," Mrs. Storey said, getting control of her tears.

"Do you have any idea who did this? Did your son have a beef with anybody at school or perhaps a gang kid?"

"Kid? He hangs out with the wrong kids, but this is no a kid. He a grown man. I tried to tell the officers, but they don't listen."

"You saw him?" Santos asked, making a mental note to have

another conversation with Patrolman De La Rosa. "So, you can identify him? Do you think if I called an artist you could describe him accurately?"

"There's no need for that," she said, sniffling.

"Why not . . .?" Melissa's question died in her throat as the mother shoved a business card into her hand. "Holy shit," she said, then pulled her radio from her belt. "Kilo-19 to Kilo-21."

After a second, Randy answered, "Go ahead, Mel. What you got?"

"You better come out here."

She saw Randy quickly exit the house and got out of the car, hurrying toward him.

"Well, you win on this one, Mel. It isn't gang related. Looks to me like a revenge killing or something," Randy said. "I just texted you some pictures." Melissa met him halfway across the yard, her face flushed.

"Well, we were both kind of right," she said. "You need to trust me more. And you owe me a brace of Coney's for stopping here. Take a look at this." She punched the business card into his chest.

Randy looked at the card and then back at Mel. "Yeah, I got one too."

"Dumbass," she said. "I just got it from *her*. White is the killer. He stopped here before us . . . about an hour ago."

Randy looked at his partner, dumbfounded, until the meaning struck home. "Holy shit. Holy shit! We gotta roll."

"Y'all need to hurry up," the woman yelled in English from the car.

"Porque?" Melissa asked.

"Because when the man leave, he say he not finished yet. I did not understand what he mean until I looked inside and saw what he did to my Christopher. My poor boy." The woman broke out into sobs again. "He's going to kill someone else."

Melissa helped the old woman out of the car. "De La Rosa!"

The young uniformed officer jogged over to them. "Get Mrs. Storey a ride to the station. I'll call in another Spanish-speaking detective to take her statement."

Randy moved away from the old woman and barked orders over the radio. "If he's there and resists, do everything in your power not to use lethal force. It's critical that I talk to him."

"Copy that, but if he's armed, no promises," the radio squawked.

"I get it, Sarge, safety first. But please try."

Randy leaned into his partner. "That is Hernandez from the tactical unit. He's en route to White's place. He'll hold him for us if he's there." The detectives got in the car and sat there.

"Why in God's name would White kill a witness?" Melissa asked.

"Why in God's name did he give her his business card?" Randy asked.

"According to Mom, to get into the house," Melissa replied. "That's when the screaming began."

"No shit."

Mel powered up her phone and looked over a sickening picture of a Christopher Storey with the base of a heavy table lamp still embedded in his skull.

What in the hell is going on here?

"We need to check on Cruz," Randy said.

"He's in a deep coma," Melissa replied, putting her hand on Randy's arm. "The jail's Lieutenant just texted me. He says he's going to handle his guys, but he said to tell you that Cruz checked out just before his guys laid a hand on him. He's making a copy of the take down video for you."

Randy took this all in without a word, but his face remained deep in thought as his mind raced. Mel knew that look, but they didn't have time for it. She woke him up with a poke to the chest.

"Crime scene is on this. We need to focus on finding the skinny black kid from the video."

"Yeah. Let's hope the tac-team finds White first." Randy's phone beeped. He pulled it open and gazed at it. "Bingo!"

"What?" Melissa said.

"A break," he says. "The tac-unit just put out a bolo on a gray 2017 Honda Accord."

"But White drives an Infiniti," she said.

"It says here that car is in the shop. He got a rental."

"Well, that's a start," Mel said, then added, "Look, this victim had to know the black kid. Kids don't do home invasions with total strangers. Hang on a second." Mel got out of the car and approached Mrs. Storey as De La Rosa assisted her into the back of his patrol car.

"Ms. Storey, one more question." The woman looked up at Melissa, her eyes puffed up. "Do you happen to know the name of Christopher's skinny African-American friend?"

"I know him, yes, but I only know his name is Rafi. I've only seen him two or three times with Christopher. I think he lives, he lives . . ." She closed her eyes and thought. "I want to say the south-side, but I can't be sure. I only know I overheard him talking about how bad his neighborhood is."

"Gracias, Ms. Storey. I'll come check on you soon."

"That would be nice. Muchas Gracias."

Melissa paused. "One more thing. Did you happen to see the man's eyes?"

MELISSA RETURNED TO THE CAR. "SHE SAID HIS NAME IS RAFI. Didn't know his last name, and that he might live on the south side."

"Now we're getting somewhere," Randy said.

"I don't know. The south side is mostly Hispanic. I'm thinking if he's black, he might be part of a mixed gang. He may be living on the East Side over by Foster Road area."

"Well, we got our work cut out and some leads," Randy said. "Shit!"

"What?" Mel asked.

"I should have had you ask . . ."

". . . about his eyes? I'm way ahead of you," Mel said. She dropped the car into gear and sped away from the curb. "He wore dark sunglasses."

NEW SUIT

6:15 P.M.
DESPERADO'S BAR & GRILL
SAN ANTONIO, TEXAS

Matthew drove around aimlessly for over an hour before an unconscious urge took over his hands. He had no idea why he turned onto San Pedro Ave, so he just went with it. The location felt . . . *familiar*. Halfway down the block, a strong need for something he could not put a name to forced him to pull into the parking lot for Desperado's Bar and Grill.

Okay. Now I get it. The lawyer needs a drink.

Matthew drove to the back of the lot, parked, and got out. He caught his reflection in the windows of the car and froze.

"Holy shit. I'm such a dumb-ass," he hissed, his eyes darting around for witnesses.

His head snapped to the right and left, looking around for any bystanders. Then in one quick motion, he removed the blood-spattered sport coat and tossed it into the backseat. Then he inspected the dress shirt the lawyer had been wearing all day.

"Fuck."

The shirt had blood spatter on it, too.

He moved to the trunk and popped it open. He lifted a black gym back out, unzipped it, and sorted through what must have been typical gym stuff. He dumped the contents into the trunk. A Fitness World T-shirt unfurled from the bag. "

Perfect," he said. He looked around again and unbuttoned and removed the dress shirt, tossing it in the trunk before pulling on the bright blue t-shirt.

So much for not standing out.

As he entered the front door of the bar, he caught his reflection in a mirror mounted on the foyer wall. Not raising his sunglasses, he could see little dark dots on his face. He spotted the restroom in the back corner, but as he stepped toward it, a group of men sitting at the bar spotted him.

"Rubeno! Como estas?"

He acknowledged them with a quick wave of the hand and a tilt of the head, then fast-paced it to the restroom. Once inside, he checked the stalls to ensure privacy, then stood in front of the only sink and leaned toward the mirror. Slowly, he removed the sunglasses. He shook his head at the tiny spots of dark blood spattered on his face and the strange glow in his eyes.

Like the smoldering embers in a fire pit, he thought. *Real poetic, asshole. Risk it or retreat?*

The sight of the red water running down the drain set off that little spark of power deep in his mind.

Fear and anger. They're catalysts for this, this . . . whatever-it-is.

His mind connected to ancient Native American tales of Skin-walkers he had read about.

"That's what I am, right?" The lawyer's voice clashed with Matthew's thinking voice. He shivered because he already believed it. "I'm a fucking skin-walker. A real one."

When the water ran clear, he pulled wet fingers through White's shiny black hair and leaned forward once again. He stood up straight, smacked himself hard across the face, and squeezed his eyes shut, praying that when he opened them, he would find himself back in his wheelchair, at home, waiting for Kristi. Slowly, his eyes opened. He looked around: no dice. The glowing red eyes still stared back at him. First in his own biological body, then into Jeffrey Cruz. Now he had become Ruben White.

"What the fuck is happening to me?" he asked of his reflection. It did not answer.

He let out a long sigh, relieved to no longer be in Cruz. That body had impulses that terrified Matthew, like he could go berserker at any moment and get angry enough to kill someone. Cruz did kill someone: him. And Kristi.

And now, so have I, he thought, starting to relive his brutal attack on Christopher Storey.

From smart-ass punk kid to terrified young man with one blow from a lamp, Christopher had immediately told him Skinny's real name and begged for his life. But then Christopher had started crying like a big fucking baby.

"Kristi didn't cry like that," Matthew had said.

Then something else had taken over. When he thought about how Christopher had just stood there and watched Cruz stomp, he struck again. Anger had pulsed through him, driven by Christopher's cowardice. That had earned him another blow. That Christopher had fled earned him yet another blow. And another, and another, until Matthew felt justice had been sufficiently served. And he had done it. Without hesitation.

One down, he thought.

He couldn't blame this one on Cruz. Fear slithered through him like a poisonous snake and set off a small, electrical buzz in his ears again. His fingertips felt numb. When he looked into his glowing red eyes, he rushed to the stall next to the sink and violently emptied his stomach contents into the toilet. While retching, he didn't hear that someone else had entered the bathroom.

"You okay, buddy?"

Matthew startled and held onto the toilet bowl with both hands. "Yeah, thanks for asking."

He waited until the man pissed, washed his hands, and left before he snatched a wad of tissue from the roll-dispenser, wiped his lips, and flushed the toilet. He pulled himself to his feet and moved back to the sink, turning on the water to rinse the bile from his mouth. He glanced again at his new reflection.

"Am I as bad as Cruz?" Words drifted into his mind like a whisper from the dark.

No. I'm not. Storey deserved to die. And so does Rafi Wilson. Matthew shuddered hard, then splashed more water on his face. He rushed back into the stall for a second round of vomiting.

Why is this happening? The power surged through his veins and seemed to answer, *Make the most of it, boy.*

Several minutes later, after his nerves had finally settled, he dried his face with a paper towel and did his best to look presentable before dragging himself out of the restroom. Then he crossed to the bar, snatched a mint from a bowl, and planted White's backside on a padded stool. The bartender, a curvy African American woman with bead-laden braids, stopped rinsing glasses and approached him with a perfect smile.

"How are you today, Ruben?"

Fucked, he thought. *I've been murdered, jailed, pulled off the great escape, and already killed someone today.*

"I'm not really sure."

"Maybe a drink will help you figure it out, sugar," she said with a wink. "What'll ya have?"

Her wink caused something to stir inside him. "What do I normally have when I'm like this?"

Two hours later, a stupid grin stretched across Matthew's face. All night long everyone greeted him with "Ruben, so good to see you!" as if he were a long-lost best friend. Matthew finally felt White's body relax for the first time since he'd taken it over. While Matthew had used it to commit murder, every fiber of his being had been tense. Being half-drunk helped Matthew release that baggage, transporting him on a new adventure that only inebriation could offer. Now he understood that White's body used alcohol as a means of escape, and Matthew happily sacrificed himself to the cause.

Within the hour, he found himself talking to the big boobs of a pretty Latina who seemed interested in what he had to say, although, she repeatedly lifted his chin, forcing him to look into her eyes instead. Interacting with a real woman set off a whole new range of sensations in White's body. And Matthew liked it. He ran his index finger along the lines of a colorful tattoo that wrapped around her arm. In the tattoo, a Japanese dragon twisted itself around a cherry blossom tree, protecting it.

"God, I love your dragon tattoo . . . the girl with the dragon tattoo!" He laughed. "Great book, you read it?"

She leaned in and planted a wet kiss on his mouth. She laughed at his bewildered look. "You were doing great, Papi. Don't screw it up now."

Doing what great? Oh, yeah, telling her my story. Maybe I shouldn't do that. But then maybe I should because she is really into . . . . Matthew couldn't finish the thought because he felt her hand rubbing his penis through his pants. White's body responded instantly.

"Where was I?" he asked.

"You were telling me about how it felt to get inside another person's body," she whispered with a squeeze on his private parts. "I want to feel what it's like to have you in mine."

Matthew stared at her and blinked, not sure what she meant. So he shrugged and continued. "Yeah, right. When I move into someone else's body, I think I can do whatever that person's body already knows how to do." He swayed in his seat. "Like this guy," he said touching White's chest. "He knows how to drive. So suddenly I know how to drive! Know what I mean?"

"Yes, I know what you mean, Papi," she whispered and

squeezed him again. Then she moved between his legs, leaned into him, and kissed him harder on the lips. Matthew felt his cock twitch in her grip when her tongue slipped deep into his mouth.

Kristi didn't kiss me like that! The thought made him feel sick and sad, so he pushed it away.

"Yes, baby. I can feel your body knows exactly what to do."

Minutes later, he and the woman were grinding against each other in the back seat of the Accord. Matthew had no memory of how they got there. Normally, that would worry him, but because of the way Rosie — *Rosie? Yeah, Rosie. That's right. She told me her name is Rosie* — squeezed and rubbed his penis through his pants, he didn't care. Instead, he kissed her back, then, feeling wonderfully dizzy, he leaned down to grope and suckle on her naked boobs.

"I like your boobies," he slurred, and then went back to suckling.

"You got some big package, Papi," she hissed. "I wanna play with it." She pushed him back, wrestled his belt buckle free, and pulled down his zipper. "Oh wow, nice." She pulled him free and gave him a few strong strokes before bending her head into his lap. The pleasure of her mouth took control over him. He couldn't resist the urge to close his eyes, reach down, and take hold of her head. A river of ecstasy roared in his ears.

Then, out of nowhere, he felt hands slide off his face. He froze, alarmed for no reason he could think of until inches from his face a hard dick stood at attention from its zipper. Matthew sprang up, leaned over the seat, and turned the rearview mirror toward him. The pretty face of Rosie stared back at him in surprise.

"Oh, my God," Rosie's voice declared. "You have got to be kidding me."

9

PLANNING

10:30 P.M.
SAN ANTONIO, TEXAS: EAST SIDE

M atthew walked into the apartment, found a light switch on the foyer wall, and flicked it on. A cold shiver of foreboding vibrated through him: once the police found the lawyer, they'd be knocking at this door.

Not sure how long that will be.

He knew he had to get out as soon as possible. He spun the deadbolt closed then turned to check out Rosie's studio, and . . .

"Goddammit!" The reflection in a mirror on the opposite wall startled him because he had momentarily forgotten he now occupied the body of a woman. He shook off the little scare and entered the bedroom where he noticed a backpack hanging from the bedpost. He resisted the urge to explore its contents and continued to the dresser. He rifled through it, pulling out jeans, a t-shirt, and clean underwear before the bras brought him up short. He held up a lacy front clasp bra in his right hand, a sports bra in his left. For a moment, he remembered how his left hand had stopped functioning around the age of ten. He tossed the memory aside. Considering what he had been through, he felt deeply grateful to be in a body that functioned like a normal human body should, and *this* body looked fantastic to boot.

Even if it is a girl, he thought.

He looked back and forth between the bras, then lowered his chin to the swell of Rosie's breasts.

"You're kidding me, right?" he whispered.

He rolled his eyes, tossed the lace bra back in the drawer, and headed to the bathroom. Under the harsh and somewhat yellowish hue of fluorescent light, he frowned at Rosie's reflection.

"You look like shit, Rosie," he said, then sniffed at her armpits and wrinkled his nose, "and you need a shower." He turned on the water and tested the temperature. Still standing in front of the mirror, his eyes took in the naked body of his new host. He cupped her breasts in his hands. The weight and silky softness aroused him. He didn't know why they felt so different in Rosie's hands than they did in White's. Without thinking, he pinched the nipples and gasped as a jolt of pleasure sparked directly between his legs. Warmth flooded into his face. He glanced around the bathroom like a kid who had just been caught with his hand in the cookie jar. Nonetheless, he had the urge, or felt her urge, to squeeze her nipples one more time, and he did, marveling at the sensation.

Kristi bending forward to kiss him on the cheek had been the only other time he had seen a woman's bare breasts. He closed his eyes, visualizing Kristi's puffy, pink nipples, and drifted off into a fantasy where she slipped her tongue in his mouth. Without conscious guidance, Rosie's right hand wandered between her legs, the fingers eagerly searched for something. When they found it, he gasped again as this new trigger sent an electrical shock, not just between Rosie's legs, but throughout her entire body. As his finger slid inside her wetness, a very different electric crackle hummed in his ears.

His hand froze, eyes shot open.

"Shit."

He knew this feeling. He'd experienced the same thing when he had moved into Rosie. This didn't feel quite as powerful as when he had moved into the lawyer, or the first time it had happened when he had moved into his killer. Sexual arousal had to be yet another trigger. He sighed and released the energy coursing through him. It dissipated just as quickly as it came on. He found this little factoid about his new power just as interesting as the prospect of sexual arousal- from the female perspective.

As he thought about his predicament, he smacked his lips together, tasting something foul in his mouth.

Rosie's mouth.

It felt dry and tasted strange. He turned on the sink faucet, bent down, and sucked in a mouthful of water. He swished it around, then spat.

"Ich, not good enough." He snatched up a toothbrush from a clear cup on the vanity, then located the toothpaste, loaded up the brush, and set to work. He stared at himself in the mirror because he hadn't brushed his own teeth since childhood. Another skill taken from him by ALS. He spat again and frowned at the sight of blood mixed in with the foam. He sorted through the medicine cabinet and removed a bottle of antiseptic mouthwash. He rinsed, the sharp sting in his gums reminding him to be more gentle next time. If there happened to be a next time.

As he moved to step into the shower, a noise brought him up short. He shut off the water and listened. Movement. He knew he had locked the deadbolt; he'd checked it twice. Panic gripped him, and the raging river of power sprang to life.

"Hello?"

He bent an ear to the door, then he heard . . . *A woman singing? Yeah.* The woman had a great voice, could really keep a tune. The angelic song wove its way into him like the call of a mythical Siren, drawing him out of the shower and to the bathroom door, all without him realizing it. When he cracked the door open, he saw a young, thin woman, with pale skin and white hair walking toward the bedroom. Her half-length t-top and low-cut jeans showed off her bare midriff in a way that set Rosie's body to tingling again.

What the hell? She has a key? This apartment isn't big enough for two.

The Siren spotted "Rosie" peeking from the door and said, "Hey there, sexy woman! I love being greeted by naked you. Can I come in baby?" Without waiting for an answer, she pushed her way into the bathroom and ran a hand down Matthew's bare arm, igniting a fire deep in Rosie's belly.

Matthew immediately wondered why Rosie would be screwing around with the lawyer if she had a girlfriend. He pushed the thought aside and addressed the Siren.

"I . . . uh, I was just getting ready to shower." Matthew felt guilty and flustered, even if Rosie's body didn't. The Siren couldn't be much older than him, the male version of him whose body was now dead. He raised an eyebrow. Now that he saw this other girl, Matthew thought Rosie to be an older woman by comparison, maybe in her late thirties or something.

"Mmmm, I'll help," the Siren purred, pressing Rosie's body to the wall and kissing her deep. Matthew melted in the woman's arms, helpless to contain the wetness as it trickled down the inside of Rosie's thighs. The power sizzled through him, riding a wave of pleasure as this totally hot girl kissed her way down Rosie's neck and gently bit Rosie's sensitive nipples. Then the Siren's fingers worked their way into Rosie's body and the electricity flowed. The girl dropped to her knees and buried her face between Rosie's legs. The woman whispered something, but Matthew only heard the river of power rushing in his ears. He thought about who this girl with a key might be, and a tiny jolt of pain shot through his head as out popped a name.

Sara. Her name is Sara.

His hands automatically caressed Rosie's breasts and pinched at the nipples again. Then his hands slid down toward Sara's head. He froze.

Don't touch her. Do not touch her. You know what will happen.

"Oooh, you *are* ready for me, aren't you baby?" the woman crooned. Matthew realized he couldn't move because each lash of the girl's tongue sent a paralyzing wave of pleasure through Rosie's body. Matthew opened his eyes and realized that he had lifted a leg to give Sara full access. Then he remembered.

"Oh shit. The police," Matthew said.

"I'll get the cuffs, baby," Sara replied.

What? Matthew thought, then shrugged off the comment and pushed Sara away.

"No. The Police are coming. We need to get out of here. Right now." He didn't know why, but paranoia shot through him. Convinced the cops were about to burst through the door, he reached into the shower, turned off the water, and collected the sports bra.

"What? Why?"

"This creep from Desperado's. I think he followed me home." Matthew shocked himself by how easily this lie came to him.

"Why would he follow you home? Did you invite him back here?"

Heat rose to his face, annoyed by how quickly his lie got beyond his control. "No, no. I didn't invite him here."

Sara's tenderness suddenly returned. "Oh, baby, did he hit you?"

Matthew blinked at the question. His breath caught with understanding. "No. He didn't hit me. He wanted to do something else to me, but I shut him down. He got pissed."

Sara took Rosie's face in her hands, looked deep into her eyes, and gasped. "Are those . . . contacts?"

Shit.

He had forgotten about the glowing irises. He ignored the question and pushed away from her. "Look. I saw him drive by. I don't feel safe.I called the police, but they're not here yet, and I don't feel safe. I just want to get out of here. Go to a hotel, just for the night." Tears sprang to the edges of Sara's eyes.

Shit. Now she's upset?

Fortunately, Rosie's instincts took over, and Matthew pulled the woman into Rosie's naked warmth and kissed her sweetly on the lips. "Come on. Come with me," he whispered and kissed her again twice as sweetly. After a moment, Sara relaxed into the embrace and kissed him back with a hunger that Matthew eagerly matched.

"I thought you were going to shower," the girl said.

Matthew slowly pulled away but grinned. "And I thought you were going to join me." Sara's radiant smile enticed him, but as much as he wanted to give in to the desire coursing through Rosie's body, *his* senses were screaming that they needed to go. Now. "At the hotel."

He bent over to pick up the clothes from the toilet seat, then rose to find the girl watching him slip back into Rosie's dress. He spun around so that Sara could zip him up. Sara kissed his back, and Matthew pressed Rosie's mind to try and recover another of Rosie's memories about this girl. The name Stephens came to the forefront, along with another sharp stab of pain. His knees buckled. Sara grabbed him by the waist and steadied him.

"What's the matter, what's wrong?"

Concern etched the girl's face, but Matthew did his best to shrug it off.

"Just a headache," he said. "I'll be alright." He collected the toothbrush and toothpaste from the sink and moved past her into the bedroom where he pulled the backpack off the bedpost. He had no idea what Rosie had stashed in there, but he had a hunch he would need it. He stuffed underwear and t-shirts into the pack, unsure as to what he really needed other than the essentials. "Sara, I need you to drive your own car."

"What? Why?"

"Because I need you to hang back and make sure that he's not following me." Matthew turned his face away, not wanting Sara to see the scarlet flush trigged by yet another lie.

"You're scaring me, Rosie. Tell me what's going on."

"I told you. I think he followed me home. Look, he drives a . . ." Matthew had to think about it. He made a mental note to start paying better attention. "A grey Honda Accord. Once you're sure I'm in the clear, call me. Then go find a hotel somewhere far away from here. I'll join you, but I've got to go by the bank first."

"I've got money. You don't need to go to the bank."

Matthew thought about all the *Without a Trace* television episodes he'd watched and leaned on them for guidance. He knew that any attempt to use Rosie's credit or debit cards would result in a paper trail. Sara had a point, although Matthew didn't think Sara's thoughts aligned with his. Not right now, anyway.

"You don't mind?

The girl stepped up to Matthew and kissed him on the lips. "You know I don't. But this isn't like you. None of it. There's something you're not telling me, and if you're that concerned, we need to call the police."

"No!" Matthew snapped. Sara yipped in surprise and took a small step back. "No police." He regretted the outburst as soon as tears welled up in Sara's eyes once more. Matthew took a deep breath, annoyed that now he had to walk on eggshells concerning this girl's feelings. "Look, I have to get out of here. I'm sorry that I got you into this mess, but do it my way, or you can leave." Even this comment came out too harsh, and Matthew thought that this kind of behavior might be ingrained in the woman he now occupied. He found the complexity of his situation, of being a girl, interesting, but shoved away the thoughts for later contemplation. "Are you in? I really need you, baby." Matthew hoped it sounded convincing.

Sara's nod came slowly, along with tears and a twitching lower lip. "Of course, I'm with you."

Matthew flashed a brief smile. "Okay then, let's go."

It will be better, he thought, *as soon as I ditch Rosie.*

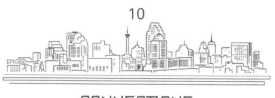

10

CONNECTIONS

12:40 A.M.
FRIDAY, OCTOBER 12TH
MILITARY MEDICAL HOSPITAL
SAN ANTONIO, TEXAS

"Oh, my God. You have got to be kidding me." His watch read 12:39 a.m., and Detective D'Agostino had just found bloodshot eyes gazing back at him from his rearview mirror. "And I haven't even started drinking yet." He shut off the engine, pulled his tired body out of the car, and shuffled across the parking lot toward a bright red sign that read: *EMERGENCY ENTRANCE: MILITARY MEDICAL CENTER.* "Where all the comatose criminals go. And their homicidal attorneys, too," he said, not caring who heard.

Once inside the emergency room's revolving door, a stone-faced MP relieved him of his sidearm. Randy slouched through the metal detector. He flashed his badge at the clerk and quietly asked to see the intake sheet. He scanned it until he located Ruben White's name followed by: *"Found unconscious in the back seat of gray Honda Accord. Condition: deep coma.*

"Cruz here, too?"

73

The clerk nodded. "First, lawyer and client. Now roomies. This your case?"

Randy nodded. "Yeah."

"What a fucking mess. I'm glad I'm not you."

"Thanks, man, I appreciate the vote of confidence." He chuckled, which relaxed the clerk, but Randy had to restrain himself from punching the asshole in the face, feeling too fatigued to even tongue-lash the man. "Which way?" Randy asked. The clerk pointed toward a set of blue doors. Randy pushed through them just as his phone rang.

"Hey, so are you ready for some good news?" Melissa asked, not waiting for his hello.

"I'm about to interrogate two guys who are in deep comas. So, yeah."

"Bartender gave us the name of the girl White left with."

"You got her?"

"No."

"I thought you said you were giving me good news."

"We went to her house, but no one was home. And before you say anything, yes, I've already set up a stake-out on her apartment. So, cool your jets. We're going to get her."

"I love your optimism, Mel," Randy replied. "Any other case, I'd agree with you, but this one is getting stranger by the minute."

"The Tac-team is taking the stake out." He heard Melissa stifle a yawn. "They'll call us the minute she unlocks the door.

"Good job, Mel. Get some sleep. I won't be here long, and I'll be right behind you." He hung up before she could reply because he'd arrived at Cruz and White's room. An MP unlocked the door and let him in. He stood there, slump-shouldered, realizing that he had no fucking clue what to do next.

Nonetheless, he walked over to the first bed. Jeffrey Cruz lay there, comatose and, yet, handcuffed to the side-rails. Randy experienced a momentary urge to put a bullet in the fucker's brain, his hand fingering the empty leather holster on his hip.

He leaned in close and whispered in his ear, "Good thing I'm not like you, right, Jeffrey?" *The fuck I'm not,* he thought, *I'd kill your punk ass in a heartbeat.*

He hoped the kid would wake up, not just because it would feel good to choke the life out of him, but because he longed for the answers that he failed to get during his first interview.

"You obviously don't believe me, Detective," Cruz had said when he'd first arrived at the hospital. That had been eight days ago.

"No shit," Randy said aloud. "I didn't believe you then, and I still don't believe you now. Why should I believe you're Miller when I got video of you beating the helpless kid to death?"

Truthfully, Randy didn't know what to believe anymore. Eight days ago, Cruz hadn't been defiant or rude. Now that he thought about it, he remembered a simple clarity in his weird, red eyes. Cruz hadn't tried to strike a bargain, something any real criminals always did. His behavior simply didn't square with a drugged-up killer. He acted more like a disappointed kid. White had acted like a kid, too, but like a kid caught in a trap. As Randy swiveled his head from one bed to the other, he couldn't shake the feeling an answer stared him in the face. He just couldn't see it yet.

He saw a box of latex gloves on a counter and slipped a pair on. He reached over and raised one of Cruz's eyelids.

"Shit, how about that? They're brown." He moved over to White and did the same thing. *They're brown, too.* He removed a penlight from his pocket to examine their eyes more closely when . . .

"You must be Detective D'Agostino."

Randy clicked off the penlight and spun around to face a haggard man wearing a lab coat and a big shit-eating grin. He extended his hand to Randy.

"How'd you know?" Randy asked, taking the man's hand but irritated by his smile. *What's so funny?*

"I'm Doctor Raymond Bishop, head of Neurology at Methodist Hospital. Matthew Miller used to be my patient, and when I heard about his murder, and then these two, well, I got involved. And here I am. I appreciate you coming at this late hour. I have exciting news to share."

"It's . . ." he checked his watch, "12:52 a.m., where else I gotta be?"

Bishop laughed a little too heartily and smiled again, not registering the annoyance on Randy's face.

"I'm sorry to seem so excited," Bishop said, "but considering the magnitude of what's happened . . ."

"You know what this is?" Randy asked, pointing at White and Cruz who were more than half-dead in their beds.

"Well," Bishop replied, "I can't be certain . . ."

"Why not?" Randy asked, his patience wearing thin. "You called me down here."

"Because," Bishop said, his tone now firm and professional, "in my twenty odd years of practice, I have never seen anything like this."

"Anything like what?" Randy asked.

"Anything like what I'm about to show you," Bishop said. He crossed to the counter, with Randy on his heels, and spread three printouts that Randy thought might be EEGs. "Do you know what these are?" Bishop asked.

"Why don't you just tell me?"

"Of course. They are EEG readouts from three patients. I don't expect you've been trained in how to interpret them." He paused, looking over his glasses at the detective. "Have you?"

For a moment, Randy thought the guy might be trying to belittle him, but even a mad scientist couldn't be that stupid. "Let's assume I don't know anything, Doctor. Please, enlighten me."

Bishop rubbed his hands together and moved to the side of Cruz's bed. Irritated, Randy frowned and rolled his eyes. Bishop bent over to the EEG machine and took a pen from his pocket, pointing to a wire.

"Okay. This machine uses these electrodes to measure brain activity." Randy's eyes followed the pen as it traced the wires from the electrodes glued to Cruz's shaved head to the big white box of the EEG. "And this monitor keeps track of his biometrics and alerts us to any changes."

"I'm tracking, Doctor. I get it. And it gives you those read-outs, right?" Randy said, sarcasm in his voice. The doctor didn't register it.

"Right!" The doctor smiled and moved back to the counter. "So, without knowing anything, I want you to look at the read-outs, side by side, and give me your analysis." Randy felt the need to punch the grin off the doctor's face.

"I told you, Doc, I don't know how to read these printouts."

"Indulge me, Detective," he ordered, which caught Randy pleasantly off guard. "You won't be disappointed."

Randy felt his face flush. He took a deep breath and bent over the papers. After a cursory glance, he squinted his eyes, traced his finger along the lines and gasped. "They're . . . identical."

"Bravo, Detective. Identical, to the last detail."

"You're right. That's unusual."

"More like astonishing. In fact, yesterday, I would have said impossible."

"Okay. Now let me guess who they belong to. One of them belongs to Cruz. Another one to White. And the third one belongs to . . . who?" Bishop revealed the names on all three printouts. The third one read, "Matthew Miller."

"Holy shit," Randy said, standing up straight, eyes wide. "How is that even possible?"

"As I started to explain, it's not. Or it shouldn't be."

"Hold on," Randy said, examining the third printout. "Miller's dead."

"Yes," Bishop replied. "It saddened me to hear that. I felt angry, actually, but between the ALS and the injuries inflicted on him by Mr. Cruz here, I suppose I shouldn't be surprised that Matthew's body was just too weak to make it."

"So, these are old readouts? Why do you have them?"

"Because Motor Neuron Diseases are my specialty," Bishop replied. "ALS is one of them. You see, Matthew couldn't have been more than eight when we met. He ended up being the youngest patient ever to be diagnosed. So, I do have a vested interest in helping in any way I can, even in his death."

"Okay, Doctor Bishop, I get it. I'm sorry if I came off as brash. But I also have to admit I'm still a little lost. It's clear their readouts are identical, but what does it all mean?"

"Now it's my turn to admit something. I have no flipping idea what's happening here. Not yet, anyway." Randy smiled at last. "But look at this." Bishop opened a file with more printouts and invited Randy to view it with him. "Breathing, heart rate, electrical brain activity, are also all in sync. If Matthew were still alive, I am certain he'd still be in sync with the other two."

"Doctor, I'm chasing my tail here. Don't you have some type of educated guess as to why this is happening?"

"Not yet. I'm sorry. I need to do more research."

Randy looked at Cruz and then back at the doctor. "Okay, Doc. Okay. I might have something. It's crazy, crazier than this." He waved a hand around the room. "When I was at the Miller residence to investigate the initial attack, and also later, when I interviewed Cruz at the jail, he refused to identify himself as anyone other than Matthew Miller."

A long silence followed as the doctor attempted to process Cruz's astounding claim. "No," he said at last. "I had not heard that, but I'm sure you'll agree that's impossible."

"And Cruz told this guy," Randy said, pointing at the

comatose form of White, "who happened to be his attorney at the time, the same thing, repeatedly."

"That doesn't prove anything."

"Until he finally went berserk and attacked."

"Wait? What?" Bishop said. "I'm afraid you lost me."

"Welcome to the Club," Randy said. "Here it is." Randy jutted his chin toward the unconscious Cruz. "A week ago, a high school classmate of Miller's — Kristi Sellers — shows up at Miller's home to find a robbery in progress. When she tries to stop it, Cruz kills her by stomping her head until it explodes." Bishop frowned. "Then," Randy concluded, "Miller, despite being stuck in a wheelchair, gets so pissed, he attacks Cruz."

"Obviously a bad idea, I assume," Bishop said, trying to regain his composure.

"Fatally bad. Cruz goes berserk and beats Matthew to within an inch of his life."

"Poor boy," Bishop said. "He was already dying."

"What?" Randy asked.

"The ALS had been progressing at an incredibly rapid pace. My colleagues and I felt that he wouldn't make it much longer because it had started at such a young age."

"What?" Randy repeated.

"Even if Matthew hadn't been attacked, it is very unlikely that he would have survived long enough to graduate from high school. He most definitely wouldn't have made it to his nineteenth birthday."

Randy thought about this information for a moment, then shook his head. "I think that info is irrelevant, Doc. Let me finish. Here's where things start to go strange." Randy began to pace. "Miller goes comatose before he dies in the ER. Hell, Cruz started claiming to be Miller while still on the stretcher at the crime scene."

"Perhaps he was lying to . . ." Bishop began, but Randy cut him off.

"To soften up the jury for an insanity plea?" Randy finished for him. "Yeah, I thought that at first. But then he, Cruz, still claiming to be Miller to the end, attacks his own lawyer." Randy pointed at White. "It happened during a legal consult in the jail, and then he, Cruz, goes comatose right there on the spot. Boom! Out!" Randy slapped his open hand on the table for emphasis. Doctor Bishop jumped. "Finally, White, who we should remember is an attorney, walked out the jail, and as best we can tell, went straight for one of the guys who was with Cruz during the Miller attack. A kid named Storey. Bludgeoned him to death. And here we are." He pointed to the comatose Ruben White.

"Are you kidding?" Bishop asked, his face ashen. "That is so bizarre."

"There's something else we have not released," Randy said softly. "And I need your assurance it doesn't leave the room." Bishop nodded. "After White killed Storey, he told the kid's mother that her son deserved to die for letting Cruz kill the woman he loved."

"Meaning Miss Sellers?" Bishop said, awestruck.

"That's the implication."

"There has to be a simple explanation."

"You keep thinking that way," Randy said, pulling out his iPhone. "Because I've got some video to show you."

SWITCH

4:15 A.M.
FRIDAY, OCTOBER 12TH
UNIVERSAL CITY
N. SAN ANTONIO, TEXAS

Matthew sat up in the bed, yawned, and glanced at the clock on the nightstand. "Damn, it's 5:12 a.m.," he mumbled. "I gotta pee." He slipped from under the sheet, staggered to the bathroom and flicked on the light. "Shit!" The high-pitched yelp emanating from his mouth startled him almost as much as the reflection of the woman staring back at him. He leaned against the wall, clutched at his chest, and took a few deep breaths to slow his heart rate. "How could I forget *that*?" A soft moan coming from the bedroom caught his attention, and he cursed his noisy outburst.

When he leaned out to investigate, a sheet-covered form, barely visible in the dark, rolled over. He'd learned more about Sara on the way to the hotel last night. He'd talked her into following him all the way to the San Antone Inn near Universal City, a solid thirty-minute drive from Rosie's house. During their talk on the phone, for the entire drive north, Matthew learned that Sara and Rosie had become lovers four months ago. They were only part-time lovers now because Sara traveled to big cities so much. Matthew, stupidly, didn't think to ask why. He heard Sara's breathing begin to slow and carefully pressed the bathroom door closed, but the latch snapped into place with a loud click.

"Dammit." He listened for a moment. When the bedroom remained quiet, he leaned against the wall and rubbed at his temples once again, causing the memory of last night's lovemaking with Sara to return. The experience had been much better than he'd imagined it would be, even though he occupied the body of a woman. Simply recalling its intensity set off a tingle deep in his belly and kickstarted the nuclear power plant deep in his mind.

Sara got him so worked up during the first orgasm, he almost ended up inhabiting Sara's body just like he had with Rosie. But he had held off, pulled back. He sensed that with practice, he might be able to control when he slipped into other people's bodies.

The Slip. He chuckled. The term sounded fitting. The slip also felt much like an orgasm: let it build it up, then cut it loose. *Like a fucking jack-in-the-box,* he thought, *Surprise!*

Last night, right after he resisted The Slip, Sara had said, "I'll never keep a secret from you." Matthew's non-reply caused Sara to look up into his eyes, searching for a promise he knew he could not make.

Thinking about it made his head hurt. He squeezed his eyes shut and rubbed even harder at his temples. He had almost told her. Everything. The younger girl possessed a sweet vulnerability that made him feel he could trust her. But not with this. Not yet, anyway. Maybe never. Matthew's eyes opened to the reflection of Rosie's body in the mirror above the sink.

"You are just too damn hot, girl," he said softly. Just looking at her reflection aroused him. *So, did looking down Kristi's shirt,*

Matthew told himself. But this had nothing to do with Kristi. He knew deep down he'd have to get over it. Once he settled the debt. He pinched Rosie's nipples and thought more about Sara. He sensed much more going on between the women. Sara loved Rosie.

Poor Sara, he thought. *You have no idea what lays just beneath the woman's skin. Me.* His attraction to the blonde girl had nothing to do with love. Or even lust. *Because she's a survivor, just like I am,* he thought.

A sudden thought that he could stay in Rosie's body and spend the rest of his life with Sara swept through him like a warm Texas summer breeze. Tears welled up in his eyes when he realized he and Kristi could have had this kind of relationship had he not been ill. None of that mattered, now. Kristi was gone. Guilt flooded his veins at the thought of taking Rosie's life for himself. Sara would figure out the ruse, sooner than later.

He felt the burn of a tear as it ran down Rosie's cheek. He wanted nothing to do with being sucked up into this weird, sci-fi drama and had no idea how to fix it.

This isn't my fault. None of it.

And in his heart, he knew this to be true. He wiped the tear away when more thoughts crowded into his mind, reminding him that he did know something: when he'd moved out of Cruz into White, Cruz did not wake up.

Why?

Maybe because drug-addicted, dumbass Cruz suffered withdrawals. Maybe because Cruz had enjoyed brutally murdering Kristi, and he deserved to die. Maybe Matthew hated being inside Cruz because Cruz had violent, sickening impulses that would not be repressed.

"Bullshit," Matthew said to himself, "because the same thing happened to the lawyer White when I accidentally ended up in Rosie." Moving from Cruz into the body of Ruben White had been like stepping barefoot on a whole new set of mousetraps.

His mind glided over the reality that he, not Cruz, had brutally murdered Christopher. Didn't matter whose body he'd used.

Matthew felt his skin prickle when he tried to rationalize killing Christopher. He thought about Cruz's obvious addiction, but the lawyer had his own closet of skeletons. Where Cruz needed drugs, Ruben's Achilles heel was alcohol. And Rosie? He guessed being in an almost perpetual state of arousal had been her motivation to cheat on Sara. He wondered if someone could really be addicted to sex and supposed that if it caused them to make bad, dangerous decisions, then yes. He rubbed at Rosie's temples again. Thinking about this shit made his head hurt.

His brow furrowed and he frowned when another thought entered his mind. He should be spending his time thinking about revenge.

He stood up straight and turned the body he occupied from side to side, admiring Rosie's profile in the mirror. The woman looked great, but he knew without a doubt Rosie's persona didn't fit what he needed in order to complete his mission. Rosie had to be replaced. He needed perfection.

Matthew studied the sad, frowning reflection of Rosie's face. "Kristi was perfect," he whispered. He stopped, listened, and heard no argument from the recesses of his mind.

Disgusted and exhausted, Matthew turned away from the mirror and started the shower, desperately trying to shift his thoughts to something other than how to get out of this mess. He let his hand drift past the plastic curtain and dangled his fingertips in the soft, warming spray of water. He tried to focus on the science behind his new ability, but the image of Cruz stomping Kristi's head commandeered his mind.

"No!" he gasped and grabbed at his chest. Rosie's heart slammed against her ribs. He fought the flow of energy that threatened to spring to life inside him. *Remember last night,* he thought. *You can control this.*

He took a deep breath to slow the flow of power and then

adjusted the water temperature again. Then he reached for the toothbrush but paused, putting it in his mouth. "Careful this time, boy," he said softly. Once finished, he climbed under the steaming water and moaned with pleasure as the scalding liquid washed away the tension and conflict building inside him. "You know what you gotta do. She tried to save you. Quid-pro-quo," he whispered. "Kristi deserves justice." Cruz's cruel smile suddenly replaced Kristi's kind one. "And that fucker needs to die, no matter what."

"Who are you talking to?" The shower curtain slowly pulled open, startling Matthew. Sara stood there naked, her blonde hair flowing down her shoulders with a sly come-hither smile on her face.

"No one, just thinking out loud," Matthew responded.

"Mind if I join you?" Sara said, waiting for an invite.

Matthew reached out, took her gently by the wrist, and pulled her into the shower. "Perfect timing."

TWENTY MINUTES LATER, MATTHEW LEANED OVER THE BED, tucking in the sheets alongside Rosie's body. He'd positioned her to look like a mummy with her arms crossed over her ribs. He leaned in close and kissed her on the lips. "I'm sorry, Rosie," he said, shivering at the new sound of Sara's voice coming out of her mouth. "But a man's gotta do what a man's gotta do."

He retrieved Sara's purse from the nightstand and moved to the tiny table in the corner of the room. He upended the purse onto the table and sifted through the contents. "Colorado ID . . ." He kept looking. "Texas ID and . . ." He held a small baggie up and examined it. "Pot?"

He snatched a roll of cash, removed the rubber band, and flipped through the money. He guessed it totaled a couple hundred dollars in mixed bills. There were also five different lipsticks, various other make-up items, and a tiny glass vial containing a white, powdery substance. He rolled his eyes and tossed the vial in the trash bin across the room. He smoothed out two wrinkled pay stubs from a local strip club called Super Stars. The name on the Texas I.D. card read Sara Stephens, but the name on the Colorado I.D., no doubt a fake, matched the name on the pay stub, Sasha Stevens. In a side pocket, he found an envelope with twenty, crisp one-hundred-dollar bills.

"So, I'm a stripper," he said. "Makes sense." He glanced at Sara's suitcase and squatted in front of it. He clicked the metal latches open and raised an eyebrow at all the skimpy outfits and shoes taking up a majority of the space. He fished around the inside pockets and found four more envelopes filled with cash. All hundred-dollar bills. "Guess you don't like banks," he whispered.

He stood up with Sara's phone in his hand and powered it up — his hand paused over the keyboard when the passcode screen popped up. He closed his eyes, took a couple of deep breaths, and relaxed. He wiggled Sara's fingers and concentrated. After a brief but sharp stab of pain in the center of Sara's skull, some semblance of numbers came to him like ghosts through the mist. He slowly typed in the access code: 1357. It worked.

"Boom," he said. "We're in, first try. I'm going to have to remember this trick."

As he flipped through files on her phone, he realized he had no idea what to look for. "Okay," he said out loud. "Why are we here? What do we need to do, and how are we going to do it?" The police were no doubt on to him by now. It wouldn't be as easy as Chris Storey had been. He frowned. Matthew wanted, no, *needed* revenge, but he didn't have a clue beyond USA Network action movies as to how to pull it off. "I don't know what the fuck I'm doing," he said. By the photos stored in her phone, Sara only slept with women. "Oh, that's going to change, girlie," he said, "because what we need to find is a man."

Matthew paced the room, feeling liberated and refreshed to find himself in a body that allowed his mind to race, almost as fast as his original brain had, without the burden of being housed in a decaying carcass. "Come on, Sara, help me think. We need someone with a skill set developed around killing and survival, someone with discipline, strength and . . ."

He stopped pacing and slapped himself on the forehead. "A soldier. We need a fucking soldier."

He hurried back into the bathroom, flipped on the light, and inspected Sara's raw, freshly showered and naturally pretty face. "Wow, I feel good. A little too good." He thought about the white vial now sitting in the waste basket, leaned in closer to the mirror, and gave himself a look of admonition through Sara's face and her red glowing eyes. He pointed at the mirror.

"Did you take some of those drugs I found in your purse?" he asked the reflection. He leaned further forward, pushed up her nose, and peered into her nostrils. *Nothing. Good.* He released the nose, wriggled it, and turned her head side to side to examine Sara's profile. He gathered up a handful of the white-blonde hair wrapped around her cheekbones and pressed it to the top of her head. He paused a moment, trying to decide if he should wear it up.

"We have to look our best if we're going hunting," he cooed to the reflection. Then her tiny, elongated ears made him giggle, thinking that, if she put on leather and metal fantasy armor, she would look like a woodland elf from *Lord of the Rings*. "You feel very different than Rosie," he said aloud. He noticed that his thoughts flowed almost as if his original brain were inside Sara's body. He opened Sara's makeup kit, his fingers buzzing with an ingrained ability to apply it. "Oh yeah. We're not going to have any problem finding Mr. Right tonight."

Matthew stopped and glared at the mirror. Something about Sara's body affected him. He raised an eyebrow when it came to him. Where Rosie's actions were dictated by paranoia, Sara had no concerns. No sense of urgency. After a moment of thought, he shrugged and went back to applying the makeup. "But it's a hell of lot better being you than Rosie the Sad-ass, White the Drunk, or Cruz the Killer. That's for sure." He smacked the lipstick, then winked at himself and said, "Let's do this!"

He slung Sara's backpack over his shoulder, grabbed her car keys off the table, and reached down for Sara's overstuffed suitcase. When he tried to lift it, it damn near dislocated his arm and dragged him to floor.

"Damn! Another good reason to find a man." He shoved and dragged and pulled the suitcase slowly, slowly toward the door. When he had one foot over the threshold, another thought came to him, and he dropped the backpack in the doorway. He grabbed the notepad from the bedside table and wrote: "*Please call an ambulance and give the paramedics this note. Transport this woman to Methodist Hospital, where she should be cared for by Doctor Raymond Bishop. He will know what to do.*" He signed it MM.

Chuckling at his inside joke, he folded the note so it would stand up straight, and then he tucked it between Rosie's fingers. "The Doc and Detectives will get a rise out of this."

12

OPTION 3

M atthew pulled into the parking lot of Sara's place of employment, Super Stars Gentleman's Club, just after 7:00 p.m. The valet recognized her, grinned, and waved. Matthew smiled and waved back, but after a quick tour around the parking lot, something inside warned him that this location might be too risky.

"Even though," he whispered to himself, "there's probably a ton of targets in there." As the word "targets" entered his mind, he lightly smacked his forehead. "Dumbass," he said. "How could I forget about the perfect place?"

Matthew's parents had taken Matthew to Fort Sam Houston on many Memorial Days. He tugged the GPS off the windshield and punched in Fort Sam. When the navigation kicked in, he started to drive again. Within fifteen minutes, a sign for the Drop Zone Cafe and Bar caught his attention. Even from the street, he saw several uniformed men and well-dressed ladies enter the bar.

Perfect. Exactly what I need. A real, seasoned military professional, and there is no better place to find this kind of man than right here in San Antonio, Texas. Soldier City. He furrowed his brow. *And I've always wanted to be a soldier.*

He pulled in and had to drive to the very back before he found a place to park. He set the handbrake and examined Sara's face in the rearview mirror, sitting upright when he realized what he did. He let out a tiny giggle that sounded totally alien to him.

"I just unconsciously performed a last second make-up check," he said. He reached into the clutch he'd selected and pulled out and applied a touch-up of lip-gloss. Once outside the car, he looked around, and after not seeing anyone, quickly adjusted Sara's breasts and pulled down her skirt just a tad. He suspected that walking in heels came naturally to Sara's body as well. He thought it easy until he felt her calves tighten up to the point of being mildly painful as she walked across the uneven surface of the parking lot.

When he arrived at the front door, he read the sign taped to the glass: "Closed for private event."

Fuck me.

A couple brushed by him; one fully uniformed soldier and one pretty lady on his arm. Matthew filed in behind them close enough to make it look like they were there together. No one noticed.

Inside the bar, he fit right into the lively party already in progress. *That explains the full lot.*

A big banner hung along one wall that read: "Happy Retirement, First Sergeant Brian Colter!!!" The event seemed to be exclusive, but Matthew felt confident that a cute blonde wouldn't be booted out for crashing it. Matthew made his way past a small group and slid into a seat at the bar. He listened for clues in the chatter around him.

"What'll ya have?"

Matthew turned to the voice and blinked at on older, burley

bartender with a big auburn mustache standing on the serving side, grinning.

"Uh . . ." He had no clue what to order. Where the cocktail menu seemed to be physically ingrained in White's subconscious, Matthew had the feeling that Sara wasn't much of a drinker. "Bud light," he said, giving the big man Sara's most winning smile.

"I.D.?"

Matthew felt heat radiate from his face. He'd rushed this morning, not remembering if he'd brought the I.D. He searched Sara's clutch and found both. "Err on the side of caution," his father had always said. So, he pressed the fake Colorado I.D. to the countertop and slid it toward the old bartender. The man scanned his discerning eyeball back and forth between the tiny laminated image and the girl sitting across from him. Matthew giggled at the man's overly dramatic inspection until he handed the card back with a smile.

"I.D. says your eyes are blue. Those eyes are *not* blue."

Matthew's heart raced. He should have left on her sunglasses. "Pretty cool, huh?" he said. "They're contacts. They glow. Should I take them out for confirmation?"

The old man scrunched up his face and shook his head. "No. Not at all. I've never seen contacts like that, but you don't seem like you're possessed."

Actually . . . Matthew thought.

"From Durango, huh?" The old man asked, placing a frosted mug under the tap.

Matthew had no idea Sara's identification card showed a Durango address. He pinched himself for not being more diligent and took the bait. He nodded.

"How do you know Brian?"

"I don't know him. I came with some friends, but now that I see him, I'd sure like to," he said.

He looked across the bar at the guest of honor. Brian

smiled as his brothers-in-arms toasted the man and rapped him on the back. A tingle of energy ignited deep inside. Exhilaration of the hunt mixed with his blood, sending a wave of excited anticipation and power through him. "I wonder if he's married."

"No, he's not married."

Matthew couldn't hide Sara's flushed face from the bartender. He didn't realize he'd spoken out loud.

"Not today, anyway," the bartender said, also watching the soldiers celebrate.

"Look at all those medals." Matthew found his mark. The man of the hour would suit his needs just fine. *Suit,* he thought. *I can change them like suits.*

"Yeah, he's won the Silver Star for bravery, twice, I think. Brain is a bonafide war hero."

"That's so awesome." He blushed again at the stereotypical blonde response that came from Sara's lips, but the bartender didn't seem to take notice. Matthew's eyes were glued on his target. He mentally willed the handsome soldier to look at him, at Sara. The soldier flashed him a quick glance with his blue eyes, just long enough for Matthew to wink. The sergeant did a double take, then grinned a perfect set of pearly whites.

This guy is perfect, Matthew thought.

The bartender raised an eyebrow and chuckled. "You work fast. Want me to introduce you?"

Matthew thought about the offer. His eyes scanned the room as he sized up the competition. There were several other apparently single women scattered about the room, all very sexy by both Rosie's and Sara's standards. "No, I think I can manage."

"I bet you can. If you need anything, Miss Sasha, I'll be right here. My name is Scotty."

The man extended his meaty hand over the bar. Matthew shook it, surprised by the man's soft skin. "Thank you, Scotty. I'll keep you posted," he said and winked.

"Good luck, young lady!" The older man winked back and moved off down the bar to fill other mugs.

Clutching his second beer, Matthew melted into the crowded bar and slowly worked Sara into a group of four women. Within five minutes, he'd confirmed his initial assessment of the women: Army Groupies dripping with estrogen and looking for their next military husband. Two more hours of hanging out and drinking with Colter's buddies provided Matthew with everything he needed to know about the man of the hour. Fifteen years of service, three deployments each to Iraq and Afghanistan, along with a two-year stint in Germany teaching Mountain Warfare. He also learned that during one of Colter's earlier deployments to Afghanistan, he'd lost part of a leg to an IED explosion. Surprisingly, despite the injury, the Army kept him on active duty. No medical discharge.

"It's a draw down in bodies," one of Colter's buddies told him. "He's getting full retirement and benefits, but they didn't make him take it because of his leg. They offered it to him." When another former platoon member recounted the details of the ISIS-planted IED explosion outside Mosul, Iraq six years ago, Matthew didn't have to feign shock. His reaction couldn't have been more authentic.

"His leg? There's something wrong with his leg?" He studied the sergeant as the man danced with two of the other women near the pool tables. Matthew decided he would never have known the soldier had an artificial leg. More importantly, Brian Colter was now officially out of the Army. According to his friends, Colter had a plan to teach firearms tactics and had already signed on with some paramilitary group to perform close personal protection for private clients. He also planned on finishing his degree. By 9:00 p.m., Matthew had positioned Sara directly across the bar from Colter. He locked Sara's icy stare on the man until they made contact. Matthew tried his best come-hither smile and winked at Colter again. Colter responded by wobbling as he looked at the men to either side of him, returning his gaze toward Matthew and pointing at his own chest. He mouthed the words, "Who, me?"

Matthew giggled and nodded his head vigorously, flashing what he hoped represented Sara's most seductive smile.

Looks like our war hero is quite drunk.

After Matthew made two or three more attempts to get the soldier to do more than glare and grin, he motioned for Colter to meet him by the restrooms. When the soldier nodded, Matthew got up and headed for the poorly lit hallway leading out to the restrooms and back exit. As he stepped into the shadows near the ladies' room, he glanced over his shoulder. Colter still watched him, but he hadn't moved. He shook his head. More dramatic action seemed to be necessary. So, he leaned back and put one stiletto-clad foot on the wall behind him. Then he arched his lower back to force Sara's small, but firm breasts up and forward. He sneaked another peek. Colter still hadn't moved.

Come on already, man! Matthew moved to get up, his only option now to physically sit in the guy's lap when, finally, the soldier got up and pushed past his party guests with his eyes locked on Sara. Matthew's heart raced and his skin tingled with that familiar electrical charge. "Come to Sara, soldier-boy," he whispered. "You can do it."

Then, with strange suddenness, Colter stood beside Matthew in the hall, and before he could even say hello, the big solider pinned Sara to the wall and shoved his tongue in her mouth. He groped Sara's breasts and pressed his groin against hers. Matthew felt himself being lifted off the ground; his feet fluttered in the open air as Colter's hands found their way under Sara's skirt. The man started to force his fingers in. Matthew tried to pull Sara's thighs closed but quickly realized Sara couldn't defeat the overwhelming strength of the man. Fear grew, and an electrical charge blasted through him.

I cannot let this happen. Is this . . . he's trying to rape me? Here? You've got to be kidding.

He focused his efforts on freeing his arms just enough to raise them up. He'd almost reached the target, when Colter slammed Sara hard against the wall.

"Hey, I thought you wanted me?" Colter said in slurred speech and kissed Sara even harder and deeper.

Matthew fought the urge to bite off the man's alcohol-soaked tongue, even though he'd shoved it so deeply down Sara's throat Matthew found it hard to breathe. With his free hand, Colter forced Sara's legs wide open, and Matthew's vision began to cloud with stars like those he had experienced in his own eyes while Jeffrey Cruz had crushed his throat. Terror flooded into Matthew, and little sparks of light danced off Sara's skin. His fear now complete, it fed the power. *I'm ready.*

"C'mon now, baby, don't be a tease," Colter said, giving Sara a chance to breathe. "You know you want me."

"You're right, baby," Matthew grunted, barely able to breathe. "But let's go out to your car."

Colter swooned and then took a long moment to process Matthew's suggestion in his drunken mind. Smiling, the soldier finally made a big mistake by relaxing his grip because the moment he did, Matthew reached up and touched the sides of the sergeant's face.

The brilliant flash of light, nauseous spinning, and spine-wrenching pain lasted only a moment before Matthew's vision cleared and he saw Sara's body going slack. He swept Sara up, amazed at Colter's strength, and kissed her to cover their clumsy move toward the exit.

"Holy shit, this dude is fucked up," he said, after he almost dropped Sara because of the drunken dizziness. He leaned against the door to steady himself and took a moment to glance toward the bar.

Good. No one is paying attention.

Then he pushed Sara and himself through the door into the parking lot where he glanced around again but didn't see anyone. He rummaged through Colter's pockets with a free hand until he found car keys. He clicked the key fob twice and a black, lifted, four-door Jeep Wrangler several rows away flashed its lights in response. He hoisted Sara's body up and over his head to his other shoulder.

"Holy shit, this dude is strong." He jogged over to the Jeep, looked around the lot, and tossed Sara into the back seat. Then he hurriedly locked the doors and hustled back toward the rear exit, hoping to rejoin the party before someone missed him. When he pulled the door open and stepped inside, another wave of nausea and dizziness slammed into him.

"Holy shit, Sarge," he said, chiding himself with a masculine voice that he found startling. "We have to sober up, man." He idled up to the bar, quickly acclimating to the soldier's body. "I'll have a cup of coffee," he said, waving to the old bartender.

"Yeah, I thought you were about ready to fall over. Did you piss the little blonde off?"

Shit, he saw me. "Nope. I gave her my phone number. She says she's going to call. We'll see."

Within seconds, four soldiers pulled up stools next to him, and one of them forced a fresh shot glass of gold-liquid-something into his hand. "To Sarge!" said the supplier, but the bartender kindly replaced the shot glass with a warm mug of coffee. "Tell them about the hairy armpit hooker you set me up with in Morocco," one soldier said. All eyes were on Matthew.

Matthew eye-balled the soldier's Class A uniform and read the nameplate. "You go ahead, Corporal Avery. It's so much funnier the way you tell it." Avery seemed over-zealous to oblige, and Matthew sat back half-listening to the tale because his mind had already lurched ahead to the moment he would find and finish skinny, fathead boy, Rafi Wilson.

"Sarge, are you with us?" Avery yelled in his ear.

Matthew pulled himself back into the world, took a swig of his coffee, and belched.

"Burpees," Matthew said, "It's time to do burpees!" Matthew had no idea where this thought came from, but he had seen soldiers performing them on YouTube, even though he had never done one.

"Burpees?" Corporal Avery asked. The others looked at him and shrugged.

"Yes, Burpees!" Matthew smiled and stood up, pushing several bar stools out of the way, before launching himself into the exercise with abandon. His comrades, his own *Band of Brothers* joined him instantly, and within a minute, every solider in the bar had cast chairs and tables aside to start busting out burpees, too. Scanning the crowd, Matthew privately thanked Brian Colter for the loan of his body, his military service, and the sacrifice he would make in the coming days in the name of justice.

13

CRUE INTELLIS

2:10 A.M.
TUESDAY, OCTOBER 16TH
SAN ANTONIO PD

Approaching the sally port steps of the San Antonio Police Department Jail, Detective Randy D'Agostino noticed the door light was out. He looked to the sky for the bright, first quarter moon, but it was already deep in the west. The sally port was thrown into total darkness. He fumbled through his coat pocket and located his small penlight, pressed the button, and lit the path as he unconsciously tightened his grip on the Miller investigation files. He couldn't stop thinking about Doctor Bishop's reaction to the video of the Cruz attack and the information the doctor had showed him in turn.

For the first time since Matthew's murder, he finally — *and without leading the witness,* he thought — had a more suitable reaction when the little flash of light appeared to leap off Miller's fingertips, apparently moving into Cruz.

"What the fuck was *that?*" the doctor had asked.

Randy would have bet a month's pay that Bishop didn't swear much, and he was pleased the good doctor asked to see that part of the video several times. When Randy showed him the clip from the jail, Doctor Bishop got very quiet, deep in thought. So, Randy laid the same line on the doctor that his partner, Mel, always recited to him during his frequent deep-thinking exercises.

"Well now! I think I smell wood burning. What do you think, Doc?"

"I don't know what to think. This whole thing is just . . . surreal," Bishop replied.

No shit.

On the top step, Randy swiped his I.D. badge across the reader. When the door didn't click open, he swiped it again and tugged at the handle. *Still locked? What the hell?* He looked up into the security camera and shined the flashlight at it while pressing the call button with his free hand, but the usually familiar buzz failed to sound off. "No power to our hi-tech security system? Really?"

He pulled out his handy, dandy, good old-fashioned building key, unlocked the door, and entered the dim hallway. The emergency lighting didn't do shit to help him see any better. He pointed his flashlight down the hall ahead of him. He stopped at the stairs, which he always took out of some need to remind his body it wasn't lazy, yawned, then continued down the hall.

Screw the stairs.

Once at the elevator, he pressed the button. No power. "Fuck me," he said, then walked back to the stairs.

He paused on the fourth-floor landing to catch his breath, then entered the pitch-black hallway; no power there, either.

"Goddamn it." The tiny beam of light cut a surreal path down the darkened corridor, and Randy took it nice and slow toward his office while waving the file folders in the air with the hope of activating the motion sensors for light. It didn't work. He shuffled the last twenty or so feet to the investigation's office where, as a test, he once again swiped his badge across the reader. No luck.

"What the hell?" He fumbled for his office key but dropped the ring on the floor. He looked up at the roof tiles, held up his hands, and said, "God? Why me? Why tonight?" He released a long breath of exasperation, bent over to pick up the keys, and struck his forehead against the door, hard.

"Son-of-a-bitch!"

Finally unlocking the door, he stepped into the office, and used the hard edges of the file folders to flip on the light.

"Good morning, Detective D'Agostino."

Randy jumped, sending files and keys flying, as he reached beneath his sport coat for his Glock 26, 9mm pistol, but two men in mottled grey combat uniforms had already drawn their weapons, racked rounds into the chambers, and had a front-site bead between his eyes before his fingers touched the grip. He almost didn't notice the attractive young woman sitting at his desk. Almost. Randy's hands slowly went up as he glared at the intruders.

"I'm sorry for the theatrics, Detective. There's no need for alarm," the woman said, just as a third man slipped in behind him like a ghost and relieved him of his sidearm. "We're all friends here. You can put your hands down."

"The fuck we are. I think I'll just keep them up, thank you very much, until you people tell me what the hell is going on." Randy didn't feel tired anymore.

As the woman stood up, Randy estimated her height to be around five feet, if that. She wore a grey ball cap with the white outline of a dragonfly sewn into it, a jet-black ponytail of hair protruded from the back. When she moved around the desk, he noticed she wore tactical pants that were tucked tightly into her boots and two, thin tank-tops, showing off muscular arms and shoulders and . . . *how cold she is.* He rolled his eyes, cursing himself at being so easily distracted. She stepped toward him, and he took an involuntary step back, right into the man who took his pistol.

"Easy buddy," the man whispered. "She doesn't bite. Hard."

Randy felt an angry blush heat his face. "Geezus fucking Christ, lady. What is this?" he said, hating the tremor in his voice. "You guys are scaring the living shit out of me. Want to prove we're friends? Have your soldiers stand down."

After a moment, the woman slowly tilted her head, the edge of her mouth curling up into the slightest of smiles. Without taking her eyes off Randy, she gave the slightest nod, and the men holstered their weapons in sync as the man behind him closed the office door. "Who are you people, and what the hell do you want?" Randy asked, more than a little frightened and not at all taken in by the exotic little succubus.

Well, not much anyway, he thought.

"My name is Jessie Richter." She lifted her chin and averted her eyes past Randy. "The guy behind you is Eric Ramos, former Marine Force Recon sniper and company helicopter pilot. The man to my right is Steve Walters, former LAPD police detective. You two should get along, and to the left, Chip Rasher, retired Army Intelligence officer."

"Is that supposed to impress me?" Randy hoped his best poker face hid how impressed he felt, and how much they really did scare the shit out of him.

The girl, Jessie, moved in front of him and looked up into his eyes as if searching for something. "I'm pleased to meet you, Detective." She offered him her hand, but Randy didn't take it. She took another half-step forward, so close it made him uncomfortable.

He found himself looking straight down his nose into her light-brown eyes and felt like slapping the sexy smile off her face.

What in the hell are you doing with a guard like this?

As if reading his mind, she said, "We work for a private military contractor called Crue-Intellis." She rested her hand on his chest and almost immediately, he felt his heart rate slowing down. "We specialize in the collection and dissemination of information, and we are going to help you with the Matthew Miller case." She stated this so matter-of-factly that Randy barely suppressed a laugh. "Please, Detective D'Agostino, you can put your hands down now."

Randy raised an eyebrow, wanting to say something smart-assed back, but in truth, her answer didn't surprise him. The case was just a little over two weeks old, and it had already become the weirdest case in existence. Why wouldn't some soldier-types break into the San Antonio Police Department and take him hostage right before offering to help him solve the case? He lowered his hands to a defensive posture in front of his torso.

"What are you a former of?" he asked. The woman didn't seem to get it and scrunched her face at him. Randy rolled his eyes. "You got a former cop, former Army man, and former Marine. What are you?"

Jessie smiled. "I'm not a former anything," she said. "I'm everything that's new and exciting about the future of intelligence." She winked at him and scooched in just a little closer.

Randy rolled his eyes, then pressed on. "And how are a bunch of mercenaries going to help me with my murder case?"

Jessie smiled, reached out her spread fingers, and stopped just before touching the back of his hand. "Matthew Miller is your killer, Detective." A tiny zap of electricity zipped from her fingers into Randy's hand, making him jump. "And we're here to help you catch him."

Randy's eyes went wide. He rubbed the skin on the back of his hand and belched out a sound somewhere between a choke and a laugh. He had seen this before on the videos, and he tried to hide his excitement.

"You're joking, right? Someone put you up to this?" Randy

looked to each of them with a huge grin, but the men with the guns and the pretty little muscle boss-lady weren't smiling back.

"No, sir. We're not joking. Matthew Miller is your killer, and he's the one responsible for the coma victims you have at Military Medical," Jessie said.

Randy had to admit, guns and shock factor aside, she had his full attention now. He narrowed his eyes and pointed a rude finger at her.

"Prove it."

"First things first," Jessie said. "Let's garner some trust. You can run us through your local FBI contact, whomever that is, and they will at least verify who we are."

"It's 2:00 a.m."

"Yeah?"

"He won't answer."

And then Randy's cellphone rang. Caller ID read Greg Chambers. He quickly answered.

Greg happened to be one of the many FBI agents assigned to the San Antonio office, and immediately barraged Randy with questions.

"Who are they?"

"Hello, Greg. I thought that's why you were calling me. I don't have a clue who they are. Who called you out?"

"The Director of the Bureau in DC. Why are they there at . . . shit, man! It's after 2:00 a.m.!"

"To help me with a case."

"Why didn't you call me for help?" Chambers asked.

"Don't get all whiney on me, Greg." Randy had known Agent Chambers for three years, and although he felt all FBI agents were know-it-alls, he liked the man well enough. "I didn't know I needed help until they showed up. And then, obviously, someone alerted you, right?"

Silence filled the line for a moment. Randy could hear Greg

typing. "Holy shit, Randy. What are you working on that these guys would just pop in?"

Randy felt his heart rate elevating in annoyance. "Look, Greg, I can't tell you anything at this moment, and I don't have time for Q&A. Besides, they obviously have enough clout to pull your ass out of bed, right? Please don't push me right now."

"Okay, okay. Don't get your panties in a bunch. Standby."

Randy listened to the clickity clack of keyboard strokes through his earpiece. Finally, Greg said, "Damn, Randy. You got some heavy hitters there." He read off the stats and credentials of those present in his office. Their identities checked out.

Randy turned his back on the Crue Intellis operators and whispered into the phone. "What about the girl?"

"She's on the list as part of some Crue Intellis team, but her file is sealed. I've searched our database. There's nothing there, man. She must be blacker than black ops."

"Actually, she has kind of an olive complexion, looks . . . Persian or something."

"With the last name Richter? Is she hot?"

As if sensing the men were talking about her, Jessie lifted a hand, stuck out her forefinger, and made a rolling motion, impatience on her face.

"Greg, I gotta go. I'm hanging up now. Bye, Greg."

"Wait! Holy shit."

"What?"

"An email just popped up. Like, just now. It's an order from my Director to assist you and these guys in any way requested. Someone woke him up to send this, Randy. Someone high up. This is serious shit. It says I am to wait for contact from my Crue-Intellis counterpart. My counterpart? What does that mean?"

"It means hang tight, Greg, and someone from this group will reach out. In the meantime, I'm hanging up now."

"Hey man, wait just a minute, if you . . ."

"Gotta run, I'll call you if I need you." Randy rolled his eyes and hung the desk phone back onto the cradle. He turned to the others. The woman, Jessie, had her arms folded across her chest, expectation on her face. "He's butt-hurt that I didn't call him sooner."

"He'll get over it," Jessie said. "We have work to do."

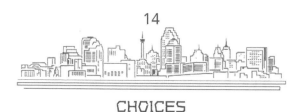

14

CHOICES

2:30 A.M.
PLEASANTON, TEXAS

Aftter driving south for over an hour, Matthew made a random left turn onto a rough dirt road that headed into dark stands of scrub oak and prickly pear cactus. He stopped the Jeep, turned out the lights, and sat for a minute to listen and look around. Only starlight peeked here and there through heavy cloud cover. He saw a street sign for Pleasanton a ways back but hadn't formulated a plan about what to do with the girl yet. He got out, opened the rear door, and stared at the skimpily clad body of Sara Stephens lying in the back seat. He watched her breasts rise and fall slowly, out cold just like Cruz, White, and Rosie.

He grabbed the girl's ankles and pulled her closer to him, causing her short skirt to climb up her legs and bunch up about her waist. Her smoothly shaven pubis-mons beckoned to the testosterone and alcohol flowing thorough the soldier's body. He positioned her ass on the edge of the seat and felt the electrical power-plant deep inside fire up on all cylinders, mixing with a level of adrenaline Matthew didn't think was humanly possible. The power swelled in his muscles. He pushed her legs apart, ran his right hand up the inside of her thigh and gently touched the soft folds of her labia.

His shaky knowledge of forensics came from countless hours watching Law and Order: SVU. Nonetheless, he knew the police would find traces of Rosie's DNA on Sara's clothes and the scratches no doubt left from Colter's fingers inside her.

No problem: I've got a plan.

He ran his left hand around her hips, then across her tight, flat belly, and finally up to her chest where he worked his fingers under the halter top and squeezed her breasts. His head fell back; euphoria enveloped his entire being. Lust coursed so powerfully through the soldier's body, it took every ounce of his being.

That would be me, keeping you straight here, Sergeant.

His head swam and the river roared in his ears. The lawyer had been so drunk, he'd barely remembered getting an erection. This guy, this soldier, turned out to be a totally different animal. He couldn't shake the thought of fucking the hell out of Sara with his new, much, *much* larger dick.

The research I've read says teenage boys think about sex every 2.4 seconds, and since I'm only seventeen . . . Kristi's face flashed in his mind, forcing him to jerk his hands away from the girl's body. He took a big step back. Heat from his face vaporized in the cool October air and slowly, the tiny motes of light rising from his skin flickered out.

"Oh, my God. What am I doing?" Embarrassment felt like a slap across the face. On two counts. Allowing the thought of molesting an unconscious girl, *that's called rape, buddy,* and feeling that even groping her equated to cheating on Kristi. "Come on, sold-ja-boy, keep it together," he whispered, pulling away from Sara and covering her. Matthew tried not to drill into the soldiers memory, as he had done with Rosie. Not because of the pain it caused, but because he felt afraid of what he might find in this guy's mind.

He rummaged around the back of the Jeep and pulled up a camouflage, tactical looking duffle bag that, at some level, he knew Colter planted it there for just this kind of situation. He opened the bag and laughed with relief. "Yeah man, that's what I'm talking about!" Inside, he found fresh underwear, black cargo pants with legs that zipped on and off, several pairs of socks, mid-height hiking boots, a soft-shell jacket, and an old AC/DC concert t-shirt. Digging a little deeper, he uncovered a small Glock 9mm handgun with a stubby suppressor can screwed onto the end of the barrel along with some spare magazines, a flashlight, paracord, and at least a dozen various flavors of MRE's, as well as other items, neatly organized throughout several interior pockets.

"What the fuck, homeboy," Matthew said. "You are some kinda fucked up, man." The words barely escaped his lips when some memory, like a ghost in the dark, reached out and touched him.

It's called a Go-Bag, you idiot.

Everything a soldier needed to survive for a few days to make it living off the grid . . . to make it . . . Matthew stood up straight, searching for the words echoing in his mind. Home. His eyes went wide, and he rushed up to look at Sara's peaceful face. "I've got to get home, to Brian's house, to my house." Then he drew in a deep breath and said, "After."

He could almost feel his careful, calculating consciousness meld with the Sergeant's tactically trained brain-matter. Understanding then came to him.

"I'm the program in his computer's hard-drive." He reviewed all the bad choices he had made already while he occupied the lawyer, Rosie, and Sara. He clucked his tongue and shook his head. "No more mistakes." From the front seat, he grabbed the bag of supplies he'd purchased while driving around as Sara had laid out in the back. He realized that he needed a plan. This was that plan.

First, he removed a box of chlorine bleach wipes, a large bottle of hydrogen peroxide, and two big bottles of iodine from the bag. Then he pulled out a small fingernail scrub brush and a medium-sized bulb cleansing device that women sometimes used to douche. "No more mistakes." He uncovered Sara's body and set to work.

4:30 A.M.
SAN ANTONIO POLICE DEPARTMENT

IT HAD BEEN OVER TWO HOURS SINCE RANDY GOT OFF THE PHONE with Chambers, and he and everyone on Jessie's crew were still pouring over the Miller case files. Randy glanced at his watch and realized that the SAPD detectives would be showing up for work pretty soon. His captain would certainly go ape shit if he caught Randy still digging into the Miller case, especially when both suspects were already in custody.

If he finds out I'm looking for an 'entity'? Yeah, game over.

"This office is going to be swarming with detectives within the next half-hour," he said. Everyone stopped and looked at him. "We need to take this somewhere else. Maybe get a little shut-eye and get at it with a fresh perspective?"

Jessie looked at her two counterparts. Walters spoke up. "That's not going to be a problem. I already have a contingency plan in place."

Randy glanced at the two men who drew down on him while they sifted through his files. Walters, the former Los Angeles Police detective ended up being much more affable than his introduction would have led him to believe. Even the former Army Major, Rasher, seemed to be pretty decent. Both men knew their way around a case file and were doing their best to convince him that Jessie was the real deal.

But the third man who'd snuck up behind Randy and relieved him of his Glock, Former Marine Gunny Sergeant Eric Ramos? Randy could almost smell the danger about the man. Randy also sensed something more going on between him and Jessie because the two worked too hard at NOT making eye contact, and barely a word passed between them.

Yeah, they're lovers, he thought.

"Force Recon sniper?" Randy said, catching Ramos' attention. "You guys do this kind of work in your off time?" Randy asked, and suddenly felt a bit inadequate.

"I do whatever Jessie needs me to do," Ramos says. "But generally, I'm overwatch. And I fly helos." Now Randy saw it in the man's eyes. The danger switch had just flipped on.

Yes, I see you man.

"He's handy to have around when things get sticky," Jessie said.

"And because he's here, I'm guessing things get sticky with you a lot," Randy replied. Jessie didn't take the bait. "I'm still kinda lost concerning what it is you guys actually do as a team, and I'm still confused about what it is *you* do and how this slip-streaming thing can even be possible."

"Here, come take a look at this." Chip Rasher reached into a small satchel, pulled out a Panasonic Toughbook computer, and slapped it on the table while the others packed up files. Randy sat next to him as the computer booted up. "What we do is provide mission support for Jessie. Here, I'll show you."

Jessie said nothing but moved from the table and walked over to the window. "Keep in mind, these clips are from helmet cams and various other surveillance devices," Jessie said. "So, they don't always show me from my best side."

Her team chuckled as Rasher continued to punch in commands. The other two men gathered around Randy and waited. When the video popped up, all three Crue Intellis men were transformed. They began to narrate the footage, NFL play-by-play style. "There. This guy," Walters tapped on the image of a large, angry looking man. "That's Jessie." Randy watched a man on the screen running and gunning with a troop of foot soldiers. Another clip abruptly interrupted the firefight: surveillance footage of Jessie seducing another target.

Randy shifted uncomfortably in his chair and glanced at the woman by the window; she seemed to be holding her breath. Then she gasped and her hand jerked to the glass pane.

"Everything alright?" Randy asked.

After a moment, Jessie let the air out, turned her head from the darkness outside, and locked eyes with him. "I thought I felt something, but it's nothing."

Randy refused to avert his eyes. He kind of enjoyed their little staring contest until a slight, come-hither smile rose to her lips. She winked at him, setting off a wave of arousal below his belt. He blinked first and understood how her targets might fall under her spell. He returned his attention to the video and watched what could only be described as porn until an all too familiar moment appeared on the screen. "Wait. Wait. I've seen this before."

"Seen what?" Jessie asked, without lifting her eyes from the dark streets of San Antonio.

"That little spark. The spark when you touched the side of that guy's face." Randy retrieved his iPhone and opened the vid. "Look. Right here."

"Damn. What is this?" Rasher asked.

"The video of the Cruz murder."

"You could have mentioned that a little sooner, Detective," Ramos said, a stern expression on his face.

"Shit. Jessie, come take a look," Rasher said.

Jessie stepped behind Randy and placed both hands lightly on his shoulders. He tightened up a little at the tiny static shock from her touch and the butterflies that fluttered in his belly as she reached past him, her breast pressing against his back, and hit the pause button on the laptop locking in an image of her nakedness on the screen. "We can get back to this, later," she said. "Play back your video." *Down boy.*

Randy scrubbed the laptop video back to the part where she touched some guys face, and then queued up his phone video. "Watch," he said. He pressed play on the laptop, then on the phone.

"That's some kind of fucked up," Ramos said. "Poor kid."

"It's right . . . there. See it?" After the men acknowledged they all saw it, Randy pulled up a second vid. "And here's the clip from the jail. Wait for it. Right . . . there."

"Very observant, Detective," Jessie said. "Now watch mine." They returned their attention to the video on Rasher's screen. "With hi-definition video, you can see the exchange of energy." She reached over him, leaning across his back again.

She's doing this on purpose, he thought. *Down boy.*

She hit the pause on the screen the moment the flash leapt from her fingers to the target's face. "That's me, or, more accurately, my consciousness slipping into his body. What you don't see in the video is the sensation during the moment of transfer." She bent down and brushed her lips against his ear. "It's euphoric and excruciating at the same time," she whispered. "It feels like your soul is being ripped from your body against your will, slammed into a steel grate, and then forced through it. It only takes a second, then you're in." She moved away, her hand lingering on his shoulder long enough to send him another little zap, making him jump.

"That's euphoric?" he asked.

"I have an earth-shattering orgasm every time. And, even though slip-streaming lasts only a couple of seconds, it feels like I'm cumming for hours."

"You know, it's a little unnerving how you can explain that

with such a straight face," Randy said. "In front of anyone." He looked at the other men. They stared back at him as if all of what Jessie could do, and how she did it, was no big deal.

"It's taken me a decade to be matter-of-fact about it, Detective. Any more questions?"

"Yeah, one. What about the coma. It looks like you go into a comatose state after you . . . slip-stream. It's the same for Matthew, but his targets don't come out of it."

"Again, very perceptive," Jessie replied. "I thought like you did when I first read the files, but now I have a theory. The difference is, when I slip-stream, I'm in a deep meditative state. I'm not unconscious, but one would think so when examining my body. I stay connected to the target by a thin, yet powerful thread of energy that allows me full control."

Randy nodded. "But that's your body. Matthew doesn't have one, so it's like . . . he's all in."

Jessie smiled. "No wonder you're a Detective Sergeant! Seriously, very good. That's my theory, too. He's all in. He has no anchor."

"How is he doing it then?"

Jessie frowned. "That's something I'd like to find out. There has to be more."

"Yes," Randy said, sitting up straight, "I need to tell you about what Doctor Bishop had to say."

"Is that the same Doctor Bishop who treated Matthew Miller? His personal physician? The same Doctor Raymond Bishop whose been blasting the internet with inquiries to every hospital in the world?"

Randy knew exactly where she was going with this comment, and his face flushed with embarrassment since he, too, had flooded the National Crime Information Center with inquiries. For all intents and purposes, he and the doc had waved big, flaming banners that they had something special going on. For all to see. And then there was his FBI Pal, big mouth Greg Chambers. Who knew what Greg might have said or done to add fuel to the fire?

No sense admitting he'd fucked up since he hadn't yet been called out for it. Randy wondered what kind of bad guys might be waiting for information. He envisioned little black widow spiders hiding in all the dark places of the world wide web. He searched his feelings and shrugged off Jessie's accusatory tone.

Too late now. And besides, he thought, *how the hell was I supposed to know?*

"Yeah, that would be him."

15

MISSING LINKS

2:00 P.M.
SAN ANTONIO, TEXAS

R andy jumped up from the couch as his phone rang. He stumbled to the window, drew open the blinds, and immediately regretted it as the harsh midday sun slammed into his stinging eyes. He glanced at his watch and had to do a double take. It was almost 1 p.m.

Holy mother of Jesus! He started to strip out of the rumpled clothes he had worn for the past thirty-two or so hours. The phone rang again. Tangled in his pants, he felt around the cushions, found the phone, and slid his finger across the answer button.

"D'Agostino." His voice cracked as if he had a hangover. *That's later,* he thought.

"Good morning, Detective. Sorry to be a pest, but I've been trying to reach you for a few hours now."

A fuzzy memory seeped into his mind of a petite, fit, super sexy mercenary chick and her co-mercenary protectors threatening to kill him, sort of, and a skin-walking, body-snatching, or whatever, killer back from the dead. "I'm sorry, Doc. Had a late night. What's going on?"

"You need to get down here. I just found out we had a comatose female come in yesterday morning, and another female is on the way."

Randy suddenly felt wide awake. "Where were they found?"

"I knew you were going to ask that if you didn't know already. See? I'm already thinking ahead . . ."

"Doc," Randy interrupted.

"Sorry. They found the first one in a hotel up in Universal City. A Hispanic woman. The other, she was a transfer . . . look, it's easier if you come down. This is very exciting," Bishop's voice dropped to a whisper. "I just ran a scan on the first woman. Same readings as the others."

"Don't say a word to anyone. There's someone you gotta meet. I'll be down there within the hour." Randy pressed the end button and saw he'd missed a call and text from Jessie Richter. He groaned and brought up the text. It read: "Good morning, sunshine, call me ASAP," and had a little smiley emoji tag at the end. His finger hovered over the dial button, but instead, he speed-dialed his partner, Melissa Santos. She picked up on the second ring.

"Are you okay?" she asked. "I found your note this morning when I got in."

"I'm fine. There's a lot of crazy shit going down related to the Miller case that we need to talk about, and there's someone you need to meet."

"Randy, Captain's gonna . . ."

"We've got a third body in a deep coma at Methodist and a fourth coming in." Randy heard Mel suck in a breath.

"Holy shit, you're kidding."

"I wish I were. Look, the captain can't fault us for looking into ditched bodies, right? If they're not related, which I'm telling you they are, then we'll ditch 'em and move on. Fair enough?"

"Sure, I'm in. At Methodist, right?"

"Yeah. Can you meet me there in about an hour?"

"Sure." Melissa hung up and he dialed Jessie.

"Good morning, sleepyhead," Jessie said, a lilt of sarcasm in her voice.

"Yeah. I already got a dose of that this morning. I don't suppose you heard about another coma victim that just landed at Methodist hospital?"

Brief silence and then, "Yes, I have. And there's a second on the way in, and that's why I've been trying to reach you this morning."

"I thought you'd say that, I . . ."

"I'll be at your place in fifteen minutes," Jessie said.

"How do you know . . ." Randy didn't finish because Jessie hung up. ". . . where I live?"

RANDY AND JESSIE MET HIS PARTNER AT THE VISITOR DESK AND quick introductions were made. Melissa glared at him with a look of absolute confusion, mixed with a tinge of suspicion, as to what this other woman had to do with the case. "You'll have to learn as you go," he told her. "Just like I did."

They were told by the hospital's greeter that Doctor Bishop could be found in room 407 and were directed to the nearest elevators. The three said nothing on the way up, but Randy could almost hear the tension winding up like an overtightened jack in the box in his partner, as the seemingly oblivious Jessie Richter stared straight ahead, lost in thought.

They found the room, and Doctor Bishop extended a hand to greet Jessie who marched straight past him and up to the bed of a dark-haired woman. She snatched up the chart from its pocket and scanned the contents.

"That's private information, you can't . . ."

Randy raised his hand to quiet the doctor. "Let her read it, Doc." He eased his way to the door and closed it as Jessie flipped through the chart.

"Rosemary Vasquez," Jessie said, and moved around to the next bed of a younger blonde girl and read, "Jane Doe".

Bishop opened his mouth to speak when Randy cut him off. "Doctor Bishop, this is my partner Melissa, and this is . . ." Randy looked Jessie up and down and struggled to ascribe a title to this tiny warrior-woman who wore tight hip-hugger jeans tucked into highly polished combat boots and a tiny camouflage half-vest that showed off her ripped abs and ample cleavage. *Not appropriate, but damn,* he thought. ". . . our associate, Jessie Richter." Randy also noticed that this time, Jessie had ditched the ball-cap. She wore her hair down and had put on some make-up, a dark eyeliner that made her light brown eyes pop. Randy decided she looked like an Egyptian goddess.

"When did this one come in?" Jessie asked, looking at the EEG monitor of the blonde.

Bishop looked toward the detective, his eyes begging for guidance on how to respond to this woman. Randy looked over at Melissa who had raised an eyebrow with that 'don't get me started' glare. Randy motioned for the doctor to answer Jessie's question.

"Jane Doe arrived about thirty minutes ago from Pleasanton. Ms. Vasquez arrived yesterday morning, but they didn't tell me about her until six this morning, and they didn't tell me about the note until a few minutes ago."

"What note?" the three others asked in unison.

The doctor reached in his pocket and pulled out a folded piece of paper. "Here's a photocopy the nurse gave me. The nurses said another detective took the original for processing.

They weren't sure who wrote it, but . . . well, read it for your-selves." The doctor handed the note to Randy, who read it and handed it off to Melissa.

"How were they found? What condition and by whom? Do you know?" Jessie asked.

"From what I am being told, they found Ms. Vasquez bundled up all neat and tidy at some hotel up in the northeast side. Housekeeping found her when they entered to clean the room. A bunch of kids found Jane Doe a couple hours ago, lying naked in a ditch close to the Pleasanton Municipal Airport. The kids were on their way to school. They thought she was dead by the way she was positioned."

"Do you know how she was positioned?" Mel asked. The doctor shook his head.

"We'll get with Pleasanton PD and the reporting officers for Vasquez and compare notes," Randy said.

Jessie had moved to the side of the bed and lifted the sheet to get a better look at the unknown girl's body. "Well, he didn't toss her out of the car. There's not a scratch on her. She couldn't have been there long. I don't see any bug bites. Are their vitals' identical?"

The doctor's face flushed red, and he looked to Randy. "How does she know about . . ."

"We'll talk about that later," Randy said. "Please, Doc, answer any and all her questions. She's here to help."

Bishop stood a little straighter, obviously prickled. "Yes, my preliminary reading is that they are identical. It also looks like the girl may have been raped. They've already taken a kit and sent it to the lab."

Jessie nodded in thought. "I'm certain he had sex with her, one way or the other." She leaned in closer and sniffed. "I think I smell peroxide. He probably cleaned her up. He's being more careful."

Mel moved to the dark-haired woman's bed. "I'm pretty sure

that this is the same Ms. Vasquez suspected of being with the lawyer, Ruben White, the night we found him in his car at Desperado's bar."

"May I see the note?" Detective Santos handed it to Jessie. She quickly read it and handed it back.

"It's signed *M.M.*," Bishop said. "Any ideas on who 'MM' might be?"

Jessie turned to face him. "It's the initials of Matthew Miller. He's the one who left the note." She reached up and gently pushed the doctor's jaw closed and returned to Rosemary's bedside. "Sloppy work, leaving a note like that," she said.

"That's impossible. I don't think . . ."

Detective D'Agostino held up a hand. "You might want to listen to her, Doctor, and we may want to talk away from the hospital. Can you come with us?" Randy asked. His partner Melissa looked at him and huffed in exasperation, her own mouth open and utter confusion written all over her face. Randy leaned in close to her and said, "Trust me, Mel, you're gonna flip."

"Not just yet," Jessie said. "Randy briefed me about what you two figured out last night, how the patients are all in sync? While I'm here, I'd like to see the EEG's from White, Cruz, and these women. I'm assuming you have Matthew Miller's on hand, his old ones. Those would be great, too."

The doctor looked to Randy again, who nodded. "Of course, I do." The doctor collected a folder off the counter, opened it, and then spread the readouts onto a small rolling table as best he could.

Jessie lined up the strips of paper and ran her index finger across the congruent markings. "This is just amazing. I would have never thought this possible. You now have a baseline for future reference. These readouts are Miller's new fingerprints, and depending on how adaptable and smart he is will depend on how many more bodies show up."

Bishop's mouth dropped open again and his face turned three shades of red from what he'd just heard. "What in God's name are you saying? You just suggested that Matthew Miller did this, is doing this, which is impossible. Do you know why?" Bishop asked, obviously flustered. "Because he's dead, lady. I'm the one who declared it. Saw him with my own eyes. You are batshit crazy."

"Sometimes I think so, Dr. Bishop, but not today," Jessie said, unfazed by the insult. She turned her attention back to Rosemary and used a finger to move hair from her face. She gently laid her hand on the woman's bare forearm and alarms screamed. Jessie jerked her hand away.

"What's happening?" Doctor Bishop asked, rushing up to her side.

"I'm not sure. I just touched her." Jessie laid her hand on Rosemary's forearm again and the alarms went off again. She pulled it away.

Doctor Bishop looked back and forth between the comatose woman and Jessie, then reached for the EEG machine. "Do it once more, when I say . . ." Doctor Bishop pressed a button on the monitor, ". . . now." The alarms howled as a freshly printed strip spat out of the monitor.

"Let's try it on the other patient," he said, and stood ready at the monitor.

Randy and Melissa watched with interest as Jessie took the hand of the blonde Jane Doe. As with the Vasquez woman, the alarms responded. "Don't let go yet," Bishop said. He let the printer run a couple extra seconds. "Okay, you can let go now."

The doctor studied the readouts for a minute or two and turned to Jessie, who now stood right behind him, looking around his shoulder. Bishop lowered the printouts and turned to face the woman. "What are you?"

16

NEW DIGS

M atthew jerked awake to a sitting position. He sat still, disoriented for a solid five seconds. His head pounded. He didn't remember where he was, how he'd arrived, and until he rubbed his face with big, masculine hands, he had momentarily forgotten that he'd taken the body of now retired Army First Sergeant Brian Colter.

He did remember his dreams. They were vivid, and he knew some of them were his, but others . . .

"Wow, you've been through some fucked up shit," Matthew whispered, wiping dried spittle from his cheek. He looked at his, Brian Colter's, hands and made fists, flexing the muscular forearms of his new body. Glancing at Colter's Suunto CORE watch, he raised an eyebrow at the time. "I don't remember ever sleeping in till 2:00 p.m., but I think this is what they call a hangover," he moaned. He pressed fingertips to both temples and rubbed in an attempt to sooth the fierce pounding going on just an inch inside of Colter's skull. "That's your bad, Sergeant,"

Matthew mumbled, recalling the severely inebriated state of Sergeant the moment Matthew took him.

Then the memory of Sara came back, and the room started spinning. He staggered forward to the kitchen sink just as his stomach let go. This had nothing to do with last night's alcohol. This resulted from the weight of his decisions and the lengths he'd gone to just to complete his mission. Matthew felt certain, no matter whose body he borrowed, he had the resolve to see this through. Until now, he'd had no understanding of how ruthless he could be. He sucked in water from the tap to rinse the bile from his mouth, grabbed a hand towel hanging off the dish rack, and wiped his face.

A voice in his head echoed another answer: *You did good, boy.* Matthew didn't know if the voice reflected his own thoughts or perhaps the sergeants. He tossed the towel into the empty sink and immediately noticed that the few dishes present were clean and organized in the drying rack. He pulled open cabinets. Everything appeared neatly organized. Same with the fridge. Glancing around, the whole place had a kind of order that only a disciplined military man, *or maybe my mother,* would have.

"Mom would love you," he said.

Matthew walked through the house looking but not touching anything. At this moment in time, he didn't feel he had the right. Not yet anyway. He worked his way to the front door, retrieved a pair of Steiner range-finding binoculars hanging from a peg at the threshold, and headed out onto the front porch. There were a few neighbors, but they were not close. He raised the binoculars to his eyes and looked around. He spotted a sign in the distance, across the dirt road. Colter's house bordered the US Army's Camp Bullis Training grounds. He listened for the sound of San Antonio to the south, but he heard nothing and saw nothing but lots and lots of trees.

I could get used to this. Maybe when I'm done.

Matthew took in the peaceful silence of his new surroundings and contemplated what he had been through so far.

He thought about the five bodies he had shifted into, how he'd killed that pussy-ass-cracker Chris Storey. His skin prickled at the thought of doing the same to Rafi Johnson. As soon as he came up with a plan. He felt motivated to get the job done, but also felt drained of energy from every crazy thing that had already happened. He closed his eyes hard and rubbed them.

The quiet of open space embraced him, allowing his thoughts to slow down and organize. He frowned when Christopher Storey came to mind. He searched his feelings for the slightest pang of guilt or remorse but felt nothing. Nor did he feel anything for the comatose lawyer or the two women he'd left behind. *Combat casualties.* The words and a flicker-vision of Kristi getting her skull kicked in echoed in his mind. They were all combat casualties, him included. Rafi Johnson would be next. Thinking about skinny fathead sent a rush of anger through him that threatened the good feeling he'd tried to cultivate. He breathed, calmed himself, and pushed thoughts of Rafi aside. For now.

He needed to learn about how Brian lived from Brian's perspective. He patted the pockets of the tactical battle dress pants he wore and found a keyring. Brian's fingers automatically located the correct one, and he slid it into the side door handle. He didn't remember doing that last night or even arriving at the house. There were two other keys. One obviously for the Jeep. He looked closely at the third.

"Where do you belong?" he mumbled.

He re-entered the house, hung up the binoculars, and slowly closed the door behind him. Holding the rogue key in his hand, he scanned the living room and wondered if most soldiers who had returned from war lived like this. Something within his host felt that being home permanently turned out to be a surreal life, whereas the battle abroad held his real life, and his battle-buddies were his real family.

The long wall in the living room had a fireplace decorated with dozens of war-zone photos of him and his friends. Iraq. Afghanistan. Germany. Some of the photos had dates penned beneath the images showing the soldier's name, date of death, and the cause.

PVT. Charles "John boy" Johns, New York, 06-18-2013, KIA-IED.

Other photos showed Sergeant Colter rappelling from helicopters or hanging off cliff ledges with what appeared to be younger soldier-students. One photo held his interest. Corporal Keith O'Connell sat in the door of a helicopter with Colter beside him. Below the photo it read, *Irish- 2-18-2014, Suicide.* The thought sent a harsh shudder through Matthew. Despite the homage to his brothers-in-arms, Matthew thought that the sergeant looked happy in every one of the pictures.

Will I ever be happy?

What Matthew didn't see were family photos, or photos with any women, or anyone for that matter, outside of the military. He did find one family photo on the wall, with him in his Class A Uniform standing beside an older man whom Matthew thought might be his father.

Perhaps Brian Colter needed a quiet house to balance out the noise of war embedded in his psyche. Matthew sensed war lurking like a shadow in an already dark place somewhere in the recesses of the sergeant's mind. It wasn't Brian who whispered to him in that tough little voice.

This is War. Like *"Go-bag, you idiot."*

To Matthew, it felt like an itch he couldn't quite reach to scratch. He thought that maybe Colter's aggression came from that dark place he kept at bay. Well, that just wouldn't do. What Matthew needed right now, to get the job done, was aggression. And Colter had plenty to go around.

Matthew worked his way into the bedroom and paused. He

ran his hand along the top flat sheet of the bed, professionally fitted to the mattress. He knew these were called hospital corners and had a flash of memory of his mother trying to teach him how to make a bed back when he still functioned as a normal kid. He closed his eyes and remembered.

"Do you know what they do in the Marine Corps if you don't make your bed right?" his mother asked, her mischievous smile reaching her eyes. Matthew shook his head. Surprising him, she grabbed the edge of the sheet. "They mess it all up and make you do it again!" She whooped and laughed and tore the sheet from the mattress. Matthew helped her fling the sheets in the air and laughed with her before going through the process of hospital corners once again.

Mama.

He hadn't thought at all about her or his father since the attack, until now. Doing so sent a wave of despair through him. He wanted to see them, to tell them what had happened. But he knew he couldn't do it. His father hadn't believed him then, wouldn't believe him now.

Because he watched me die.

He envisioned what would happen the moment he approached them and tried to tell his story, which happened to be the truth. His father would quietly get up, go into the bedroom, and call the police. Maybe someday he'd be able to approach them. But not now. *Not ever,* the voice hissed from that deep, dark place.

He needed to talk to someone about this. Someone who would listen, and even more importantly, believe him. The fleeting moment of emotion passed like a warm summer breeze through the forest. Coldness, to the depth of his bones, returned.

Matthew tugged open a nightstand drawer and found a Keltec .22 pistol with a silencer mounted on the barrel laying inside. Colter had wrapped the gun in some kind of treated cloth. He set the keys on the nightstand, carefully removed the weapon, and somehow knew to keep his finger off the trigger. Without thinking about it, he snapped the handgun up to a ready position with both hands at his chest. He pressed it out, aligning the sights at his reflection in the dresser mirror opposite the bed. He tilted the pistol to the side and press-checked the slide, viewing a round in the chamber.

"Shit."

Matthew had never held nor shot a pistol — or any gun for that matter — in his life and felt both shocked and impressed with Brian's ingrained motor skills.

As if he held some sacred thing, he placed the gun back in the drawer and pushed it closed as a sense of urgency crept up on him. His head slowly turned toward the large walk-in closet. He flicked on the light and stood in the doorframe, visually taking in the contents. There must have been ten pairs of blue jeans and dozens of pressed plaid shirts hanging above a few pairs of combat boots lined up on a little bench secured to the outside wall.

His eyes were drawn to an olive-green military footlocker squatting on the floor against the back wall of the closet. Not the old-fashioned wooden type his dad had in the garage to store old car parts, but a big, heavy waterproof bin with a brass I.D. tag that read 1st SGT B. COLTER riveted to the front. He snatched up the keys, stepped in, and shoved the hanging clothes aside to get a better look at the box.

"Well, well, what have we here?"

A battle helmet loaded with electronic devices sat on some dark green but ornately embroidered cloth draped over the lid. He picked the helmet up, pulled it onto his head, and fastened the chin strap. He picked up the green cloth and unfolded it. He inspected the geometric shapes sewn into the large cloth.

Shemagh.

The word came from deep inside the soldier's head: *A head-cloth to protect your hollow noggin from sand and heat.* Or perhaps,

Matthew thought, he knew about the shemagh during one of his own Call of Duty gaming sessions.

His hands automatically folded the cloth into a triangle, and within a few practiced moves, he had the cloth expertly wrapped around his face. Moving the bin around, he saw it had wheels. He grabbed the thick end-handle and rolled it out into the living room, dropping it beside the couch.

He flipped the night vision goggles down, and Brian's fingers knew exactly where to go to turn the EVNG unit on. Nothing happened. He unwrapped the shemagh, removed the helmet, and tossed them both on the couch. There were two padlocks on the front latches.

He pulled out the keyring and looked at that third key again. Slipping the key into the lock, Matthew felt both like a criminal going through someone's private life as an intruder, and equally elated, like a kid opening presents at Christmas.

Unlatching and slowly lifting the lid, he let out a breath he hadn't realized he held at the sight of another Glock pistol in the top left tray. He picked it up, looking at the number '19' stamped into the slide, the numbers 9x19 stamped into the top of the barrel's chamber. This gun looked to be bigger than the one in the go-bag, except the end of the threaded barrel had no silencer can.

There were a bunch of spare clips, 'Magazines', the voice reprimanded, and a couple boxes of ammo. A latched, lidded tray took up the right of the locker. It had stenciled printing on it that read, "SAFETY FIRST- No ammo in cleaning area". He lifted both trays out and placed them on the floor next to the trunk. He reached into the main compartment and pulled out one neatly folded uniform, a heavy body armor vest with the tag "IOTV-Level 4" on the collar, knee and elbow pads, and a matching camelback hydration bladder. Upon closer inspection of the vest, he noticed another single key and a piece of paper with an Amman Road address pinned on one of the molle straps. *Yeah. MOLLE: Modular Lightweight Load-Carrying Equipment. You betcha.* He removed the key and paper and stuffed them into his cargo pocket.

In the very bottom of the box, pressed into fitted foam, he found an M16 style rifle broken down into two pieces; a short barrel with another suppressor screwed on the end and the grip with stock attached. *Lower receiver.*

"Yeah, yeah, I got it," he told the voice.

He picked up the parts and looked closely at the lower receiver. Matthew guessed that Colter filled the engraving on the side of the rifle, ".300 Blackout", with dark red enamel paint. He also found at least a dozen loaded magazines. He removed the rifle parts and somehow knew to press the barrel and gas tube into the upper receiver and twist. Once clicked in, he extended the rear stock and looked closer at the rubber coated scope labeled 'ACOG-BAC' already mounted on the top rail. Without thinking about it, the soldier's fingers automatically located the 'on' switch. He pressed the button and whipped the rifle to his shoulder, taking a bead on the kitchen faucet. He turned off the reticle, leaned the rifle against the couch, and went back to the body armor.

A large combat knife hung from the molle loops on the front of the vest. He grasped the handle and pulled. The ink-black blade hissed from its sheath. He examined it closely. The blade had a thin film of oil, making it look sleek. And deadly. A tinge of excitement seeped into him as he gently scraped the cutting edge against his forearm. The hair fell away.

He laid the blade on the coffee table, found a small waterproof box in the bottom of the footlocker, and opened that, too. Inside, he found a small bottle of honing oil and a grey whetstone. Matthew opened the bottle, squeezed a thin line onto the length of the stone, and picked up the knife. He had never sharpened a knife before, but the soldier's hands moved with a practiced rhythm and drew the belly of the blade across the stone, easing the beveled edge straight across the oily surface. He found the coarse hiss of metal against stone had a soothing effect on him. As he let the soldier's ingrained skill take over sharpening the blade, thoughts of Rafi Wilson seeped into his mind. An answer had not yet come to him on how he should handle that business.

"But you know what to do, don't you Sergeant Colter?" he asked.

No answer came from the little voice. Matthew took that as a kind of silent agreement, and the blade moved more swiftly across the stone.

17

TEAMWORK

3:30 P.M.
SAN ANTONIO POLICE DEPARTMENT

As Randy and his partner escorted their new entourage of mercenaries into police headquarters, they didn't make it ten feet past the front desk when the duty sergeant called out to him.

"D'Agostino! Your pals need to get visitor badges."

They all turned toward the desk. Jessie watched as Randy stepped up to handle the badges when the duty sergeant leaned forward and pointed at Randy. "Detective Santos can take care of that," he said. "The Chief wants you in his office. Now."

Jessie leaned in close to Randy as they approached the visitor desk. "You in trouble?"

Randy took in the smirk on her face. "Since you arrived, most likely."

Jessie watched as Randy headed toward the elevators. She motioned for her team to move a few more paces away to have words. She raised her chin and eyebrows as Detective Santos turned from the desk and approached.

"I need your creds. For the visitor badges," she said.

Without a word, the group retrieved identifications and handed them over. Melissa raised an eyebrow at Jessie concerning the awkward silence but said nothing as she turned on her heel and walked back to the desk.

"What do you think about them?" Jessie asked, looking into the faces of people who had saved her life on more than one occasion.

"I like him. Both of them," Chip Rasher said, shrugging as if he had nothing further to add. Jessie looked to Steve Walters.

"I'm with Chip," Steve said, then added, "Look, if the doc and detectives hadn't put out feelers for their strange case, we might have missed this all together. It seems to me they're both on board. I trust them."

"What choice do we have?" Eric said, leaning in close, his voice lowering to a whisper. "What are your thoughts, Jessie?"

Jessie looked away from her team toward Melissa and the Doc and turned her head just in time to see Randy step onto the elevator. "I can't say I like them, or don't like them. I'm sure they're all good people. My concern is that I'm not sure they're going to be on board with what we have planned."

"In all fairness to them, it's going to depend on Miller's response as to the feasibility of our plan. What's your problem with the detectives?" Walters asked.

"They want to take him down. They can't see beyond the bodies, and that's not fair to Matthew. None of this was his fault."

"Of course it wasn't, and it's up to us to convince the detectives that they need to retrain their brains," Walters said.

"In my humble opinion," Eric said, "I think that's going to be your job, Jessie."

The group nodded and waited. Jessie let out a slow hiss of air, shrugged, and also nodded.

"Besides," Walter's said, "it's too late to pull support now anyway. Our cat is out of the bag."

A FEW MINUTES LATER, RANDY ENTERED THE CHIEF'S OFFICE AND moved to sit in one of the big library chairs in front of the desk. "Don't sit down, you're not going to be here that long." The Chief looked to be in an irate mood. "I'm not sure what's going on, but some Department of Defense types are asking for my full cooperation in allowing some folks from a company called," he looked down his nose and through the reading glasses at a note on his desk, "Crue Intellis, to assist you with the Miller murder case."

Randy opened his mouth to speak but the Chief threw up his hand. "Ah, ah, ah! No, do not say a word. Some fucking bureaucrat called the Governor of the State of Texas and advised me to keep out of it, reminded me that I don't have a top-secret security clearance, but you do." Randy couldn't hide the shock on his face, he had no idea he had any military clearances whatsoever. "The Governor also felt the need to duly inform me that your case, an easy open and shut murder, is now a Department of Defense matter." Randy moved to speak again, but the Chief cut him off.

"Department of fucking Defense, D'Agostino? Are you fucking kidding me? NO, Randy, close your mouth. I don't want to know. I am too busy for this shit. Just do what you have to do and get these people out of my building as soon as possible. From what I had previously understood, your killers are already in custody. How in the hell did you fuck this up?" The chief held up his hand again, although Randy hadn't yet opened his mouth. "No. Don't tell me. I am frightened to my very core to even ask. I don't know what the hell is going on, and I don't care. You get this fucking mess cleaned up, ASAP, you got me?"

"Yes, sir," Randy said, hoping the veins pulsing on the Chief's forehead and neck didn't burst. He thought the term 'mess' to be quite the understatement. *If he only knew.*

"You are dismissed." The Chief turned his back to him, and Randy cautiously backed out of the office, reeling at the depth of Jessie's apparent influence.

Minutes later, Randy headed toward the service desk where three uniforms, two males and one female, were showering Jessie with attention. Steve Walters and Chip Rasher appeared much more professional as they chatted with the desk sergeant.

"Where's Eric?" Randy asked.

"He went to pick up our in-house FBI agent at the airport, and they are going to meet with your pal, Greg Chambers, about his big mouth," Walters said. "Your partner took the doc upstairs already."

Randy nodded and thought future favors might end up running thin with Chambers. At least for now.

"You have an in-house FBI Agent?"

"Yes, well, sort of," Rasher said. "Let's just say he retired from the bureau, but still kept his active status. It comes in very handy. We got a CIA spook or two as well."

Randy didn't know what to say, so he chose not to say anything at all.

The group headed to the elevators. Jessie held up her visitor pass and raised a sardonic eyebrow at Randy.

Randy rolled his eyes. "Don't look at me like that. You should have had them the first time we met," he said. "And we need to talk about this government clearance thing."

"Hey, I told you this is some serious shit," Jessie said, smiling. "Nothing like having friends in high places."

Randy shook his head. "God, please take me now." Jessie chuckled.

They made their way upstairs to the investigations conference room, where Doctor Bishop and Detective Santos were already waiting, reviewing the EEG strips and the preliminary rape kit results from the lab. Steve Walters hoisted a waterproof Pelican briefcase to the table and twisted the heavy latches open. He removed a handheld scanning device, turned it on, and passed the flat sensor over every surface in the room.

"There are no bugs in here," Randy said. "Our recording devices are in plain view."

Walters raised an eyebrow. "Yeah, that's what we always say, too." He continued his scan and stuck a small, black suction cup to the lens of the sole video camera in the corner of the room unplugging the desktop microphone that squatted in the center of the table. "You can't be too careful." After putting it in the corner, he turned away from the mic, and the scanner alarm went off. Everyone stopped and looked at Walters. He raised his finger to his mouth, signing for quiet, then ran the scanner over the mic once more. He flipped it over and dug at something embedded in the base. It took him another minute and use of his pocketknife to pry a small button from beneath. He pulled out what looked like a metal envelope and slid the button inside.

"You've got to be kidding me," Randy said. Melissa just sat there, looking stunned.

"You were saying?" Walters asked.

"Who would want to bug the conference room?"

"Well, looks like someone else is interested in your investigation, Detective," Jessie said. "Thanks to all the NCIC and Internet traffic about strange comas and suspects claiming to be victims." Jessie held up her hand to silence Randy's protest. He was getting used to the gesture. "I told you, this is some serious shit."

"Well, we're clean now," Walter's said as he packed up the scanner. "But the sooner we get to our new base of operations, the better."

"New base? You people really do live a rich fantasy life," Doctor Bishop said.

Everyone turned to the doc, who sported a most serious look of doubt and dejection.

Jessie looked back to Walters, who gave the okay, and then

moved to where they were sitting. "I can see you're both skeptical," she said.

Santos shrugged. "I can't say I'm not. I'm the kind of person who needs hard proof," she said.

"How can we not be?" Bishop added. "You suggest that my former patient, Matthew Miller, whose death certificate I personally signed, is alive and well and inhabiting the bodies of other people to seek revenge."

Jessie leaned over and snatched up the EEG strips, held them in front of the doctor's face. "And this evidence isn't enough?" Jessie asked, switching her gaze to the paper in the doctor's hands. "And let's not forget the reaction of the monitors when I touched them." Both Bishop and Detective Santos raised an eyebrow, obviously remembering the EEG alarms when Jessie touched the two women's bodies.

"What that tells me," Bishop said, "is that we should be running tests on you."

"Maybe another time, when I'm in the mood to let you poke and prod me," Jessie replied. "Who knows, it might be fun." The doctor's face flushed wildly.

Mel rolled her eyes and shrugged. "It is about as farfetched as anything I've ever heard," she said. "But hey, if Randy believes it, I'm along for the ride,"

The doctor shook his head, looking almost angry. "You're all nuts."

"How about we perform a little test, so we can move on. What do say, Doc?" Jessie asked. Bishop and Mel looked tentative. "This will only take a minute. I promise I won't hurt you."

They both looked at Randy, whose face twisted up, desperate to keep from laughing, "Look, either you guys can take my word for it and believe it, because it's true, or stand up and learn like I did. Stop being such wimps."

The doctor shook his head again but relented and slowly stood up. Santos followed and stood next to the doctor as they both faced Jessie, who pushed her hands toward them, palms up. "Give me your outside hand, please." The doctor threw another pleading look at Randy, appearing as if he were about to cry. Randy didn't hide his shit-eating grin, waving the doc on. Walters and Rasher crossed their arms to watch, but they were not smiling.

Jessie grasped one hand from the doctor and one of Melissa's. "I need you to hold hands," she said.

"This is preposterous," the doctor grumbled.

"I promise not to tell your wife you were holding hands with a hot female detective," Jessie said and winked at Santos. The doctor blushed.

Melissa grinned and snatched the doctor's free hand. "I'll be gentle, honey."

"You're all insane. I don't . . . " Bishop stopped in mid-sentence.

The sudden change of their facial expressions alerted those watching that Jessie had already seized them.

Randy leaned in toward Steve Walters and whispered, "I would bet a paycheck they're feeling a wave of warmth creep up their arms right now. "

"Oh, there's no doubt," Steve said, watching detective Santos's reaction with interest.

Jessie's eyes were closed, and Randy wondered if she found it harder to control two bodies, or even if Jessie could do something like that.

"I need you both to take a deep breath and relax," Jessie said. They did, and as if on cue, both heads fell back slowly as they let out a unified long, slow breath.

Randy could almost see Jessie forcing her energy into the disbelievers to take control of their breathing and heartbeats, adjusting their individual biorhythms to be in sync with her own. *Just like she did to me back in the office.*

"Oh, my God, I feel it," Santos whispered. Bishop said nothing.

"There, good, I've got you," she said. "Relax, Doctor. Go with the flow."

Their faces told those around them what they were experiencing. At that moment, he had no doubt Jessie bathed them in a wave of calm. And then together, all three of them frowned. Jessie abruptly switched gears. Randy chuckled because the doctor's knees trembled, his cheeks blushed furiously, and Randy almost pulled his iPhone out to get a picture of his partner as she clutched herself in front of the occupants of the room. Melissa looked about to fall over as she moaned softly. The doctor's eyebrows twitched.

Jessie looked relaxed, like she might be in some serene state of meditation, and immediately, her two subjects fell into step, three heads falling back slightly, in sync. Randy knew Jessie had complete control, but seeing it unfold before him, firsthand, reminded him to close his mouth.

He glanced at Jessie's entourage, who weren't paying a bit of attention to their amazing teammate. Randy returned his attention to Jessie, Mel, and the doc. Their eyes closed, they sported small, peaceful smiles, then suddenly their faces twisted into what could only be described as fear. Randy guessed that Jessie had just fired a warning shot across the two nonbeliever's bows. After another few seconds, Jessie opened her eyes, apparently cutting herself off from the others because their eyes opened too. Jessie finished off the demonstration with a mild electrical shock just as her hands slipped out of theirs. They both gasped just as the connection terminated. Doctor Bishop's eyes shot open, and he glared at Jessie.

"And what do you think, now?" Jessie asked.

This time, Doctor Bishop reached out and took up one of Jessie's hands, stepping closer to her. "Oh, my God. That was . . . that was incredible." He paused, looking embarrassed. "I'm sorry for being so closed-minded," he said. "I am at your service."

Smiling, Jessie turned to Detective Santos who desperately continued to try and hide the squeezing of her thighs together, her face mildly flushed. "And how about you, Detective?"

Melissa waved a hand back and forth in front of her face. "Oh, I'm in. Sign me up for some more of that." She looked sideways at Crue member Steve Walters and winked.

Randy glanced at Steve and saw him smiling back.

Well, well, he thought, *always time for a little lovin'.* Randy then spoke up. "Good to hear. Now that we're all on the same page, the Chief wants us out of his building and has ordered me to wrap up the case." He looked at Jessie who shrugged and had a *"who, me"* look on her face. "Steve, you said something about another base of operations?"

"Yes," Walters said. "I've got a place lined up and a remodel crew is already there retrofitting the floor to fit our needs. We can head over there now if you like. Construction has already started."

"Construction?" Detective Santos asked.

"Yes," Rasher chimed in. "As soon as we realized that Miller was a Walker, we pulled some strings and found the perfect spot to set up shop. We've got a lot of equipment to organize if we're going to find him fast," Rasher said.

"Mel, we need to find Rafi Wilson. He's next," Randy said. He made a mental note to thank his FBI contact, Greg Chambers, for identifying Wilson through their database . . . if the man ever talked to him again after today.

"I've already got the task force out looking for him at all last known addresses. I have some other ideas as well and will hit the south side for a few hours," Melissa said, still looking flushed from her "Jessie time".

Randy raised an eyebrow. "We don't even know whose body he's in."

"Yet," Jessie said, "but we will soon. He's sloppy. Inexperienced. He's bound to trip up, no matter who he's Walking in."

"There's so much to do, so many angles to cover. I'm not sure the handful of us are enough," Randy said.

Jessie grinned and shook her head. "Great minds think alike, Randy, because I've taken the liberty of calling in reinforcements."

"Reinforcements?"

"Yes, we've already got a call in. The rest of the Crue will be arriving at Stinson Airfield tomorrow around 1500 hours."

Randy remembered the Chief's warning. The man all but pressed Randy's back up against the wall on this. Having more boots on the ground that were *not* SAPD might be a wise decision after all.

"So, let's see what the tactical unit uncovers tonight. We can get a fresh start in the morning, after everyone's well rested."

Jessie nodded. "You're right. I'm pretty beat, too. But why don't you introduce us to your tac-team. Maybe we can ride along and help."

Randy nodded but felt it might not be a good idea. He opened his mouth to speak when Jessie interrupted him.

"Don't worry. We won't embarrass you."

18

RAFI

5:00 P.M.

SAN ANTONIO, TEXAS: EAST SIDE

Matthew watched Rafi Wilson through the Steiner binoculars and jotted the number 166 down on his notepad. He placed the binos on a small table mounted into the center of the van's floorboard and leaned down to rest his cheek on the stock of Colter's 300 Blackout rifle. Looking through the scope mounted on top, his eye focused on the magnified image of Rafi's fat head, and he gently laid his finger across the trigger. He had no concern for the sound of a gunshot; the barrel length suppressor would contain the noise and allow the bullet to maintain accuracy over the short distance to target. He held the crosshairs steady on Rafi's forehead, and a distant voice echoed in his mind, telling him no adjustments were necessary.

Just squeeze.

He put pressure on the trigger and stopped right at the breaking point. This was a two-stage Geissele custom trigger with a 1.5-pound breaking weight. At this point, he could blink too hard and the bullet would be headed downrange. He released it, flipped the safety on and sat up.

"No," he said. "Too little effort for too little reward. What we are missing here is balance."

He pulled the combat Bowie knife from its sheath, ripped a sheet of paper from his notebook, and ran the edge of the paper across the bevel of steel. The blade hissed as one sheet of paper magically became two. A flash of Kristi's head being stomped and Rafi standing there doing nothing to help made Matthew's hand tighten on the leather grip of the knife.

"No, Mister Johnson. I'm not going to shoot you today. This death needs to rise to a level worthy of vengeance. This death requires a personal touch." He picked up the binoculars and resumed his surveillance.

Finding Rafi turned out to be much easier than he'd anticipated. He followed Christopher Storey's directions to the letter, mildly surprised to find skinny fathead standing on the exact corner Storey said he would be. It had been a week since Kristi's death.

And mine.

It didn't take a detective to see that Rafi had become complacent, and after an hour of surveillance, Matthew hadn't seen a single cop in this shitty part of town.

So far, everything appeared to be going as planned. Stealing the van, his new mobile operations center, turned out to be an exciting adventure in its own right. He had never stolen anything in his life, and until he and the van moved bodly down the road, he hardly remembered stealing it.

He left Brian's house to search for Rafi driving the jeep, but thinking about what criminals did on TV, he knew using his primary vehicle was a stupid, amateur thing to do. So, he took the long way around, ending up in a public parking space downtown, close to the Alamo.

The urge to walk around the city felt almost as strong as the lawyer's need for a drink. Or Rosie's need to fuck. He parked the Jeep between two bigger pickup trucks, then rummaged through Brian's go-bag. He pulled out a grey zippered hoodie and looked around before getting out of the Jeep. He put it on, covering his head and checking to see how much of his face showed in the Jeep's rearview mirror.

As he headed for the elevators, he noticed some people lined up, waiting. He moved past them and took the stairs. He'd been a child, maybe eight years old, the last time he'd used stairs. He smiled at the sensation when the pads of his feet, *well, his foot,* struck the steps. He set off down West Market street until he spied the van, door open, engine running, in front of The Hotel Contessa. Not a single person appeared to be paying attention as he got in, closed the door, and drove off. Just like that. He glanced at his inside mirrors and didn't even see the van's owner step into the street, waving his arms frantically. Once he turned the corner, he was gone.

The van suited his mission perfectly. There were no windows in the cargo area, and the owner had the presence of mind to bolt a small worktable to the center of the cargo bay floor. He pulled off I-35 near what appeared to be an industrial area, looked for Cameras mounted on the corners of buildings, and when he didn't see any, pulled into an alleyway and dumped the flowers out the side door. He drove back to the downtown garage and parked at the loading area adjacent to the garage, put the hazards on and unlike the van's owner, he locked the door. He vaulted the stairs two at a time, reveling in the exhilaration of running, and had to restrain himself from whooping and yelling his joy at the top of the stairs. He retrieved his rifle case and ammo bag from the Jeep. That part of the mission had gone way too easy. Just like pulling the trigger would have been.

Matthew returned to the driver's seat. Rafi and four other males were standing in front of an old, closed-up diner located at the corner of North Polaris and East Commerce streets on the east side of downtown San Antonio. An eerie orange glow painted the front of the tattered white building as daylight faded. The vagrants passed around a joint and were laughing and jack-jawing. Matthew thought they looked like chickens because their heads twitched and jerked about when something alarmed them. They froze and looked ready to run until they were convinced the police were not coming. Then they went back to strutin' and cluckin'.

Christopher Storey's information had turned out to be accurate, so far. If Rafi continued along his reported modus operandi, he should leave the corner in the next few minutes and walk to his aunt's house in the three-hundred-block of Belmont, just a little over two blocks away. Matthew thought about the moment Christopher parted with the information.

"You're lying, the police will go there first," Matthew said, the lamp poised to strike.

"No, no, please . . . she's like his second or third aunt. Rafi's mom hates her and doesn't know we hang out there. She gives us pot, and we make runs for her. The police don't know her. I swear."

At first, Christopher acted like an insolent little smart ass. He gave "Mr. Lawyer" the run around until Matthew backhanded the kid so hard, he fell back into the wall. The kid tried to run, but Matthew stopped him in his tracks with the heavy base of his mother's favorite ceramic lamp. With each successive blow to Christopher's head, the buzz wound up in Matthew's ears and adrenaline had flooded into him. He'd bent over and inspected Chris's face, which had appeared to be bisected at a crazy angle across his nose and skull, but amazingly, the kid still pleaded for him to stop.

"Does it really hurt that bad? Kristi didn't act like it hurt. Not once did she scream or cry out while you let your buddy Jeffrey kick her head in. So, stop being such a pussy." The words, "Pluh, please," gurgled through Chris's throat as his one remaining and functional eyeball rolled around aimlessly in its socket.

Sick of the whining, he delivered a flurry of blows to Christopher's head until the noise coming out of him stopped. Killing Storey gave Matthew the polar opposite feeling to pulling the trigger for Rafi. In Chris's case, the end result felt like too much work for too little reward. Revenge should be sweet, right?

He lowered the binos and searched his vernacular for a word or words to describe the encounter, and then snapped his fingers. *Embarrassing. Fucking embarrassing.*

Movement in front of the old store startled Matthew. He glanced at his watch. 10:56 p.m. He shook his head at the disappointing representation of humanity standing across the street. "I mean, I just literally sat here watching you guys entertain each other for eight fucking hours. What a bunch of losers."

It also dawned on him that he didn't really remember what he had been thinking about this entire time, and that concerned him. But finally, Rafi left his pals.

"Fuck it," he whispered. "It's time to say hello again."

Matthew settled in again, raised the binos to his eyes, and waited until his target made the left onto North Gevers Street. Matthew eased into the driver seat, turned the ignition key, and the van sputtered to life. He pulled the knob on the left side of the steering wheel that activated the headlights. He pulled the shift lever, so the little red line matched up with the big "D", and let off the brake. He chuckled at the action, still fascinated over picking up the ability to drive from his hosts and smiling at the sensation as the stolen van rolled forward.

A thread of nervous energy ignited the little power plant deep inside his mind. For a moment, he thought he'd lost his target, until the headlights picked up the faint glow illuminating Rafi in the distance. Matthew followed at a steady speed and passed Rafi, careful not to look at the boy in fear of spooking him. He turned right onto Belmont and stopped abruptly under the streetlamp. He opened the door, stood on the footstep, and looked around. Not a soul walked the streets. He reached into the bag between the van seats, drew out the little Keltec .22, and after one more scan of the area, took aim at the overhead street-light and squeezed the trigger. *Pff, pff, pff, pff.*

The shots were silent, but the light blew out in three. He jumped back behind the wheel and drove quickly up the block. He pulled the van off the road a few houses past the aunt's, pushed in the headlight knob, and got out. He checked his waistband, pulled the hoodie over his head, and proceeded on foot, back towards Gevers.

Matthew smiled in surprise at how Colter's natural night-vision seemed abnormally good. His smile turned into a grin as Rafi's form rounded the corner, then walked forward into perpetual darkness.

Right on time.

Matthew's skin crawled with a mixture of excitement and electrical energy as he maintained a leisurely pace toward his target. He took a quick glance at the aunt's house as he passed – the lights were on inside, the porch light out. He didn't see anyone. He felt so amped up, he had no doubt he could slip into skinny fat as soon as he laid hands on him.

But that is not going to happen.

Time slowed down as the distance closed between them. Even at a little under twenty yards away, Matthew sensed a change in Rafi's gait. Rafi's street senses kicked in, and the kid stepped off the sidewalk, giving Matthew a wide berth. Matthew smiled at the gesture and nodded.

With each step, the tension wound up tighter as the gap closed. Ten yards, then five. Sensing the danger, Rafi moved to bolt but not quick enough. Matthew launched sideways and snatched Rafi by the wrist. Using momentum, Matthew spun the boy into a choke hold, cutting off his air in mid-scream.

Matthew relished the incredible strength of the soldier, man-handling the spindly boy with ease. Matthew lifted until

Rafi's feet dangled several inches off the ground. He kicked at the soldier's legs, striking one firm but ineffective blow on Matthew's carbon fiber and steel right shin. Matthew squeezed harder, and Rafi's body twitched and danced like a marionette.

Matthew hissed in Rafi's ear. "I've got something for you, Mr. Wilson." He cranked down with his left arm on Rafi's throat and pulled the blackened Bowie knife from a sheath at the small of his back with his right hand, presenting the oiled blade in front of the boy's eyes. Rafi flailed with such a renewed effort, it reminded Matthew of how he'd fought for his own life against Jeffrey Cruz while sitting in his wheelchair. That seemed so long ago.

"Let's end this," Matthew said. "For Kristi. Remember her?" Matthew raised the chin and slid the knife across Rafi's exposed throat with such force, air hissed and fluids sputtered as the blade severed the windpipe. Matthew shuddered as the steel edge ground against the bone vertebrae. He held Rafi for a moment longer, waiting for the fight to evaporate. And then he let go. His body flopped to the ground, jerking and twitching the last of its life energy away. Personally, Matthew had never been one for gore. But the sight of Rafi's open throat and gushing blood did not faze him. He thought that perhaps his mind had finally bonded with the sergeant's body.

He squatted down and placed a hand on the dying boy's convulsing chest, regretting not being able to see the life go out of Rafi's eyes, as he had unwillingly witnessed with Kristi. He reached up and wiped at the unbidden tears in his eyes with his blood-soaked sleeve.

"Consider your debt to her paid in full, asshole."

He started to move but settled back down and leaned in close to the dark mask of Rafi's face. "Oh, and when you get to hell, tell Christopher I said hello, and let him know Jeffrey will be joining you both soon."

Rafi's body stopped moving.

Matthew stood up and mechanically reconnoitered the dark street as he walked back to the van. He glanced again at the aunt's house and saw the flittering light from a television through the large, curtain-covered bay windows.

He wondered if his aunt would miss Rafi. If his death would shock her.

He reached the van, quietly pulled the door open, and climbed into the plastic covered seat. He looked at his watch, saw that six minutes had elapsed and smiled.

Much less work, much more reward.

He took a deep, satisfying breath and pulled the rearview mirror down. The backlit, bloody irises burned dully, but not as bright as to when he had first slipped into a new body. A fresh, bright red streak across his face appeared to glow from the dashboard light. He looked down at his blood-soaked body. He credited Colter for the idea of covering everything with plastic. He looked once more into the face of the soldier staring back at him and gave a solemn nod to the reflection.

"Thank you for tonight, Sergeant Colter. I look forward to and appreciate your continued support." Matthew saluted. "Because Jeffrey Cruz is not going to be that easy."

He plucked some baby wipes out of a box on the passenger seat, wiped the blood from his face, fixed the rearview mirror, and drove slowly out of the darkened neighborhood.

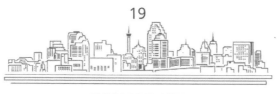

19

IMPATIENCE

6:30 A.M.
WEDNESDAY, OCTOBER 17TH
SAN ANTONIO, TEXAS: EAST SIDE

Randy squatted beside the sticky pool of blood soaking into the ground and watched the station wagon with Rafi Wilson's body pull away. He folded up a photo of the victim printed from the original Miller crime scene and stuffed it in his pocket.

In the video, the Johnson kid did nothing to hurt Kristi Sellers or Matthew. They just stood there and then ran. Randy knew what Miller was thinking now. Storey and Wilson's cowardice was their crime. Randy tried to put himself in Miller's shoes. Lying there, witnessing the bloody death of your girl. And those two not doing anything about it. Matthew had died that day, too.

The thought of the dead coming back for revenge muddled Randy's thoughts. Dead or not, Miller had crossed the line. Unique ability or not, Miller had labeled himself a bonafide murderer. Randy considered for a moment that perhaps the death of Storey and Wilson might be his fault. For not believing

Matthew as he laid there strapped to the gurney in his house, desperate and trapped in the body of Cruz. Thinking about how no court of law would ever believe the impossibility of it all made his head hurt. But he knew one thing for sure: somehow, someway, Miller had to be put down.

And then he had Crue Intellis and Jessie Richter to deal with. He had no intention of allowing them to continue coddling and making excuses for Miller. For a kid who had spent most of his life in a wheelchair, Miller took to murder just a little too efficiently for his liking. And it pissed him off.

Randy's partner, Melissa, handled Wilson's family, who spent the morning screaming and howling to the press about how their son didn't deserve to be murdered like this. Rafi may have been far from innocent, but Randy made up his mind to be on their side of this; the kid did not deserve to die.

JESSIE WATCHED RANDY FROM ACROSS THE STREET THROUGH A pair of binoculars while Eric stood outside the car, video camera in hand. Jessie felt a hundred and ten percent certain that Matthew wouldn't show up to the crime scene, as so many other criminals tended to do. She knew the kid didn't think he had committed any crimes. Matthew only wanted revenge. Pure and simple revenge.

Detective Randy D'Agostino, however, had a train of thought that was not in line with Jessie's, and she didn't like it. She watched as the coroner's lifted Rafi Johnson's body off the ground, coagulated blood sticking to the body like some thick, shredded red rubber band. They loaded what was left of the boy onto the gurney with an almost forced gentleness.

That's for the camera's, and family, Jessie thought.

As Eric filmed the crowd, Jessie watched Randy. Even from this distance, she saw his distress at the situation boiling, though. No matter what she had explained, he just wasn't getting it. He hadn't really vocalized his displeasure of her plan. But his body language spoke volumes. Jessie wasn't sure how much longer she could keep Randy in her circle if he didn't stop looking at this like a fucking detective.

She liked that he was smart. That even against all logic, he had figured out something special was going on with Matthew. She didn't like that the dick side of Randy wanted to take the kid down. He was too much a cop to unwrap his head. It wasn't his fault, but Jessie couldn't let this train of thought go on much longer. Jessie liked Randy well enough. His partner, Melissa too. But this relationship had been born of necessity, not by choice, and that made her have to work twice as hard.

Watching Randy get up and head to his car, an idea sprang into her head. "Eric, get in. Take me over to Randy before he takes off."

RANDY GOT INTO HIS CAR AND PULLED AWAY FROM THE CRIME scene when a flat-grey GMC Yukon pulled up, blocking his path. Jessie Richter got out of the truck and jogged up to the passenger door, opened it, and hopped in.

Just fucking great.

"Mind if I ride with you to the morgue?" she asked.

"Not necessary. Santos is meeting me there."

"All the better," Jessie said, then fastened her seatbelt.

Blood filled Randy's face. He gritted his teeth, threw the car into drive, and sped off down East Commerce Street. As unbelievable as the entire situation kept evolving to be, he had murders happening in his city that he could not ignore.

"Is there something bothering you, Detective?" Jessie asked.

Randy took a couple of deep breaths and launched into a tirade. "You know, when you and your thugs showed up, you said you were here to help me catch this guy, and since you've arrived, we've had two more comatose victims and one more dead kid."

"I've been thinking about this, too," Jessie said, apparently not understanding Randy had directed his rage at her. "We still have to identify him before we can catch him. Now that we know he's not abandoning his mission, we need to lay a trap."

Jessie said this with a cold calm that pissed Randy off even more and caused his frustration to boil over. "Look, lady, I don't have time for games. This guy is on the warpath, and you're supposed to have the inside edge. So, what's your plan, other than to stand around and watch me flounder?"

Jessie didn't take the bait. "I do have a plan, and like it or not, this is a game. The longer he goes unidentified, the more collateral damage there will be. Right now, he's in control, and we both know there is nothing we can do about it except to ride it out. I'm still your advantage. You won't catch him without me."

"You're pretty fucking narcissistic."

"If you don't want to play, Detective, then I'll take care of this myself. So, either stop your bellyaching and man up, or step aside."

Randy lifted his foot off the gas to slam on the brakes with the intent of kicking her out of the car when she threw up a hand.

"Stop," she said. Randy shot an angry look her way and saw her demeanor had changed. Her face looked calm. Almost submissive. "Randy, please stop the car."

Randy pulled to the curb, red-faced and ready to punch her, especially since she didn't have her bodyguards here to protect her. Jessie looked him straight in the eyes and spoke in a serene tone.

"Look, I'm sorry. I didn't mean to insult you. We have only just started working together, and I can only imagine how frustrated you are. But you have to believe me, you are getting worked up because you are still thinking inside the box. You're not going to win if you don't let those old habits die and learn to walk the edge of insanity where I live each and every day." She reached out, touched his hand, and shocked him.

He jerked his hand back. "Hey! Knock it off. I'm sick of your parlor tricks. I don't think any of this is funny. People are fucking dying, lady."

"I don't think it's funny, either. You were not the only one out last night trying to find the Wilson boy. All of us were out canvassing the streets with your people. And we failed. I know you think I'm a cold bitch, but I'm with you. The boy didn't need to die. But he did, and we both know there's one more to go."

Randy knew all too well that Jeffery Cruz was next. He cursed his desire, more like a deeply ingrained need, to save the only one of the gang who deserved to die. It seemed that Cruz's future traveled on an inexorably final path. At this point, Miller seemed unstoppable. "More if you count the innocent people he cycles through to get at him," he said quietly.

Jessie nodded. "You also know I can do more than tricks. So can Matthew Miller. You've been shown the proof. You've seen a glimpse of an unimaginable truth, but you're still thinking like a detective, not like him." She reached out to touch him again, but he pulled back.

"Keep your hands to yourself, lady."

"One more time, Detective. I promise I won't hurt you, but I need to show you something else. What you're really up against. Remember your office?"

She reminded him of the calming effect she'd forced into him when they first met, where he gave in and could sense the words "trust me" echoing in his mind. He also recalled the control she had exerted over Mel and the doctor.

I sure as fuck don't trust her now.

She gazed at him with those ridiculously sexy light brown

eyes, and after a moment, he relented and slowly forced both hands toward her.

"I need to show you more than I've shown you or the others. I need you on my side, Randy, because I'm on yours." Randy furrowed an untrusting brow at her. "Come on, now, play the game." A slight smile raised her lips.

He shook his head slowly, rolled his eyes, and gave over his hands. "Okay, I'm ready, show me what you got this time . . ." A burst of white light blinded him before he finished his sentence. His body felt like it moved, and then slammed to a stop.

Am I falling?

His reached out with his hands and his feet flopped and shuffled beneath him as he tried to regain balance because he stood on the curb. Outside, leaning on the car in front of the Bexar County Morgue.

"What the fuck, Jessie! What did you do?"

"I took you for a spin," she said flatly.

Randy's equilibrium slowly caught up, and a wave of fear shot through him as Jessie tried to support him. He shrugged her hand off like a child throwing a tantrum. Jessie stepped back and folded her arms across her chest.

"What? Why? What the fuck, Jessie, you took me for a what?"

"A spin. Not a long one. I felt you needed a little more insight as to what we're up against."

Randy's head stopped spinning, and he let go of the car one cautious hand at a time. His eyes widened at the understanding that felt like a slap across the face. "I thought you said that to shift into someone, you had to, well, you know . . ."

". . . seduce you? I'm strong enough now that I only need to have physical contact with someone to take them. I use sex because, when uninhibited, the target's guard is completely down. It's the easiest way in and out, so to speak, and it's also the best way to explain away the time slip." Jessie had him locked in her most serious, not smiling this time, gaze.

Randy looked at his watch. Two hours had passed. "I'm not even going to ask what you've been doing for the past two hours."

"Well, I called Melissa and asked her how Wilson's family was holding up. She said as well as can be expected and asked, well, your thoughts on me. So, we chatted a bit. She's kinda cool, Randy. I like her." Randy rolled his eyes. "After, I asked her to meet us here when she finished up. I then stopped by your apartment and changed clothes."

Randy hadn't even noticed that he now wore tan khaki's and a polo shirt instead of his grey slacks and dress shirt. "You went to my apartment?"

"Yes. Look at your phone. There's video of our little outing."

"I'll take your word for it." *But I'm sure as hell going to look at it later.*

"Your partner is on her way and should be pulling up any second, but that wasn't the point of the exercise." She moved close to him and looked up into his face. "Now you have experienced slip-streaming like no one else. You've been hijacked and used at my leisure. And unlike the hundreds of others I've done it to, you are the *only* one," she gently poked him in the chest, "who knows it happened."

Randy had no idea what to say. He had absolutely no memory of his down time. Jessie reached up slowly and pushed his mouth shut. "I'm stunned," he said, "and now I get it. Matthew is unstoppable."

"I wouldn't say unstoppable," Jessie said, a serious look on her face. "So, think like him now, Randy, and tell me what his next move will be. If you could control what you just experienced, what would you do next?"

He turned away from her and rubbed his face and neck. He knew with deep certainty that Jessie was right. He was neck deep in a game and in way over his head. "I'd be going after

Jeffrey with everything I had. He's the last one. No matter who I have to go through."

"Bingo," she said, and smiled. "So, let's get inside and take a look at the latest victim, and maybe between us we can get a sense of what's coming. Then we lay the trap."

20

POST KILL

6:30 A.M.
BOERNE, TEXAS

Staring at Brian Colter's naked reflection in the mirror, it shocked Matthew to see his skin covered head to toe with the red stickiness of Rafi Wilson. He scrunched up his nose and smacked his lips at the metallic smell and taste in his mouth. It was also surprising to find that he still had his stomach, not on his knees in front of the toilet throwing up, like he had with the lawyer. He also felt satisfied.

Very satisfied, he thought and stepped into the shower.

As the steaming water cascaded down his back, he propped his hands on the tile wall and watched, mesmerized as the blood swirled slowly around his feet before finding its path into the drain. He shampooed his hair and thought the biggest revelations of tonight's mission was how easy planning, execution, and killing came to him through the soldier.

In contrast, he felt he had operated by the seat of his pants while in Sara, and almost couldn't think because of the ingrained paranoia in both the lawyer and Rosie. Then it struck him: He could change out a body like changing clothes.

"New suits," he said and chuckled.

The water calmed him and gave him a clarity he did not possess in his own, disease-ridden carcass. He understood that although he may occupy a new body, his consciousness had no choice but to play by the rules of his host's ingrained physical and biological attributes, as well as restrictions. So far, they had all served him well.

God had given him another chance, although he remained uncertain if the man upstairs sided with him. Or maybe this was a test of faith. He thought about his mother and their weekly, involuntary trips to Mission San Juan Capistrano—forced subjugation to the word of God.

He remembered Romans 12:19, "Do not take revenge, my dear friends, but leave room for God's wrath, for it is written: 'It is mine to avenge; I will repay,' said the Lord." The crystal-clear memory of that verse sent a violent shudder through his body.

Why did you give me this gift if not to seek revenge on your behalf?

Perhaps God had nothing to do with this? The science behind his ability made it easier to understand. This just seemed so much bigger than science. He slapped his hand against the tile wall and decided at that moment to make the most of his gift, even if he ended up getting caught or killed. He didn't feel righteous or anything, but certainly, God would lay a path of escape before him. Both he and Kristi deserved that much.

Matthew set to scrubbing his hands with a small brush, soaped up for the third time, and after another thirty minutes, finally stepped out of the now ice-cold shower. While brushing his teeth, he walked back into the bedroom to the television sitting on the dresser. He picked up the remote, pressed the power button, and turned up the volume.

Breaking news about a body discovered on the East side of San Antonio stopped the brushing. He stood there watching the camera pan from the reporter to a body covered with a yellow medical blanket.

"Neighborhood children found the body just before sunrise and rushed home to call the police," the reporter said.

The camera then zoomed out and focused on someone Matthew recognized: Detective Randy D'Agostino. Matthew listened intently as the detective proclaimed this murder as a senseless killing and finally asked viewers to call police with any information.

Matthew pointed the toothbrush at the television screen. "You're a fucking liar, Detective. You know exactly why the boy was killed, don't you?" He reached for the remote and shut the television down.

Matthew moved back into the bathroom, spat into the sink, and stood naked in front of the full-length mirror hanging on the inside of the bathroom door. He studied the tall, muscular body before him. He flexed and tightened the arms, legs and torso and inspected the striations and vascularity of Colter's body with interest. He moved closer to the mirror and inspected the Army 101st Airborne tattoo and Army Ranger tattoo below it. Lifting his body up by the balls of his feet, he was impressed with the almost human robotic carbon fiber and stainless-steel prosthetic limb attached to his right leg just below the knee. He nodded at the reflection, quite satisfied with his new "suit".

"Now we're ready to complete this next mission," he said. "Time to tear Jeffrey Cruz apart."

10 A.M.
BEXAR COUNTY MORGUE

JESSIE, RANDY, AND HIS PARTNER MELISSA WATCHED DOCTOR Bishop verbally engage the Medical Examiner from the wrong side of the glass. Behind the two medical professionals lay the body of Rafi Wilson. A moment later, the medical examiner exited the room and marched past Jessie and the others, grumbling something about a smart-ass know-it-all. Bishop waved his entourage into the room.

"OK, obviously, as the lead detectives, you're permitted to be present for the autopsy," Bishop whispered. "He's just not going to allow you to examine the body without him here. I've given him my professional assurance there will be no contamination or tampering."

They all looked behind them at the large picture window, which framed a grumpy looking M.E., his arms wrapped about his torso, as if holding in his anger.

Jessie nodded at the man who glared back at her. "That's great, but I have a feeling we won't be here long."

Following Doctor Bishop's lead, Jessie pulled two bicep-length nitrile gloves from a box on the instrument tray and donned them. She moved in close as the doctor slowly lifted the chin up and back, exposing the open throat. "This is the work of a professional–a seasoned combat soldier," she said.

"Yes, it's a clean cut, done by a powerful person," Bishop added.

"So, you think he's in a soldier now?" Melissa asked.

"Look at the sweep of the blade, the depth of the cut. Only a pro would know how to do this. Someone who's done it many times, practiced at it." She picked up each arm and inspected the man's arms, wrists and hands, then soft-probed the skin of his torso, "There's no bruising, no sign of a struggle, no second or defensive cuts. It happened quick."

"I'm surprised he didn't severe the head," Bishop said. "The cut mark into the vertebrae is deep."

"A fucking soldier," Melissa said. "Just great."

"It makes sense," Randy said, "and there are thousands to choose from in San Antonio."

Jessie backed up from the gurney and pulled her gloves off. "He wants to succeed," she said. "I don't need to see anymore. Let's get outside and talk."

Randy waved the M.E. in. The angry looking man stomped back in. "Thank you, Doctor, you can take him now. I appreciate your accommodating us," Randy said.

"Can you have someone call us with toxicology and if you find anything else unusual?" Mel asked.

The medical examiner grunted with a nod and called in another pathologist to begin the official autopsy as Jessie and the others exited into the hallway. Detective Santos had a sour look on her face.

"What's on your mind, Mel?" Randy asked.

"Look, I'm having a hard time wandering around outside the box. I get that he can transfer his consciousness into someone else's body, but even if Matthew is controlling the body, how does he know how to kill like this? The kid has been in a wheelchair most of his life. You don't learn this from video games or television violence. You learn this through experience."

Jessie looked at her with empathy. "I completely get what you are saying, but we've already discussed the answer for that. He retains the pre-trained skillsets of his hosts. I think we can all agree that combat military types, not to mention Navy Seals, Special Forces and the like, have the skill instilled into them through years of training. They can kill you in their sleep. We, meaning Walkers, have full access to skillsets. We can also tap into some memories of our hosts."

"You can read our thoughts?" Melissa asked.

"No, not read your active thoughts, but I can tap into a hard-wired, solid memory. Part of having access to the host's skillsets is part of their memory, too."

"But killing like this? It's just hard to fathom."

"He's on a mission of revenge. He's using the soldier to his full advantage." Melissa and even Doctor Bishop looked confused. "I learned about this part of the shift phenomenon by accident myself," she said and pulled each one in a little closer as the pathologist walked by. She kept her voice low. "It's just like driving a car or riding a bicycle. Once you get it, you got it. You train your body to do it to the point you no longer have to think about it. The soldier is Matthew's bicycle." Detective Santos looked doubtful, and Randy didn't seem to be paying attention.

"Here's an example. A few years ago, we were on a mission in Afghanistan. I flew a helicopter out of a terrorist compound to escape capture. At the time, I did have some rudimentary training on flying helicopters, but not Russian helos. I just got in, started flipping a bunch of switches and went. I didn't think about it. The body I occupied just did it naturally, through years of repetition and deeply ingrained training. I only started thinking about it when it came time to land, and I almost killed us all."

"I didn't see that video," Randy said. "You escaped in a helicopter? What the hell from?"

"I had just beheaded a Taliban's Jihadist spiritual leader. It was time to leave."

The color drained from Melissa's face and Jessie reached up, patting her on the shoulder. "The point is, the body's highly trained skillsets usually come with the territory. I think it's the best benefit of slip-streaming, and it looks like Matthew Miller is catching on quick."

Melissa's brow furrowed and she hissed, "So you're telling us that we need to lay a trap for a seventeen-year-old kid with the body and skill of a professional soldier, who's going after a comatose detainee locked up in a supermax military medical facility?" She looked back and forth between Randy and Jessie. "Are you fucking kidding me?"

"I see your point. We're going to have to plan this to minimize casualties," Jessie said.

"Casualties?" Melissa asked, her voice up an octave. "I'm being sarcastic. Casualties?"

"Because he's going to do suicide by cop," Randy said.

"I think you're both wrong." Melissa paced the hallway and looked for answers on the linoleum floor. "I think you're underestimating him."

"How so?" Randy asked.

"You don't think that with his newfound ability, he'll want to go on existing? I mean, when you think about it, he can live as anyone. Hell, he can live forever if he plays his cards right. If I was him, I wouldn't go out in a blaze of glory."

Jessie looked at her and nodded. "That's great thinking, Detective. You could be right. But we still have to anticipate that he's going after Cruz one way or another. Breaking into the military hospital will be a piece of cake for him, but getting out? Once he blows his cover, that won't happen," Jessie said.

"We don't want him to escape, but what do we tell the soldiers and doctors at the hospital? Don't mind us, we're just hanging out for a corporeal assassin. As soon as he shows up, we'll take it from there?" Melissa asked.

"Yeah, that's a problem. I don't want him trapped in the military or jail infirmary, either. That won't be good for me," Jessie said.

"I'm not talking about him being trapped. I'm talking about stopping him." Melissa's frustration apparently fell on deaf ears.

"Oh, we'll stop him, but we're not putting him down like a rabid dog. I've already told you. I will help you catch him, but he's mine to do with as I please once we do.

Melissa's face turned to a fun shade of beet red. "You're insane. This guy's a fucking killer, he's . . ."

Randy cut her off, ". . . let's make it easier for him."

"Oh great," Melissa said. "You're taking her side on this?"

"You know she's right, Mel. We've got a deal with Jessie. You're going to have to trust that she's on the right side of this also." Randy gave his partner the "we can't win, knock it off" look. "So, here's my idea . . ."

As Jessie listened to Randy's plan, a smile tugged at the corner of her mouth. "I'm liking the way you think, Randy. Your timing is perfect."

"Why?" Randy asked.

"Because our reinforcements will be here around 2:00 p.m."

"Good. We can use some other sounding boards because you're both fucking crazy," Mel said.

21

DATE NIGHT

2:00 P.M.
BOERNE, TEXAS

M atthew pulled the bore brush through the barrel of the .300 blackout rifle thinking, *How in the hell am I going to get into Military Medical Center?* More importantly, *How the hell am I going to get out?* His cellphone rang and startled him into flipping the cleaning rod across the room and dropping the upper receiver on the floor. He snatched up the phone and saw a photo of a girl with the name "Anna" on the screen. *Pretty.* He took a deep breath and answered. "Hello?"

"Hey stranger," the female voice said. "Long time no chat. This is Anna."

He had no idea who Anna was or what to say and wanted to kick himself for answering. His face got hot, and he poised his finger over the END button. He almost pressed it when she spoke again.

"Are you there?"

"Oh, yes, I am. Sorry."

"You don't remember me, do you?" Matthew said nothing. "We met a couple weeks ago at the Rodeo Bar?" Matthew still said nothing. "You gave me your number because you said you'd probably lose mine, and it seems like you did, so I just thought I'd call to say hi. So, hi!"

Matthew, not remotely prepared for this kind of call, still considered hanging up. He had a mission to plan, and it aggravated him that a cute girl with a cute voice could distract him so easily.

"Oh, yeah . . . hi. Uh, not much, I mean, I'm not doing much. Just sitting around, sort of. What are you up to?" He cringed and rolled his eyes, relieved she had no way to see the beet red, stupid look on his face.

Why am I even talking to this girl?

Elbow deep into cleaning the rifle, he had shit to do, and he just didn't know what to say.

"Well then, I have perfect timing," she said.

"You do?"

"Yes, I'm just sitting around, too, and I thought I'd give you the opportunity to make it up to me for blowing me off."

"Opportunity?"

Opportunity? What?

"By taking me to dinner," she said. "Some place nice."

He wanted to hang up on her. *I really do NOT have time for this shit. But ugh! I can't hang up!* "Hang on a second," he said, and punched up the photo app on Brian's phone.

He flipped through the pictures and stopped at a photo of very sexy brunette with Brian at a bar. Although the photo is dated from two weeks ago, some tingle of recognition within Brian's body tells Matthew that this is Anna. *She is stunning.* Her straight black hair and jet-black eyes reminded him more of a Native American than a Latina. And her boobs were big. That or she wore a really small top to get attention at the bar.

She had your number, didn't she, Colter? he thought.

"I'm sorry . . . hh, Anna. I didn't mean to blow you off, but to be honest, I completely forgot. I've had a lot going on lately." *You have no idea.*

"So how about now?"

"Now, like in right now?" A trickle of sweat sprang to life on Matthew's temple. Not only had he never been on a date, but she now put him on the spot to deliver. He looked around the living room. He had everything from the footlocker spread out all over the place, ready for maintenance. "Now isn't good, I'm sorry. I'm in the middle of cleaning my place."

"I thought you just said you were sitting around."

"Well, I mean, doesn't cleaning count for sitting around?" Matthew was digging a hole for himself, and he knew she knew it!

"That's true, but if that's your idea of sitting around, then you can come over and clean my house," the girl said and giggled.

"How about four o'clock?" Matthew asked, and cringed again.

What the fuck am I doing?

"What? Clean my house? Sure! Are you gonna wear a sexy maid outfit for me?"

The girl sniggered at him on the other end of the line, and that bead of sweat rolling down his temple somehow turned into a stream. Butterflies invaded his stomach as he talked to this girl. He felt like an inexperienced, stupid kid.

Because I am an inexperienced, stupid kid.

"No, I mean, dinner, and maybe I'll clean your house in the maid outfit if you ask really, really nice." *That's better,* he thought, but honestly, he didn't have a clue about what the hell he was doing.

"Are you sure? You sound super busy, just sitting around and all."

"Yes, I'm sure." *No, I'm not. I'm fucking terrified.* He had a tough time wrapping his head around how talking to this girl made him so nervous considering what he had already been through, you know, killing punks and lesbian sex and all.

"You're not going to blow me off again, are you?"

Now she sounded serious.

The thought of spending time with a pretty girl sent a familiar slow burn to the pit of his stomach, and it struck him that he should enjoy time in this new body, especially because he didn't anticipate being in it much longer.

"No, I'm not going to blow you off. Do you want me to come and get you?"

"Well, yes. I think I deserve that, too. I love Jeeps! Can we go downtown to the River Walk? I haven't been there in a while, and I think it will give you an opportunity to prove I'm right," she said.

"How did you know I have a Jeep?" Her mention of Brian's vehicle set him on edge.

"Well, we made out next to it when you gave me your number." The girl went quiet. "Maybe I'm making a mistake, if you don't remember that, then . . ."

"No, I just forgot we were by the Jeep. That's all. I think I had too much to drink that night." Matthew hoped his recent experience in the severely inebriated version of the sergeant would ring true.

"Yeah, you were pretty drunk. So, the Riverwalk, then? Maybe you'll prove I am right."

He couldn't recall how old he was the last time he was at the Riverwalk, but he did remember walking it on his own two feet. He also remembered the boat rides and ducks. And the ice cream.

"Right about what, exactly?"

"That there is more to you than just a studdly body, and that you're actually interesting, intelligent, and not just another roll in the hay."

"What if you're wrong?" Matthew asked and had no clue where the bold comment came from.

"Then it sounds like a fun night in the barn, regardless. We both win."

Matthew laughed at the woman's brash confidence and decided he could use a little of that, too. He thought about his short time in Rosie and Sara and how he'd enjoyed the physical contact.

"Hello, you still there?" Anna asked.

"I'm sorry, sure. I'm looking at my contacts in the phone, and I don't have your address, can you text it to me? I will pick you up around four o'clock."

AFTER ADDING THE ADDRESS TO HIS CONTACTS, HE THOUGHT about Kristi and a wave of guilt vibrated through him. Kristen would have never been his girlfriend. But he loved her.

I still love her.

He renewed his oath and promised to avenge her, but for the moment, he forced thoughts of her aside. Fantasies about this strange woman ran wild, and his body responded to the thought of rolling in the hay with her, although he had no clue where to begin. He felt certain Brian's body would know how to respond if it came to having sex, but for some strange reason, Matthew remained nervous about this girl.

Who knows, perhaps she'll end up being an asset.

He tossed the phone on the couch, retrieved the cleaning rod, and picked the barrel back up. Glancing at the clock, he saw he had plenty of time. When he reached for some cleaning fluid, he realized that he had lined up all the cleaning supplies from the footlocker in an organized manner.

He raised an eyebrow and said, "Do we have a little OCD

going on here, Brian?" He plucked a cotton pad from the kit and ran it through the barrel's bore a couple of times.

In an instant, he felt something wrong. He slowly laid the barrel down and held his hands out in front of him. They were shaking, and suddenly his chest tightened, and the room closed in around him. He stood up and ran out the side door and into the yard where he took deep, deliberate breaths.

What the fuck is this?

Doubt about his next mission, meeting Anna included, turned into anxiety and fear flooded into him. His skin tingled and the rush of power built up in his ears. Something deep in his mind made him think this might be PTSD and wondered if maybe *he* was the one, not Colter, suffering from it. He searched his feelings for guilt, for killing Storey and Wilson, and maybe for how he'd dumped Sara's body in the ditch. This felt wrong, terribly wrong, but he just couldn't figure out the nature of the problem with his heart slamming about wildly inside his ribcage.

A few more minutes of deep breathing brought the pounding in his chest under control. He went back inside, directly to his bathroom, and splashed his face with cold water. He opened the medicine cabinet and found a half-empty bottle of Paxil, an anti-depressant he happened to be intimately and unfortunately familiar with — his mother used it, or more appropriately, abused it. He took a pill out and paused just before popping it in his mouth. He remembered how his mother turned totally worthless when she took these pills, which became more frequent as his condition worsened.

Come on, man, you don't need this shit. Get a fucking grip.

He dropped the pill back in the bottle and tossed the whole batch in the trash. He went back to the kitchen, snatched another beer from the fridge, and returned to the couch in front of the disassembled rifle.

"We got work to do soldier," he said. "Time to focus man. Time to fo-cuz."

He lifted the knife used to cut Rafi's throat and looked closely at the razor-sharp edge. He'd already cleaned off all the blood and sinew and started to sheath and stow it but paused. He picked up the whetstone, oiled it, and slowly drew the length of the blade across the grainy surface, just as he had before. As he suspected, the hiss of metal against stone had an immediate soothing effect. The soldier's heart slowed, his hands steadied, and Matthew found comfort in the sound and rhythm as he honed the blade's edge.

"I'm with you, man. I'm with you," he murmured. His insides unwound, and Matthew smiled at the sensation of his consciousness and the body of the soldier syncing up. "Wow, that is such a great feeling," he said out loud and returned to work, preparing the tools of the soldier's trade. Matthew and Brian were now one, united in the noble and worthy cause of locating, and then killing, Jeffery fucking Cruz.

After my date with Anna.

22

IRON CACTUS

4:30 P.M.
STINSON FIELD
SAN ANTONIO, TEXAS

J essie pointed toward the huge AC130 Gunship as it leveled off at about a hundred feet over the runway. Randy glanced over at Melissa and Doctor Bishop. With their mouths hanging open, they were obviously impressed with this show of force from Crue Intellis.

So am I.

He also noticed that the former LAPD guy, Steve Walters, and Mel were standing very close together, smiling and giggling like a couple of teenagers. Randy had never seen his partner so touchy-feely with any man before, and their obvious mutual attraction made him uncomfortable, in a brotherly sort of way. The plane roared overhead, and Randy's hands shot up to cover his ears. The wings tilted back and forth in a salute as Jessie bounced on the balls of her feet and waved. Randy also thought the plane looked way too big for the old WWII airfield.

Jessie leaned in closer to Randy and yelled over the noise. "I bet the neighbors around here are shitting their pants about now," she said, motioning with her hands at how low the plane flew.

"Nah, this is a small airfield, but we get big old warbirds out here every year. They're used to it."

"Really? Warbirds?" Jessie said, nodding with a sardonic look on her face. "Well then, I'm sure you'll like what's coming next."

As the plane touched down and taxied toward them, a smaller vintage warbird came into view. Melissa stepped forward eyes wide with astonishment. She also started bouncing up and down with the kind of excitement one gets when meeting a movie star.

"Holy crap, that's a B-25 Mitchell," she said. "That's yours?"

"Now I'm really impressed," Walters said. "Good I.D., Mel. It's not 'ours', per se, but it does belong to the pilot, who also happens to be our CEO."

Mel looked flabbergasted. "Your boss flies a WWII bomber?" As the plane flew low over the group, Jessie and Melissa waved. "I see the .50 cals. Wow, that's so cool."

"Those guns are fully operational," Jessie said, and leaned in, "and loaded."

"That is seriously badass," Mel responded and continued, "It's a B-25J, one of the few clear-nosed B-25's still flying." Melissa caught Randy's glare and punched him lightly in the arm. "Don't look at me like that. Did you forget I'm a Navy brat and my great-grandfather flew one of these in the Pacific Theater?"

Randy threw his hands up in a defensive posture. "Hey now, no need to get feisty. I'm onboard. It's very cool."

Everyone watched in silence as the smaller bomber taxied in and parked under the wing of the bigger C-130. Jessie jogged out to the flight-line to meet her boss as the ramp of the big cargo plane lowered. Two flat-grey GMC Yukons drove down the ramp and swung around to meet the group. Dr. Bishop's eyes were still wide. The SUV's doors flew open, and the Crue

Intellis team bailed out of the vehicles wearing big smiles. Randy thought the way they walked told a different story; these guys were ready for a fight.

Steve Walters motioned the Crue team to gather around. "Guys, this is Dr. Raymond Bishop, Detective Randy D'Agostino, and his beautiful partner, Detective Melissa Santos." Randy felt the heat come off his partner from two feet away and chuckled at her reaction to Walter's pass. "They are handling the Miller Case you've all been briefed on. Jessie has been revealed, necessary for us to find Miller. Our job is to support them with the full extent of our resources."

Randy measured up the Crue Intellis team as they exchanged happy greetings. Two of them were women who looked to be cut from the same cloth as Jessie, and the men all appeared to be seasoned soldiers. Except for one — a stereotypical surfer with long blonde hair and a dark tan, wearing surfer baggies and an Iron Maiden t-shirt.

That one belongs on the beach.

Hands extended for quick introductions as Jessie, her boss, and a tall, beautiful blonde woman walked up.

"This is Jon Daly, CEO of Crue Intellis and Krys Johanseen, our VP of Operations," Jessie said.

Randy shook Jon's hand. "Sir, I have to say, I'm impressed. I appreciate you bringing your team down here, but I certainly didn't expect all this." He looked toward the two planes and at the military contractors standing around them.

"I can see the word 'overkill' on your partner's face," Jon said. Randy glanced over at Mel.

"That's not her overkill look, sir. She's in awe."

Melissa's eyes were glued to the World War II bomber. "I love your B-25, Mr. Daly. My great-grandfather flew them in the war. Pacific. Can I have a closer look?"

Jon smiled and shook her hand. "First of all, you can both stop calling me 'sir' and 'Mr.'. I prefer Jon, and I'm intrigued by your interest in the B-25, Detective. Other than my lovely partner, Krys, she's my favorite thing to talk about."

Krys unwrapped herself from Jessie and stepped up to hug Randy and Melissa but held each of them in her grip just a little too long. Randy felt some kind of warmth come from the woman. It made him think of Jessie. "I feel like I know you both already. Jessie speaks very highly of you." Randy saw the look on Mel's face—she felt it too.

"Detective Santos, I'll be happy . . ."

"Please, Jon, call me Mel."

Jon smiled warmly. "Mel, I'll give you the grand tour of the Mitchell. We'll make time over the next couple of days to take a ride." Melissa's eyes lit up, causing Randy to laugh. "But if you don't mind, I'm famished, and we all have a lot to discuss. We haven't caught Miller yet, and there's a lot to do." Jon's comment struck a nerve in Randy.

How was I supposed to know that my killer had supernatural powers, who would have ever believed it?

Jon raised an eyebrow at Randy. "You have found some remarkable information, and you've handled all of this very well, Randy. I'm looking forward to working with you to catch him. Now let's get going, I'm starving."

Randy appreciated the comment, but he still felt a bit underqualified for the task. "Thank you for that, Jon. We'll do our best to keep up and be helpful. You like Tex-Mex?"

Jon grinned and rubbed his belly. "My favorite!"

"Great," Randy said, "because I've made reservations down on the Riverwalk."

5:30 P.M.
SAN ANTONIO RIVERWALK

JON WATCHED HIS TEAM ENTER THE IRON CACTUS MEXICAN Grill and reflected on how it had been over ten years since he'd last visited San Antonio. He thought the big city with the small-town feel hadn't changed much, other than being more crowded than he remembered. This was a first visit for some members of the Crue.

Since Jon knew his team might be dealing with a current or former soldier, he had put together this team of battle-hardened operators, with the exception of Steve Walters and their in-house FBI ambassador, Mario Cabrisi. He smiled at how the team covertly went into action, casually finding tactical seating positions along the patio wall and entryways. Cabrisi went into the building, came out, and nodded. Once settled, Jon pulled out the seat for his partner, Krys, and sat beside her, confident any number of his Crue had his exposed back covered. He glanced at each member of the team and smiled with satisfaction.

"You've brought your best for this adventure," Krys said. Jon glanced at her and winked.

"I get more than I pay for." Then he glanced at Rasher, who stood a little away from the group near the river entrance. "Rasher. Can you at least smile a little? Remember sensitivity training?" he asked, a half smirk on his face.

Retired Army Major Charles "Chip" Rasher perked up at the comment. "Sensitivity training? What's that?" He grinned and Krys rolled her eyes at him.

Jon watched the man slip back into his serious, situationally aware self and remembered when Chip first came to Crue Intellis. It took a couple of years for the man to let go of his demons and loosen up. Incredible nav-skill set aside, Jon smiled at how close he and Chip had become over the years. Especially after their discovery of Jessie some ten years ago.

He glanced back at Eric Ramos, his former Marine Force

Recon and current helicopter pilot, and even though the man looked to be giving Jessie his full attention, Jon saw he only half-listened. Not due to lack of interest in what Jessie had to say, but instead, Jon saw Eric's busy eyes scanning the tourists every fifteen seconds or so. For threats. Jon never said a word, nor gave his blessing, when he and Jessie came to him several years ago to confess that they had become lovers.

"You're grown adults. As long as I don't see it affect your judgment, then you have my blessing. Just keep it discreet," he had said. More of a daughter to him, Jon had every confidence Jessie could take care of her own heart. She knew he would be there for her if, or when, that heart got broken.

Jon also gave Eric a lot of credit for sticking by her side, knowing what Jessie often had to do to succeed on her missions. Jon sighed, knowing he would lose the bet that one day they would marry and make a little one for him to train up. But there was always hope.

The waiter arrived with menus, big baskets of tortilla chips, and bowls of salsa. Everyone ordered drinks and pointed to Jon when asked about the tab. Jon nodded and grinned.

"God, I love these guys," he said.

Krys leaned in and kissed him lightly on the cheek. "And we all love you right back," she whispered. "Keep playing this right and you'll get the bonus package of thanks tonight."

Jon snatched Krys by the neck, making her laugh with surprise, and pulled her in for a passionate kiss. "I can't wait."

Two other Crue members, Marc Samuelson and Taina Volkov, recruited from the Air Force Security forces, were also a couple. They had proven themselves exemplary on combat rescue missions, both credited with saving Jessie's ass. Twice. Marc happened to be twenty years Taina's senior, but the age difference didn't seem to get in the way of their relationship. They took up positions across from each other and covered the main dining room area on the far side of the restaurant.

Jon turned his attention to the interaction between Detective Melissa Santos and Steve Walters whom he'd recruited from the LAPD almost fifteen years ago. Jon had no memory of Steve giving attention to any woman since his wife had passed six years ago from cancer. The two were deep in conversation, and Jon thought he saw the same light in Steve's eyes he still witnessed every day in the eyes of Krys. Jon nudged Krys's knee and pointed at Steve and the detective with his chin. Krys glanced over, doing a double take of surprise, followed by a huge grin.

Juanita Washington, former CIA and now his in-house intelligence analyst, sat on the other side of Doctor Bishop. The two were already engaged in deep conversations about the doctor's findings from the coma victims at Military Medical and the two women at Methodist hospital. After one more thorough scan of the Iron Cactus, Mario Cabrisi sat next to the doctor.

Then, of course, there was Jessie.

"She looks so happy," he whispered.

Krys caught his comment and leaned in. "She is, generally, but I sense she's also frightened."

Jon nodded and picked up his frosty cold *Dos Equis* beer. "That's why we're here," Jon said, then raised his glass. "Here's to a smooth, easy mission for the rough-riders." Jon and Krys clinked glasses, then looked over at Jessie. He thought about the time he and Jessie had met, or more appropriately, how he'd rescued her in Myrtle Beach, South Carolina over ten years ago.

As if sensing Jon's thoughts about her, she looked toward him, grabbed the armrests of her chair, and sat up straight. Her face morphed into . . . what? Pain? Jon sat up too, his quick movement setting the others to following his gaze.

Jessie's eyes went wide with fear and her face twisted in pain. Then she fell.

23

CROSSED TERMINALS

6:30 P.M.
SAN ANTONIO RIVERWALK

As Matthew looked past Anna at the Riverwalk, he took a second to run his finger along the brim of his ball cap, checking to make sure the infrared LED lamp mounted there still worked. He hoped the internet article claiming LED lamps could fool street-side cameras wasn't complete bullshit. For the past few days, he had been extra careful to cover his tracks. He felt silly about that now. On the other hand, after taking in the fancy neighborhood, he found himself grateful for all the cash Sara had because that meant he wouldn't need to use Brian's credit cards.

"The Iron Cactus is right around the bend," Anna said. She reached out and took Matthew's hand, pulling him out of his reverie. "I'm really having a great time, Sergeant Colter. Thank you for bringing me down here."

Matthew brought her hand to his lips and kissed her fingers. "I am, too. I haven't been this relaxed in some time," he said. He pulled her closer to him and moved in to kiss her lips. She lifted herself up on her toes and met him halfway, her huge onyx eyes luring him in. Matthew had a brief flash of Kristi, which Anna shoved aside by wrapping her arms around his neck, pulling herself up, and kissing him deeply. Matthew felt the taught muscles in her back and her hard nipples against his chest.

The staff sergeant likes.

She pulled her hips into his, and in a moment, her feet were off the ground.

"Oh wow," she said. "I haven't been kissed like that, ever."

Matthew looked down into her face and removed a strand of hair from her eyes as he settled her onto the ground. "Me neither. That's only the second real kiss I've ever had," he said.

"You're such a liar!" She punched him gently in the arm and held onto his hand as they made the turn and headed into the restaurant.

"I'm not lying. I swear to you, it's kind of a long, weird story, but . . ." Matthew stopped in his tracks.

"Ow, Brian, you're hurting my hand," she said. Her nose wrinkled in pain.

Matthew's stomach clenched, and he felt slightly dizzy. "Oh, shit, I'm sorry." He glanced at her, kissed her hand again, and tried to move forward, but he found himself clutching Anna's arm to maintain his balance.

Anna looked frightened. "What's wrong?"

Matthew took another step onto the patio, at the same time searching for an escape route. "I'm not sure. Let's get to a table." After another step, a man, a soldier-type who stood sentry just inside the gate, made direct eye contact with Matthew. He nodded in acknowledgement, but when the man nodded back, a wave of pain struck Matthew hard, shooting through his limbs and filling his vision with stars. It took all his willpower just to stay upright. He repeated the visual assessment of his surroundings and discovered a second sentry at the other end of the patio. Before he could determine what that meant, a woman seated at a table about halfway down the patio grabbed at her stomach and then fell to her hands and knees, almost pulling her table over on top of her. As she retched violently on the ground, the two sentries as well as the two men at her table rushed to her side.

Worse than the pain, Matthew felt overwhelmed with panic. It had everything to do with this woman.

"We have to go, Anna. Now!"

WHEN JESSIE GRABBED HER STOMACH, EVERYONE STOPPED talking and turned their attention to her. Jon and one of the two men seated at her table knelt beside her.

Jon whispered, "What's wrong? What can we do to help?"

After a groan, Jessie doubled over and pulled the patio table off its legs as she fell to her knees on the hard-tiled floor. Juanita Johnson and Doctor Bishop rushed to her side as Rasher, Santos, and Walters quickly fired off hand signals in an effort to establish a perimeter. Jon took a moment to watch Ramos, Samuelson, and Volkov attempt to seal the exits but realized there was too much space and too many people to cover before returning his attention to Jessie.

"Talk to me, Jessie. What's going on? Do you need a medic?" he asked.

Sweat poured down her face as she tried to answer but instead wretched again, bringing up what remained in her stomach. "I . . . I don't know," she said, at last. A lost glaze filled her eyes, then she wretched a third time. "Something just slammed into me. Not the food, it's something else." She took Jon and Doctor Bishop's hand and used them to pull herself to her feet. She drew a shaky breath and looked around. "It's passing."

"What's passing?" Jon asked.

"The feeling that just blasted through me, like, like . . ." Jessie replied. "I can't explain it. But it's passing." Her head shot up and she pointed toward the interior of the restaurant. "Actually, the feeling is headed that way."

Rasher calmly scooted close to Jessie. Santos and Walters were at his back. "What are we looking for, Jessie?" he whispered.

"I'm not sure." She used her finger to trace an invisible trail along the river. "It felt like . . ." She paused and shook her head. "God, this is going to sound stupid. But some kind of weird force or power slammed into me." She pointed to the waterway again. "I sensed it coming in from the river but didn't notice anything until it passed right through me and then went into the dining area." Her eyes started to clear. "Male. The power was definitely male. It felt like slip-streaming, or like being slip-streamed into by someone else." Her eyes went wide.

"Matthew!"

Chip scanned the restaurant, intensity in his eyes. "We'll search," he said.

"I'm guessing he will be affected like Jessie," Jon said. "Look for someone in pain, man or woman."

"I don't know how I know, but I'm sure he's in a male."

Rasher, Santos, and Walters moved with focus across the covered dining room and bar at a slow, deliberate pace.

At long last, an embarrassed waiter rushed up and offered to assist. Jessie waved him off. "I'm sorry. I can't explain. But it's not the food, I promise."

"Just bring some ice water, please," Krys said, as she righted the table. Jon grabbed Jessie's elbow to guide her to a seat. Jessie grabbed Jon's hand and snapped to attention. Then she motioned to Ramos and Randy and said, "You guys come with me. Everyone else just stay here. We'll be right back."

Samuelson and Volkov nodded and quickly took up positions on either side of the patio, subtly palming their concealed Glocks.

"Jessie, go get him," Jon said.

Jessie moved onto the Riverwalk and toward the nearest street side exit to Crockett Avenue. Randy and Ramos stayed close, scanning as they moved.

"What are we looking for?" Randy asked.

"A man. I can still sense him, but just barely. He's lingering."

They took the steps up to the street two at a time and turned south onto St. Mary's. Jessie glared at all the passers-by like they owed her money. She glanced down West Crockett Street, shook her head, and then began hurrying straight ahead, fast. She rushed around the corner of East Commerce Street but then slowed and finally stopped in front of the Aztek Theater where Walters, Santos, and Rasher met her coming from the other direction.

"We went through the restaurant, down Crockett, and down an alleyway when we saw you heading south. We didn't see anyone acting abnormally, Jess," Chip said.

Jessie stood still and stared down Commerce toward Navarro. "It's gone. The feeling is gone. Miller's gone," she said.

The group looked at each other.

"What do you mean, he's gone? How do you know it's him?" Randy asked.

A dark shadow crossed Jessie's face and Randy stepped back.

Chip whispered in his ear. "Smart move. You were about to meet her killer side."

"He might not be in a man, but I'm positive it's a male presence, very strong. Don't ask me how I know. This is the first time I've experienced anything like this. It just felt too similar. It's got to be him."

"Are you okay?" Eric asked, a concerned look on his face.

Jessie shot him a small smile and nodded.

"Don't kill me, but when you say presence, what do you mean? A ghost?" Randy asked.

After a beat, Jessie said, "I've never experienced a ghost, but

I'm going to say no. This felt physical. Like I said earlier, it's kind of like what I feel when I slip-stream, like an electrical charge, but . . . shit, guys, I can't explain it, but I don't believe in ghosts."

The group surrounded her like a protective wall. So seeing no one near, Jessie rubbed her thumb and forefinger together until electricity began to dance between her fingertips like miniature lightning bolts. Melissa and Randy gasped, which inwardly pleased Jessie to see the shocked looks on their faces. "You guys know what happens if you jump a car battery and cross the wires?" she asked. Everyone nodded. "That's what it felt like."

"Let's get back and fill in Jon," Rasher said and began to lead the group around the corner, but Jessie pulled up short.

"You feel him again?" Melissa asked.

Jessie didn't answer because she focused on a male figure well over a block away. He stared back at her from the corner of the old CVS building.

Eric saw the figure, too. He waved everyone off, then glided in next to Jessie. Eric tensed, ready to run.

"Want me to go after him?"

"No. He's too far away." Then the man seemed to melt into the shadows. "Now we have a new problem," she said.

24

ANNA

Matthew hissed through gritted teeth. He put a hand on Anna's waist and guided her to the front of the restaurant, straight to the stairs leading up to the street. As he nudged Anna upward, he paused to glance toward the patio. People Matthew guessed were part of the woman's group helped her to her feet. As she raised her head his way, he fought off a wave of nausea and vaulted up the last few steps to push his way onto Crockett Street. His stomach calmed and dizziness subsided as soon as he made it through the door. He looked around to gain his bearings and recounted at least five more soldier-types in the shop. For the first time since Jeffrey Cruz had crashed through his door, fear gripped him. He grabbed Anna's hand and hustled them past the back of the Aztec Theater

"Brian, stop," Anna said. "You're scaring me."

But he couldn't stop. He had to get away from the woman responsible for the lingering pain and sickness and back to where he parked the Jeep on Navarro Street. "Don't let go of my hand," he said right before taking an abrupt turn down an alley-

191

way. Without looking back, they exploded out of the alley and turned left onto Commerce. Anna said nothing, but she did not resist. "I'm sorry," Matthew said. "I'm scared, too. I'm trying to put us at a safe distance."

"A safe distance from what?"

Matthew glanced at Anna and saw terror etched on her face.

"I'm not sure. Anna, please. I'm not going to hurt you, I promise. I don't know what else to say. I need to figure out what's going on myself. Something's not right," he said. They had traveled two-thirds of the way down the block when Matthew pulled Anna into the vestibule of the CVS. "In here, quickly. Stay silent, be still." She stared at him, and he could smell her fear. Matthew shook his head and waited. "She's still out there," he said. "I can feel it."

"Who's out there?"

Matthew put a finger to her lips. "Shhh, I'm serious, Anna, please." After a minute, Matthew took a deep breath and stepped from the alley onto Commerce. He looked up the street in the direction they had come from. No one there. So, he reached to pull Anna behind him when a woman, *the* woman, stepped around the corner, feet shoulder width apart, fists clenched at her sides. The both froze. "Wait," he said as every muscle in the soldier's body tensed, ready to bolt again. As the woman stared back at him, a man slowly emerged from the same corner and stood behind her; neither of them moved toward him. After a few moments of measuring each other up, Matthew slid back into the shadows of the covered archway. "They're not going to come any closer, but we've got to go."

"What kind of trouble are you in, Brian?"

"I didn't realize there might be trouble until five minutes ago," Matthew lied. He hoped the shadows hid his blush from Anna. Without waiting to find out, he pulled her from the archway into the CVS and marched them through the store to a rear door with a lock bar that read, "Emergency exit only, alarm will sound." Matthew paused, but Anna shoved the bar and charged through the door. The alarm didn't sound off. From the alley, they hurried back to Market Street, then doubled back onto Navarro, and finally to the public lot to Matthew's Jeep. He half-sprinted to the car and opened the door for Anna. Matthew noticed her eyes darting right and left, looking for an escape route.

"You don't have to come with me. I understand if you're scared. I'm sorry I got you into this. I didn't think . . ."

"That's the problem with men," Anna replied, holding her ground, "they don't think."

He reached for his wallet. "I'll call an Uber for you, if you want, but I have to go." Then he quickly checked that the infrared lamp on his cap and the one on the Jeep's license plate were still working. This strange woman appearing out of nowhere made him feel even more grateful for the precautions he had taken.

Who the hell are you, lady?

"I went along with your little terrifying escape, Brian. I think it's only fair I know what the hell is going on with you," Anna said. Then she climbed into the passenger seat and closed the door behind her. Despite the bold gesture, her face didn't look angry. Matthew knew that face. He had seen one like it before. A face filled with terror.

They had been driving for over an hour before Anna sensed that Brian needed to talk. She figured this to be a good thing because it took her that long to convince herself that the guy might be suffering from simple PTSD.

As if there is anything simple about PTSD.

She didn't want to believe his strange behavior had anything to do with what had just happened at the Iron Cactus, but she had no clue what had just happened. They just ran around a lot, with Brian apparently in fear for his life. Anna saw the woman standing in the street but didn't think she looked menacing enough to scare the likes of Brian.

"Park at the curb, up here at the Hideaway Coffee Grille," she said. "We need to talk, and you're not getting away without feeding me something."

She did her best to give him an authentic smile, but he didn't even look at her. He focused on parking the Jeep instead. After shutting off the engine, she watched curiously as Brian reached up and turned on his little cap light that didn't light up at all. She didn't ask him what the contraption was for, even when he had gone through the same ritual back on the Riverwalk. She watched him hop out and have a look around.

When he finally opened her door, she joked, "Are we all secure, Sergeant?" But when he scanned her face for sarcasm, she changed tactics. "I'm serious," she said. "If you don't think it's safe, we'll go somewhere else."

Brian looked right and left once more before he said, "I think we're okay." But when they entered the coffee shop, Brian assessed every one of the occupants. At first, she mistook his behavior for paranoia, but then she understood.

This is what professional caution looks like.

She thought Brian acted kind of like a bodyguard or, better said, a soldier on a mission. They made their way to a couch at the back of the house, then ordered coffee and sandwiches.

"If I had any idea this would happen, I wouldn't have gotten you involved," Brian said.

"Involved in what?"

"It's hard to explain."

Anna folded her arms across her chest and glared.

"Had I known there were others, like me, I wouldn't have agreed to see you."

"Others . . . like you? What do you mean?" Anna asked,

wondering if she should punch him in the face and run out the door.

"I've tried to tell other people, from when it first happened. The EMTs, the police, the lawyer, even Rosie, but no one believes me."

When Brian finished with a blush, Anna realized that she was no longer scared of him. Freaked out a little, maybe, but not frightened. If this man were a cold-blooded murderer, or serial killer, she'd be dead already and not sitting beside him in a very public café watching him blush. "If it didn't happen to me, I sure as hell wouldn't believe it. So, what's the point in telling you? You won't believe me, either."

"Believe what, exactly? I don't think it's fair to make up your mind about me. You don't know the first thing about me. I haven't started screaming yet, have I? And you're not even going to give me a chance?" She searched Brian's eyes, but he didn't seem convinced, so she leaned in and looked him in the eyes, taking his hand. "Why don't you start from the beginning? I promise not to judge you, but if I feel like I need to, I will get up and walk out. Fair enough?"

"Fair enough," Brian replied in a brand new tone of voice. To Anna, he no longer seemed like the badass soldier from the bar, no longer the sexy, confident man from the Riverwalk. No, he suddenly seemed more like a kid.

After another quick scan of the room, Brian scooted in closer, took a deep breath, and locked eyes with Anna. "My name is Matthew Miller."

25

NOT WHAT, BUT WHO

8:30 P.M.

CYPRESS TOWER

SAN ANTONIO, TEXAS

Afixter checking in with security on the first floor of
Cypress Tower, Randy stepped onto the elevator. It was
an older building but still the administrative center for the
largest food retailer in all of Texas, HEB Grocery, and so blessed
with the accompanying prestige. Randy was finding it hard to
imagine the connections Jon Daly must have used to get space
on the top floor. When he stepped off the elevator, he had to do
a double take.

Am I on the right floor?

The steel wall directly in front of him appeared to be part of
a ship's bulkhead, with hatchway, knee-knocker and all. To left
of the hatch, a pair of old wood-veneer double doors lay against
the wall covered in bubble wrap. There was a strong odor of
fresh paint and an even stronger odor of burnt plastic. He
looked up into the lenses of two video cameras mounted in the
ceiling corners, thinking, *You guys must have just moved in.* Then
he noticed the full-size hand scanner mounted in the steel wall

next to the hatch and reached out with a tentative fingertip to touch it.

"Hey, Randy," a voice crackled from an unseen speaker. "I'll be right out."

The door clanked open and out stepped Steve Walters. David West, the surfer kid Randy had met at Stinson Field, was with him.

"Hey, man, welcome to SA-HQ," David said. "We'll get your hands scanned into the system so you can come and go as you please."

"When did you guys have time to install part of a battleship up here?" Randy asked.

"Oh, we have lots of these lying around at home base," David replied. "We flew it in and dragged it up the stairs last night." David chuckled at the surprise on Randy's face. "You are too easy, man. We used the crate elevator on the other side." David reached up to high-five Walters, but Walters ignored him. David frowned. "You old cops are all alike: no sense of humor."

"Oh, I've got a sense of humor," Randy said. "I'm just still in shock from the bulkhead." He ran his hands along the glossy grey paint. "I'm seriously impressed. This is way cool." He held up his hand. David smiled and completed the high-five.

"No worries, man. It's all good," David said as he punched in a code into the screen and turned to Randy. "Okay. Put your right hand on the scanner and stay still." Randy pressed his right hand to the cool glass surface and watched the red scanner beam complete several passes. Finally, the panel lights blinked green. "Okay, man, you're good to go," David said, then he stepped over the knee-knocker and disappeared into the back offices.

"Follow me," Walters said, interrupting Randy's impulse to follow David. "Melissa's already here. She's reviewing street side cameras with Jon and Jessie right now."

"You have access to the city cameras?" Randy asked.

"And all the cameras available from towns surrounding San Antonio," Walter replied.

Once inside the offices, they walked across bare concrete floors and down roughed-out hallways before finally turning a corner into a conference-sized room. Randy gasped at the twenty or so large LCD video monitors lining the walls. Some of the Crue members from last night, including Jon Daly, were still securing wires and installing components.

"Hey, Randy," Jessie said from behind a monitor.

He smiled and then mouthed the word "wow" at her. Over his head, everything above the door looked to be sprayed with a heavy, dark grey soundproofing material. Thick cables ran down from a hole in the corner.

Which means they've got some serious equipment on the roof, Randy thought.

The cables were plugged into some type of transfer box affixed to the pipes above. The cables snaked from the box down to the individual desktop computer stations in the center of the room where other Crue members were already hard at work.

"Quite the command center, Jon. You guys work fast," Randy said.

"After what happened at the restaurant," Jon replied, "I didn't want to waste time."

"The view up here is great." Randy noticed that the office window provided the team with a panoramic view of one giant parking lot and Metropolitan Hospital in the distance. He took a moment to enjoy the cloudless night sky filled with stars despite the streetlights in the parking lot below, then he reminded himself that Dr. Bishop was at Metropolitan Hospital right now treating Rosemary Vasquez and a yet-to-be-identified blonde girl. It was reassuring to know that the unconscious duo of Jeffrey Cruz and Ruben White were still on lockdown at San Antonio Military Medical Center.

Meaning they were chained to their beds. Good.

"So where are we at?" Randy asked.

"We're still going through the camera views all along the River Walk, especially in front of the restaurant," Melissa said. Randy walked over to the screen and looked at the images. "That's the guy, right there."

"That's the only view? Why can't I see his face?" Randy asked.

"He's using a small infra-red LED lamp to disguise himself," Jessie said.

"Have we identified the girl he's with?" Randy asked.

Mario Cabrisi, the former FBI agent, leaned out from behind her monitor. "Hey there, Randy. We're working on her now. I've sent her photos over to your pal, Greg Chambers, at the local bureau office. He keeps pestering me to give him something to do, so I'm having him run it through the facial recognition program. We should get a hit soon."

"That task won't shut Gregory up for long," Randy said.

Mario shrugged. "He means well. We just needed to get him refocused. Slipping him tidbits of info and giving him time-consuming tasks like this will hold him over for a while. Best to keep him close to the vest." Randy nodded. "As soon as we get her ID'd, I'm sure we will track her down."

"Don't forget that I'd like to be there when you pick her up," Jessie said. "I need to make sure Matthew isn't slip-streaming through her."

"What makes you think it's him and not her?" Randy asked.

Jessie pulled Randy in front of her and then brought up a still shot from the dining room camera of the restaurant. It showed a man looking toward Jessie's table right after she fell to the ground. Despite the fact that the image was barely in frame and the face was so grainy that no amount of enhancement would ever bring it into focus, Jessie said, "It's him. I'm sure of it."

AFTER HAVING LISTENED WITHOUT INTERRUPTION THROUGH almost two hours' worth of coffee and finger food, Anna stared at Brian, searching for the right words to respond to his fantastic tale.

"You don't believe me," he said.

Anna didn't shake or nod her head. Instead, she furrowed her brow and continued to stare. Prior to this conversation, she had thought the man across the table was a seasoned war veteran named Brian Colter. Now he'd asked her to believe that he was a scared-shitless teenager named Matthew Miller. Not a split personality, but the real persona of Matthew Miller who had somehow become locked inside a body that he had accidentally "hijacked." If that weren't bad enough, during the course of his fantastic tale, Miller had admitted to murdering two people. Two people, who according to him, had totally deserved it. It sounded a lot like revenge to Anna.

But the weirdest thing about this, she thought, *is that none of the revenge shit scares me.*

What did frighten her was that his story was too much like tales she'd heard as a child. In fact, that similarity was terrifying.

"Don't put words in my mouth," Anna said. "You had your chance to talk, but I'm not ready to say anything yet."

"Why not?"

"Because I'm thinking!"

Anna got up, stretched, and then walked over to the counter to refill her coffee before returning to the table where she continued to ignore "Miller." She had to put up a finger several times to stop Matthew from saying anything while she struggled to process all that he had told her. After several minutes, she moved over to his side of the table, sat down close, and searched his face. Finally, she said, "I believe you." If he started laughing and told her this was all a big joke, she was going to stab him in the face with her fork.

Matthew folded his arms defensively and raised an eyebrow. "Really?"

"Yes, Matthew, I believe you. I do. And I want to help you." After the words had slipped from her lips, she knew they were true. That felt good. She knew that she could help Matthew in ways he would never think of.

Well, I hope I can.

"You? Help me? How?" he asked.

Despite the uncertainty of it all, a wave of certainty washed over Anna. She felt inexplicably drawn to this man. Sure, there was a physical attraction, but they hadn't been physical yet. No. Being with him had awakened something from her childhood, something she thought she had lost long ago, something she wanted back.

"I want you to come with me to meet someone," she said.

"Who?" he asked.

"I'm not going to tell you just yet," she said. To forestall his objections, she added, "You've asked me to trust you. Now I'm asking you to trust me. Besides, the less you know about this guy I'm taking you to see, the better. All you need to know is that I think he might be able to help."

"No, Anna, I'm not —"

"You're not what? Not going anywhere with me? Not going to meet anyone? I'm the one with something to lose here. You said your life is over. If that's how you feel, why not take a chance? Because I don't believe it's over."

"How do you know?"

"I don't know. But from what I've heard about Army Rangers, they never give up."

"I'm not an Army Ranger. Colter is and . . ."

"And you're stuck inside of him, so use that." Matthew closed his mouth on whatever protest he was about to make, and his eyes went blank. Anna recognized the thousand-yard stare; she had seen it on her grandfather's face a thousand times. "If you can't trust me, you got nowhere left to go, nothing left to do, but spiral out of control. Good luck with that. Sounds like you're already well on your way. And good luck finding anyone else who believes you."

Anna scooted out from the table and stood up.

He reached out a hand and grabbed her arm. "What exactly do you believe?"

Anna didn't sit back down fast enough to hide the shadow of fear that crossed her face. One part of Anna felt confident but another part of her was screaming *Run!* Then, thanks to another wave of certainty, she regained her composure, leaned into Matthew, and began to whisper in his ear.

"I'll tell you what I believe. I saw all three stories you told me on the news. Two people brutally murdered. A poor girl left in a ditch. Anybody else would think you're batshit crazy, hungry for attention, wanting to take credit for things you didn't do. But I believe you. Why? Because I know you did it. Why? Because I feel your need for revenge. But I also feel how scared and confused you are. Because so much has happened so fast. And, yes, I know you haven't told me everything yet. Listen. I don't want to end up in a ditch, Matthew. So why would I go with you? Because my instincts tell me that I can trust you. You're going to have to figure out if your instincts tell you that you can trust me."

Matthew discreetly wiped his eyes with a napkin and took a deep, shuddering breath. "They're probably going to identify you from the street cameras," he said. "Soon."

"Then we'd better leave now," Anna replied. "I need to pick up a bag from my place, and you should do the same."

"A bag? Why?"

"Because we're going to be gone for a few days."

Matthew's brow furrowed. "A few days? I don't have time —"

"You have all the time in the world, Matthew. There is no need to rush in for revenge. Give me a chance. Let me help."

After a long moment, Matthew nodded. "Okay, I'm in. But at least tell me which way we're headed."

Anna smiled. "West. We're heading west, young man."

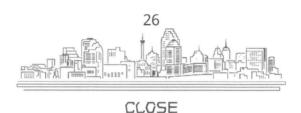

26

CLOSE

7:15 A.M.

THURSDAY, OCTOBER 17TH

UTSA STUDENT APARTMENTS

Randy, Eric, and Jessie stood on the threshold of Anna Chee's apartment facing a young girl who Randy thought looked worried and indignant at the same time. "When was the last time you saw your roommate?" he asked her.

"Like a week ago. Why? Has something happened to her?" she fired back.

"We're not sure," Randy said. "That's why we're here. We need to find her. To make sure she's okay. May we come in?" For a second, he thought the girl was going to start crying, but when she stepped back and motioned toward the small living room with an open hand, the three barged right in.

Jessie made a quick visual scan of the room and pursed her lips. Then she subtly shook her head at Randy. "Not here, not her," she said.

"We covered that," the girl said. "I just told you, I haven't seen her in like a week."

"Why did it take you so long to realize she was missing?" Randy asked.

"Because we're on different schedules. We don't have any classes together."

"So when did you start to suspect that she might have gone somewhere?"

"Just this morning."

"Why?" Jessie asked.

"Because I noticed some of her things had disappeared from the bathroom."

"Which room is hers?" Jessie asked. After the girl pointed at the door, Jessie slipped on a pair of clear gloves and Randy and Eric followed suit. She turned the handle. It was locked.

"She always locks the door to her room. So do I," the girl said. Jessie pulled a small tool from her belt buckle and stuck it in the door lock, manipulating the tumblers. "Don't you guys need a warrant for that?"

"We're worried about her safety and time is against us," Randy replied, then tried to gauge her reaction. Her befuddled expression convinced him she was clueless. Finally, he heard a click and turned to watch Jessie push the door open. He reached out and held Jessie lightly by the shoulder, then leaned in himself to take a quick scan.

Clean floor. Made bed. No immediate signs of foul play. "Can you tell if anything's missing?"

"No. We don't go into each other's rooms when one of us isn't home. Her rule. Not mine."

"Look," Randy said.

"Why?"

"Will it hurt to try?"

The girl peered through the doorway and said, "I think her backpack is gone. She usually hangs it off the end."

"How would you know? I thought you never came in here?"

"I said, when she's not home. When she's here, I do. We're

not that weird." She finally entered the room and began to move toward the closet.

"Stop," Randy said. "I'll do that." He opened the door. "Okay. Come look, but don't touch anything."

The girl leaned in and studied the interior of the small closet.

"Yes."

"Yes, what?" Jessie asked, annoyed.

"Yes, what do you think? Yes, there are clothes missing from here, too. And, I know because we're the same size and sometimes we share."

"Anything else?" Randy asked.

"She has a rolling suitcase."

"Where?"

"Usually, right there," she said pointing at the right back corner of the closet.

"So, it's gone, too?" Jessie asked. The girl shrugged an "isn't that obvious" gesture, as she watched Eric pop open Anna's armoire.

"Do you know where she might have gone?" Jessie asked.

"No clue."

"So, she never tells you where she's going?" Randy asked.

"No, she usually does."

"Have you ever gone anywhere together?"

"Weekend getaways."

"Where?" Jessie asked. Randy sensed she was doing her best to keep her tone as level as possible with this smartass girl.

"Port Aransas. Houston. Nothing big."

"So, where is she?" Jessie probed.

The girl folded her arms across her chest. "I just told you. No clue. Maybe she went to visit her family."

"Do you know where they live?" Randy asked, cutting off whatever ugly thing seemed to be on the tip of Jessie's tongue.

"No clue."

"Bullshit. No idea?"

"I don't know. New Mexico somewhere. Maybe."

"Well, shit," Jessie grumbled.

"Is it my fault Anna didn't talk about her family?"

As Eric opened Anna's dresser and began to probe the contents softly, Jessie said, "Well, could you at least tell us if she had a boyfriend?"

"I could . . . fine. She's got lots of guys after her but nothing steady. She's spent the night with some but never here. And she's never been gone more than one night." The girl's eyes suddenly welled with tears. "Great. Now I'm worried."

As Eric continued to check the dresser and Jessie started in on the nightstand, Randy guided the girl into the living room and called his partner. "Melissa, I need you to do background on Anna Chee. And see if you can get an address in New Mexico."

The roommate touched Randy's arm and said, "Anna told me she's a full-blooded Indian and she grew up on a reservation. I thought she was kidding, but maybe not?"

Ten minutes later, having learned next to nothing, Jessie and Eric exited the apartment. Randy was right behind them, but he turned and stopped at the threshold. "Please call me right away if you hear from her," he said, handing her his card.

The girl reached out and took it, biting her lip as she nodded. "And you'll call me if you find her."

"*When* we find her, you bet."

After the girl slowly closed the door, Jessie said, "Dammit. We're so close."

"Closer than you think," Randy replied, pulling an envelope from his back pocket. "Found this on the kitchen counter." He held it up.

"Window Rock, Arizona," Eric said, reading the return address.

Jessie took the envelope for a closer look at the upper right corner. "That's a Navajo Art postage stamp."

Randy smiled. "That's right."

DURING THE FIRST FEW HOURS OF THEIR ROAD TRIP, MATTHEW poured out his life story like the flood waters from a broken dam. Anna laughed, cried, and reeled back in fear as he related the tale of his broken life. They both cried when he talked about Kristi, and Anna felt a surprising pang of jealousy shoot through her. She convinced herself that she wasn't jealous of Kristi but of Matthew because he was able to love someone so much.

"You should have told her, even if she rejected you," Anna said.

"My mom would love you," Matthew replied. "She said the same thing. At the time, I couldn't handle the thought of it. Now I'll never know. That's the only regret I have."

As they pulled into a gas station near Midland, Texas, Anna offered a silent prayer for Matthew's secret love. After they fueled up, Matthew suggested they get a couple of hours sleep, and Anna realized that sharing his story had worn him out. "I'm fine," she reassured him. "You get some sleep. I'll drive."

After they switched places, Matthew said, "I've been blabbering about myself all night. Tell me about you, Anna Chee."

"There's not much to tell, really. Besides, this trip is about you, and I'm still taking it all in." She hoped he wouldn't press the matter.

Because there is more to tell. So much more.

And, for once, she got her wish. When she turned her head to look at him, the poor boy was fast asleep. She studied Matthew's face, wondering what in the hell she had gotten herself into. When she thought about how her initial attraction to Brian Colter had been strictly sexual, she had to stop herself from laughing out loud. Now she was enveloped in a life-and-death struggle. Possibly involving her own life. Definitely involving the lives of others. Suddenly, her world revolved around this other-worldly teenage boy in a man's body.

Hours went by and there was still way too much going on in her head. And when she glanced at the sergeant wrapped in her Pendleton blanket, his head propped up against the passenger window, he was still totally out. *Bastard.* Sleep was not coming for her any time soon. She was still struggling to convince herself that bringing him home was the right thing to do. After all, he had no idea she was a card-carrying member of the Navajo Nation. All he knew was that she had moved to San Antonio to go to college. Again, she almost had to laugh at that. He had no idea that she was the child of a Hopi mother and Navajo father. The middle child. Though, he would have no idea why that would be important. No idea that she grew up in the spiritual center of the Navajo Nation. No idea how much time she had spent learning Navajo traditions. No idea that she had completed her Kinaalda, her rite of passage into womanhood. No idea that her oldest brother, grandfather, and great-grandfather had been Hatalii. Spiritual leaders. Secret medicine men of the Navajo Nation. Anna still remembered the day that her great-grandfather had travelled on foot with other Hatalii to a distant corner of the reservation. Anna had trailed behind them, until she had gone too far to go back alone.

"I can hear you. You might as well come out."

"Where are we going, grandfather?" she had asked.

"To perform the Blessing Way for your cousin."

"Why?"

"She is soon to be a mother. She and her unborn child need positive energy and good fortune."

"But that's a job for women, not the —"

"Ssh. Do not speak our secret name. It is rare for us to get involved, but when the ceremony needs to be powerful, we do."

"Why does it need to be powerful?"

"There are signs your cousin and her baby will need special

protection. That's why we have spent the past five moons bartering with neighboring tribes for everything we need today."

"When did you first hear me following you?"

"From your very first step."

"Why didn't you send me home?"

"Because you are one of the things we need today."

The memory of her great-grandfather's love for her brought tears to her eyes. She wiped them away so she could see the road and stick with the memory. Great-grandfather had been right. The ceremony had been powerful. The Hatalii ritual had caused ghosts to appear and begin to speak.

"Grandfather!"

"Ssh. I know. I know you can see them. That is because it is your presence that has summoned them."

"But I can hear them, too," she had whispered. When her great-grandfather's mouth opened in surprise, she realized she was the only one who could.

"What do they say?"

His face had shone with such pride, she hadn't been able to tell him the truth of what she heard. The Dineh people would go the way of the Buffalo and be lost forever to the ways of the white man. So, she had lied.

On the way home, great-grandfather hold told her, "At your Kinaalda, you will become one of us."

"But I can't. I'm a girl. No girl has ever been Ha —"

"Ssh. Do not be afraid. It is your destiny."

"Why me?"

"Because you are deeply connected to the spirit world."

And he had been proven right again. But Anna hadn't felt afraid. She had felt ashamed that she had used her great gift to lie to all of them, but especially to him.

She thought about how, as a kid, she was connected to the spirit-world and her great-grandfather. Not now.

So what if I can communicate with the spirits of the dead? How does that help me? How does that help him? Great-grandfather is long dead, but grandfather might be able to help, Anna thought. *Yes. Because he is Hatalli. He would know what to do. Because if the Dineh' Hatalii' can't help Matthew, no one can.*

ANNA SMILED AT THE WASH OF PREDAWN SKY COLORS JUST AS SHE turned the Jeep north onto Old Highway 84. When she saw the first rays of the morning sun illuminate the peaks of the Santa Fe Mountains, she breathed a sigh of relief.

I'm home, she thought. *Bringing Matthew here was the right thing to do.*

"How you holding up?" Matthew asked, his voice startling Anna from her thoughts.

"I'm good. Going to stop at Eagles Nest for fuel."

"Eagles Nest? Where's that?"

"Another hour north. By the way, we're in New Mexico now. We just passed Santa Fe."

"How much longer until we get to where we're going?"

"Are we there yet? Are we there yet?" Anna teased him. Matthew smiled back at her.

Now that she knew the truth, and believed it, the man sitting next to her looked different than the man she had kissed on the Riverwalk. Moreover, now that she thought about it, he was completely different than the man she had danced with all night at "Cowboys" two weeks ago.

"I have a question," Anna said.

"Shoot," Matthew replied, folding up Anna's Pendleton blanket and putting it in the backseat.

"Do you feel or sense anything about Brian?"

Matthew's face grew dark. "Yes. I think I was dreaming about battles and stuff. Iraq. Afghanistan. And . . ."

"And?"

"Well, when I took him . . . I was in that girl, Sara, remember?"

"Yes."

"Well, let's just say that he's pretty aggressive when he's drunk. Once I was in, I felt that aggression. It wasn't pretty."

"What did you do?"

"I sobered his ass up, that's what."

"But you . . . never mind." She cut herself off. Sure, she didn't want to upset Matthew. But mostly she didn't want to think too deeply about what he had done. She was frightened by the idea that she might have done the same thing.

"Once we stop, you can drive again," she said, totally changing the subject.

"Great," Matthew said. Anna could tell by his tone of voice that he was just as eager as she was to let the matter drop. She realized that he probably had a pretty good idea what she was going to say. So, when he poked her in the leg in an obvious attempt to change the mood, she played along.

"Ouch!"

"Did that really hurt?"

"No."

"Well, guess what? Before I 'hijacked' the lawyer, I had never driven a car before."

"No way. You're good at it."

"I know. Know why?"

"Because you're just that good?"

"No. Because when I hijack somebody, I get instant access to their skills."

"Like their muscle memory?"

"Exactly."

"Very cool."

"No shit. And I love driving!"

Anna locked eyes with Matthew. She wanted him to know

that not only was she still on his side, she was still attracted to him. She reached out, took his hand, and squeezed it in a way to make sure that he got the message. She wasn't sure she succeeded because Matthew was already looking out the window with that thousand-yard stare.

27

DINEH

2:00 P.M.

WINDOW ROCK, ARIZONA

A s he gazed out the windshield at the flat, hi-plains desert, yet another flashback shuddered through him. This one of a knife cutting through Rafi's neck. He rubbed at goose-bumps rising on his arms, thankful that he hadn't told Anna it wasn't the soldier's aggression that had provoked him to murder Rafi as brutally as he had. *That's all on me.* Sick of his thoughts, Matthew poked Anna gently in the leg. "Anna. Wake up."

"I have to pee," she mumbled.

"Well, that works out, then," said Matthew. "We need to stop and get fuel." Just before the exit, he saw a sign for Ship Rock.

"We're almost there," Anna yawned. Matthew didn't ask where, although he wanted to. He pulled the Jeep into a gas station, which looked more like part-Indian-trading-post and part-motel. A "For Sale" sign in the window of a customized International Scout 80A parked on the motel side caught his eye. With his chin, he pointed to the classic 4x4, admiring its desert tan paint job and the 4x4 goodies it looked to be loaded with. "When we're done here, I want to have a closer look at that."

Anna yawned and leaned against the Jeep as Matthew operated the pump. Then a coyote howled in the distance. "I thought they did that mostly at night," Matthew said.

"Know a lot about coyotes, do you?"

"Just what I've seen on Discovery or Animal Planet," he confessed.

"Coyote, the trickster," Anna said.

"What?"

"I'm taking you to my home to meet my great-grandfather, Ben Chee, Senior. My dad is named after him. Anyway, Grandpa will explain it to you."

Caught off guard by the sudden change of subject, Matthew leaned closer to her and searched her face. "So, I'm guessing Grandpa Chee is some kind of Navajo shaman." Anna's mouth fell open, an amazed look on her face.

"Why would you think that? I didn't say anything about being Navajo."

He hung the nozzle on the hook, laughing softly and turning to look at her. "No mystical Indian magic here. While you were sleeping, there were, like, a dozen signs announcing this place as Navajo Country."

Anna punched his arm but then took his hand in hers.

"When I first met you, you know what I thought?" Matthew asked.

"Who is this gorgeous woman, and why is she looking at me like that?"

"Sure. But after that, I thought about a painting I'd seen as a child of a beautiful Indian maiden."

"Oh, that's so sweet."

"It was called White-Buffalo Woman, I think."

"And culturally insensitive. White-Buffalo Woman? Seriously? Where did you see that?"

"I don't know. From some culturally insensitive kid's book that I read." He smiled at her and got a big smile in return. "Besides, who other than some holy man would believe me?" A shadow crossed Matthew's face. "Do you think he'll believe me?"

"I don't know," she replied.

"Wow. That's reassuring."

"He used to believe in me, and that's what I'm counting on," she replied.

"I guess we're about to find out."

"Yup. He'll either accept you or shoot you as you walk through the door."

"Great," Matthew said. "Well, before I die, I want to see that Scout."

FIVE HOURS LATER, AROUND 4 P.M., THEY APPROACHED THE outskirts of Window Rock. They entered from the Arizona side, now driving the Scout; the Navajo at the Motel had been more than happy to make the trade. Matthew eased the Scout up a winding hard-packed road that slowly curved up to a modest, goldenrod-colored adobe sitting at the base of a butte.

"That's it," Anna said. "That's the house I grew up in. Been in our family over a hundred years. That old wooden fence surrounding the house continues down the slope into the valley. You can't see them, but I bet at least two dozen sheep are grazing down there right now."

"This is the first adobe I've ever seen," he said as he parked. "What's that thing on the roof? An air conditioner"

"No. A swamp cooler," Anna replied, climbing out of the car and stretching a little bit.

"A what?"

"Okay, it's a kind of air conditioner."

"Thought so."

"But a kind of air conditioner that cools the air using an evaporator."

"Right, an evaporator. I get it."

"And the evaporator brings moisture into the house which is great because —"

"Because we're in a desert. I noticed," Matthew said from his seat behind the wheel. Anna noticed the concern on his face and laid her hand gently on his leg.

"You getting out? You look nervous."

"Yeah. Thoughts of being shot by your grandfather have crept into my mind," he lied. In fact, the face of Jeffery Cruz had just flashed through his mind, and now, with anticipation of the meeting to come, his skin immediately tingled, and that scared him. As he concentrated on calming himself, several children of different ages ran out of the residence, straight into Anna's arms. They screamed with excitement and climbed over one another to hug her. A moment later, they moved to the driver side of the Scout and dragged Matthew out. As they swarmed him, he couldn't help but notice their outfits were straight out of an 1880's photograph. In the middle of them stood a tiny girl, no more than three, who held her arms wide and pumped her hands open and closed.

"Yo-lailh, yo-lailh," she said.

Needing no translation, Matthew hoisted her into his arms. "Hello, what's your name?" he asked.

The little girl responded with a most serious frown as she stared into his face. To Matthew, she seemed to be inspecting his deep red eyes and lightly colored skin.

"You're on your own," Anna smirked, as the children led her and Matthew to the house.

In the front room, Anna's extended family greeted Matthew with a healthy mixture of warmth and irreverence unique to the

Navajo. It took Matthew a moment to notice the elderly man standing in the back of the room.

Grandpa Chee, for sure. The old man looked to be in deep contemplation, or seriously angry. Even as Anna hugged her grandfather, he continued to stare in Matthew's direction.

He must be trying to decide if he should get his shotgun, Matthew thought. Matthew maintained eye contact with the old man and suddenly, his breath caught in his throat.

Why do I feel I know you, old man? He couldn't pin-point how but guessed this might be some residual memory of his host, Brian. Or maybe the old man was just trying to scare him. *It's working,* he thought.

More men, both younger and older than himself, continued to pour into the house. These men, like the men already present, with the exception of Anna's grandfather, gave Matthew a cursory glance and a wide berth. He tried to convince himself that they were afraid of him, afraid of a white man, but it felt more like they were simply sizing him up. Finally, the crowd became so large that it spilled toward the back half of the house dragging Matthew along with it.

After several rounds of shuffling, several groups of men and women moved into what appeared to be the dining room and settled around a rustic wooden table. For some reason Matthew couldn't put his finger on, the table felt familiar, but the women surrounding him on his side of the table did not.

An elderly woman and her middle-aged companions seated to his right contented themselves with placid stares, but the teen girls to his left violated his personal space with pleasure, squeezing his biceps, proclaiming him handsome, and barraging him with personal questions. "Are you a soldier?" "Do you have a job?" "What happened to your leg?" "How long have you been dating my cousin?" "You want to have children with her?" "Have you kissed her?" As Matthew deflected their questions, he tried to eavesdrop on the men across the table, but they were speaking Navajo and refused to acknowledge him.

But the small children were drawn to Matthew like iron filings to a magnet. They wormed their way under the table, dragged him away from the women, and wrestled him to the ground. Their horseplay was not entirely gentle, and Matthew found himself liking it.

Playing with the little ones reminded him of how he used to roughhouse with the neighborhood kids before the Motor Neuron Disease had forced him into a wheelchair.

Finally, the elderly woman shooed away the children and pulled Matthew to his feet with surprising strength. Her companions guided him back to his seat, again not as gently as he thought they would. After he sat, they forced a cold coke and a plate of fry-bread into his hands. The honey-drizzled bread felt and tasted strange and sticky. When he attempted to wash it down with a swig of coke, the double-sweet sugar-rush felt like an army of ants were crawling beneath the skin of his face.

As he recovered, he sensed being watched. Sure enough, when he peered into the front room, he found Grandfather Chee watching him over Anna's shoulder. The frustrated look on Anna's face told him that she hadn't gained any ground. Three sugared-up boys took advantage of Matthew's distracted gaze to claw him to the floor for a second time, but when a strong voice said, "Yee-naaldooshii," they froze, then scattered like beetles looking for a place to hide. That left Matthew on his back looking up at the jean-clad leg of Grandpa Chee, his boots inches from Matthew's head.

When the old man frowned down upon Matthew and repeated, "Yee-naaldooshi," a middle-aged man behind Matthew stood up so quickly that his chair flew into the wall and shattered. This man wrapped Anna in a tight hug, pulling her close to his side. Both looked as frightened as Matthew felt. Matthew guessed the man was Anna's father and confirmed it when he said, "Why do you say this, Father?" Matthew then saw the resemblance between them. Old man Chee held up his hand to silence his son right before the front door flew open, and four Navajo policemen armed with M4 carbines rushed in. The threatening way the lead officer, who looked like a younger version of Anna's father, trained his M4 on Matthew caused tears to well up in the eyes of the roughhousing boys. Matthew felt a wave of guilt and sadness envelop him. When that same officer pulled the M4's charging handle and rammed its muzzle against Matthew's forehead, the teen girls began to scream. The elderly woman and her companions quickly corralled the teens and the children into the backyard. Matthew, not knowing what else to do, raised his hands in surrender, not at all surprised to find the officer's name tag read R. Chee.

"To your knees, bilaga'ana," R. Chee said.

As Matthew rolled from the floor onto his knees, he felt Colter's prosthetic leg forced into an uncomfortable angle. Then an officer behind him stepped on the leg and the discomfort turned into searing pain. Matthews eyes clamped shut as the pain drove straight into Matthew's brain and cranked on the power. Matthew slowly opened his eyes and looked at his captors. Everyone gasped at his now brightly undulating red eyes.

"So much for helping me, eh, Anna?" he said. He glared at Grandpa Chee as he spoke and took just a little pleasure seeing the man squirm, trying with all his will not to break eye contact with Matthew.

Before Anna could rush forward, her father snatched her by the arm to restrain her. In English, she yelled, "Grandpa, what have you done?"

The old man ignored her and continued to circle Matthew, evaluating him until, at last, he whipped a knife from his belt. The sunlight filtering through the window glinted off the polished silver blade directly into Matthew's eyes. In a flash, the old man had moved behind Matthew and held the blade firmly to his throat.

"*Déjà vu,*" Matthew whispered to himself, thinking of Rafi Wilson.

"This Yee-Naaldooshii is not my sister," Grandpa said to Anna. "He is a different one. But I know him. I met him at the time the Bilanaga murdered my sister." Then he turned back to Matthew. "Yee-Naaldooshii, Skinwalker, what lies have you told our Anna? Why are you in our house? What do you want?" Before Matthew could reply, Chee had spun back to Anna. "Why have you brought this creature here?"

Tears in her eyes, Anna said, "I've been trying to tell you, Grandpa. I brought him here so that you could help him."

Chee furrowed his brow and chuffed at his granddaughter. "Skinwalkers are evil," he said.

Matthew had caught the old man's comment about Matthew not being his sister. Without completely understanding it, he decided to ask, "Was your sister evil?" The knife tightened against his throat and he felt a trickle of blood run down his neck. "Go ahead, old man, I've already been killed once. I'm ready."

"No, Grandpa! He's a good man. Just like Auntie Abigail was a good woman."

The tension of the blade against his throat relaxed. A little. Matthew guessed the notion of his sister struck a nerve, but he had difficulty wrapping around the old man's comment about a visit. *What visit? He was a child? What the hell is he talking about.*

Anna's father stepped past his grandfather with a chuckle and said to Anna, "Abigail? Our mythical Great-Auntie Abigail? That's just a story he used to tell to scare us. Skinwalkers aren't real." But Matthew saw the man's eyebrows rise in uncertainty when he looked into the strange fire he knew burned in Colter's eyes.

"Quiet, Junior. Listen, and learn," the old man said. Matthew felt the tip of his knife pressing the soft tissue under his tongue as the old man slid around to the front side of him. At a nod from Grandpa Chee, the officer who had stepped on Matthew's leg moved in. He quickly secured Matthew's hands to the top of his head and rammed the barrel of a pistol in the back of his neck. "Move, Skinwalker. I dare you." Matthew ignored the officer, and instead locked eyes with Grandpa Chee, seeing the soldier in him plain as day.

"How did you come to be in this body, Skinwalker?" the old man asked. Then he grasped Matthew by the side of the head and whispered, "Lie and I will know it. And I will bleed you out right here in my dining room. Got me, white man?"

"So, you believe it then?" Matthew asked.

"That you are a Skinwalker? Yes. But there is more."

The tension disappeared from Matthew's shoulders. He sat back on his crossed feet, tears welling up in his eyes. When he glanced at Anna, she mouthed, *Go on.* Matthew released a long breath and started talking. "I first took the body of my killer just before he choked me to death and ended up getting caught by the police." Matthew choked out the words in a sobbing laugh. "I woke up trapped in the body of my enemy. I didn't know I had this . . ." he looked to the floor, searching for the right word, ". . . power until that moment. After a week or so, I escaped and went through a couple of more bodies." The room fell silent.

"Women, too," he added, causing everyone present to gasp, except Grandpa Chee.

"What I want, more than life itself, is to exact revenge on the criminals who killed me, and my . . . friend." He glanced again at Anna and saw that she had started to cry. "I had taken a woman's body for a short time. That made it easier for me to find this soldier. He is the best tool to complete my task. So, I seduced this soldier and then I took his body."

Chee looked deeply into his eyes, totally unafraid. The pain in Colter's leg almost overwhelmed him, but when Matthew shifted his weight to get more comfortable, he got the hardened steel pistol barrel jammed into the back of his head again. Matthew shook his head. "You don't have to be scared of me. I'm not here to hurt you."

"Really? How many people have you killed already, Skin-walker?" Grandpa Chee asked.

"Two, but they deserved it," Matthew replied. "I hijacked three other bodies, but they aren't dead. All of them are in a hospital in some sort of coma. Don't ask me why. I don't know why."

Chee stood up and turned to face his granddaughter. "You need to go outside." When she hesitated, Grandpa Chee snapped, "Now! We will discuss this only among elders who follow The Dineh' Way."

Anna looked like she had been slapped, but before leaving, she trudged over to Matthew. The tears rolling down her face broke his heart. "Don't worry about me," he said. "Thank you for trying." Despite his brave words, he couldn't hide the fear lurking behind the soldier's eyes.

"Please believe me, Matthew. I had no idea this would happen."

"Out!" Chee commanded. "This no longer concerns you." Anna's father, still looking shell-shocked, pulled Anna into a hug as he led her out the back door.

"You don't have to be such an assho —" Matthew started before a rifle butt crashed into the back of his skull. "What are you doing?" Matthew slurred, fighting to remain conscious.

"Yee-Naaldooshii, you must pass the Enemy Way."

Then stop hitting me, he thought just before he surrendered to the darkness.

28

ENEMY WAY

6:00 P.M.
STINSON AIRFIELD
SAN ANTONIO, TEXAS

A fter helping the Crue Intellis team secure the last Yukon in the cargo bay of the C130, Randy walked down the ramp and noticed Jessie sitting on a large transport box. She seemed focused on watching the sunset, but she also had something that appeared to be flipping around in her hand. Thinking she wanted some alone time, he backed away to give her a wide berth, but when she spotted him, she waved him over. As he approached, he heard a *click-click-click* as the object spun around. Then he saw it. "You're pretty good with that butterfly knife. Something you learned while on a mission?"

"Nope," she said. "Learned this skill on my own. Ever used one?"

After he shook his head, Jessie gave him a half-hearted smile. She scooted over and patted the empty space she had just opened up. When Randy sat too close and their legs touched, he felt a trickle of electricity flow from her skin into his leg, though he might have been imagining it. She flipped the knife closed and handed it to him.

"Wow, it's lighter than I expected."

"It's a Benchmade Balisong," she said. "I find doing aerials with it relaxes me." He attempted to manipulate the Filipino knife but dropped it. As she retrieved the knife, she said, "Careful, don't cut yourself. Turn it like so, let the guard fall, then rotate and spin. Try it again. Relax your hand." Her comment had sent a little jolt of feeling somewhere between envy and fear right through Randy, but when she took his hand in hers, he sensed something bothered her. "I'm scared, Randy."

"You? Scared? No way." But in truth, he could see she struggled to control it. He knew better than to press her, so he focused on the knife. After a couple more fumbles, the blade spun around a full turn, the handles closed properly behind it.

"You did it," Jessie said, cocking her head to the side, smiling.

Randy smiled back and did it again. After several more successful spins, he picked up the pace until he lost control again and almost did cut himself. "Okay. I think I'm done," Randy said and handed the knife back to her. In her hands, the blade spun so fast it became a blur. Then she stopped the knife suddenly and closed it.

"Whether you believe it or not, Randy, I am scared. At one time, I was naive enough to believe that I might be the only one who could slip-stream. And now there's this dangerous kid out there trying to survive, bent on revenge."

"We're doing everything we can to catch him, Jessie."

"I'm not afraid he'll get away."

"You're not? But I thought . . ."

"I mean, yes. I am afraid of that. But that's not my biggest fear."

"Then what is?"

"I've been running around all hi-speed super-spy girl for over ten years. I kid you not, Detective, throughout my time working with the Crue, no one remotely close to being a Walker popped up on our radar. Like we told you, we looked. And now Matthew-after so long a time . . . I didn't see him coming. I should have been better prepared for this. And we can't be the only ones. That's another thought that scares me."

Randy thought about what she said. Unfortunately, it made sense. "Maybe Doctor Bishop's research will help us find others. We've uncovered identifiers, right? Seems like the residual side effect is coma. And the biorhythm thing."

"That's concerning, too. Remember back in your office? I don't leave my targets like that. Bewildered and usually under arrest, but not comatose. What this kid is doing . . ."

"Jessie!" The voice that had just rung out from the airport terminal behind them belonged to Juanita Jonson. She jogged over and handed Jessie a piece of paper. "We found them."

"You're sure this is the address?" Jessie asked.

"We found it through Anna Chee's college registration. We had a drone do a fly over and confirmed a dark colored jeep. It's got to be them."

---

6 :00 P.M.
WINDOW ROCK, ARIZONA

WHEN MATTHEW'S EYELIDS FLUTTERED OPEN, HE SQUINTED FROM the bright light above him. But when he tried to cover his face, he couldn't move — his arms and legs were strapped to the table. He turned his head left and right, trying to figure out where he was. His attempts to move caused his head to pound. In response to his movement, or maybe not, the light flicked off.

"Why are you doing this?" Matthew demanded, trying to

mask the fear that caused his skin to prickle. Then drums and voices began to sound off in the dark.

Is that singing?

Barely audible at first, a rhythmic chorus of native voices slowly got louder. He breathed deep and tried to relax. His pupils gradually adjusted to the near darkness until he could make out the walls of a large room through the shadows. Then he felt the energy begin to build until he knew that he would be able to slip into the first person he laid hands on. He didn't feel angry, and he found it interesting he didn't really feel afraid anymore. But something brought the power forth. He was ready.

"This is the story of my sister, Abigail," old man Chee's voice said in the darkness, cutting through the song that quieted but did not stop as he spoke. "She was fourteen years old when it happened. Our Apache cousins invited her to attend their annual coming of age ceremony down at Mescalero Reservation. The year was 1948, and I had just turned six years old. We were allowed to be there, even when we were so young because the Apache Sunrise Ceremony was open to all our people. So we went to the Tribal Grounds for four days of celebration. We all danced. We all ate. Our young women attempted, failed, and succeeded in many private trials to prove our courage. We loved those days because we knew that we were all working together to keep our traditions alive. We wanted to give our young women a chance in this cruel, white world. But I was too young to protect my sister, and she was taken from me because the Sunrise Ceremony was open to your people, too." By the last line, Grandpa Chee had approached Matthew's bedside and whispered in his ear. Matthew flexed his fingers to see if he could touch him, but Chee wisely remained out of reach.

"I'm sorry for your loss, sir," Matthew said, his quavering voice betraying his attempt at bravery. "But what does that have to do with me?"

"Because you were there. Let me help you remember."

A blinding light flicked on, forcing Matthew to close his eyes. Several pairs of powerful hands seized his head and wrenched it back, leaving his mouth open and his throat exposed. He felt a wooden cup press to his lips as the singing and now drumming grew louder once more. He squeezed his lips tight, but fingers squeezed his jaw hard to pry his mouth open. A second later, he felt a hot liquid — smelled and tasted like shit with a hint of honey — pour into his mouth.

He choked and sputtered on the foul broth, but the fingers forced his jaw closed and pinched his nose shut. Matthew bucked and squirmed and tried to vomit but the hands held tight until he swallowed. The wretched potion burned in his sinuses and caused his eyes to water. And the hand still wouldn't let go. They wouldn't even let him scream. A minute later, maybe more, Matthew felt his body start to relax. The singing quieted, leaving only the soft beat of the drum now in sync with the throbbing in his head.

"Young white boys from Albuquerque had come, they said, to bear witness and celebrate with us," Chee said. "But even my six-year-old eyes could see how disrespectful they were. They sat in the back of their truck and drank whisky. They passed the bottle to some of our Indian boys who did not follow The Dineh' Way. But I did not recognize the danger these white boys posed until it was too late."

Matthew tried to understand what the old man said, but his voice echoed in his ears, sounding as if it came from far way, getting more distant with every word. The sweet smoke filling his nostrils made his eyelids heavy and turned the white light above him into all the colors of the rainbow. He wanted to make up for those white boy's lack of respect, but his head spun as dizziness seized him.

Grandpa Chee continued. "Those boys followed us home,

forced their way into our Hogan, killed my mother and father, and held my sister down, taking turns raping her."

And then to his right, Matthew heard . . . *Shots. Explosions. Machine gun fire.*

But when his head flopped back to the left, he could hear men nearby singing in a language he did not know, yet he understood it to be a death song.

So — why am I'm running?

"Move, move, MOVE!"

That must be why.

"Sergeant Colter!" someone called in a strong male voice, and Matthew's eyelids, no longer heavy, shot open to the blazing light and heat of a desert. Furnace hot winds muffled the sound of gunfire and explosions as ghosts that looked like soldiers ran for cover in slow motion.

"Brian, goddammit! What are you doing? Fall back!"

Matthew, at last, fully alert and awake, stood in Brian's body wearing full combat gear and held a large machine gun in his hands. But when he looked to his left, he saw the Navajo hogan a short distance away.

That's impossible, he thought. *Is this time travel?*

"Colter, are you injured? Lie down, we'll come and get you!" a voice called to him over the wind.

He felt the urge to run to the hogan but forced himself to walk steadily toward it. After he stepped inside and closed the door behind him, the world outside went silent. When he turned, he startled at the sight of a young girl — *Abigail* — pinned to a large wooden table, *the same table I sat at today,* by a young, yellow haired man who held her firmly in place. Matthew saw the girl's eyes glaze over with a look of resigna- tion. Of defeat. The other man with dark hair mounted her from behind. Matthew forced his eyes away but saw two adults — *Abigail's mother and father* — lying on a bed pallet along the far wall. They were covered in blood. Movement caught Matthew's eye. A small boy — *Abigail's brother, great-grandfather Ben Chee Senior at age six* — looked up at him with tear-filled eyes from underneath the blankets. Matthew tried to move toward Abigail, but his feet were locked into place. "Let me loose. I can help her." His voice sounded muffled to his own ears as if speaking into a pillow. Smoke blew into his face from somewhere, and when he fanned it from his eyes, he noticed his hands were translucent, almost ghostly.

The dark-haired boy finished, and laughing, moved into position to hold Abigail by her arms. "Go get some, Blaine," the dark-haired man said. And the yellow-haired man took his turn. Matthew couldn't watch but wasn't able to turn his head away either. A voice drifted into his mind. *Watch. Learn.*

The blonde man finished quickly, pulled up his pants, and buckled his belt. The other man released Abigail, who stood up as if nothing had happened and smoothed the front of her long skirt.

"We can't let her go, Blain," the dark-haired man said. So, Blain crossed to the center of a hogan and grabbed the handle of a large skillet on the stove while Abigail just stood there with a look Matthew knew too well. He had seen it in the reflection of Colter's face: the thousand-yard stare. Blain slowly pulled the heavy pan from the burner. The screech of metal against metal sounded so loud that it forced Matthew to cover his ears. Matthew looked at Abigail, who just stood there, then she looked at Matthew and smiled.

"You can see me?" he asked, his voice still muffled. Abigail nodded then turned her gaze to her little brother in his hiding place. She brought a finger to her lips and walked past Blain toward the door Matthew had entered. Tiny motes of light floated from her skin. *Soul-shifter, Skin-Walker, Lightning Dancer.* The words drifted to his mind from some far-off place. Matthew gasped then called out to her. "Abigail, run!" But his voice was lost to the void.

The dark-haired boy stepped into Abigail's path and put his hands on her shoulders. "Where do you think you're going, whore?"

Matthew threw himself against his invisible restraints and managed to take a step toward her, but with a tiny flicker of her head, Abigail redirected Matthew toward her brother.

"I said, where you think you're going, bitch? And what you looking at?" Then the man slapped her across the face. Hard. Abigail smiled at Matthew, then looked her attacker in the eyes.

Matthew understood and, surprisingly, was able to move to little Ben Chee's side. He crouched down beside little Ben, who looked at him. "Can you see me?" Matthew asked.

Ben nodded and said, "ch'įįdii". Ghost.

Ben turned his eyes toward his sister, then started to cry out. Matthew quickly wrapped his left hand around the little boy's mouth as Blain stepped up behind Abigail and raised the skillet to strike. Just as Blain brought the pan down, Abigail raised her hands up and touched the sides of his face. Matthew gasped at the wave of electric light as it sprang from Abigail's fingers, and he knew she had escaped into the dark-haired boy an instant before the skillet crushed her skull.

Matthew watched the dark-haired boy's eyes turn bright red and thought, *Abigail owns that body now.* Little Ben, fury on his face, bit down hard on Matthew's hand, threw his blankets off, and screaming like a choking animal, raced toward Abigail's body right before it fell to the floor. Blain turned to attack little Ben, but his eyes merely widened in surprise when his dark-haired friend leapt toward him and drove a knife into his neck. Matthew grabbed Ben but failed to shield his eyes from the relentless strikes Abigail delivered to Blain's face and neck. When, at last, Blaine's body fell, it landed awkwardly on top of Abigail's corpse, twisting his neck at an angle that allowed Matthew and Ben to watch the life seep out of his greying eyes. The dark-haired boy knelt beside Matthew and, with an electric, but soothing touch, gently removed his arm from around little Ben.

"Abby!" Little Ben said and rushed into the arms of the new body she possessed.

In Navajo, the dark-haired boy said, "Little brother, you must tell the police that you stabbed the boy who attacked me. But you must not tell them about the boy whose body I just took. Do you understand? I need time to get away." Matthew felt unnerved that he could understand the language.

"Don't leave me, Abby," six-year-old Ben Chee said.

"I promise, Ben, I will always be close, but you must be brave now." Little Ben tried to stand tall as he choked back his tears. "Go to Aunt Margaret's house for help. It's not too far." Then she hugged Ben tight once more before tearing herself away. Matthew pulled the boy to him and held him as he sobbed. When Abigail opened the door, the howling wind and sounds of battle from that other time and place returned. She turned in the arched doorway and said to Matthew, "Come with me, ha'go." Matthew hesitated to leave the six-year-old, surrounded by his dead family in a blood-soaked room. "Ha'go. Come now."

"See you in about seventy years, old man," Matthew said as the dark-haired boy pushed him through the door into the hot light of the desert that bathed him in a swirl of color —

"Ch'ínádzííd, Matthew Miller, WAKE UP!"

Matthew's eyes shot open. He blinked tears away and found himself sitting cross-legged on the floor, naked, breathing hard, and drenched in sweat. He tried to focus his vision on several men sitting inside the shadows wearing the masks of ancient native gods. He raised his left hand to admire the blood pushing through the old scar.

"So, you are alive, Skinwalker. Welcome back," said Ben Chee, now a great-grandfather once again.

29

A STEP AHEAD

2:00 A.M.
FRIDAY, OCTOBER 18 TH
WINDOW ROCK, ARIZONA

"We're three clicks out."

The whisper of Chip's voice in the headset startled Jessie. She pressed the transmitter button on her throat and said, "Copy." This particular comms set up made Chip's voice sound as if it came from inside her head, even though Chip, Detective Santos, and Steve were in the vehicle ahead of them.

"Let's go dark at one click out."

She glanced over at Sean, who was driving, then Eric strapped in next to him, and finally to Randy who sat beside her on the backseat of the Yukon. Half the team wanted to simply knock on Chee's door and ask to speak to Matthew. The other half wanted to take him down by any means necessary. Jessie just didn't want to lose him again. She still had no plan on how to get close enough to speak with him, and she had no idea what she was going to say when she finally met him. Randy's fuddling with his night vision goggles interrupted her thoughts. She reached over and assisted him with adjusting the straps.

"This is the power button," she said. "Whatever you do, don't turn on your NVG until after we go dark."

"Unless you want to be flash-blinded," Eric added.

"*OK, we're at one click out,*" Rasher said.

Eric turned and flashed the thumbs up signal before pressing the switch on his own throat mic. "Time for night vision, folks. Pull over and let's do this," he said.

The vehicles stopped and turned out their headlights. Everyone waited a moment for their eyes to adjust to the darkness. Jessie glanced out the window and thought the night vision goggles might not be needed. One could almost read a book by the brilliant splash of starlight in the Arizona night sky. When everyone else had their NVG's down and ready, Randy's hands crawled around his pair, feeling for the power switch. Jessie reached over and placed his finger on the button.

"Power is here, but don't press it yet," she said.

"Sorry, I've never been part of a raid quite like this."

"Don't worry. You'll get used to the green light after a minute or two," Jessie reassured him as the cars rolled forward into the darkness.

"*The Chee residence is up against that bluff. It's the only house around,*" Chip said.

"We'll exit about 800 meters out and go in on foot," Eric said, taking command.

At exactly 800 meters, the team pulled their vehicles off the road and hid them in a shallow creek bed. The headlights went out. A moment later, the occupants of both vehicles bailed out together, all dressed in black multi-cam uniforms. Eric and Steve carried tranquilizer guns, but the rest of the team brandished Kriss Vector 9mm Sub-Machine Guns. Jessie reminded herself of how much she liked the Kriss because of its small size, folding stock, and because the 9mm rounds wouldn't over-penetrate. She double-checked the suppressor can screwed onto her threaded gun barrel to quiet any necessary shots and nodded in approval as she watched everyone else perform the same check.

"Let's do this," Rasher said, and everyone but Eric moved up the small hill toward the house. Eric walked over to the two San Antonio police detectives.

"Randy, we need you and Mel to stay here with the trucks," Eric said. "When we call you, come straight up the driveway to the house, fast." Melissa and Randy both looked to one another through their goggles, nodded, and moved into position beside the driver's door of each vehicle.

Jessie glanced behind her to see Eric doing the Groucho walk, impressed how, even with his knee's bent and feet rolling heel to toe across the ground, he was able to move so smooth and quiet going uphill in the High Plains landscape without tripping over something. Eric quickly closed the gap, catching up to the team, and as one, they quietly worked their way up the bluff. At about ten meters out, they separated to surround the house. Four of them took up the perimeter while Jessie and Sean swung around to the front to look for vehicles. Sean disappeared into star-shadow as he relayed the license plates.

"*We got a van and two pickup trucks,*" he said over the walkie while Jessie stood dead still, listening.

"*No Jeep?*" Randy asked over comms.

"*No Jeep,*" Sean replied. "*We confirmed this is the correct address, 10-4?*"

"*Yes,*" Steve said. "*We crosschecked Anna's college papers. It's all we have.*"

"He was here," Jessie said. "There's a lingering presence. I don't sense him now."

"*You're sure?*" Chip asked.

"I'm sure. There's a weird, lingering presence, but not his," Jessie said. "Goddammit, he's —"

"Why don't you just come out and show yourself, Yee Naaldooshii?" asked a voice from inside the house. Jessie thought it sounded like an old man. "I know you're out there," the voice continued. "I can feel your energy."

Jessie looked at Eric through the NVG and shook her head.

Dammit it all to hell!

She pointed at him to stay put and indicated her intent to step to the front porch. "Maintain positions until I know more," she said.

Eric nodded. Radios clicked. She took a few cautious steps up to the dark corner of the house and peeked around it. She let out a long, slow breath as an old man sitting in a rocking chair on the porch glanced in her direction and waved at her.

Dammit.

"I'm at the lower corner of the property, Jess," Steve said. *"That old man wasn't there until just now."*

"I'm going to turn on the porch light," the old man said. "Might want to shut off your NVG's. Your friends can come out, too. I have some cold Cokes here. It's not safe to be creeping around the High Plains desert at night. Even though it is October, it's still too hot. The snakes are out."

Fuck me!

Jessie flipped the SMG's safety on, slung it over her shoulder, and pulled off her night vision goggles. She took a deep breath, then stepped out from the darkness with her arms spread wide.

The old man eyed Jessie up and down, sat back in his chair, and folded his arms across his chest. "A lot of attention for one skinwalker, don't you think? You could have just knocked." The old man had a small smile on his face. "At least you're prettier than the other one."

"He's dangerous, sir," Jessie replied. "We can't afford to take any chances."

"He's less dangerous than you, I think. You are a Skinwalker, too, but different. I haven't decided how you are different, yet."

"How can you tell?" Chip asked as he moved into view from the shadows. He reached into the cooler and tossed a can of soda to Sean who just then stepped out of the dark. Sean snatched the can out of the air, popped the top, and took a long draw.

Jessie noticed that the old man didn't so much as flinch at the sight of the two heavily armed men. "She has a stronger life energy than any of you. The other one is strong, too, but a different kind of strong. I'm not sure how to explain it." He looked the group over. "Besides, you all make too much noise. I could hear you from a mile away."

Sean chuckled.

Jessie started to step onto the porch, but she stopped suddenly when she felt the familiar electrical charge tingling at the edge of her senses. It felt different than she remembered from the Riverwalk. "Are you —"

"No," the old man replied. "I am not a Skinwalker. But my sister was, so maybe you are sensing that, as I sensed your kind."

"You mean our kind," Jessie said. "It's in your blood, too."

"I suppose you are right. But I don't have the gift. I haven't seen a Skinwalker since 1948, when I was six years old. Now two a couple days apart. I'm either blessed by the great spirit or cursed. Please have a Coke." He held open the cooler lid and Jessie reached in and took one.

"Blessed or cursed how, sir?" she asked.

"Please. Do not call me sir. I was an enlisted man; four tours in Viet Nam and a trainer for Desert Storm. So, you can all just call me Grandpa. Look," he said, "I'm not going to hurt you. You can have the others come out. We can all have a little pow-wow."

Steve keyed the mic on the radio and called for Melissa and Randy to drive the trucks up to the house. Sean joined Jessie on the porch and extended a hand to the old man. "Thank you for your service," he said.

The old man took the hand and shook it. "You, I did not hear," he said.

"Damned Delta Force" Chip said. "Always the superstars."

"The other Skinwalker. Where is he?" Jessie asked.

The old man leaned forward in his chair and squinted at her. "He's gone."

"But where?" Steve asked.

"I don't know. He said he had something to do, some business in San Antonio to take care of. Maybe he's there."

The two Yukons pulled into the driveway. Randy and Melissa walked up to the others in the group.

"Two more. You all came here looking for a fight."

"We came prepared for a fight, sir," Randy said. "Not looking for one."

"Why was he here?" Jessie asked.

The elderly Navajo stood up slowly, leaned in even closer, and looked directly into Jessie's eyes. A bead of sweat rolled down her temple. She forced herself not to blink. "He was here to understand and say hello to an old friend," he said.

"He has friends here?" Eric asked, also coming in from the shadows.

"In a sense," the old man replied. He frowned and suddenly he looked sad. "We met when I was six. He's the same skinwalker who came to our hogan and kept me from getting killed. I remember biting him on the hand. It is strange. He hasn't aged a day."

"What you're suggesting is impossible," Jessie said.

"No more impossible than what you, the boy, or my sister can do," he said. He turned and opened the door into the house. "Why don't you all come in? I'll tell you a story, and perhaps have answers for your questions."

FIVE HOURS LATER, JESSIE'S TEAM HAD RETURNED TO THE AC-130 and prepared to take off. Jessie sat at the ADS ramp panel, her hand pulling the controller back and raising the ramp into the closed position. Thoughts of the old man were still swirling through her head, but the whir of ramp gears put her into a trance. When Randy came up behind her, she jumped.

"Sorry. Didn't mean to startle you."

"I thought you were buckled in," she said.

"I just got an email from Doctor Bishop. You need to read it."

Jessie released the controller, took Randy's cellphone, and read the email he had pulled up for her.

"Dr. Bishop, I would like to meet with you at your earliest convenience to discuss my condition as well as the current situation this ability has put me in. I have recently learned something that may have an impact on the others in your care. I need to be assured our client/doctor relationship is still intact, considering my biological body is now deceased. I require absolute discretion and secrecy and must have your word that your detective friend will not be notified. The future of the others, save one, will depend on your cooperation. You have twelve hours to respond. If I do not hear back, I will assume you have alerted the others, your comatose patients will die, and you will never see or hear from me again. Sincerely, Matthew Miller."

She handed the phone back to Randy. "Doctor Bishop needs to agree."

"It's a set up," Randy said.

"Of course, it is. This guy is always two steps ahead of us. It's up to us to figure out what the set up is."

"He's going to try to distract us so he can get to Cruz."

"Perhaps, but we'll need to come up with other scenarios as well."

"But he can't think we're that stupid," Randy said.

Jessie nodded. "I agree with you. We can discuss on the flight home. Go buckle in, Detective, we're ready to take off." She finished securing the ADS ramp and then opened the panel mic and said, "We're ready to go, Sam."

"Roger that. You coming up to the flight deck?"

Jessie loved flying the big cargo plane, but she also knew Sam had a crush on her. He gave her flying lessons every time they went up and despite being professional at the controls, he never let her leave without a mostly harmless flirt. Today, she couldn't shake the feeling of trouble ahead. "I have to pass, Sam. We've got planning to do back here. Maybe next time."

MATTHEW WATCHED THE BIG CARGO PLANE TAKE OFF THROUGH his binoculars. When he lowered them, he noticed that Anna, sitting next to him in the front seat, had a worried look on her face. He glanced in the rearview mirror to check on her brothers Rudy and Charlie in the back. They had helped take him down in Old Man Chee's house and joined the singing circle during the Enemy Way ceremony. When the ceremony went in a different direction than any of the Navajo Hatalii had expected, they had taken it in stride. So, he wasn't surprised to see that their faces were more eager than nervous. When they leaned forward from the back seat, he passed the younger brother Charlie the binoculars.

"That's some kind of firepower coming for you, Skinwalker," Charlie said, passing the binoculars to his brother, Rudy.

"Who did you piss off, man?" Rudy adjusted the focus on the binoculars. "That's an AC130 Spooky gunship," he said, still looking, "One bad mamba-jamba."

"I don't know who they are," Matthew said. "But now we know one thing for sure: I'm not alone."

They watched in silence as the plane banked to the east, its gleaming surface dimming until its image evaporated out of sight.

"What now?" Anna asked.

"I've already got a plan in motion, but I'm going to need your help."

Anna reached over and touched his hand. "You know I'll do whatever I can."

"How about you two?" he asked.

"We're in, man," Rudy said. "Who would turn down a chance to work with a real Skinwalker?"

"Especially when he's out for revenge," Charlie said with a laugh that neither Matthew nor Rudy shared in.

"I'm not a murderer," Matthew said, and Rudy punched his brother in the arm a second time.

"What he meant, Matthew, is we understand your mission," Rudy said.

"Hell, yeah. I would do the same thing," Charlie added before Rudy silenced him with a glare.

"You have our full support," Rudy said. "And we can get more help if we need it."

Matthew entwined his fingers with Anna's and then pulled the back of her hand to his mouth to kiss it. She looked worried. She had reason to because there was no doubt she would not like what he had in mind.

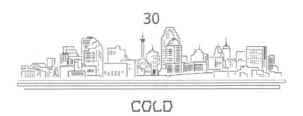

30

COLD

San Antonio, Texas

Despite his reluctance, Jon departed San Antonio to negotiate new contracts, leaving Jessie and the rest of the team to wrap up the mission. Another week had gone by since Ship Rock, and everyone paced the floors of their make-shift office because nothing about the mission had been wrapped up. That was a problem. Jessie hadn't heard a word from Matthew since the email to Doctor Bishop. All trails and contact had gone cold. No more comatose bodies showed up, anywhere. Not CONUS, or Continental United States, or anywhere else in the world as far as any intelligence report gleaned. She didn't believe that Matthew had tricked her into coming back to San Antonio simply so he could escape. No. He had something else in mind. She looked out the window toward the lights of Metropolitan Hospital, deeply troubled that Matthew's slip-stream victims, Ruben White, Rosie Vasquez and the Jane Doe were still in a coma.

You're not done yet, are you?

She had been checking in with Grandpa Chee once a week, but his answer never changed: "I haven't heard from or seen either of them." Jessie liked the old man. Over the past few weeks, he had become more than a source of information. A loose friendship, of sorts, formed between them. Perhaps it was the bond of her ability. But after Crue Intellis informed her that some of Anna's brothers and cousins had dropped off the grid, she had the feeling Grandpa was hiding something. She felt sure that family came first, and she couldn't fault the old man for that. At that moment, her phone rang, fortunately, because her thoughts were leading her down a dark and distrustful path. Unfortunately, because the caller ID put a knot in the pit of her stomach.

"Hello, Jon."

"Hey, Jess. How are things progressing?"

Jon hadn't pressed her for results, but she also knew he had a business to run. Jon gave her a lot of leniency due to the special circumstances. "I'm sorry, Jon, it's like we've hit a wall here. He's dug in. I'm not sure what else to do but wait him out. On a good note, no other bodies have been reported over the wire. None that stand out with the signature coma, anyway."

"We've used up our favors with General Evans. He had to reallocate the drone and satellite coverage from Arizona to more pressing National Security targets. He's sympathetic and agrees with your assessment of Miller, but we're out of time."

"He's been more than patient. As have you, but I don't want to give up on this, Jon."

"Who said anything about giving up?" Jon asked. "Remember the idea Randy came up with a few weeks ago?"

"Which one? Randy's come up with lots of good ideas." Jessie stopped pacing and sat down at her desk.

"That's true," Jon said. "The one where we made it easier for Miller by getting Cruz and White out of the military hospital."

"Yes, I remember," Jessie said. "We tried everything. It didn't work."

"It did work," Jon said.

"What? When?"

"Just now. I'd been pulling some strings and finally got Doctor Bishop in front of a federal judge this morning."

"You did that . . . this morning? Are you here in San Antonio?"

"No, we did it in DC. San Antonio's Federal Judge is here for a conference. I flew Doctor Bishop in yesterday. I didn't want him to tell you, in case we failed."

"And?"

"The good doctor blinded the poor judge with science."

"Meaning?"

"Bishop convinced the judge to sign an order to have Cruz and White moved from the Military Medical Center to Metropolitan."

"How?"

"By getting him to believe that Cruz and White would never come out of their comas."

"Wow," Jessie said with a nod of the head toward the hospital. "Boy did I underestimate the Doc.

"We all did. He did something that never occurred to us. He told the judge some of the truth. Namely, that his best chance of helping Rosie and Sara would be to bring all four coma patients to the same location so that he could study and monitor them together."

Jessie felt both blown away and relieved. "That's fantastic, Jon, thank you so much."

"Get the team together at the office and watch the six o'clock news. We're working with the local TV stations who have agreed to broadcast the move locally. The murders are bizarre enough to warrant good media coverage. I'm willing to bet you a big Texas steak dinner that wherever Miller is at, he's paying attention to home. Hopefully, he's running counter-surveillance on you, too. Let's see if he takes the bait. Time to get frosty."

But the six o'clock news came and went, as did the eleven o'clock. Then a day. Two days. A week.

Crap, Jessie thought, *it didn't work.*

EIGHT DAYS LATER, JESSIE STILL PACED THE HALLS OF CRUE Intellis' San Antonio satellite office. She groaned aloud, causing her teammates to turn to her. But when she stomped out of the room mumbling something about joining Steve in the control room, Randy returned his attention to the stacks of police report files growing on his and Melissa's honorary Crue desks. The Police Chief may have loaned them to Crue Intellis, but he hadn't removed the requirement to investigate burglaries, robberies, or other incidents from their work loads. Randy's eyes glazed over until his phone rang, startling him.

"Hi, Doc! Any news?" he said into the receiver. After listening for a moment, he whispered to Mel, "Go get Jessie and the others. Matthew has taken the bait." When Melissa returned from the control room a moment later with Jessie and Steve Walters in tow, Randy punched the speaker button and said, "Go ahead, Doc, you said Miller called."

"Yes," Bishop said, "I just hung up with a man claiming to be Matthew Miller." His voice vibrated with excitement. "I'm a bit unnerved," he admitted. "It was really him."

"You recorded the conversation, right?" said Randy.

"Of course. He spoke to me through some voice modulator, trying to disguise his voice. Which seemed strange and totally unnecessary given the fact that his biological body is deceased. He should have thought of that. Well, maybe he had a different reason for disguising his voice. I'll have to think about that. But it's going to be difficult to determine that reason since we still don't know whose body he's in."

"You sure it wasn't a prank call?" Randy asked, concerned by Bishop's rambling.

"Yes. Yes. It was him. I'm certain of it. He knew things that only I know. Well, things that only Matthew and I know. So, yes, yes. I'm one hundred and ten percent certain. It's him."

"Good," Randy said.

"But there's a problem."

"Go ahead. What is it?" Randy said.

"He wants to meet me at my Lockhill-Selma office tonight at 9 p.m."

"Tonight? There's no way we can do this tonight. We're not ready," Melissa said, looking around the room.

"He knows what he's doing," Jessie said. "He's got us off balance, and he wants to keep us this way."

"I told him I had plans with my wife tonight, which is true, but he didn't want to hear it. He told me flat out that this is my one chance to have all my questions answered. He said it's tonight, or never, so I agreed. Was I wrong?" Bishop asked.

"No, Doctor, that's fine. Are you okay with us taking him down in your office?" Randy asked.

"I'm not worried about that. I'm worried about his 'no detective' clause. I'm worried about saying the wrong thing and tipping him off."

"Don't worry. Text me the address and we'll be there in an hour," Randy said.

Randy hung up the phone and turned to face the group.

"We need backup at Metropolitan Hospital . . . in case this is a distraction and he goes for Cruz," Melissa said.

"Chip and I will take that post," Sean Parker said and bumped fists with his partner. "You guys call it in and let them know we're coming. Send the P.D. units home. We don't want a cop getting hurt over this," he added over his shoulder as they exited.

"He dragged this out so he could catch us unprepared. And it worked," Jessie said.

"I wouldn't have expected anything less," Randy said. "Let's get going."

THE TEAM HAD ANTICIPATED THAT MATTHEW MIGHT BE WATCHING the building, and therefore, any sign of police or strange activity entering the doctor's office would instantly red-flag them. Although they were lucky enough to gain discreet access to the same building, they would have to cut through three offices worth of sheetrock to get next to Bishop's—and that just wasn't an option. Logistic issues aside, their time to prepare had expired. Steve Walters and Marc Samuelson gave the doctor a crash course in setting up pin-head sized cameras and microphones, and by the time Doctor Bishop set up the last camera, there were only fifteen minutes left before Matthew's scheduled arrival.

"How's that?" Doctor Bishop said as he positioned the last pin-head camera in the upper corner wall of his office.

"*Step off the ladder,*" Detective Melissa Santos said. Bishop raised a hand to the mic implanted deep in his ear canal, nodded, then got off the ladder. He moved to his desk and sat down.

"*That's perfect Doc,*" Randy said. "*Good job.*"

DOCTOR RAYMOND BISHOP BRISTLED AT THE SITUATION HE agreed to be put in. He felt guilty about betraying Matthew, and the detectives had pulled out all the stops to convince him that his patient was physically dead, and he really didn't have an oath to the corporeal spirit of Matthew Miller. Raymond didn't believe it. Not for a second. But he decided to go through it anyway because Matthew, too, had crossed the line. Raymond couldn't see that Steve Walters from Cure Intellis and the two San Antonio Detectives were putting the final touches on video monitors that controlled all the cameras and microphones he had just installed, but he knew they were working on it. They said if something went wrong, they would be to him in seconds. He knew that was a bald-faced lie. He unlocked the door leading to the back alleyway of the office building, but if the team were forced to maintain a safe enough distance as to not be discovered by Matthew, he knew that ultimately, he was on his own.

"*Let's mark the time at . . .*" Steve paused, "*6:40 p.m.*"

"*Marked,*" Melissa replied.

Raymond felt as if he were going to be sick. Matthew would be here any minute, and the thought of having a conversation with his dead patient terrified him. He reached across the desk, pulled Matthew's file toward him, and slowly opened it. Clipped to the inside cover was a photo of the two of them, during Matthew's last visit to the hospital. Bishop's heart thumped harder in his chest and his eyes welled up at the memory. The boy knew he was going to die, yet always had a smile for everyone he met. Now, by some miracle, magic or some unexplainable science, Matthew still lived.

And killed people.

"*You okay, Doc?*"

The sound of Detective Santos's voice in his ears sent such a violent jolt through his body, the file jumped out of his hands, paperwork flew, and the first expletive to pass his lips in thirty years involuntarily escaped his lips.

"*Good one, Doc, I don't think I've ever heard you cuss, before,*" Randy said.

It annoyed Raymond that Randy, and most likely the others, thought there was anything funny about it. He had momentarily forgotten Jessie was watching the cameras from somewhere close. He reassembled the file, got up, and went to the office kitchen and soaked a dishtowel in cold water.

"There is nothing funny about this, Detective," Raymond snapped back. "I'm not okay. I'm terrified. I've never been part of a sting before." He walked back to his desk and sat down, leaned back, and placed the cold cloth across his forehead. "Matthew's going to be here in a couple of hours and the closer it gets . . . I'm not sure I can do this."

"You're right, Doc. It's not funny. I'm just trying to get you to relax. I apologize," Randy's voice said quietly.

"He didn't get in touch so that he could kill you. He contacted you because you took care of him when he was a child," Santos said.

"So?"

"So, he trusts you."

"And I'm about to break that trust," Bishop said.

The comms were quiet just a moment too long. *"If it's not a ruse and he actually shows up here, you have to believe that he's doing it because he thinks he has a chance. We have all talked about this. He can't make it without you. If he's going to survive what's happened to him, he's going to need your help."*

"I suppose you're right." Raymond felt certain that Matthew reached out to him because he needed help. That still didn't mean the others would make it through the door in time to save him if Matthew had other ideas.

BY SEVEN O'CLOCK, STEVE, CHIP, RANDY, AND MELISSA — TWO blocks away at a bank building — were loading into a plain white van that Jon had rented for the sting. After they settled in, Eric, who sat beside Jessie, showed Steve a map of the area around the hospital on his phone. After a quick nod at Marc and

Taina who were unpacking bino's and NVGs, the group began to study the map.

A moment later, Steve leaned over and said to Eric, "Why don't you take Jessie into this residential area here?" He pointed to an area near the medical plaza. "It's a quick in and out and should be far enough away so that Miller can't detect her." Jessie nodded. "But close enough to get back here when we catch him. Chip, Randy, Mel, and I will take him into custody. Marc and Taina, you guys stay put here. Once he's inside, come up West Avenue from the bank on the corner of Military Drive. Chip, you post up here," Steve tapped the screen, "across from the medical plaza. Take overwatch with bino's and night vision, then make your way in once the doc has him in the office."

Randy piped in over comms. *"I'm calling the duty Sergeant and am going to ask him to hang out near West Ave and Lockhill Selma, just in case. And hope he doesn't report back to my Chief."*

"You ready, Doc?" Steve asked over his mic.

"As ready as I'll ever be," Doctor Bishop replied.

"Oh shit," Melissa said. *"I almost forgot about the gloves."* The team outside couldn't see her reach into a duffel bag overflowing with camera gear as she pulled out two pairs of absurdly awkward, elbow-length gloves. *"These babies are heavily insulated. Same gloves used by powerline workers."*

"Good thinking, Mel," Steve said. "I'll be back with you and Randy shortly. One last thing: whatever happens, do not allow Miller to touch you."

"Oh, just great," Bishop said over the comms. No one in the van could see that the doc had leaned back in his chair and had once again thrown the cold cloth over his forehead. "Just fucking great."

31

TABLES TURNED

9:15 P.M.

CASTLE HILLS MEDICAL

SAN ANTONIO, TEXAS

"He's late," Jessie said, slouching down lower into her seat. *"God's rot, Jessie, you about gave me a heart attack,"* Doctor Bishop said.

Jessie rolled her eyes and slouched down further in the seat of their surveillance van and tapped relentlessly at the screen of a tablet she held in her lap, used as a remote monitor for the half dozen wireless cameras placed in and around the doctor's office. She shook the tablet, as if doing so would chase away the fuzzy picture she had to deal with.

"We're at the limits of the camera's range," Eric said, sitting beside her, a placid look on his face. "Want me to pull a little . . ."

"No!" Jessie snapped, not intending to sound so harsh. "I don't want to take any chances. I don't feel Matthew now, and I'm guessing he can't feel me. So let's just stay put."

Eric nodded. "Roger that."

"Hold the phone, folks," Chip's voice chirped over comms. He

positioned himself on the farthest end of the medical plaza's parking lot, amidst other vehicles, well out of sight. *"There's a Mustang convertible pulling in now, right up by the doc's office. It's dark in color. One occupant."*

"Okay everyone. Let's keep comms clear, stay focused. Chip, you make the call," Randy said.

Jessie knew Randy, Mel, and Steve were somewhere in the office, but she wasn't certain how close to Bishop they were able to get on such short notice. She keyed her mic, "So it's not Miller?"

"Not unless he's changed bodies again," Chip said. *"Looks like a female."*

Eric looked over at Jessie who nibbled on her low lip, her brow furrowed in concentration. He reached up and keyed his mic. "Chip, can you get up on the car, see if there is anyone else inside?"

"Roger that," Chip said. Then a moment later, *"Shit!"*

"What's wrong?" Eric asked.

Chip said nothing, so Jessie flipped the video screen on her iPad to Chip's wifi bodycam. She watched as he pulled a roll of duct tape from a bag in the front seat of his rental, tore off a piece, and slapped it over the interior light. She saw him gently open the door, slip out, and could hear the click as he carefully pressed the door closed. She tilted the screen toward Eric, and they watched as he slipped across the street, pressing his body up against a thick oak tree.

"Careful Chip," Jessie said, pointing at the top corner screen. "The woman's looking behind her in your direction." She turned the monitor toward Eric who nodded. The comms were quiet a long moment as Jessie watched while the woman turned away and walk to the front door of Doctor Bishop's office.

"She's at your door, Doc," Jessie said, switching cameras to the interior lobby. Jessie saw the doc's backside as he approached the door, the office lighting bright enough, and the camera's low-light abilities good enough to get a clear view of the woman's face. She used the camera button to snap a couple of good photos of the woman. "Randy, sending you some pics. Maybe you can send to your pal Greg Chambers, see if he can start working on her identity."

"*Copy that,*" Randy replied, quietly.

"*This woman is about five-foot-six, a pretty, very pretty brunette with long, straight black hair, dark-skin, looks to be mid-twenties. She has a thin briefcase,*" Bishop said.

"That's Matthew. It's got to be," Jessie said. "He's taken the girl. Doc, do everything you can to get him into your back office."

"*Did you unlock the back door, Doc?*" Chip asked. "*After she's seated, I'm coming in the front, I'll hang in the waiting area as back up.*"

"*Yes, yes! Please, shut up,*" Bishop said, his voice firm.

"*Recorders are on, and all cameras still up and running. We're ready,*" Steve Walters confirmed. Jessie wondered how ready he could be. She had no idea where in the building Steve and the other two were.

"*Yes, may I help you?*"

Jessie looked at Eric, who raised an eyebrow. "His voice sounds calm," he whispered. Jessie nodded.

"*Hi! You must be Doctor Bishop. I'm Anna. Anna Chee,*" the woman said, her voice crisp through the hidden microphones. "*I apologize for being late, but Matthew had something come up at the last minute and can't make it. He asked me to come and share information about his research with you. He said you would find it fascinating and that he would reach out to you tomorrow if you're interested in continuing conversing with him.*"

Jessie recognized nervous body posture when she saw it, and the doc was covered in it.

"Please. Come in," Bishop said and opened the hallway door wider. The young woman stepped past. "If you don't mind, we'll talk in my office." Jessie watched Bishop, then the woman, leave the camera view and switched to the unit placed in the far corner of the hall in time to see the doc enter his office first and the girl follow up behind.

"*For a teenager, he's got outstanding taste in women,*" Chip said.

"Keep the channel clear," Eric snapped into his mic.

DOCTOR RAYMOND BISHOP TURNED TO FACE THE WOMAN AND swallowed hard as the pretty girl smiling at him from the other side of his desk carried herself with an air of absolute confidence. Raymond didn't want to believe that it was truly Matthew who stood before him because the long spaghetti straps and plunging neckline of the bright yellow sundress this woman wore worked as a team to reveal ample cleavage.

Stay focused, Raymond! Stay Focused!

"I'm disappointed Mr. Miller couldn't make it," he said.

"I am too, Doctor," Anna said, smiling. "I have heard so much about you. Matthew explained that you were his first doctor, and that you were with him to the end."

This comment caught Raymond by surprise. "Yes, well, we do have quite a bit to talk about, as you might have guessed." He motioned a hand at the leather chair placed strategically at an angle from his desk. "Won't you sit? Would you like something to drink? Water? Perrier?"

"Thank you, no," Anna said, and with the practiced grace of a lady, sat straight backed on the edge of the leather chair, legs pressed together to one side. Raymond didn't buy it. It was one thing to take and use the skills of someone else, but quite another to have something as cultured and practiced as sitting for a professional interview when you're an eighteen-year-old teenage boy. Something just wasn't adding up.

"You're doing a great job, Doc. Keep it up."

Raymond flinched ever so slightly at Mel's voice in his head, and hoped Anna, or Matthew didn't catch it.

"So, I'm sorry. I'm bad with names. You said your last name was Chee?"

"Yes, sir. Chee. Anna Chee. I'm a research student at UTSA, working on my Master's in Sociology."

"That name, is it Native American?"

"Yes, it is!" Anna smiled at Raymond's attentiveness. "It's Navajo. I'm a Navajo."

"Ah, I see. Well then, I'm curious as to how you and Mr. Miller are acquainted."

"Well, we met at a dance hall and became friends," she said. "When we were getting to know each other, he told me about his research, how he worked with you on the nature of bio electricity and human consciousness. I found it fascinating! And here I am!"

"Yes, and here you are," he said. The problem was, Raymond hadn't a clue about what the woman was talking about. He knew something of the research, but it had little to do with his line of work. "So, let's see what you have to share, shall we?" Raymond glanced at Anna's feet, where she had set the thin leather messenger bag. As Anna bent forward to retrieve the case, Bishop found himself leaning forward and over his desk to get an unfettered view of her braless breasts. Heat filled his face and he sat up straight, not able to hide the embarrassment over his adolescent knee-jerk and sexist behavior.

Anna smiled when she caught the doctor averting his eyes, then walked around to his side of the desk and put four EEG readouts in front of him. Bishop's eyes widened.

"These are from Cruz, White, Gonzalez, and the blonde girl

we call Jane Doe," he said, as he tried to assimilate the oxygen levels and vast array of other biometrics noted on the readouts. "Where did you get these?"

A look of confusion crossed the girl's face. "I'm not sure what you mean," she said.

"Miss Chee, it's a simple question. Where did you get the readouts?"

Anna looked befuddled. "These are from the four subjects you are studying at Methodist Hospital. Matthew gave them to me. He said you hadn't seen them yet, and that the information they contained would confirm all of your questions."

"Ask her when he was at the hospital," Jessie said over the mic.

"When?" Raymond asked. "When did he print these?"

"Why, just a few hours ago. He said you two spoke after they moved the murderer, Jeffery Cruz, to the hospital." Raymond could almost hear the group collectively suck in their breaths, as he did now.

"That was four days ago," Jessie said.

Bishop said, "I was there during the transfer, Miss Chee, and I don't remember speaking to him. As a matter of fact, I haven't seen Matthew since . . . since . . ." Raymond swallowed hard, "Well I haven't seen him in some time."

"He said you'd ask about that," Anna replied, reaching into her bag again. This time Raymond watched her hands, not her breasts. He let out a long sigh of relief when she pulled one additional sheet of paper from the bag instead of a pistol. She handed the paper to him. "Matthew said to give you this." She flattened out a new, separate EEG read out beside the others in front of him. "This was also printed a few hours ago."

Raymond raised an eyebrow for only a moment before retrieving Matthew's old medical file from his desk drawer. He thumbed through the document until he found what he was looking for. An old EEG taken by Raymond himself a few years ago. He lined the two papers up for comparison.

"This is remarkable. It's identical! It really is him!" Raymond couldn't contain his smile, and neither could the girl as she returned to her seat.

"He also said you'd believe him, since no one else would."

"He's here. Miller is here," Jessie said, her voice laced with urgency.

Randy's voice chimed in over comms. *"Yes, we know, he's in the doc's office."*

"No, you don't understand."

ERIC LOOKED OVER FROM THE VAN'S DRIVER SEAT JUST AS JESSIE'S face turned ashen and she vomited into her lap. As he reached into the back to grab a towel, Jessie looked past him out the window and said, "Oh, no." A white pick-up truck slammed into the door and rocked the van up on two wheels. The impact instantly shattered Eric's left arm and snapped both their heads so violently that they passed out.

Two men dressed in grey mottled combat uniforms, their faces covered by matching shemaghs, bailed out of the truck's rear seat, ran to the van, and jerked open the passenger door. They slashed Jessie's seatbelt with a knife and dragged her onto the ground where they flex-cuffed her legs and hands. Then they slipped a large, metallic-looking sleeping bag over her body and zipped it up. One of the men hoisted her small frame over his shoulder and dumped her like an old rolled up carpet in the bed of the pickup.

Eric regained consciousness just in time to watch the truck speed off down the street. He reached up and pressed the mic key on his headset. "They . . . got . . . Jessie" was all he managed to broadcast over the radio before he passed out again.

Randy and Steve drew weapons and rushed into Bishop's office from the hallway door. "On the floor, on the floor!" Steve shouted an instant before Chip burst into the room from the lobby door. He also had his weapon drawn, and he pointed it directly at Anna who sat nonplussed and defiant.

"I don't understand. What is this?" Anna asked.

Melissa jerked Anna out of the chair by the hair and flung her to the floor. "Now do you know what this is?" Santos hissed.

"Watch her hands," Randy said, as Steve put his knee into Anna's back and wrenched one of her arms behind her.

"Ow!" Anna said. "You're hurting me!"

As Melissa struggled into the hi-voltage gloves, she felt the bucking young girl start to slip out of her grip. "Someone cuff her hands. I can't hold on."

Chip reached in and drove his thumb and fingers into the crease of Anna's collarbone. She whimpered and stopped kicking. "Stay still, missy, I'd hate to accidentally snap your neck," he said.

Anna stopped resisting. "You're hurting me. Why are you doing this?" she wailed. In an instant, her defiance had turned into overacted sobbing. "I don't understand."

Melissa removed the mitts from her hands and slid them onto Anna's. Then she duct taped the mitts together, and she and Randy hoisted the girl, still wailing, onto her feet.

"Quiet!" Randy yelled. Then he brought his free hand to the mic and said, "Status?"

Marc Samuelson turned the grey Yukon left onto La Rue Ann Court. "We're pulling up now, oh my god . . . Randy, get over here ASAP." Residents from the surrounding homes were already gathering in the dark cul-de-sac. Some were using flashlights to look inside the van while others were chattering away on their phones. Taina Volkov launched from her seat and grabbed an EMT bag from the back of the Yukon. She rushed to the caved in driver door of Eric and Jessie's van where she found a man she guessed to be a local resident, trying to stabilize Eric's head.

"Are you an EMT?" the man asked Taina.

"Yes, I am," Taina said. "Thank you for helping. Let's get this neck brace on."

Marc approached the mangled door and leaned in. "Randy and Melissa are on their way."

"He's bad, Marc. He's really bad."

As the ambulance pulled away, Randy walked up to bystanders who were all busy recording video on their phones. "Folks, please, did anyone see what happened?" he asked, still taking in the scene.

A San Antonio fire engine and a city ambulance that had arrived less than five minutes earlier already had the scene lit up with flood lights. Randy glanced at Marc, who comforted Taina on the sidewalk, as a tow truck worked to drag the destroyed van onto its flatbed. A small boy walked over to Randy and tapped him on the leg.

"You the police?" the boy asked.

"Yes, I am," Randy replied.

"I got video of the truck."

"Truck?" Randy asked squatting down to look the boy in the face at eye level.

"Yeah, it was dark, but it was a pick-up with heavy bars on the front," the boy said. "I was taking out the trash and texting a friend. I saw the truck parked in front of my house. It was too dark to see the color, but it looked kinda grey, or white. My dad always said to get information when I see something suspicious, so I activated the phone's camera and zoom! The van took off. I about freaked out when it slammed right into the side of that van. Two guys got out of the truck, wearing towels around their heads and soldier uniforms. They ran to the van, then came back carrying something. Something big. They threw it in the back of the truck. It looked like a body all wrapped up. I recorded the truck leaving."

"Can you play back the video for me?" Randy asked. And the boy did. The video appeared dark and blurry, but Randy knew his tech could improve it. "What's your name, young man?"

"Brian."

"Where are your parents, Brian?"

"They went to the store. Should be back any minute."

"How old are you, Brian?"

"Ten. Are you going to arrest me?" The boy took a step back, fear etched on his face.

"Well Brian, you're pretty smart for a ten-year-old. And pretty brave, but these were bad men who did this. We don't want them to find out you took video. So, if you give me the phone, you'll have nothing to worry about."

The kid looked at him with wide eyes and nodded quickly, then handed him the phone.

"You take it. I don't want any trouble. My dad's going to kill me."

"Why?"

"That's his phone."

Randy took the phone and saw that the video the kid had taken had been queued up so he pressed play. His eyes were glued to the screen as the kid leaned in and gave the play-by-play. His brow furrowed in anger as he watched the attack on Eric and Jessie.

"Wait right here, young man," he said, then stepped away and activated his throat mic. "Mel, you on?"

A moment later his partner answered. *"Yeah. Just putting Miss Chee in the back of the cruiser."*

"Looks like we have an eyewitness. A kid. Can you come and get his statement? I think I scare him a little."

"No shit," Melissa said. "What's new?"

32

QUESTIONS

Amman Road Warehouse
Boerne, Texas

A low, muffled hum lured Jessie from a dream where she floated just beneath the waves of Myrtle Beach. Her eyes wanted to stay closed, but the sun forced her to open them. When she did, her vision blurred, and water stung her eyes. Something felt attached to her face, filling her mouth. The realization that she was really under water struck her like a vicious slap. Terror seized her. Disoriented, with no use of her hands or feet, she tried to scream, but only bubbles came out as she struggled against bonds she could not see, her arms stretched overhead, her feet secured at the ankles.

"Calm down," a soft male voice said. *"Keep thrashing about like that and you'll put a kink in the air hose."* Jessie heard the words as clearly as if they were coming from inside her head. She bit down, felt rubber between her teeth and breathed. She understood. Scuba regulator. After a couple of deep breaths, she stopped wriggling and then took stock of her situation. She had been sealed inside a big water tank and stretched tight. She felt certain she was horizontal, like a skinned rabbit on a campfire

skewer. She was also naked. She blinked and concentrated on calming down.

"I'm going to release the restraints," the voice said, and once she stopped moving, she felt the binds at her wrists and ankles ease. *"Peel the tape off your mouth. There's a full-face mask you can talk through in a bag at the bottom of the tank. Once you're loose, take off the straps and put on the mask. You'll need to remove the earplugs first. You'll hear better without them once the mask is on."*

Jessie knew this voice, even though she had never heard it before. *Matthew.*

She shifted her jaw muscles until she felt the deep-seated wireless earplugs. Reassured by this small truth, she lay still. After allowing her shoulders to relax, she pulled the rubber tubing off her wrists and ankles, but when she attempted to stand, she hit her head on the top of the tank. She lowered her head and pressed the breadth of her shoulders against the lid with all her might, but the lid refused to budge. Realizing she had no other option, she reached for the blurred image of a bag in the corner of the tank and pulled out a full-face scuba mask. After one last deep breath, Jessie ripped the tape off her mouth and used the air in her lungs to clear the water out of the mask. Then she secured the straps around the back of her head and breathed in the cool, compressed air. Her vision now clear, she squinted and tried to peer outside the tank, but the light shining through the lid of her transparent coffin was simply too bright and only provided the reflection of her naked body in thick Lexan walls.

Of course, the sun, she thought, her brain starting to function again.

"Put the rubber tubing and earplugs in the bag," Matthew said.

She shoved the tiny plugs in the bag right away, but she ran her fingers along the smooth stainless-steel disks attached to the ends of the tubing before stuffing those in.

"There is a small hatch above you dead center. Push the bag through it."

She heard a loud click in the water and looked up. As she groped for the spring-loaded door, she realized that the large steel blocks attached to the rubber tubing were affixed to the center of the side walls by magnets. She found the door and pushed the bag through it, extending her arm all the way to her elbow and counting to ten, slowly.

"Get your arm out of the hatch."

Jessie hesitated two more seconds before she pulled her arm in and returned to a kneeling position at the bottom of the tank.

"What do you want with me?"

The bright overhead light suddenly went out, throwing her into total darkness. Then, a small focused beam lamp turned on directly above her, bathing her form in a harsh, surreal light. At the same time, another small spotlight outside of the tank clicked on about twenty feet away. A male figure stepped into the light, turned toward her, and stood at what she recognized as standard military parade rest. The man looked tall, muscular, wearing fatigue pants and a tight-fitting t-shirt. The beam of light over his head created harsh shadows, but even through the mask and walls of her cage she could see a familiar light in his eyes.

Definitely the same man I saw on the river. So, why don't I feel anything?

"Is there a reason I'm naked?" she asked.

"You seem to be comfortable in your own skin," Matthew replied. *"I don't have that luxury."*

He was right, of course. Jessie understood. Matthew's physical, and most certainly emotional stability had been taken from him through violence. The attack on the van suddenly came back to her.

Eric, oh God.

What Matthew had done to capture her and how he had

secured her in the tank made it clear that he was as dangerous as the Old Navajo accused her of being.

"You hurt one of my crew to capture me. That wasn't necessary," she said.

"*Really?*" Matthew sounded amused. "*And deploying an elite tactical force to Grandpa Chee's house was?*"

"We couldn't take a chance. You killed those two boys . . ."

"*Fuck you, lady. How dare you lecture me?*"

Right again. How many men, or women for that matter, would avenge their own murders if they could?

"What is the condition of my teammate?" she asked.

Matthew turned his head as another man, shorter than Matthew, wearing mottled grey Battle Dress Uniform, BDU, pants and a shemagh wrapped about his face, stepped up to the edge of the light. The man whispered something to Matthew and slipped back into darkness. Matthew breathed deep and turned his attention back to her. He walked toward her and stopped within ten feet of the tank. She braced herself for the nausea that did not come. Like a shark, he slowly circled the tank, not taking his eyes off her.

When Jessie could no longer endure the silence, she asked, "What do you want, Matthew?" She saw a slight smile rise on his face.

"*That's easy. I'm surprised you feel the need to ask. I want to know who in the fuck you work for and what you want with me,*" he said, his words hot with warning.

Jessie persisted. "What's the condition of my teammate?" she asked again.

"*You're in no position to ask questions, Miss Richter, but you will answer mine.*"

Suddenly, the air stopped flowing into her mask. When she sucked in and got nothing, her eyes went wide. Matthew let her flail in the tank for a full twenty seconds, then nodded. When the air came back on, just as suddenly, she gasped.

"Fuck you, Miller." Jessie hissed, seething in anger. The little generator kicked in. Her skin began to tingle. Then nothing. The energy had nowhere to go. *It's the water.* "You're using water as an insulator?"

"Very good! You know, I'm learning that this soldier has quite the skill-set, but it was clear that science is not his strong suit. It sure is mine. I'm very proud of this tank."

"So, the water allows us to get closer?" she asked hoping to distract him from her guarded but careful visual sweep of the tank.

"It's not just water. I used pure, deionized water, circulated through filters below the tank. That's why you're not floating."

She spied a vent seated in the floor, ran a hand over it as casually as she could and felt the rush of water flowing in. On the opposite side of the tank, she spotted the outflow vent.

"Pure rubber tubing to secure your hands and feet, and polished stainless steel. No pollutants. On such short notice, it seemed the safest way to see you up close and personal," he said. *"It was all theory until I put you in there."* Matthew stepped right up to the tank and peered in at Jessie. His glowing red eyes intentionally wandered her nakedness. Jessie didn't flinch. Then he slapped the side of the tank, making her jump. *"I'll ask one last time, who do you work for and what do you want with me?"* He started circling the tank again.

Jessie had known for weeks exactly what she wanted from Matthew, but now that the tables had been turned, her former ideas evaporated from her mind. "Why didn't you just make contact if you wanted to talk? This is a bit overboard, don't you think?"

He stopped at the back of the tank, forcing her to turn and watch him. His eyes were riveted to hers this time. Jessie did not blink.

"Remember the restaurant?"

"How could I forget?"

"I'm not stupid, lady. I knew, well, the soldier knew he was being hunted." Matthew waved a dismissive hand at the tank. *"This situation is all on you. However, I'm starting to believe that our encounter at the restaurant may not have been as random as we both thought."* He returned to the spotlight and stood again at parade rest. *"At first, I chalked it up as dumb luck, but the more I learn about this ability we have, the more I believe in fate."*

Jessie felt inwardly satisfied that she got Matthew talking, at last. If she could just keep him talking long enough, the team would find her, provided the hydrogen-powered GPS implanted between the muscles of her forearm worked. Since the tiny transmitters utilized her body's nervous system as an antenna, she hoped that exposing her arm to the air would be enough. "Matthew," she said, "I know you were a victim. You and Kristi Sellers. No one knows better than me of how shocking the first time — I call it the slip-stream — must have been for you, but your rampage has got to stop."

"DOES IT?" he cried, clenching his fist to his sides and starting to pace. *"How can you even say that to me? Last chance, lady. Who do you work for and what do you want?"*

"My name is Jessie Richter. I work for a private military company called Crue Intellis. We specialize in the collection of intelligence, and I'm just like you."

"Just like me?" The deep rumble of his laugh sent a thread of fear trickling though her. Goosebumps rose on her skin.

"That's not what I mean. I . . ." She felt stupid and pathetic. So, she took a moment to regroup before she spoke again. She pressed her hands against the Lexan and leaned forward. "Before you came along, I didn't know there were others like me. Who can do the things we can do? You have to believe me. Until you came along, I thought I was the only one. I want you to come with me, Matthew. With us. Look, I'm not sure how we're going to work it out, but you need to learn to control the slip-stream. The group I work for can help you. You can have a new life, Matthew. But you can't have that life if you kill Jeffrey Cruz or leave any more bodies in ditches. So, I'm asking you to let him rot in a prison cell chained to a bed."

Matthew snapped his neck to the left, popping the vertebrae in his neck. *"That's a lot to ask, considering, well, you know, that he fucking killed me and all."* His voice had calmed. *"How did you learn about your ability?"*

"By accident."

"How?"

Jessie didn't hesitate to tell the story. "I was seventeen making love for the first time with my boyfriend and it just happened. Scared the shit out of me."

"How did you end up with a bunch of mercenaries, or whatever the fuck you are?"

"I was kind of like you are now," she said, relieved to keep him talking. "Scared of my ability and making bad, dangerous decisions that led to me getting badly beaten and almost raped. That's when I was rescued by my boss, the CEO of the company I work for."

"No need to be cryptic. That rescuer would be Jon Daly, CEO of Crue Intellis, right? Don't look so shocked. I hacked your phone. Well, I didn't have anyone to rescue me. I sat in my wheelchair like a lump of shit and watched Jeffery murder Kristi and couldn't do shit about it. But I can do something about it now, and you're asking me to stop? I'm not sure I should stop. I'm not sure I want to stop."

"Matthew, there is so much more you can do with your ability. It looks like you've already proven that. I'm not going to lecture you on revenge. I'm well versed . . ."

"So you've killed people, too," he interrupted.

"To save my own life, yes. Never as revenge. But I've done other things I'm not proud of. You can have a fresh start. We can give you the positive purpose you need. That's why I've come for you." Jessie hoped she didn't sound as desperate as she felt. She placed both hands on the wall of the tank and pleaded to him. "I want to help you. I swear I'm telling you the truth. Jon and the others with me, they agree. We want you to join us. We can learn from each other, we could . . ."

*"Do incredible things together? I bet we could, yes. Who knows what the two of us . . ?"*His voice trailed off for a moment as he walked back to the center of the spotlight and resumed standing at parade rest. *"What do you do for your company, Crue Intellis?"*

"I cannot tell you in detail. But I mostly gather intelligence on enemies of the United States, both domestic, and abroad."

Matthew chuckled. *"So, let me get this straight. You're a spy?"*

33

ENEMY REVEALED

STINSON FIELD
SAN ANTONIO, TEXAS

As soon as Jon received the call from Steve Walters, he packed up and flew the B-25 straight to San Antonio. Krys sat in the co-pilot seat, her eyes glued to the GPS tracking system. Jon had the unit custom built and retrofitted into the old plane's instrument panel. It even had the modern heads-up satellite display that allowed Krys to work on finding Jessie without having to talk about it. More than any other Crue member, Krys knew that Jessie's nervous system had more than enough power to keep the implant running for weeks. She glanced at Jon. He appeared so focused on the clouds outside, so deep in thought and worry, she kept her mouth shut, not wanting to add to the stress by talking about how the last time they had used the system was to find Jessie.

The tiny tube transmitters used a nitrogen powered battery activated by crushing the walls of the module. Once the battery turned on, the system relied on the body's natural bio-electrical nervous system to keep it going. It lasted a week in normal human beings, but the ampule in Jessie had still been active from her last mission for weeks. They hadn't thought to check it before travellitravelingng to San Antonio, and Krys knew Jon kicked himself for the oversight. So she remained silent, and searched.

Upon landing, Krys walked across the tarmac toward Randy and Melissa who were ready with an unmarked police car. She hugged the two detectives and looked back at Jon. He didn't even look their way. Instead, not able to hide his anger, he marched up the cargo ramp of the Crue's AC130 gunship. Randy started toward the plane, but Krys put a hand on his arm.

"Randy, you should stay here until you're called," she said, a worried look on her face. "They'll need your help later, but don't board the plane just yet. We would hate for there to be a conflict of interest."

Randy watched the ramp slowly rise off the ground, and Krys saw the goosebumps rise on his forearms, either from the high-pitched whine of the ramps motor, or his mind working overtime to guess what might happen in the cargo bay.

"Do you know how many cases I could have solved if I had been allowed to employ "questionable interrogation techniques?"

"Well," Krys said, then carefully added, "As much as I don't like it, Jon has proven to me time and time again that sometimes it's necessary."

"Right," Randy said, "but I get it." He reached down and unclipped his badge from his belt and stared at it. "Conflict of interest." He hopped up on the lid of a nearby fifty-gallon drum and heard what sounded like a terrified yelp from inside the plane. He shivered at the sounds coming from inside, and Krys reached out once more.

"You don't have to stay."

Randy looked at her and smiled. "No, ma'am. I'm going to do

what any good cop would do in this situation," he said. "I'll wait."

Krys took a deep breath, hugged him once more, and drove off with Melissa.

Jon walked past Chip without a word while Sean Parker closed the cargo ramp behind him. He marched straight up to Anna Chee, grabbed her by the face with both hands, and lifted her entire body out of the jump seat. The woman squealed in fear. He leaned in so close their noses almost touched. She stared back at him, the resolve in her eyes already starting to waiver. He turned her face to the right and left, examining her bone structure like some predatory animal sizing up its prey, and squeezed.

As a former Selous Scout from the long defunct Rhodesian Army, Jon was no stranger to torture, pain or death. It had been years since he had to perform or endure these up close and personal tasks. It surprised him how effortlessly it all came back, but thoughts of Jessie steeled his resolve. Jessie's uniqueness aside, she meant more to him than just being the Crue's most valuable intelligence asset. Every team member felt the same way about her. Jessie had hijacked their hearts as easily as she had hijacked the bodies of her targets. Once you were in Jessie Richter's sights, you had no hope of escape.

He held Anna by the face as the tears started to flow down her cheeks and thought about the first time he had met Jessie, how vulnerable he promised she would never become again. He squeezed harder, forcing another whimper from the girl. The violence caught Chip and Sean off-guard. They had never seen Jon this angry before, but they sat back, said nothing, and observed.

"Where is she?" he growled then ripped his hand from her

cheeks and dropped her back in the jump seat. "I'm only going to ask you once more," Jon said. His calm demeanor sent a visible shiver through the girl. "Where is she?" The girl shook but did not break with Jon's glare.

"I'm not sure. When I asked what he was planning, he told me it would be in my best interest if I didn't know."

Jon's hand struck so fast that Anna didn't have time to cry out again before he had grabbed her by the throat and begun to squeeze. Her eyes bulged. Her tears flowed. Her mascara streaked across her wet face as she groaned in agony.

"I don't know you, young lady, but I want you to look in my eyes." Anna tried, but couldn't meet Jon's intense stare. "I said, look at me!" Anna finally managed to lock eyes with him as she struggled to suck in air from under his grip. Jon felt the terror pulsing through her neck at 160 beats per minute. He pulled her face close to his. "Know this and believe it: I don't give two shits about your life. And the way I see it, your boyfriend used you as bait to capture her. So, he doesn't give a shit about you either."

The look in Anna's eyes shifted to concern and Jon relaxed his vice-like grip.

"That's not true," Anna rasped. "Do whatever you want. It doesn't matter. I already told you the truth."

Jon slapped her with his free hand. "I don't believe you."

Chip piped in. "Lady, as God is my witness, if Matthew hurts Jessie, *you* are going to pay for it."

"I don't know where they are. I had nothing to do with her."

"Bullshit," Chip added.

"You're in this up to your pretty little neck," Jon added.

"Jon," Chip said, "I think we need to find out how tough she is."

"You don't scare me, bilaga'ana," Anna spat. "I'm telling the truth. He said he only wanted to talk to her. He didn't say anything about kidnapping her. I'm telling the truth. I had no idea he was going to hurt her. If I knew, I would tell you because he promised . . ."

"Promised what?" Jon asked, letting go of her face.

"He promised to get help," Anna said, working her jaw.

"Help for who?" asked Jon.

"The lawyer and the other girls," Anna almost yelled. "I don't think he was lying to me when he said he was worried about them. But . . ." With her mascara-streaked eyes, she suddenly appeared to Jon as a fragile, frightened zebra. He leaned in once more. "Stop, please stop!" she whimpered, flinching from another strike that didn't come. "Aren't you listening to me? I'm telling you the truth! I told him I would do whatever it took to help him, but I didn't know he would hurt anyone."

"Bullshit," Chip said again. "You knew he had already killed at least two people."

"Two people who deserved it," Anna said, suddenly bold again.

"That wasn't his decision to make," Jon said.

"Wasn't it?" Anna shot back.

"Besides, Cruz killed Kristi," Chip said. "Those boys didn't do shit."

"They sure as hell didn't," Anna said. "They just stood there and watched. The way I was taught, cowards deserve to die. What about you?"

Chip had no response.

"Who's he working with?" Sean asked from the shadows of one of the plane's frame ribs. He had been quiet up until now. "Those guys in the video. They were dressed in grey battle dress uniforms and knew what they were doing."

Anna said nothing.

"This is bullshit, Jon," Chip snapped. "She's mad at her fucking boyfriend, but she won't tell us who he's working with?"

Jon tilted his head to the side and glared at Anna. As much as he wanted her to tell him what he needed to hear, he felt she was telling the truth. His satellite phone rang so he released Anna and stepped back. "What do you have, Steve?"

"We sent the kid's video clip to David. He enhanced it enough to figure out the truck was stolen from Budget Rental. Mario's running the image of the driver through the FBI's facial recognition database. It's pretty darn clear. The other men's faces were covered and too dark for the analytics to work, but the driver's face is good enough. All military personnel are in the database, so it's just a matter of time before we identify him."

"Great work. Any news on the GPS tracker?" Jon asked.

"No sir, not yet, but we'll find her. She's too smart."

Jon hoped like hell Steve was right.

"Email me the scanned images," Jon said. "His girlfriend isn't giving him up." After the image came in, it took a few minutes to upload due to the size of the hi-resolution enhancement. Jon filled the frame of his iPad with the image of the driver and presented it to Anna. "Is this your boyfriend?" Anna nodded.

Chip caught a glimpse of the screen. "Jon, can I see that?" Jon handed him the tablet. "No way. No fucking way. This is just insane." Jon and Sean looked on as the blood drained from his face. "I don't believe it."

"You know him?" Sean asked.

"You're damn right I do. His name is Brian Colter. He was my top Sergeant in Iraq and Afghanistan. He just retired last week, I think." Chip ran his fingers through his hair and sat in a jump seat. "Boy, do I have a story to tell you."

"Get Randy in here," Jon said just as his phone rang again. The caller ID showed the number for the local Command Center. Jon put the call on speaker. "Jon here. Please have something good to tell me."

"I got one ping, Jon," Krys said. "Off a cell tower up in Boerne, Texas. Then it died. I've captured a satellite image of the area and the tower is closest to a string of warehouses on Amman Road. She's somewhere in there, Jon, I'm sure of it. I've already submitted the request for a Reaper. They said they can have the drone airborne in two hours, on station in four."

"No, that's too much time. We'll be there long before it does. It's all-hands-on-deck time. Have Steve and Detective Santos head that way."

"They are on duty at the hospital," Krys said.

"Right," Randy interjected as he climbed up the ladder into the belly of the plane. "I'll get them relieved by a uniformed officer." Everyone, including Anna, glared at him. "Hey, it got quiet, so I guessed she had either talked or was dead." He pulled himself aboard and smiled. "Glad to see you talked, young lady, would have hated for your death to cause me to become a corrupt cop."

"You know the area?" Jon asked.

"Sure. There's a shooting range I go to not far from there. Lots of warehouses," Randy said. "Hold on." Randy retrieved his cell phone and dialed up his partner.

"What's up?" Mel asked.

"I need you to call in a uniform to relieve you, or even hospital security if they're not close. I'm texting you a map. You and Steve go north on Blanco Road, then turn left onto Amman Road. Keep an eye out for that white pickup truck. You guys would end up being on the only escape route from the east unless you know the backroads, and I'm betting Matthew doesn't know his way around that area."

"Copy that," Melissa said. "We'll be rolling shortly."

After texting the map, Randy slipped the phone into his belt clip and looked at Jon. "What's next?"

"Krys, we're rolling. Call if you get any change in the signal." Jon hung up and confronted Anna. "One last chance, young lady. We need to know which warehouse he's holding her in."

Anna shook her head and said, "I swear to you, I don't know. He never told me about a warehouse."

"She's a liar, Jon," Chip said.

"We'll find out. Load her up. She's coming with us." Jon pulled his sat-phone out of his flight bag and started dialing. When the line picked up, he said, "General Evans, I need a favor."

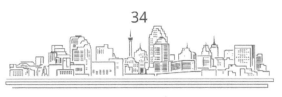

34

DOORS IN THE DESERT

Warehouse Row
Amman Road
Camp Bullis, Texas

J essie watched as Matthew sat on a blanket, straight-backed and crossed-legged in the center of the spotlight.

"C'mon now, Jessie. It's no time to be shy. You probably know more about me than I will ever know about you. It's time to share a little." He nodded at the dark shadows around him and laid his hands on his knees, palms up. "Tell me how you came to be a spy."

A soldier dressed in grey camo fatigues stepped into the light and handed Matthew a cylindrical speaker. Matthew examined the cylinder, pressed a button on the side which activated a bright, neon blue light that pierced the darkness. He placed it on the floor beside him, peeled off the headset and handed it to the waiting soldier who slid back into the shadows.

"Can you hear me?" Jessie nodded. "Say something," he said.

"I can hear you."

Matthew smiled and removed his t-shirt as two other soldiers drifted into the light like grey ghosts. One had a bowl, and the other carried half of a large clam shell with something in it. They placed the objects on the ground beside him. "Crue Intellis. Tell me about it. Don't lie and don't skip anything." He tapped the side of his nose with a finger. "I'll know if you do."

The soft beat of a drum crept into her hearing as an old Indian man walked into the circle wearing a red breechcloth, moccasins, and a thick headband with a single turkey feather sticking up from the front of it. His bare chest appeared to have glyphs that had been either tattooed or etched into his skin. At first, she thought it might be the old Navajo, Ben Chee. But no, this was a different man. The Indian dropped to both knees in front of the shell, pulled a knife from the waistband of his breechcloth, and struck a flint. Sparks flew into the shell, setting the contents aflame. He picked up the shell and blew lightly into the smoldering contents. The small bundle glowed, and thick smoke rose up into the darkness. He stood and started a slow stomp dance, stepping in time with the drum. He used a fan of feathers to spread the thickening smoke around Matthew.

"Don't mind him," Matthew said. "Go on. We don't have much time." He picked up the bowl and put it to his lips. With a grimace, he tilted the vessel back, chugged the contents, and looked as if he were about to wretch.

Jessie took a deep breath of compressed air and shivered at the sight before her. Matthew lifted a hand and rolled his index finger in front of him, coaxing her to speak. Jessie settled onto the floor of her tank as she searched her memory. "I was twenty years old and running my own Crossfit box, that's a gym, of sorts, and working nights at a restaurant when my sister showed up at my apartment door."

"Louder."

Jessie shrugged and continued. "Her boyfriend beat her so badly, her left eye swelled shut, the right shoulder dislocated, and he bruised her head to toe."

Matthew's head flopped forward and his hands twitched.

"Go on, I'm listening." His voice now sounded slurred, but he raised his head slowly and smiled.

Are his eyes glowing?

RANDY TURNED THE YUKON ONTO I-35 AND SPED NORTHWARD. Jon and Chip sat on each side of Anna in the back seat. Sean Parker rode shotgun and operated comms between them and the second Yukon containing Crue members Marc, Taina, and two others Randy didn't know. Everyone was armed to the teeth. Jon finished attaching his throat mic and pressed the transmitter button. "Marc, you on back there?"

"Yes sir, we're right behind you."

"Keep comms clear. Chip's got a story to tell."

"Go on, Chip, let's hear it," Jon said. Sean Parker placed a handheld unit on the seatback and keyed the mic.

"I'm telling you, this story is even stranger than what Jessie can do, that's why when I learned about her, it didn't shock me. Not one damn bit."

"So tell the story already," Parker said. "Everybody standby." Jon and those in his truck turned their radios off. Parker cycled the mic once more. "Go ahead," he said, and everyone in the Yukon gave Rasher their rapt attention.

Rasher closed his eyes, let his head fall back and thought a moment. Then he spun the tale.

"I'll never forget that day. It's so crystal clear in my mind, like it happened yesterday. But this was in 2006. It was dawn but still blistering hot at zero seven hundred hours. We were holed up in the Panjwai district of Kandahar, Afghanistan.

"My unit had been assigned as part of a joint US, Afghan and Canadian strike force called operation Medusa, and the Canadian's felt they had something to prove . . .

CAPTAIN RASHER POINTED TOWARD WHAT APPEARED TO BE THE sturdiest mud wall available and motioned for his machine gunner, Sergeant Brian Colter, to take up position. The sergeant silently cozied up to the cover and threw his weight against it to test the wall's crumble factor. He shrugged and leveled his M264 light machine gun at another, identical wall less than twenty-five meters across the street. Minutes prior, a handheld Raven drone confirmed dozens of Taliban insurgents lay in wait on the other side. From the short distance, Sgt. Colter looked over at his captain, pushed a button on his throat transmitter, and whispered, "Mike 1, in position."

"Tango-Lima-1 to Raven-1," Rasher whispered into his mic.

"Raven-1, targets confirmed, they are directly across from you Cap'n," the drone operator said with an eerie calm to his voice, "and more are crawling into position."

Rasher nodded and turned to look at Colter, then keyed his mic. "Whenever you're ready, Sarge, cut loose."

Colter let out a long, slow breath as he increased pressure on the trigger. The absolute silence was wrecked by the mechanical dragon being unleashed at the enemy. Despite earplugs, the sound was deafening. Colter moved the front site of the gun back and forth along the lower part of the enemy wall. Chunks of mud ripped away, and the rest of his fire-team joined in.

The enemy combatants behind the wall across the wide street did not turn and run. They fought back with ferocity and confidence, firing their AK-47's over, around and through the holes the sergeant had just created for them. In turn, 7.62 rounds pierced Colter's mud wall and grazed the top of his shoulder and helmet.

"Goddammit!" Colter yelled as he thumbed his throat mic. "Captain, I'm moving, my cover is turning to shit."

Captain Rasher gave Colter the thumbs up and looked

through the growing hole in his own wall. He pointed to another building twenty meters to the right with the three Afghan National soldiers fighting behind it.

Rasher keyed his mic, "That location seems to be holding up," he yelled over the gunfire. "Can you get there and cover us? We'll follow." Colter nodded, bundled up the machine gun, and prepared to sprint. "Lay down cover for the Sarge," Rasher said over comms. "Now!"

Colter dashed out and kept low as friendly rounds whistled over his head and enemy rounds skittered in the dirt at his feet. At the halfway point, about twenty-five yards out, directly between the enemy and safety, Colter stopped dead in his tracks and stood up straight.

Rasher noticed this and involuntarily stood upright himself. "Colter? What the fuck are you doing?"

One bullet whizzed by Rasher's head and another ripped through the sleeve of his uniform. He raised his arm to look at the streak of blood, then ducked down into the rubble at his feet, keeping his eye on Colter. His eyes went wide as enemy bullets that should have cut the man to pieces were instead being absorbed into some sort of energy field surrounding him.

The machine gun slid off Colter's shoulder into the dirt.

Rasher watched helplessly as his best soldier dragged his feet through the yellowish dirt toward the enemy.

"Colter! What the fuck are you doing? Colter! Are you hit? Goddammit man, MOVE, MOVE! MOVE!" Rasher directed the others in his team to concentrate even more fire at the Taliban who now took pot-shots at the sergeant. "Fuck this," Rasher said as he peeled off his ruck. He tapped the helmet of the Corporal crouched next to him. "Jammer, let's go get him."

The Corporal acknowledged his Captain by slipping out of his ruck and looking through a smaller hole in the wall. "Cap'n, what's wrong with the Sarge?"

"I don't have a fucking clue, but are we letting him stay out there?"

"No way, sir. Let's go!"

Both men loaded fresh magazines into their M4 carbines and did a final check of the mags on their battle-belts. They looked to the confused faces of several other men, Afghan nationals included. "Cover us with everything you got," Rasher said. The men nodded in unison, raised their weapons over the wall, and fired.

Rasher placed a hand on Jammer's shoulder and both men locked eyes. "On three, two, one."

The two men sprinted into the open and zigzagged toward Colter. The air around them sang as rounds whistled past going in both directions. As they closed in, Rasher saw the sergeant reach out and grab a thick piece of rope suspended in thin air. They rushed in to rescue him but slammed into an invisible wall so hard that they were thrown backwards to the ground. Dazed and confused, both men attempted to sit up, but froze when a large wooden door formed up around the rope Colter still clung to. The now full-sized door floated about a foot above the ground. All weapons fire stopped. Even the Taliban fighters couldn't resist standing up and pointing toward the American and the door.

Rasher sat up on his knees and reached out to the invisible wall. Pain shot into his hand and sparks leapt from the barrier. "COLTER! Brian Colter!" Rasher yelled. He was close enough to see Colter's head flopped to one side and drool edge out his mouth onto his shoulder. Oblivious to the battle around him, the sergeant tugged at the rope and pushed the door forward.

"What the . . ." Rasher rubbed his eyes and focused on what appeared to be the interior of some sort of dwelling. There was a rough-hewn wooden table in the middle of the room, an antique wood stove in one corner, and a handwoven rug hanging on the far wall.

"Looks like an Indian hut of some kind, from the Old West," Jammer said.

The entire street of soldiers from both sides gawked as the Sergeant stepped into the phantom room and pushed the wood door closed behind him. The latch clicked so loudly that everyone watching flinched as the door and Sergeant Brian Colter evaporated into the hot, acrid air.

PARKER SAID, "YOU ALL HEAR THAT?" AND RELEASED THE MIC button.

"That's one incredible story," Taina Volkov's voice said over the radio. *"Crazy."*

"And you never saw him again?" Anna asked, her eyes wide at Rasher's story.

"We did. Some little kid found him four hours later, lying face down in the middle of the street right where he disappeared. Lucky for Colter, that was well after the Taliban and NATO forces moved on. They notified me that he was transported to the medical tent. Other than a fresh bite mark on his left hand– looked to be from a child– he didn't have a scratch on him and had no recollection of the incident.

"Did you report it?" Jon asked.

"Absolutely. Along with about thirty other American, Canadian, and Afghan soldiers. They debriefed Colter for a couple of days, but never spoke to him about it after that. The whole incident ended up buried by the higher ups. We were given the code of silence threat, and honestly, until now, I haven't thought about it in years." Everyone in the truck went silent, their eyes fixed on either Rasher, or the photo in his hand.

"This is incredible. Impossibly incredible."

Everyone turned to look at their would-be prisoner, Anna Chee.

"I'm not saying you're lying. I'm saying it's impossible," Anna said.

"What is it?" Parker asked Anna.

"That's the same story my great-grandpa told us as children," Anna said. "But his tale was from the inside of the hogan. That's what we call the kind of homes we used to live in. They're round-shaped." Anna squirmed in her seat due to her hands being cuffed behind her back.

"It's the other part of his story," she said, pointing her chin toward Chip. "The way great-grandpa told it, he was just a small boy when a soldier from another time and place came through the door of his family hogan. The soldier was covered in sand and a battle was being fought outside until the door closed. He said the soldier protected him while two white boys raped and killed his sister, my great aunt Abigail. My great-grandpa bit the soldier on the left hand."

She took a deep breath and looked into Chip's eyes. "Oh my god," Anna said, "That would mean —"

"Matthew traveled back in time, and somehow slip-streamed into Brian on the battlefield," Jon said. "It's too close to your stories to have any other explanation."

"I wonder why the old man didn't say anything about Colter when we visited him? He told us all about Matthew, but not the soldier he occupied," Parker said.

"Because he was trying to help Matthew," Anna said. "Had he known that Matthew would kill your friend, I'm sure he would have told you everything."

"How can this be? If Matthew's in Brian Colter's body now?" Chip added. "I mean, I was there, and I'm totally onboard with Jessie's ability, but this is crazy."

"I'm not even sure Jessie has a total understanding of what she can do and why she can do it. We can't discount the possibility Matthew can do even more, which just adds to the problem," Jon said.

"How did this happen?" Randy asked. "This visit Matthew made to Brian's past?"

Anna frowned at the question. "I wasn't there for any of it. They wouldn't allow me to attend."

"Attend what?" Jon asked.

"My grandfather and the tribal medicine men, they call them the Hata'li, performed a ceremony on Matthew. It's called the 'Enemy Way.' It's supposed to chase off demons and evil spirits attached to a person. I asked Matthew about it. He told me about a dream battle in Afghanistan and how he saw the hogan appear in front of him. He walked to it, pulled open the wooden door, and went inside where he witnessed the murder of Grandpa's sister, Abigail through Brian's eyes. I figured the drugs they use for the ceremony gave him a more vivid visualization of grandpa's story . . ."

She turned slowly, her eyes fixed on Chip.

"But with what he saw ten years ago, Matthew wasn't telling grandpa's story, it's his own," she concluded.

"So why Jessie? Well, I know why, but why this way?" Randy asked.

"That's not fair," Anna said boldly. "You should have seen the look on his face when he first encountered Jessie on the River-walk. I didn't see a big, bad soldier. I saw a terrified boy. I don't agree with the way he did it, but that's kind of on you."

"From an outsider view," Randy interjected, "I don't see how this is the Crue Intellis's or Jessie's fault. Your boyfriend has already killed three people, and others are in comas. He's far from innocent."

Anna leaned back. "Yes, he has, and I don't like it either, but there's not a law on the books that prohibits a dead man to come back and avenge his murder. We've checked."

"Okay, enough," Jon said. "Points taken on all sides. My only interest right now is to keep Jessie from becoming one of those casualties." He turned to Anna. "He has her because he knows she can do the same thing, but what does he want? According to Jessie, they can't be in the same room together."

Anna shook her head. "He only said he needed to talk to her. About what he calls the Slip."

"That's what Jessie calls it. Slip-streaming. She slips in and streams her consciousness through the body of the host."

Anna didn't respond, but spoke slowly, "Actually, he seemed excited about meeting her. I think that part was genuine. He also promised no violence. I would not have gone along with any of this otherwise."

"Excited? Why?" Sean Parker asked.

"After two days with the Hata'li, he told me he learned something new and exciting about his gift, and he had much more to learn. When he came down from the high-plains desert — the Hata'li have a secret long-house hidden in the mountains up there — something about him seemed different. When I first discovered who Matthew really was, I saw him as an angry, frightened boy, so focused on revenge. Rightfully so in my eyes. But when he returned, he had changed."

"Turned even more violent," Chip said, "adding kidnapping to his murder resume."

"Not even close," Anna said, looking offended. "He told me he might have a way to help the lawyer and girls. To connect with them, maybe even release them."

"Funny way of showing he wanted to help," Chip replied. "He killed my pal and took Jessie by force."

Anna looked at them all a long moment. "I'm really sorry for that. I swear to the Haashch'ééh, I had no idea he planned any of this. But you have to believe me, your girl will be fine. I'm certain he won't hurt her."

"How can you be so sure?" Jon asked.

"He's found someone he can relate to. Someone just like him. He needs her."

35

ANSWERS

AMMAN WAREHOUSE
BOERNE, TEXAS

J essie hadn't thought about the retribution against her sister's ex-boyfriend for years. Drawing the memory out from its locked away place made her shudder.

"Any day now, Miss Richter. Time is ticking," Matthew said, the beat of the drum steady.

Jessie sensed that, somehow, her story followed along with the beat of the drum being struck by men barely discernible in the shadows just outside Matthew's circle of light. As the men continued chanting in their ancient dialect, the old man leaned in from the darkness and blew smoke on Matthew. Jessie drifted off . . .

SHE FOUND HERSELF STANDING AT B & T BANK IN MYRTLE Beach, South Carolina. She looked at her hands first, then at the reflection in the window where the eyes of Terry Hoffman were looking back at her.

You can do this, she thought. *Terry is a class 1-A asshole and disrespectful to women. I have to be the asshole.*

She pulled the door open, marched up to the counter, placed her folded up Crossfit Myrtle Beach duffle bag on the counter, and slid Terry's ID across to the teller. Jessie adjusted the sunglasses she wore, hoping the teller couldn't see the glowing red eyes behind the lenses.

"Can I help you, Mr. Strong?" the teller asked.

"Yes, you can. I'd like to make a withdrawal," Jessie said.

"I'd be happy to assist." The teller fetched a slip of paper and handed it to Jessie. "Would you please fill out the withdrawal slip?"

Jessie felt her face turn red. Then she recovered herself. "I need an account balance, too. Checking and savings."

The woman punched keys on a computer then jotted numbers down on a small piece of paper and slid it, along with Terry's ID, back to Jessie. Jessie's brows furrowed in disappointment. The numbers written on the paper read $4,356.04, in checking and 35,000.00 in the savings account. Less than forty grand.

What the fuck? Is that all?

She started to second-guess if her efforts were worth the trouble.

"I'd like to withdraw it all." Terry's voice cracked nervously.

The teller raised an eyebrow. "So, you want to close your account?"

Jessie thought about this a moment and looked at the slip. "No, don't close it. Leave the six bucks and four cents. Please."

The teller called the manager.

"Is there a problem, Mr. Hoffman?"

Jessie thought the manager looked pretty smug as he approached, a look that suggested he might refuse her request.

"No, there's no problem, I just want my cash," she said.

The manager huffed, then rolled his eyes and looked down

his nose at Jessie. "State law is that you must fill out the proper IRS form for any cash withdraw of over ten thousand dollars."

Jessie looked at Terry's watch and decided it was time for Terry to help out with this situation. "Listen," she read his name-tag, "Dan. I don't give a fuck what has to be filled out, just do what you gotta do. Get me my cash now and stop wasting my fucking time."

The blood drained from the manger's face. "Yes, sir, Mr. Hoffman, right away." He nodded to the cashier and dropped his voice to a more acceptable tone. "Sir, it's just that you've been banking with us for years and this is the first time you've withdrawn such a large amount of cash. Ever."

Jessie seethed with annoyance. She didn't have a lot of time and needed to get this done and get back to her own body.

"I don't understand why you're stalling," Jessie said.

"I'm just concerned —"

"I don't care about your concerns. Mind your own business. How long will this take?"

"Shouldn't take more than thirty minutes, Mr. Hoffman."

Then Jessie remembered something, felt her pockets, and pulled out a set of keys. "While you're doing admin, I'd like to go to my safety deposit box."

"Yes, sir, right this way."

Jessie entered the vault room and waited for the manager to use his bank key in concert with the key in Jessie's hand to pull out one of the largest drawers in the wall. "Fuck this is heavy," she groaned. "Very heavy." She hoisted the box onto the steel table, unlocked the lid, and opened it.

"Hole-ee-shit-ski," she hissed, and then opened her duffle.

Within thirty minutes, Jessie pulled into the parking lot of her Crossfit box. She looked around for nosey neighbors, rushed inside, and stuffed the duffle bag into the far recess of a closet in her tiny office.

On the drive back to Terry's house, she felt the power crank up over the mixed emotions of exhilaration and terror as they flowed through her at the same time. She felt so amped up that even from this distance, she felt sure she could slip back into her own body right now. She had never stolen anything in her life, and she had never seen so much money. She entered the beach house and knelt beside her own half-naked body lying on the floor of his living room. She shivered at the sight of herself, then picked up her limp body and tried to remember how she and Terry were standing before she hijacked his body. A wave of guilt crashed into her. The rapey aspect of doing herself while in the body of a man she despised not only felt wrong, it wasn't working. It would come. It had to come.

She called the police, still searching for the spark she needed to activate the little generator that had gotten her into Terry's body in the first place. Within minutes, the police arrived and the panic set in . . .

Matthew's voice pulled Jessie out of her memory. She gasped at the realism of the recollection, to the point of even feeling the echoes of pain lingering, radiating in places Terry Hoffman had bruised and beat her some ten years prior. A first for her, she had never had such a vibrant recollection before. "What the fuck *was* that?"

Matthew smiled and spoke to the old Indian in a language she didn't understand. The Indian looked at Jessie and nodded. "So, you shifted into your sister's boyfriend and stole his money. How much again?"

"About a hundred and fifty thousand dollars," she said.

"That's a lot of dough," Matthew replied.

"Yeah, I suppose." Jessie decided not to share how she could have had more or how most of it ended up going to her abused sister.

"But you got caught."

His voice whispered in her ear. The energy from Matthew's eyes cut through the space between them and raised goosebumps on her naked flesh.

"Yes, I got caught. But not until a couple of days after I took the money. When he figured out what I had done."

"You were beaten and almost raped." Matthew's hands and upper body were trembling. The drumbeat picked up in tempo and volume. "Because you panicked and shifted back too soon." Matthew seemed to be having difficulty speaking now.

"You call it shifting?" Jessie said. "I call it slip-streaming."

"Slip-streaming." Matthew's chuckle sounded forced. "I like that better." He coughed violently. "Was it worth it?" His question sounded rushed, and his molten red eyes glowed even brighter.

"I underestimated him and paid the price. But yes. To protect my sister, it was worth every painful minute."

Jessie's brow furrowed and she would have gasped, if not hindered by the full faced scuba mask, as she watched Matthew's entire body start to vibrate. His voice, too. Like he just stuck a metal fork into an electrical socket.

"I'll try to remember not to make the same mistake," he said. An unearthly groan emanated from him, making Jessie shudder again.

"I think we're going to have to take a rain check on how you became a spy." His head fell back, and he growled in pain with each deep breath. "And one more thing . . . I'm sorry about your teammate, the driver of the van, I didn't intend to kill him."

"Eric?" she whispered, caught completely off guard by the revelation. "He's dead?"

Jessie put both hands on the wall of the tank and watched as the soldier Matthew occupied convulsed so hard it appeared as if his actual body, not just his consciousness, was slip-streaming, fading in an out like something from a sci-fi movie. "I'm . . . sorry," Matthew said.

"NO! You motherfucker! No!" Jessie screamed into the mask. The electricity flooded from her skin and began to heat the water around her. Her fists, slowed by the mass of liquid, could only pound softly on the walls of the tank. Her tears flowed. Rage surged. But her lightning remained stymied by the water.

The drumbeat quickened. The chanting grew louder. The old Indian dancer blew more smoke into Matthew's face. Then another sound, not part of the music, reached Jessie. It took a moment for Jessie to identify the low hum and a familiar thwack-thwack-thwack of a helicopter that began to vibrate through the water and into her body. Jessie dug deep and found a new source of power. Sparks shot from the motors pumping air into her mask as the water around her began to boil. She willed the power inside her to escape the confines of the tank: she directed her life force straight at Matthew.

The walls of the tank shook and Matthew froze. His eyes rolled back into his head and his face contorted with pain. He screamed and fell back into the old man's arms. The Indian quickly pulled a long, stone pipe from his waistband, took a deep draw from the mouthpiece, and breathed this white colored smoke into Matthew's face right before a full-size military Humvee careened through the sliding doors of the warehouse. Jessie screamed. Matthew's eyes went wide, and the drone of the helicopter drowned out the beat of the drums.

Chip and three Army Rangers bailed out of the Humvee and leveled their M4 carbines at Matthew, the Old Man, and the drummers. Sean and three more Rangers slid down ropes hung from the unseen chopper and immediately split up to sweep the warehouse. Jon, Randy, and three other Crue members arrived just in time to witness Jessie's water tank explode.

Jessie howled with rage as she spilled out onto the concrete floor like an escaped eel.

"Ya' 'at 'eeh, Jessie Richter," Matthew said, his voice a loud moan. Jessie grabbed his foot and clawed her way up his body to his throat. She gasped at the realization she felt no illness, felt no counter-power, and then she knew. She was too late: Matthew was gone.

JESSIE, WEARING NOTHING BUT AN OVERSIZED BDU SHIRT, STARED at the unconscious form of Brian Colter, lying on a gurney near the warehouse doors. Anna stared at him, too, but Randy kept her handcuffed to the big Hummer. Chip, beside the gurney, had his carbine slung over his shoulder, letting Sean keep Colter in his sites. Jon stepped up to Jessie and put his arms around her shoulders. "He's gone, Jon," she whispered, just loud enough to hear.

"What do you mean?" Jon asked.

"I don't feel his presence."

"His presence? He's right there," Chip said.

"That's not —" A raspy inhale from Colter cut Jessie off. The soldier instinctively started to pull at his restraints.

"See," Chip said, holding him down, "He's still —"

"Major Rasher? Is that you?" Brian asked.

Chip's mouth fell open, but after a quick glance at Jessie, he said, "Yeah, Colter, it's me."

"Where am I? Why am I strapped down?" Fear did not etch the battle proven soldier's face, his being restrained did not make him a happy camper.

Randy stepped to the other side of the gurney and said, "Relax, Brian. I'm Detective D'Agostino, San Antonio Police. We're pressed for time here, and we need your help."

"Where the hell am I?" He pointed at the soldiers guarding key points in the building. "Who are they?" At a sign from Jon, Melissa let Anna out of the Hummer. But when she rushed to Brian's side, he didn't even glance her way.

"We'll tell you everything, I promise," Chip said.

"But right now," Randy cut in, "we really need to know what's the last thing you remember?"

Brian closed his eyes.

"Colter, stay with us!" Chip ordered.

"I'm not going anywhere. I'm trying to remember. It's like I've been locked in a dream or something. I remember being at my retirement party and getting really drunk. And then . . . I'm not sure if I was dreaming or what, it's all so foggy. Can I have some water?"

The medic lifted a canteen to Colter's lips. After a quick sip, despite his promise, Brian passed out again.

"What do you think?" Jon asked, keeping a close eye on Jessie who appeared to be in a trance.

"Matthew told me that Eric . . . Eric was . . ." Tears filled her eyes, Jessie couldn't ask the question.

"No, Jessie. I'm sorry. Eric is gone," Jon said. "You didn't know?"

"No. I blacked out when the truck hit the van."

"I'm sorry, Jessie," Jon said again.

She crossed her arms to stop herself from wiping away the tears rolling down her cheeks. "It's okay. I hoped he was lying, but I guess I knew deep down he was telling the truth because he apologized."

"Matthew apologized?" Jon asked. "What for? Why?"

"For killing Eric. He said he didn't mean for Eric to die. That was right before — Oh shit!"

"Right before what?" Randy asked.

But Jessie's eyes were lit by a private epiphany. "Oh, my God, who's at the hospital?"

36

NOT TODAY

METHODIST HOSPITAL
SAN ANTONIO, TEXAS

The security guard closed her book and sat up straight in her seat at the sound of alarms going off inside the hospital room. The instant she cracked open the door to peer in, all went quiet. She stepped in and inspected the monitors of the four comatose bodies; two men chained to beds and two women who were not.

She didn't know a thing about the monitors, but it looked obvious to her that the vital signs were all in sync. Listening to the perfect syncopation of the beeps, she shuddered at the speculation as to why. She shook her head and pulled the door closed behind her. The moment the door latch clicked, all of the alarms went off again.

She slowly pushed the door open, leaned into the room, and gasped at the four bodies convulsing and gyrating in their beds. Tiny sparks were dancing and popping on the murderer Cruz's body. Arcs of electricity shot off the handcuffs and crawled along the metal handrails.

"Holy mother!" she shrieked, crossing herself as she leaned

back out the door and looked down the hallway. Not seeing anyone, she yelled down the hall. "Duty Nurse! You need to get down here!" She heard no response and looked back just in time to see the lightning race into the little blonde girl. She stepped into the room, pulled out the push to talk cellphone given to her by one of the men who had previously stood guard before she arrived. She pressed the button for Detective D'Agostino.

"D'Agostino, go ahead."

As instructed, the guard pressed the button and waited a full second before speaking, and wishing she had more instructions, she tried to keep her anxiety under control. "Hey Detective, it's the guard from the hospital. Donna. Donna Prinz. Something weird is going on."

"Chip, who's at the hospital watching Cruz and the others?" Jessie asked.

"A hospital security guard. Said her name was Donna. I gave her my EPTT phone since Sean has his."

"Randy, you've gotta call someone to get there now."

Randy's phone beeped loudly. "It's Chip's phone. She's using the radio." He pressed the green button, then held the phone up for everyone to hear.

"Detective, something's wrong, you gotta, oh my God . . ." Terror laced the woman's voice.

"Donna, slow down. What's happening at the hospital?"

"I'm not sure. I heard an alarm, and all the bodies are shaking like they are plugged into an electrical socket. Wait, they just stopped."

"She's holding down the mic button," Sean said. They all heard another alarm go off in the background.

"Now it's just that Cruz guy. I think he's having a seizure, and I mean he looks like he's going to break his back." She finally let go of the mic button.

"Donna, I need you to stay calm. Let go of the green button after you talk. You copy?"

"Yes, sir, sorry, I'm okay. Oh, my God."

"Did you call the nurse?" Randy asked.

"Yes, but I think she's on rounds . . . wait." Listening to the panic in the woman's voice, Jessie shook her head. *"Cruz's body just stopped. Holy shit, some electrical bolt or something just jumped from Cruz to that lawyer, and now his body is shaking. Now the dark-haired woman. Oh my god . . . the nurse is coming, she's almost here."*

"She needs to get out of there," Jessie said.

Randy pressed the transmit button and said, "Donna, get out of the room. Secure the door and wait for help. Uniformed officers are on the way."

"Wait, now it's in the little blonde girl. Nurse! Come quick!"

"NO!" Randy yelled. "Get out! Have the nurse lock the door!"

"Hey, it's okay. It looks like one of the girls is awake."

The radio went silent.

ROSIE VASQUEZ'S EYES SHOT OPEN. SHE GRIPPED THE BEDRAIL, groaning as she sat up. Groggy and confused, she looked around the room gripped by confusion. Her eyes wandered to the wide-eyed, mouth-agape female security guard.

"Where am I? What happened?" She moved slowly to get out of the bed. The guard rushed to her bedside, pulled the bedrail down and retrieved the radio from her pocket. She fumbled with the transmit button, then said, "Detective? Are you there? One of the females is awake, talking. Do you want to talk to her?"

"Donna listen . . ." Randy said, but the guard cut him off.

"I think they are coming around, Detective,"

Rosie stood on wobbly feet and looked at the blonde girl in the bed next to her. Suddenly, both the guard and Rosie screamed as threads of electrical energy sprang from the blonde girl, arcing off the bedrails as her body convulsed and bounced violently off the mattress.

"Sara, oh, my God, poor baby, what has happened? Officer, what's going on?" Rosie said, and reached out to touch the younger girl's hand. As soon as she did, the girl's body stilled.

"Donna, don't touch them. Get out of the room, now," Randy said, his electronic voice breaking up from yelling into the mic.

Rosie moved to the side of the bed and bent over the girl she called Sara, kissing her lightly on the lips. "Please help her. Call the nurse. Help her, please, please . . ."

Donna ran to the door and waved for the nurse coming around the corner to hurry.

The nurse called out as she approached. "I've called Doctor Bishop! He's on his way."

"Okay, Detective. Sorry for the scare. It seems to be good now. The nurse . . ." then nothing.

Pow! Pow! Pow!

That sounded like gunshots? Am I dreaming?

The report and concussion of gunfire forced Donna's eyes open. A blurry figure, Donna saw the young blonde standing up on the bed of Jeffrey Cruz, screaming wildly in a fit of rage. And she was pointing a gun . . . *wait just a minute.* Donna struggled through the throbbing in her head to move her hand to her holster. She fingered the empty hole where her duty weapon should have been. *Oh damn.* The gun went off three more times before Donna slipped back into darkness.

OVER AN HOUR LATER, UNIFORMED POLICE OFFICERS STOOD IN THE hospital room, now only containing three patients. Randy, his partner Melissa, Jon, and Jessie were also present, doing their best to handle the aftermath.

"I don't remember being struck," the guard, Donna said. She held an ice pack to the side of her head and groaned. "And I can't believe what I just saw, and I can't believe the bitch stole my gun."

You're lucky Miller didn't shoot you with it, dumbass, Randy thought, but only said, "At least no one got hurt." He patted Donna sympathetically on the shoulder and crammed himself into the security office alongside Doctor Bishop, Melissa, Jon, and Jessie. They were all watching the hospital security director impatiently as he manipulated the controls of the security cameras. Jessie stuck her hand out behind the man's back and rolled her finger in the air.

"Ah, here we go," he said, finally managing to queue up an image of Donna outside the door just before the alarm went off the second time. "Yeah. This is where it starts. No audio. Sorry." He pushed play and in the background of the wide-angle video, EEG lights began to blink and bodies went into convulsions, one after the other.

"Jessie, do you know how he's doing that?" Jon asked.

"Negative. I'm at a total loss," Jessie replied. Her brows furrowed on her darkened face, arms folded across her chest. These were the first words she had spoken since leaving the warehouse.

"We were so close," Randy said.

"Yeah, and I don't have a clue what to do next," Jessie sighed.

"I'm still blown away that this is even possible, even knowing what you and Matthew can do," Doctor Bishop added.

The video continued to roll. Rosie woke up and kissed Jane Doe.

"Did Vasquez identify Jane Doe?" Jon asked.

"Yes," Randy answered. "Vasquez is alert and cooperative. Jane Doe is her ex. Sara Stephens."

In the video, Sara sprang from the bed like a jack-in-the-box, roughly shoved Rosie aside, and snatched up the metal IV bar. She glided forward, bringing the steel rod back like a baseball bat. They all stared slack-jawed as Sara rushed forward and struck Donna in the side of the head. Vasquez scrambled toward her former lover in an obvious attempt to stop her attack. She was rewarded with a swift elbow to the face that knocked her out. The blonde squatted beside Donna, expertly defeated the safety locks on her holster and belt, pulled out Donna's pistol, and stole her handcuffs.

"Look at that," Jon said. The gun went straight up into what's called the Sul position, ready to press out and fire from the chest. The blonde did a quick assessment for others in the immediate hallway, then marched over to Rosie, seized her by the hair, and dragged her to the nearest bed. It only took her seconds to handcuff Rosie to the rail. Sara laid the pistol down on Cruz's chest and climbed onto his bed before picking the Glock 9mm back up and leveling it at his head.

Melissa pointed to the bottom of the screen. "Wait. Look at Rosie."

Rosie came around and desperately tried to pull off the cuffs. She looked as if she were screaming at Sara as she pointed at Cruz. Even without the audio, it was obvious that Rosie begged Sara not to shoot.

Behind Randy, Jessie twitched with impatience and then forced herself to be still. She watched, stoic and silent, as Sara gripped the gun with both hands and fired one round.

Sara paused a moment, as if struggling with a decision, before firing six more rounds into the pillow around the head of Matthew Miller's killer. She leapt from the bed, landing in a Spider-Man-like crouch, then stepped over the unconscious security guard. When she entered the hallway, the nurse, on her cellphone, came into view. Sara ignored her and slipped out the emergency exit on the opposite side of the hall. The video cut out for a second, then picked her up again on the loading dock of the hospital, now dressed in a hospital gown but still armed with Donna's duty pistol.

"She covered her exit with the tactical precision of a professional soldier," Jon said and wrapped a consoling arm around a stiff and visibly angry Jessie Richter.

"She might look like a stripper, but she handles the gun like a pro," Melissa said.

"He learns from his hosts," Jessie said. "He's chosen her for a reason. I'm sure we'll learn why soon enough."

Randy watched the hospital security director click through more surveillance videos until he found one that showed Sara slipping between the trash compactors and bending down out of view. A moment later, the hospital gown floated into the bin and Sara Stephens emerged wearing a tank top, jeans, sneakers, a ball cap and dark glasses. She slung a backpack over her shoulder and tossed the Glock into the dumpster.

"He planned this well," Randy said. "We'll need to review the tapes from when Cruz and White were initially transferred here. Think he was in Colter?"

"I'm sure of it," Jessie replied.

They continued to watch the video as Sara reached into the backpack, pulled out a set of car keys, and in a surprise move, turned to face the camera and walked toward it where she could be clearly seen. She reached into the back-pack, pulled out a cardboard sign and unfolded it. Jessie gasped. The sign read "See you soon, Jessie." Then, suddenly, Sara made a quick, quarter turn and looked off into the distance for a full ten seconds while folding up the sign, stuffing it back in the pack.

"Something got his attention," Jessie said.

"We'll look at the other cameras when we're done," the video op said. Then, slowly, Sara turned to the camera once again. The whites of Sara's teeth glowed from the shadow of the ball cap's bill. She grinned, flipped off the camera, and walked off into the streets of San Antonio.

"Imagine that," Jon said.

"Mel," Randy said, "would you ask CSI to get out there and retrieve Donna's duty weapon? Have them process it for prints and get it back to Donna. We don't need to take it tonight. We need to focus on finding everything we can on Sara Stephens." He turned to face Jessie, and for the first time since he had met her, Jessie's face had a defeated look. "We're not done yet," he said. "We'll track Anna and Rosie's movements. And we will find Sara Stephens. We're all over this, Jessie, we'll find him." Given what he had just witnessed on the video, Randy was not sure he believed his own words. He saw doubt in Jessie's eyes, too.

Jessie and Randy locked eyes. He wasn't fooling her one bit, certain he looked as frustrated and defeated as Jessie. She turned to her boss.

"Jon, he's taken slip-streaming to a level I didn't know was possible. I hate to repeat myself, but I don't have a clue how he does it, and I don't know what to do next."

"I just think he's a fast learner," Jon replied, though deep in thought. "Reminds me of someone else I know."

"It's not the same."

"It's exactly the same. Have you forgotten? Don't you remember the time a suspect told me an unbelievable story of how a twenty-one-year-old young woman had cast a spell on him? When that physically- and emotionally- battered woman accepted my offer of help, I had no idea of what I was getting into, either. Look at you now, ten years later. You have done things no one would have believed possible. Because *you*, Jessie Richter, are an impossibility." Resting his hands on her shoulders, Jon looked deep into her eyes. "I know you, Jessie. Don't beat yourself up over this. We've learned a lot today."

Tears welled up in Jessie's eyes. "Now we have another

impossibility on the loose. He doesn't need to physically touch someone to shift. Incredible."

"As much as I want to put a bullet in him," Jon said, "he was thrust into a situation worse than anything any of us could imagine, you included. Remember, he's still only an eighteen-year-old boy. Your pursuit forced him to slow down and think. The positive side is he listened to you. I think you're underestimating your influence on him. He could have killed Cruz. He could have killed you, but he didn't."

Jessie blinked out a single tear, a familiar hardness returning to her jawline. "But he did kill Eric, and he needs to pay for that."

"Look at me, Jess," John said. Through his palms, he could feel anger and hate welling up inside his protégé. "You said Matthew didn't intend to kill him. That doesn't make it any easier, perhaps it's Matthew's way of trying to tell us all that he's not a cold-blooded killer."

"I'm not giving up on looking for him. He's going to pay," Jessie said, as if she hadn't heard a word her boss just said. "He kidnapped me. He killed Eric. That makes him the enemy."

"Let's not forget that you were prepared to do all of that to him as well, and he knew it."

"I don't care, Jon. I'm going to find him, and he's going to pay."

Jon didn't press the issue. He knew that Jessie needed to cool off and grieve. "Correct me if I'm wrong, but what Matthew can do . . . he must have learned it from someone, right?" Jon was talking about the old Navajo, Ben Chee. An understanding look traveled from Jon to Jessie to Randy and back to her. "Well, you're going to convince that person to teach you." Jessie nodded. "Randy, Mel? I know you don't work for us, but I really feel you guys are part of the team, now. We're going to pack up the Cypress Tower command center, but I'm going to arrange for you both to have direct comms to our home base."

"What if more coma victims start popping up? What if he's not done?" Melissa asked.

"We can't 'what if' this," Jon said. "Matthew is still in control. We have to wait it out. Again." Jon's phone rang and he stepped off to answer it.

Randy put his arm around Jessie and pulled her in close. "So, are you going?"

"I'm not sure yet."

"C'mon, Jess. The old man invited you back when you were ready."

"I'm not sure I'll ever be ready. But I am sure that I'm not giving up the search for Matthew Miller."

37

THE WATCHER

9:30 P.M.

METHODIST HOSPITAL

SAN ANTONIO, TEXAS

Jon exited the hospital with Jessie wrapped in his arms, as Randy and the rest of their team followed close behind. The group shuffled across the parking lot, slow and silent. To Jon, they looked beaten. He knew they had been through worse, much worse, but the revelation of not only another Walker, but one who could slip-stream without physical contact, felt deeply demoralizing. Losing Matthew to the night had been bitter. Ten feet from their vehicles, Jessie stopped cold. Her back straightened and she pivoted toward the east. She snatched Jon's hand and squeezed so hard he winced.

"What is it?" Jon asked. "Is it him?"

In an instant, his team went from defeated to on-point and frosty. They surrounded Jessie and drew their sidearms, holding them high and ready as they scanned the parking lot.

"Which way?" Randy asked.

Jessie pointed with her chin to a dark space between buildings about two blocks away. "Over there, somewhere."

Moving as one, the group slipped behind the Yukon, using the bulk of the big, grey SUV and its bullet proof windows for cover. Sean skulked to the dark side of the vehicle and opened the door without a sound. Several seconds later, he emerged from the shadows wearing a pair of NVG's and holding a short-barreled rifle with a built-in silencer. After scouring the lot in all directions, his head suddenly snapped left. Jon could almost feel it as Sean zeroed in on something in the distance, someone perhaps, between the hospital, and the highway.

"What do you see?" Jon asked.

Without taking his eyes off his target, Sean eased behind Jessie and whispered, "I thought I saw something move in that direction."

"Jessie, what's going on? Talk to me," Jon said.

"It's not Matthew. It's a male, but this feels different."

Melissa slowly pulled her radio from her belt clip and keyed the mic. "Rope-thirty-two, if there are any tac-units in the area of Metro-Methodist and I-35, can you cruise through discreetly. Repeat, discreetly. Repeat. Just cruise through."

A few seconds later, an answer. *"Copy. This is Tac-21. We're a few blocks away, en route. What are we looking for?"*

Mel looked to Jessie, but her eyes were focused into the dark. "Jessie?" she prompted her.

Jessie flinched, and then rubbed her bare arms. "I'm sure it's not Matthew, but he's watching us."

Mel keyed the mic again. "Just cruise the area between Eyrie and McCullough, closer to the I-35 frontage road. Shake down anyone you find. Male or female."

"See Mel, you're catching on," Steve said. She rolled her eyes, but with a smile.

"There's usually a lot of homeless in this area. But nothing yet."

"This guy could be posing as homeless," Jessie said.

Jon and Randy nodded, so Mel said, "Just stop them and let

us know. We're only a couple blocks away and will back you up."

After a few moments of almost unbearable tension and silence, a dark-colored Ford Mustang cruised into view and then almost immediately disappeared behind the buildings Jessie had identified. Melissa keyed the mic. "That you in the 'stang?"

"10-4. There's no one out. We'll keep our eyes peeled. Another unit is headed this way."

After several additional agonizing minutes, Jessie let out a long breath. "It didn't feel like random power floating through the air," Jessie said. "It's being . . ." she searched for the word, ". . . focused." Jessie shuddered and flexed her fists at her side. "Dammit. He's gone."

THE MOMENT THE ASSASSIN, QUON, PUT HIS FINGER ON THE trigger, the blade of a knife met the right side of his neck while a black-gloved hand, attached to a thickly muscled forearm, shot out in front of him from the left, batting away the long silencer tube that made up the length of his sniper rifle's barrel.

"Don't even breathe," a British accented voice said.

Quon closed his eyes for a moment, disbelief gripping him. Not once, ever, in his forty years of doing this kind of work had anyone ever sneaked up on him. Not even his dead wife, who had even greater stealth than he.

"Move cautiously," the voice said, "or die here. I really don't care either way."

For a moment, Quon accepted that dying would be preferable to capture, but he just had to see the face of this man who had bested him and foiled his moment of revenge.

Besides, he thought. *There are others.*

Quon's team hid somewhere in the shadows beyond, waiting to hear the bullets before moving in to capture the girl, Laina Main, as he knew her to be. While he waited, he sensed the man was watching for the girl as well. Just as Quon and his team had been doing for over a month. The inept police had all but escorted Quon to the Main woman, and he wondered if this man, this Watcher, wasn't here for the same reason: For her special powers. Now that the moment had passed, surely, the others would come to his aid. It would be best to surrender now in order to kill this man, up close and personal, in the next few minutes.

"Slowly, careful, put your hands behind your back." Quon did so, surprised at how quickly the handcuffs went on and a leather strap had been lashed around his throat.

Less than five seconds, he thought. *Amazing.*

A bag went over his head next, and then, quiet filled the room. Quon mentally timed that within the next few minutes, his team would barrel through the door if they didn't already have this Watcher next to him in their sights. But time ticked by, and Quon, just like the man who had just bested him, waited. Quon wondered if perhaps this man might also be going after the girl for the same reasons. The gods only knew that the incompetent police had put enough information into the world, he felt truly surprised he hadn't had to fight his way to the girl sooner.

Quon decided the new entry into the èmó arena would be too much of a distraction, although he knew Chen would be interested in what Quon had gleaned. But now, hearing vehicles start in the distance, he realized the man was here to protect her.

But why?

Quon had canvased this place thoroughly, as well as the dark places his team were supposed to move in from. Quon had given them instructions to wait until he took out the Delta

Force and Army Ranger guys with the rifle, and then moved in to finish off the others and snatch the girl.

He let a soft groan escape his lips–Chen would not be happy. It appeared to be the realization the man who bested him had been waiting for.

"Your friends are all dead," The Watcher said. "They weren't as quiet as you, but they weren't as skilled as you, either. So I dispatched them all as they were setting up. Their bodies are in the trunk of my car. All five of them. It's amazing what you can get away with in the shadows of San Antonio." Quon did not take the bait, although he knew the man told the truth. He was one of six total. None of them, however, were his friends. He felt the man lift the bag from his neck, and almost choked on the large ball gag stuffed into his mouth. After fastening it around his neck, the man, the Watcher who would kill him in the coming hours, tightened the bag around his neck. Quon made up his mind then and there.

No matter what he asks, no matter what he does to me, I will take what I know to the grave.

"Enough chit-chat for now," The Watcher said. "We can explore deeper conversation, later. Right now, it's time to go."

WITH THE NIGHT VISION GOGGLES ACTIVATED, ALEXI VALENTIN pressed hard with his mind until Jessie Richter, standing in the parking lot in the distance, stopped cold. He chuckled at the reaction of the team surrounding her and in observing their quick response, he guessed that the Asian team he dispatched an hour or so earlier might have had a harder time with this group than they had anticipated. He found it exhilarating when he discovered the Chinese assassins setting up on the hospital using his own property as a sniper nest.

What luck, he thought.

But no. This had nothing to do with luck. In all his years, Alexi had experienced much stranger situations than this. He slid back, deeper into the shadows of the third floor of the building. He turned his gaze to the man he had captured an hour earlier, hog-tied and bound in the corner. The radio squawk got his attention again.

"There's no one out. We'll keep our eyes peeled . . ."

The police transmissions between the lovely Detective Santos and the Tactical Unit sounded as if it originated from the center of his head as it came through the bone-conduction headset he wore. He reached up and lowered the volume. Watching Jessie and the others slip into the Yukon and depart, he hardly felt satisfied with what he had learned about the woman so far, or the Miller boy. But now, he had to deal with the quite unexpected assassin.

Alexi hoisted the small man to his feet, positioning his long tanto battle blade into the small of the man's back so if he tried to struggle, or flee, the sudden movement would bury the blade deep into his kidneys. He wouldn't last ten minutes with that kind of wound, and Alexi felt certain the assassin had a keen understanding of this ancient method of moving prisoners. The Asian did not resist.

"We're going to a more private location," Alexi said. "Somewhere we'll be free to chat, and you'll be free to scream."

After making his way down the three flights of stairs to the front exit doors, he pulled out his key, unlocked the huge wooden door, and stepped into the foyer vestibule which had been long ago covered in vines and growth. Alexi had purchased the building and submitted plans to begin work on renovations in the coming fall. It was a perfect location, just north of downtown, and less than three blocks from Methodist Hospital.

He stood the gagged man up in the doorway and closed and locked the door behind him, but before he could separate himself from the shadows, he observed a red mustang creeping slowly down the street. Holding the smaller man next to him, he moved right up to the edge of the shadow, inches from where the streetlamp's illumination cut through the black like a knife. If the cops pulled a flashlight, they would see both of them. If the man he had captured was as professional as the watcher imagined, he would bet his considerably long life that he wouldn't move, either.

"Isn't this exciting?" he whispered to his prisoner. The man made no sound, didn't twitch a muscle. The Watcher's heart thumped in his chest, exhilaration from this little cat and mouse game. He worked to restrain the fit of laughter ready to leap from his mouth. All from the joy of the chase.

The car slowly passed him. "I'm here. Right here," he whispered. Close enough to see two men through the darkened windows, Alexi saw the forms of the men's heads as they looked in his direction, and just maybe, if they had unrolled their windows, he would have been caught.

But not tonight.

The unmarked car slipped around the corner and the Watcher stepped into the light. He stood, feet shoulder width apart, spread his arms and laughed. "So close," he said quietly to his captive. "You guys were so close."

As he pulled his prisoner across the street to his own vehicle, one of many plain looking, nondescript cars he used for occasions such as this, he felt pleased that he didn't have to kill the police officers. It had nothing to do with bodies already taking up all the room in his trunk. He searched his feelings even deeper, not sure if he itched for a gun battle, or knife fight because it had been so long since he had experienced one-on-one combat. The men in the trunk hadn't had the opportunity to defend themselves. He clucked his tongue, self-acknowledging that he always supported the local police.

He started his car, turned the volume of the police scanner up, and headed for his warehouse to entice his quiet passenger into a deep, engaging conversation. Alexi had so much to think about. Regarding Matthew, he hadn't had a clue as to the boy's existence until his murder and the spectacular revenge killings after. The excitement of it, compounded by the unexpected capture of this wayward hitman ignited his soul-shifting power to full-on jet-engine thrusters. The energy reverberated through him as if he had accidentally stuck his finger in a light socket. As he approached his warehouse, he thought that certainly, Jessie and Matthew had a nickname for their power, too. But what they didn't know was that some could do what others could not. Alexi had learned that the hard way.

After all these years, he had time to hone many uses for soul-shifting. He knew Jessie also had his ability to sense others using their gift. There were limits to how far away someone could be for him to feel it, but in years past, he had been hundreds, even thousands of miles away and had received signals. But Matthew? His shift felt spectacular, to the point he had almost passed out from the unbidden power surge at the very moment of Matthew's transference. Alexi guessed that the feeling overwhelmed him because the incident happened in his own back yard.

Tracking the fumbling police investigation also turned out to be easier than expected. It wasn't their fault. They had no idea what they were dealing with. But when Jessie Richter arrived? Now that turned out to be a pleasant surprise. He still had yet to learn how Matthew escaped Jessie's far reaching, and obviously well supported grasp. Those Crue Intellis guys were good. No doubt exploiting Jessie for her skills. Alexi took a deep breath to quell the thread of anger that rose up in him at the thought.

Jessie should be their master, not the other way around.

He glanced over at the quiet man lumped in the seat next to him and punched him in the arm. Hard. "We're just tripping onto all kinds of excitement today, aren't we?" The assassin made no sound, but Alexi sensed he understood English.

He had lost track of Jessie many years ago and knew that one day he would inexorably run into her again. But to run into her here? In his own backyard? Being chased by assassins and chasing the new kid, Miller? He smiled, drummed his fingers on the steering wheel. The gods certainly favored him. He approached the garage, punched in the code on his remote, and glanced around for passers-by as the door slowly crawled up and open. Pride for Jessie welled up in him. She had finally found a useful purpose for her tool, one that had kept her off his radar for these many years.

He parked the car, closed the overhead door, and donned the pair of night-vision goggles again. The moment the sensor turned out the warehouse light, he activated the NVG's, opened the passenger door, and jerked the assassin out of the seat, dragging him across the concrete floor to another room. He pulled the handle of the walk-in freezer, tossed the man inside, and closed the door behind him.

Standing over his prey, he flicked open the blade of a folding knife, cut the clothes off the man's body, and let him lie naked on the frosted floor a few minutes until he looked ready.

Once the shivers from the twenty-nine-degree room set in, Alexi said, "I'll be right back." A moment later, he returned and observed the assassin hadn't moved a muscle and appeared to be controlling his breathing.

Alexi hoisted the man from the ground and shoved him into a steel chair bolted to center of the freezer's floor. He hand-cuffed one foot to each steel chair leg and did the same with his wrist binding to the vertical bars on the seat-back.

He ripped the hood off the man's head, but only managed to get the man to glance at him before returning his gaze straight ahead.

"You're a tough one," Alexi said. "I like that."

The assassin said nothing.

"Well, you already know you're a dead man. So we might as well cut the chit-chat and get straight to the point: Why were you setting up on . . ." Alexi caught himself. He wasn't sure if this man knew Jessie's name and didn't want to give anything to take with him to the afterlife. "The woman."

The man said nothing. "I'll leave you here for a few minutes to contemplate my question."

Alexi left the room, returning thirty minutes later to find the Asian still staring forward with the glum look on his face. The cold didn't appear to bother him.

"Well now," Alexi said, "it seems you are very highly trained, indeed. Perhaps this will help loosen your tongue." Alexi picked up the bucket he had brought in earlier, stirred the slushy water around inside and dumped it over the man's head.

Of course, the assassin screamed and said something that brought a smile to Alexi's face

"So that was Mandarin Chinese," he said. "We're making progress!" Alexi bent forward at the waist, planted his still gloved hands on his knees and looked into the prisoner's eyes. "Wèishéme kàngjù?" *Why resist.* That got a reaction out of the man, whose eyes shot toward Alexi, then just as quickly moved to straight ahead.

"Cāo nǐ." *Fuck you.*

"See? It's so much easier when we have a dialogue between us," Alexi said, pulling a folding chair from the back wall of the freezer, forcing it open and sitting before the Asian, then he grinned. "You know you're not going anywhere, and I know you speak English. I, myself, speak about twenty-five different languages and some dialects that have been long lost to the sands of time." The man said nothing, but Alexi took note of the ice crystals forming on the man's now blueish skin as he spoke.

"I noticed the tattoo on your arm. It's the old Quin Dynasty, yes? So you have lived and will die for Old China, then," Alexi said, in fluent Mandarin, and continued. "Let me tell you what I have learned about *you* in the short time we have been together. You have formal training in Ninjutsu, which isn't really Chinese at all. So I'm guessing you spent most of your youth learning the art in Japan." The assassin made no sign of admonition.

"You're an old school assassin. And since you fly the Quin flag, I would say that you are working for one of the Chinese underground crime families, not the government." The man still did not flinch. "But which one? Are you part of the San Ho Hui? The Old Triad? Come now, let's work something out here. We may have something in common, and we can prevent what will surely be inevitable in the next hour." Alexi abruptly stood and walked around the man, whose eyeballs now followed him.

"Perhaps Three Harmonies? Heaven and Earth? I used to do work for them back in the day, you know. In the mid 1700's. I was a smuggler. And a damn good one. No? Not them? Surely, you don't work for 14K or the Tai Huen Chai? You don't seem like the drug-runner type to me."

"Perhaps the Hōn?"

The assassin's body tensed, cracking the ice on his skin, and he glared at Alexi, who sat back down in front of him and grinned. "Ah, so it's the Hōn, then. I have never had the pleasure of dealing with them, but they are known for undermining authority. Yes! There it is, I see it all clearly now! That is what you are loyal to—a new China!" Alexi frowned, cocked his head to the side, and drew out his next words. "How noble."

QUON DID HIS BEST NOT TO SHIVER, DESPITE THE COLD SEEPING into his bones. Satisfaction filled him knowing the black man had yet to extract more than a racial slur. The perfect Mandarin had been a surprise, however, and surely, Quon misheard the man as having dealings with a three-hundred-year-gone crime syndicate. Suddenly, the Watcher jumped to his feet, flipped the chair around, so that his chair back faced him.

The Watcher sat up straight, clapped his hands together three times and closed his eyes. Air hissed from the black man's lips as he his hands went through several, ancient martial arts movements that only a trained Kung Fú assassin like Quon would recognize. It was a sign of preparation. He watched, mesmerized, as the Watcher's hands moved faster, and the endless stream of air coming from those black lips formed a vapor that hung in the freezing air, then he quickly brought fist to open hand, bowed toward Quon, and opened his eyes.

Quon gasped and fought his restraints

"Èmó," he said. He had seen that once before. In the Benefactor's representative. A man called Tano. An èmó he had killed weeks ago.

"Shì de, èmó," The Watcher replied. *Yes. Demon.* "I promise you an honorable death, now tell me what you know."

Quon braced himself, and the torture began.

EPILOGUE

Alexi Valentin finished writing the address on a yellow index card, pierced the center of the card with the pointed end of a vintage, WWII Fairbairn-Sykes commando knife, then rammed the blade to the hilt into the chest of the dead, almost frozen body of the Chinese assassin he had killed during an intense, and ultimately productive interview.

He took one last look at the man, and the five other bodies he had tossed to the back of the walk-in freezer a few hours ago, and closed, then locked, the door to allow the freezer to finish its work. He had slit open the chests of the men on the freezer floor from groin to gullet to allow their bodies to cool and freeze quicker in the twenty-two-degree room. The assassin cuffed to the steel chair bolted into the center of the freezer's floor would take a bit longer. He locked the walk-in freezer's door behind him and headed toward his small, but well furnished office in the back of his San Antonio warehouse.

Although Alexi rarely used the office, the room had been kept spotless by his trusted and extremely well-paid staff. He passed the stainless-steel refrigerator, stocked with his favorite beer and wine, and decided to wait until he got home to celebrate. He entered the full-sized bathroom at the opposite side of the room, started the shower, and retrieved his phone before stripping out of his blood-soaked clothes. He pressed a button that speed-dialed a number. While the phone rang, he continued to strip then proceeded to hum a little tune he had learned years ago.

Too many years ago, he mused.

"Yes, Mr. Valentine, how can I help you?" the voice on the other side asked.

"I have a freshly hunted hog that will be ready for processing in seventy-two hours. I will need the individual parts freeze-packed and mailed to the address pinned to the carcass. There are five other hogs I decided not to process. Dispose of them as you see fit. You have your key?"

"Yes, sir. I have the key. Does the Crown Vic need to be washed, sir?"

Alexi rolled his eyes at the oversight. "You take such good care of me," he said. "Of course, it needs a thorough washing, inside and out. It's still too warm out, so the car needs to be taken care of after I leave, which will be in an hour."

"Yes, sir. Of course. We'll take care of it."

"Thank you."

"My pleasure, Mr. Valentine. Have a wonderful rest of your evening."

The man hung up, and Alexi set his phone on the sink counter, then he proceeded to stuff his soiled clothes into a red plastic bio-hazard bag. He tested the temperature of the water, stepped into the shower, and began the gruesome task of scrubbing blood from his skin that his clothing hadn't seemed to repel. He smiled thinking about that old tune and humming it again as the soapy, bloody swirl of water circled down the drain.

When finished, he toweled off, pulled a fresh pair of pressed slacks and silk shirt from the small closet and dressed. After tying his black Beck dress shoes, he picked up the plastic bag and walked back to the freezer. He unlocked the door and peered in.

"Don't worry gents," he chuckled, "my staff will take care of you in a couple of days." He had to give credit to the assassin–he had kept quiet until Alexi finally revealed himself. But in the end, he caved.

They all do, he thought. He tossed the red bag in and locked the door behind him.

He walked past the Crown-Victoria to his daily driver: a 2018 Jaguar F-Type, painted blood pearl, climbed in, and pressed the start button.

"Damn I love this car," he said. He punched in the code to open the garage door, pulled out of the warehouse, and waited for the big roll-up door to close behind him before taking off into the San Antonio streets. It was well after 2 a.m., and he usually saw plenty of homeless people roaming about the streets. Not tonight.

He turned onto Saint Mary's street, gunned the engine a couple of times for effect, then headed toward downtown to his next destination. As he cruised the city streets, he contemplated the information he had obtained from the assassin. His little girl, Jessie, had grown up and apparently caused quite the ruckus in the Chinese underground. The thought of Jessie triggered more thoughts of the other one, Matthew. Although not of his blood, any and all Walker's on this earth were *his* children.

As he drove, he opened the convertible top and admired the old buildings. He slowed down as he approached the Alamo, and like he did every time he passed it, he wished he had purchased the old fort when had the opportunity. He hadn't foreseen the growth of this big city with the small-town-feel. S.A., as the locals called it, might have been the seventh most populous city in the United States, but it ranked number one Nationwide for serious crimes.

He pulled up to the curb of the Majestic Theater and glanced up at the old, original Marquis. He remembered the day it went up and had personally paid for its restoration and upkeep.

Beautiful, he thought.

He looked around, but didn't see a soul in the streets, not even the homeless. He glanced at his watch, and although the valet parking service didn't run cars at three in the morning, he waited. Within five minutes, a young man looking as fresh as if he had just started his day, pushed through the Majestic's main entrance doors and hurried to the driver side of the car, opening the door.

"Good morning, Mr. Valentine," the young man said.

"Good morning, Kevin," he replied. He got out and fished a small clip of folded cash from his slacks, peeled away two, one hundred-dollar bills and handed it to the young man. "Kevin, can you have it cleaned up? Keep the change," he said. He knew Kevin would hand wash, wax, and vacuum the car himself and wouldn't spend more than an hour on it, but he liked the boy, and knew he was working his way through college. Alexi never went to college, per se.

"Yes, sir. I'll have it ready in a couple of hours."

"That's fine, Kevin. Thank you."

"Thank *you,* Mr. Valentine. Have a great morning, sir."

Alexi pulled the large glass door open and strode across the grand foyer, making a quick visual scan of the great room before entering his private elevator. Alexi had commissioned and challenged Straus Elevators to create a lift that operated absolutely silent–its movement barely perceptible. Straus did not disappoint. As if someone closed the door to a room, then opened revealing his penthouse, he chuckled at the lack of sensation each and every time.

Like Magic!

He stepped off the lift and glancing at the dozens of hand-held cameras carefully placed around the penthouse, their technology spanning the ages. Some were in glass display cases, others seemingly tossed onto open bookshelves. Not one appliance, countertop, or shelf went without some type of camera.

He draped his coat across a barstool, walked up to a six-foot-tall wooden cabinet and admired the beautiful mosaic on the door. Made from hundreds of meticulously carved puzzle pieces, he reached out and quickly manipulated the sliding parts around and into an impossible sequence, unlocking the door. Inside sat a large safe that took up every inch of the cabinet's interior. He entered a long numeric code into the keypad, and when the light turned green, he twisted the handle. *Psssst.*

The door popped open, releasing a cool breath of air from within the temperature controlled vault. Swinging the door open, he carefully removed an ancient bottle of 1727 Rüdesheimer Apostelwein and gently worked the cork top free. He slid a wine goblet off the rack and poured himself perhaps a shot's worth of the venerated elixir.

Swirling the contents within the goblet, he brought the lip of the glass to just below his nose, breathing in steady and deep. *Perfection.* He carried the bowl of precious liquid to a large veneered double door with a carved sign above it that read, *Tempest et Locust*–the Room of Time. He held the glass up to the sign and said, "Here's to proof of life, once again," and took a small sip, relishing the wine and the moment.

Sensors detected his entry and activated several strategically placed mercury-vapor accent lights mounted in the ceiling. As the light increased, two eight-foot-long light tables, slanted back-to-back, also flickered on in the center of the room.

He marveled at the drama of light each time the bright, 5000-degree Kelvin lamps from the tables battled the warming MV lamps for luminous advantage in the spacious room. He smiled, appreciating the subtle drama as the centuries old hand-carved furniture and the even older woven tapestries sprang to life when the glow of modern and ancient light touched them. Alexi was enchanted with being able to observe a different effect each and every time he entered.

It truly is the little things in life.

He took another sip of wine and redirected his attention to dozens of transparencies ranging in size and age, strewn across the plexiglass tops of the light tables. He picked up a loupe and examined one or two before meandering to the walls of his gallery, where news clippings from the London Gazette dating as far back as the early 17th century, and handprinted photographs both in color and black and white, decorated the spaces between the tapestries and fine art.

On the opposite side of the room hung a huge, modern map of the world. It was littered with at least a hundred numbered flag pins, each placed to catalogue an adventure or offspring dating back as far as his earliest memories. He faced the map and pondered it before taking the final sip of the ancient red.

Looking at the pin-flags pressed into the map, he guessed that for each pin, several more adventures and hosts had slipped through the cracks of memory and time during the 2400 years since his rebirth.

One of his few regrets during his perennial life was not having kept track of his earlier exploits.

Well, what I've done will have to do.

He set down his now empty wine glass and pulled a leather-bound journal from the top drawer of an authentic Louis XIV corner table. He laid it onto the book stand and opened it to the latest page of entries. Again, he thought about the amazing and terrible things he had done.

I have fought alongside kings, sailed the oceans to every shore, and loved the most beautiful women and men on the planet and there is still so much to do!

Staring at the map, he thought that for the most part, world history had been recorded adequately. He also pondered how much history had not been recorded at all, or worse, history that had been either twisted to meet political or religious needs or destroyed to hide the truth.

He glanced at a bookcase standing to the right of the map

and selected a paperback from the shelf. Book one of Brian Sadler's fictional series; *Casca: The Eternal Mercenary.* He thumbed through the pages and chuckled. He found the thirty or so adventure novels incredibly entertaining to read and uncannily familiar. Probably because Alexi knew the factual Longinus personally and had been present on Golgotha's Rock when Longinus pierced the heart of Jesus. A bonus in Alexi's life had been when he ended up in Vietnam serving with Sadler for one brutal tour. He had no idea the man was a writer.

Although, he was a fair singer, as I recall.

Alexi reached for the Roman spear mounted on the wall next to the map and pulled it free of its mount. It was old, very old. Hefting the weight of it in his hands, he took a stance and thrust upward, bringing the hand-forged iron tip an inch from the ceiling. He wasn't sure if it was *the* spear or a replica he'd made for that jackass Adolf Hitler back in 1940.

So long ago, but not really.

He replaced the spear and shook his head. He still couldn't understand how Longinus had ended up becoming such a big deal, nor how the Jew had ended up becoming the most powerful religious symbol on earth. He certainly believed that Jesus was the son of a god, but he wasn't the only one.

He slid Sadler's book back into its slot and returned his attention to the ledger and a box of flag-pins. He dragged his finger down the page to his last entry, made last month, and assigned a new number, entering the name Jessie Richter in the log, right below the name of Matthew Miller. He jotted the log number on a colored flag and stuck the pin in the center of San Antonio. The tracking device he placed on the mercenaries' Yukons would tell him where she was really from, but there was plenty of time for that.

Always plenty of time.

Thinking about Matthew and Jessie, he felt impressed with his recently found great, great, possibly even greater, grandchildren and pondered as to how he hadn't detected the girl for the past ten or so years. Following Matthew around gave him a new understanding into his young progeny's mind-she needed the company of others. Like Matthew. Like *him.*

Alexi felt equally thrilled that the Miller boy had bypassed the second level of taking and seemed to be close at mastering the third, and how the two came to interact. These two, the first time he had come across two, together, were elevated to being the most special of all his children. Both were ready to take the next step. Alexi would help them.

He closed his eyes, rubbed at his temples, and reached back into his memory. His training and practice had lasted over a millennium before he could perform the third level of taking. And even with all that training, he more or less had stumbled upon the ability rather than learned it.

I must make time to meet the Navajo.

He lowered his head, closed his eyes, and drifted off, his body swaying slowly side to side. He sorted through his vast catalog of experiences, an uncountable number of takings, and searched to find some similarity with Matthew. He shook his head and clicked his tongue at not being able to come up with a parallel.

Although he had forgotten many of his earliest or random taking experiences, he remembered the first. It had happened a little over twenty-four hundred years ago, and the memory of it was still so vivid in his mind, it felt as if it had happened yesterday.

ALCALES, FIRST SON OF VALENTIN, GREW UP IN THE PORT CITY OF Ephesus, in what was now known as Turkey. The night it happened, the night he was reborn, he had been a young boy who had just celebrated his fifteenth birth year and gone through the Greek ceremony of manhood. Alexi's brow furrowed in anger at reliving the memory of when screaming tore him from sleep.

He leapt from his sleeping flat and stood in the shadows of a small window of his family's cottage. His eyes widened and tears rolled down his face as he watched fire ravage the orchards and vineyards his family had tended for over four generations of Greek or Persian rule.

Roman foot soldiers and mounted cavalry were already deep into sacking the city's center. He ran to the main room only to find his mother and father gone. He went back to his room and told his two little brothers and only sister to be very quiet and to wait for him.

He opened the door and heat from the fires washed over him. He looked up at an iron-tipped spear cradled in a rack above the door.

"When you can reach it, you can fight with it," his father had told him. He reached up, but his fingers only just touched the ancient, hand-carved shaft. He jumped once, twice and knocked the weapon free. The heavy steel tip came first and stuck in the dirt floor right between his feet. He let out a long hiss and shook his head.

"Wouldn't father be proud of a son skewered by his own spear," he whispered.

Bright fires danced with dark shadows. The scene beyond his door a waking nightmare. His heart raced and he forced himself to stand tall. "I can do this, I can do this," he told himself but didn't believe the words even as they passed his lips. In the distance, his older brother engaged a soldier and pierced the Roman through the chest.

"Brother!"

With a rush of courage, he ran twenty lengths from the house and stumbled over a body, falling hard to the ground. His hands slipped on something slick and he struggled to kneel.

Looking at his blood-covered hands, he looked closer at the body and cried out when he realized it was the hewn body of his mother. Sobbing uncontrollably, he bent down to caress her face when the anger took control of him.

He leapt to his feet and turned right into the chest armor of a Roman solider who was balancing his father's still convulsing body at the end of a spear twice the length of the one he held in his own hands.

He screamed and hatred flooded through him. It was an intense feeling unlike anything he had ever experienced. He was so distracted by it, he did not remember driving the entire spearhead through the Roman's neck. Hate driven adrenaline had his nerves dancing on end, and he watched in grim fascination as the surprise on the soldier's face gave way to the greying eyes of death. Watching this man's life slip away, the first man he had ever killed, gave him deep satisfaction. He tried to keep the soldier on his feet, just as the soldier had done to his father, but did not have the strength to balance the weight of the man.

As the Roman's body fell, a powerful force jerked him backwards by his long black braid. He was lifted off the ground and spun around to face yet another, even larger soldier who had come to the aide of his comrade. Alcales reached up to hold onto his own hair, lest this giant of a man pull it from his skull. Knowing himself to be at least three lengths in height, this man could not have been less than five and held Alcales aloft single-handedly.

The soldier pulled him closer, nose to nose, and studied his face as a child would look at a fascinating new toy.

"You struck true, boy," the soldier said in his own village dialect. The Roman did not sound angry or vindictive. He spun Alcales around, pulled him right up against his stone-like body and growled in his ear. "Now you have tasted battle, and after bearing witness to your talent with the spear, I'm afraid I cannot allow you to live. But I *can* offer you the honorable death of a soldier."

With his free hand, the Roman seized Alcales by the throat and squeezed. Bones popped in his neck, and a numbness followed. He tried to call out but could not breathe. Stars shot through his vision, and his legs twitched as he dangled in the air from the man's grip. He felt the tip of something sharp enter his ribcage from behind.

"I know it hurts, little warrior. There is no dishonor, you may scream."

Alcales did not remember the scream, but he knew it had left his body, closely followed by his life-force.

"Time to die." The soldier drove the blade fully into his body. He felt the hilt against his back and at the same time, the tip of the gladius scraped the inside of his ribcage before the searing heat of pain set in.

I am not going to die like this.

Alcales was taught to embrace death when the time came, and to never go quietly.

Power surged through his body. Atropos, the goddess of death, whispered in his ear, giving him favor. A stronger, more electric pain shot through him as this god-sized man eased the blade free from his back. Alcales felt the power of Zeus at his fingertips, and with his last breath, he arched his back and reached up to gouge the man's eyes out. His fingers just barely touched the sides of the soldier's face.

A brilliant light blinded him like an explosion of white flame. His stomach turned over, and he wretched as he was flipped up and around. What sounded like the crack of a legionnaire's whip went off deep in his head, and he knew something inside him had broken.

Am I dead?

He gasped as air flowed into his lungs. His vision slowly cleared, and a lifeless body hung in his arms. He dropped the body in a pool of blood and howled at the realization that the body at his feet was his own.

"What is this?" he asked in a familiar voice, the voice of his killer.

He stepped back and found he now possessed the body of the Roman. He looked at his massive arms and flexed every muscle. *Zeus has rescued me.* The lightning still pulsed through his veins as he went to one knee and called out to the mightiest of gods.

"Oh great Zeus, I am your servant, what will you have of me?"

There was no answer. He stood, taking in the death and mayhem around him. He knew then what must be done. He turned and saw a soldier ready to pierce the heart of his neighbor with a spear. Alcales furrowed his brow and called out to the Roman, "Wait!"

The shock on the soldier's face as Alcales's new, powerful hands wrapped around the man's throat made him want to laugh. He lifted the man off the ground, shook his head from side to side as if scolding a child, and with a roar, crushed the soldier's neck. He tossed the body ten lengths and looked down at the frightened man at his feet.

Euphret, his father's oldest friend, looked up at him in terror and confusion, then knelt and bowed down low. "Have mercy, great Roman," he said in broken Italian.

"Euphret, it is I, Alcales, son of Velentin, and I have been granted this body by the great God Zeus. I will not harm you, but you must take as many as you can and flee to the south pass. I will arrange transport for you when I can."

The old man shook in terror at the feet of this insane demon of a soldier before him. The soldier took a knee and gazed into the old man's eyes and smiled. Euphret reached out slowly and touched the Roman's face. "Alcales? Is that you? Your eyes, they glow. Like Lava"

"It is I, old friend." He lifted the old man from the rubble and gently stood him on his feet. "Your life and the life of your family begs you do as I say. Will you save them, or will you stay here and die?"

Euphret nodded and reached up to caress the soldier's black beard. "I don't understand," he sobbed. "How can this be? What will you do?"

"I cannot say why I have been blessed. I only know that now is the time for revenge. Now go!"

The old man stumbled forward, found his footing, and fled to gather his family. Alcales walked to where his former broken and bloody body remained. He bent a knee, stroked the long hair, and said a silent prayer for his own passing.

Zeus must have understood I was too small and too weak to defend this injustice, he thought. He rose to his full height, straightened his back, and found his father's spear, still imbedded in the neck of the first man he had killed.

He stood on the soldier's head and wrenched the blade free. Turning to face the slaughter of his people, he gripped the spear in one hand and the bloody gladius in the other. He spread his arms wide and took a deep breath.

"I will make you proud, Father," he said.

A smile rose to his lips, and the killing commenced.

Did you enjoy Enemy Walks?
I would love it if you'd leave a review!

Ever want to know how Jessie became a spy?
Get the prequel, Enemy Mine for free here!

Book four in the Jessie Richter series is on its way...

ALSO BY STEPHEN EAGLES

Enemy Mine: A Jessie Richter Prequel

Enemy Walks: Book 1

Enemy Way: Book 2

Book 3 (Title Coming Soon)

ABOUT THE AUTHOR

Stephen Eagles is the author-alter-ego of a US Navy veteran, former cop, and former wildlife educator who draws heavily from his interesting and unusual life experiences, including (but not limited to) working in Naval Intelligence during the Cold War, as a homicide detective in South Florida, as a licensed NRA Law Enforcement firearms instructor, and as a professional master-class and eagle falconer.

Throughout his law enforcement career, he explored his Native American roots alongside his grandmother and danced the professional pow-wow circuit for several years where he made many life-long Navajo, Seminole, and Lakota friends.

Stephen currently lives in San Antonio, Texas with his lovely and supportive fiancé, Michele. Sign up for Stephen's newsletter at https://www.stepheneagles.com where you can get a glimpse of current and future projects.

Stephen considers himself a common-sense conservationist and stays active in common sense approaches for protecting our natural resources and wildlife in the US and throughout the world. Visit his friends at the VetPaw.org. Stephen also contributes directly to Wounded Warrior Project and the USO. He encourages you to donate to these or other Veteran organizations as well as to support your local POLICE.

When Stephen is not writing, he's honing his firearms and defensive tactics skills and trying like hell to get back into Crossfit shape. But more often than not, you'll find him stuffed in a corner of some small San Antonio coffee shop, iPad in hand, clicking away at the keyboard.

ABOUT THE ENEMY WAY SERIES

In 2009 while working as a contract falconer and Cross-fit instructor in Chicago, Illinois, Stephen experienced *"The Slipstream"* at exactly 0300 hours during an intense and vivid dream. He sprang out of bed, cracked open his MacBook Pro and started writing. This book is the result of that long endeavor and the Jessie Richter series just keeps growing into what is quickly becoming its own "Walker Universe". Stephen plans on collaborating with his growing fan base and other authors to develop and craft exciting spinoff character stories.